ATLANTIS

Dedicated to
PHYLLIS PLAYTER

JOHN COWPER POWYS
ATLANTIS

faber and faber

This edition first published in 2008
by Faber and Faber Ltd
3 Queen Square, London WC1N 3AU

Printed by CPI Antony Rowe, Eastbourne

All rights reserved
© Estate of John Cowper Powys, 1954

The right of John Cowper Powys to be identified as author of this work
has been asserted in accordance with Section 77 of the
Copyright, Designs and Patents Act 1988

This book is sold subject to the condition that it shall not, by way of
trade or otherwise, be lent, resold, hired out or otherwise circulated
without the publisher's prior consent in any form of binding or cover other than
that in which it is published and without a similar condition including this
condition being imposed on the subsequent purchaser

A CIP record for this book is available from the British Library

ISBN 978–0–571–24212–2

CHAPTER I

There had been an unusual tension all that Spring night in the air of the arched corridor that led into the royal dwelling. It was a weird, hushed, premonitory tension, the sort of tension that implies a secret fore-knowledge shared among a number of so-called inanimate things. It was the sort of tension that strikes human beings as ominous, and from which all sub-human creatures instinctively shrink.

Even when the phantom-light that comes before dawn and is known in the island of Ithaca as "Lykophos" or "wolf-light," touched with its ghostly greyness that silent portico the tension did not relax. Some chroniclers would no doubt declare that if this palace of the aged Odysseus had been on the mainland, or if Ithaca had been a larger island, the elemental vibration that was bringing this tension would have been less active. This is extremely doubtful. Such chroniclers would be laying too much stress upon the purely physical capacity of the inanimate to convey the shock of far-away outbreaks, and too little stress upon whatever it may be in the composition of any form of matter that partakes, however faintly, of the nature of emotional consciousness.

The corridor which was thus affected that Spring night was a narrow one but it was about eighty feet in length and its arched roof was reached by—it would be incorrect to say "was supported upon"—six huge pillars. These pillars were not of great height, for the arched roof was low; but they were of colossal girth and were by no means identical in appearance.

In fact the first impression any stranger who visited the House of Odysseus received from them was that they had been dragged to this royal entrance by long-forgotten generations of slaves and had belonged to more than one pre-historic temple in the primal age of the Island of Ithaca, an age so fabulously remote that these terrific pillars had probably beheld creatures that were neither gods nor men nor centaurs nor satyrs moving about beneath them.

The entrance to the corridor was from a garden of very ancient olive-trees, at one side of which was the slaves' burying-ground. The stones that supported the entrance-arch were so enormous that they made the porch itself look just what in all probability it was, the mouth of a subterranean river that aeons ago had dried up.

A stranger entering it could make out at once the half-open brazen doors at the end and at most hours could feel the fragrant smoke emerging from beside the throne and floating out down the row of pillars.

The tension at any rate that welcomed that particular dawn had been created, so it was gradually made evident, by some world-upheaval that was nearer human consciousness than the most insidious constituents of these last eddies of wood-smoke that were at that moment being wafted out between those brazen doors from the whitening ashes of the fire by the empty throne, nearer human consciousness than even the sepulchral mist that at this hour was slowly drifting in over the stunted olive-trees from the slaves' burying-ground.

Whatever was the nature of the revolutionary event that was happening or was just going to happen, and however important it may have been or was going to be for human consciousness, one thing can be counted upon as certain: it meant absolutely nothing to the dust of the dead slaves out there in that unhistoric enclosure. What did it mean to those Six Pillars? Now this was a significant question. To dispose of those centuries-old layers of slave-dust not a great deal of nourishing soil had had to be disturbed; but with these Six Pillars it was a different matter.

Odysseus himself, who had known them from childhood, and whose homesick imagination had turned to them again and again under the walls of Troy and in the Nymph-tended gardens of

Circe and Calypso, found it impossible even now, as he went out or came in between the polished rondures of their preoccupied surfaces, to imagine them as anything but still erect in their majestic immunity, whatever convulsion at the heart of the island might make the rest of his home a heap of ruins.

But if the aged lord of that place could himself only too easily imagine its final desolation and see in those Six Pillars its only lasting memorial, by what tremors of vibration or currents of magnetism was the appalling tension caused that now filled that corridor?

One of the most startling things in human experience, whether the person be old or young, occurs whenever such a person is left alone for a while with another of its species who is sunk in sleep. It is then that the wakeful one suddenly becomes aware of the chasm that exists, a chasm resembling a crevasse in scoriac rock, between its consciousness and a consciousness like its own that is functioning in a completely different dimension.

There are some who find themselves questioning when they are fully awake, but of course they may have been influenced during their sleep, whether it is true that of all the things in the world the most precious is human consciousness. The champions of human consciousness defend its preciousness on the ground that it is consciousness alone that makes it possible for one living creature to respond to the feelings of another living creature.

Among ourselves however there are so many varieties of consciousness that it would seem as if it ought to be possible for us to relax the thought-pattern of human beings, or perhaps stretch it a little, till we could pass into the consciousness of a fish or a reptile or an insect or even of a plant or a tree.

Indeed if we have known the weird discomfort and strange uneasiness of the isolation of a brain awake lying close to a brain asleep, we have also known the annoying frustration of our complete failure to feel what the inanimate entities around us feel.

In the pre-dawn of the February day that brought this odd tension into the corridor of the palace of Odysseus the human sensibility that was really needed before any adequate solution of the mysterious shock lately received by this portion of the earth's surface could be obtained was the peculiar and special sensibility of a virgin who had never known a man, in other words of an old maid, a sensibility that the mere experience of copulation, whether resulting in pregnancy or not, wholly destroys, a sensibility that is as impossible for a mother as it is for a father.

The only human beings in the corridor at this hour were neither paternal nor maternal, nor were they on the watch. They were both male and they were both asleep. Thus it was left for the last of the six enormous Pillars to give the first articulation to the curious suspense that pulsed from one end to the other of that corridor.

One aspect of this magnetic vibration was naturally outside the Sixth Pillar's field of awareness. We refer to the possibility that being so rocky an isle Ithaca may simply have been the highest peak in an under-sea range of precipitous mountains and that thus, whatever it was that had happened whether of a psychical or of a physical nature, whether an insurrection of Titans or a revolt of Women, the news of it had travelled by way of Ithaca from the extreme East to the extreme West and from the extreme North to the extreme South.

The Sixth Pillar was the one nearest the olive-trees and the slaves' burial-ground outside the porch; and it was the furthest from the throne-room inside the porch. Its difference from the rest lay in the fact that it had been hammered and chipped and scooped and carved by none other than a son of the great craftsman Hephaistos, who was himself the son of Zeus and had been endowed with a peculiar sensitivity much nearer human awareness than anything possessed by the other five. So sensitive indeed was the Sixth Pillar that this particular Spring-night had seemed to it as long as three ordinary nights.

In this mood of nervous apprehension it had been distressingly aware of all the other entities in that corridor. One of these was an extraordinary-looking club from the Nemean forest on the mainland. Another was a still-living olive-stump, not more than a foot high, growing between two flagstones in the centre of the corridor.

A third had a quite different sort of identity and was a small brown moth with a way of flying that sometimes was faint, weak, fluttering, drooping and drifting, and at other times was jerky, violent, desperate, almost suicidal; while the fourth among them was just an ordinary house-fly.

All these had been struggling frantically for five hours of suspense to convey to one another, each with its own private interpretation, their particular *version* of the terrific shock that was now turning that dawn in the palace of the King of Ithaca into such a shattering experience.

"How extraordinary it is," the Sixth Pillar pondered, as it felt a breath of cooler wind, "that these two human bipeds, this simple Tis and this sly little rogue Nisos, can go on sleeping quietly among us here like a pair of acorn-surfeited swine, when someone or something who has a friend outside is telling us in here what the dawn-goddess has just confirmed, namely that things have begun to happen in our universe that may prove to be the beginning of its end."

Having uttered these words in a tone that was barely distinguishable from a sad soft air that had just crossed the slaves' graves, the Sixth Pillar decided that until new revelations should reach it, it would revert to the hieroglyphical if egotistical problem that was dearest of all to its un-roofed heart, namely the mysterious "U" and "H" carved upon its pediment which had been interpreted for generations as meaning "the Son of Hephaistos".

Further and further into the corridor, implacably moving from pillar to pillar, and throwing a phantom-like chilly greyness over the dark flagstones as she moved, came the dawn-goddess. The one solitary ancient olive-stump that grew inside the corridor near its entrance and thrust forward one crooked bough like a raised hand with fleshless fingers lifted by a long-dead corpse from between the flagstones, could not hinder the dawn's ashen-pale luminosity from enveloping it but it hardly seemed to be welcoming this pallid illumination.

On the contrary it seemed to be imploring the dawn to

approach more slowly so that the awkward nakedness of its reluctant resurrection should not put either of them to shame. Between this corpse-like protuberance from beneath the floor and an enormous fire-blackened club that was propped against the inner side of the low entrance-arch there was now flitting through the grey light a small but alert house-fly.

This small creature seemed as conscious of the unnatural tension as was the over-vigilant Sixth Pillar itself. For though the little fly appeared to be using the resurrected bough solely for the purpose of cleaning its front legs, the visits it paid to the formidable club resting beside the entrance-arch were clearly actuated by a quite different motive.

Obviously what was urging the fly in this case was the necessity it felt of talking to somebody about this tension who had a philosophic mind. But the awakened house-fly was not the only insect in the place who feared, like the Sixth Pillar, that there was some planetary catastrophe imminent, either happening now, or just going to happen.

There was also a very disturbed light-brown moth. This moth seemed for some definite reason of its own to avoid alighting upon the olive-stump; but it also, like the fly, kept paying repeated visits to that Heraklean weapon by the entrance.

It must have been clear to the Sixth Pillar by this time that the dawn-goddess was not going to reveal to them anything beyond what they had all instinctively known, namely that something momentous, something that probably affected them all, had really occurred; otherwise the Pillar would hardly have relapsed into her ancient ponderings about those letters that had been engraved ages ago upon her marmoreal flesh. They must have been engraved there before she had had time to become a conscious, separate, inanimate entity. In fact they must have been engraved when all she felt was what her mother, the earth, felt.

Meanwhile the two human sleepers, lying discreetly apart on their goat-skin mats, one the middle-aged cow-herd, Tis, and the other the princely boy-helper of the household, Nisos, were both vaguely aware, even in their dreams, that psychic disturbing tremors of some sort were troubling that rocky palace and probably that whole rocky island.

What this especially simple cow-herd and what this especially alert princely house-boy would actually do, if, their dreams shaken off, they found themselves conscious, whether they understood its nature or not, of a catastrophic, all-affecting event, remained to be seen. None of their sub-human neighbours, animate or inanimate, not the club, not the olive-stump, not the moth, not the fly, had any doubt about the existence—for they had all learnt it from pleasant and unpleasant personal experience —of a very considerable gulf or gap or lacuna between the feelings, impressions, intimations, instincts, and, above all, reasonings, of all human beings, and their consequent action.

"It all depends, my pretty one," whispered the olive-stump to the house-fly as the latter in its agitation tried to clean its left back leg by brushing it against its gauzy transparent right wing, as it laid its square black head sideways against the smoothest portion of the upspringing shoot, "whether Nisos had a visit from Hierax his pet hawk while both you and I were still fast asleep."

"Why doesn't Pyraust come to ask you things like I do?" whispered the fly to the olive-shoot.

The older creature hesitated a moment. Then he said: "Because, Myos darling, she knows that I know who sends her here."

The fly, who had balanced itself very carefully on its front-legs and had begun to clean both its back-legs with its gauzy wings pressed its huge black head still closer against the skin of the olive-shoot and allowed its unemotional staring black eye to drink up the conversation that was now proceeding between the brown moth and the club of Herakles.

"I suppose you don't want to tell me who sends her?" whispered the house-fly. "I don't mind telling you at all," replied the other, "or anyone else either. It is Enorches, the High-Priest of the Orphic Mysteries who sleeps in the big ante-chamber of Athene's Temple where Telemachos ought to sleep. Instead of which Telemachos sleeps in that hut you pass on the left as you go in."

"Why does the Priest of Orpheus take that big ante-room for himself?" asked the house-fly, standing perfectly still now and staring at the brown moth whose wings were fanning the queer slit that went down the upper portion of the club of Herakles.

"That's for Athene to answer, little fly," replied olive-shoot with a curious hissing sound, as if its sap was seething.

"My Lord Telemachos has let himself be wheedled and worked upon by that Orpheus Priest ever since our Lady Penelope died. She would have scarce endured to see it."

"You're getting angry," said the fly to itself. "By Zeus I believe if that Priest Enorches came in now you'd split into two and spurt poison over him." The olive-shoot *was* getting angry and it wished it had wings like the fly so that it could accompany the fly to where the club was leaning.

"The Club is surely," thought the olive-stump, "watching us now while it listens to the chatter of that silly little moth-girl Pyraust." And the fly said to itself: "How tiresome it is that so many learned and scholarly philosophers have no eye into which you can look and read their thoughts! I've seen my own eyes reflected in a hundred different things and I may say without boasting that they are fierce and implacable. But even I can't read any living creature's thoughts with them. Now why is that? I can't even read the thoughts of that silly little moth. Now why is it that I am no good at expressing the stern and majestic authority through my eyes which I feel so powerfully in the pit of my stomach? Isn't it a funny thing that a person should feel inside him feelings that he can't express in any possible way to other creatures? As for this poor amphibium of a half-in, half-out olive-shoot, it seems totally devoid of all real insight, it can only see through the inflamed pores of its touchy skin!

"And over there, within a dozen buzzing flaps of my wings, rests that great Club of Herakles as it has done for seventeen years I Yes! as it has done ever since Penelope died. Eurycleia must have seen it for seventeen years balanced between those out-jutting pieces of quartz!

"All those years—think of it!—it has been keeping its position, upright and invincible, leaning first to the right but still upright, still straight and unbending; and then, just a tiny bit, to the left, but still straight and unbending! Aye! How I admire thee, O great Club!"

And the fly went on to think how it would love to throw some charm or spell over the Club that would force it to make known to Odysseus how this cunning Orphic Priest was ousting Telemachos from the great hall of the Temple! It longed to ask the Club how it could refrain from calling upon its former master Herakles, now that it was clear that the old Odysseus was beginning to lose his grip upon the sequence of events.

Thus as strongly moved in its heart as it was in its mind, the fly stared at the archway beside which the Club was resting. Meanwhile the great Club was being slowly aroused from a dim obscure and puzzled sleep by the approach of the dawn-goddess, that tiptoe-footed daughter of Helios Hyperion, whose rosy fingers were still pressed against the palms of her hands.

"So I am still myself," was the first clear thought of the great weapon. "Yes, I am still myself." And it began deliberately recalling that far-off day when Herakles snatched it up from a fire-burnt portion of that Nemean forest on the mainland when he was struggling with the monstrous lion.

The club had been seriously blackened by that fire; but long before the fire had touched it it had been deeply indented by the trailing and twisting around it of a honeysuckle intruder who eventually would have possessed itself of it entirely and have transformed it from a noble pine sapling, half-strangled by a deadly honeysuckle, into a flourishing honeysuckle beautifying a wretched dead pine-trunk already blackened in some forest-fire.

"Still myself," continued the great weapon in its slow confused awakening under the gradual approach of dawn, "still old Dokeesis—who was embraced in that far-off forest by God knows what treacherous neighbour-plant, but who is still able to fit himself as easily into the hand of an older hero as into the hand of a younger hero; Yea! by the gods, and into the hand of a mortal hero as into the hand of an immortal one!"

Pondering thus, the fire-blackened, well-polished club, deeply furrowed into rounded grooves and convoluted curves by the parasitic plant which had so assisted or impeded—who can say which?—its natural growth as to endow it with what resembled a female bosom, found himself recalling his feelings, when, years and years ago, he was washed up by the waves on the coast of Ithaca.

Broken pieces of sea-bitten wreckage from far older vessels than the one upon which the sea-god's wrath had most recently been wreaked were strewn about him on the strip of shore beneath the rocky promontory where he lay. Sand-crusted fragments of seashells together with wind-tossed wisps of foam and salt-smelling ribands of slippery seaweed had drifted by pure chance and were piled up by pure chance against the rounded wooden curves of his female-looking bosom.

Just because he was the latest object to be cast up out of the deep upon that shelving shore the club of Herakles had felt in some dark and deep sense humiliated as well as ill-used.

It was curious, he thought, that this ancient feeling of humiliation should return to his consciousness at this particular moment of this February dawn; but as he tried to analyse what he felt, for the club had grown almost morbidly introspective during these long years of peaceful relaxation with his head resting sometimes against a piece of quartz to the East and sometimes against a piece of quartz to the West, he could only repeat over and over with a proud, furtive, sly, secret detachment, "I am myself", and as he did so he felt detached not only from the service of Odysseus, but also, and this struck him as something quite new in his experience, from the service of his old master, the demi-god Herakles. He had therefore two introspective riddles about himself to ponder on as this cold pale light of this early dawn moved from pillar to pillar. Why should there be any sense of humiliation in his memory of surviving, in the way he had, the wrath of Poseidon?

And why should he be feeling this savagely cunning, ferociously sly sense of detachment from the service of *any* master, while at the same time he had such a self-confident sensation of power; of power to serve a mortal hero like Odysseus, quite equally with power to serve an immortal one like Herakles?

"Perhaps," he said to himself, "I have spent so many days and months and years with my head drooping and slipping and sliding and sinking, first to the east and then to the west between these glittering blocks of quartz that when I try to form any clear-cut explanation of my real inner feelings I just swing from the extreme of shame to the extreme of self-confidence.

"But that seems a silly explanation when I think of the pride I felt in throwing my life into every blow I struck for Herakles, and when I think of the shame that shivered through me as I lay, like a swollen and bloated baby's rattle, half-covered by seaweed, between two rock-pools, and felt the swishing of sea-gulls' wings brush against my bare cheeks and my bare stump-end."

But it was at that moment that the awakened consciousness in the club of Herakles decided that common decency as well as common courtesy, not to speak of prudence, demanded that he give some flicker of attention to the small brown moth that for the last half-an-hour, indeed long before any light entered that corridor, had been struggling to tell him things that concerned them all.

"*What's that?* You imp of Erebos? What's that you're telling me now? Isn't it enough that for more years than I can count I've been listening to you, and listening to your mother's and your grandmother's and your great-grandmother's chatter about this infernal Priest of Orpheus who has ousted every other prophet and seer and soothsayer and omen-reader from the Temple of Athene, that I must now treat you seriously; and begin solemnly answering a whole series of ridiculous questions about the end of the world?

"*What's that*, you silliest of insects? No, of course I've felt nothing of the kind! Have I felt, do you say, that the world was coming to an end as soon as the sun was up? Of course I've felt nothing of the kind! Don't I feel it now, you ask, this terrible news? No! I certainly *don't* feel it! I feel the confounded tickling of your tisty-wisty wings against my old life-crack; that crack from outer to inner, I mean, from what's going on to my consciousness of what's going on, that began when He—and if you don't know who *He* is you'd better get back into your baby chrysalis as soon as you can!—hit that great roaring Beast over the head in that Nemean wood.

"It's ever since then that my hearing's been so good. Curious, isn't it? Shows how wisely old Father Zeus governs the affairs of the world, eh? And so this blasted fool of an Enorches thinks the world's coming to an end does he? He'll soon learn the opposite if that great Son of Zeus whose business it is to purge the world of those who try to bring it to an end comes this way again!"

"Please, please, *please*, great Club," pleaded the little Pyraust in her most tender tone: "Please believe me when I warn you that there is serious danger ahead for all who fear the gods."

The voice of the club of Herakles shook with wrath. "I tell you, silliest of girl-moths, that this world of ours is founded forever on the will of Zeus the Father of All, he who wields the thunder and lightning, he who kills and makes alive, he who can cast those who refuse to serve him into the lowest depths of Tartaros; and Tartaros, you must remember, O most misled and most infatuated of small moths, is as far below the earth as the earth is below the starry heaven! Think, little whimperer, think, what it must have meant to an enemy of Zeus and of the Olympians when he felt himself falling, falling, falling, falling, even as the monster Typhon must have felt himself falling when, with Etna on the top of him to keep him perpendicular, down, down, down, down he went, down to a place—and don't you forget it, little flutterer with a wren's eye!—that is as far below the kingdom of the dead as *that* is below the earth!

"Yes, you flipperty-flap of an insect, what you've got to realize is that the Kingdom of the Dead is the Kingdom of Aidoneus; and that Aidoneus is the brother of Zeus and as much under his will as you and I are under his will.

"It is by the will of Zeus, as well as by the help of Queen Persephone, that Aidoneus keeps the ghastly myriads of the dead in control and compels them to submit to their fate. And do you know, you flicker-fan, what their fate is? What yours will be, yours will be, *yours* will be, if you flap at my crack of quietness, or disturb my groove of wisdom any more!

"But if you ask me, you silly flitter-fluff, what *their* fate is now, and what *yours* will soon be, I cannot answer.' Shadows they are and shadows cover them,' as I heard Herakles muttering once when we brushed the dead leaves from his lion's skin. Have you forgotten, O grain of sand on a pair of wings, the story of how our old Odysseus called up the Theban Prophet Teiresias from among these shadows?

"And how the Prophet had to drink blood before he could speak? So much for the most intellectual of mortal men when it comes to real knowledge! *Drink blood* is what *they* have to do, little brown one, drink blood! Is your precious Priest of Orpheus prepared to do *that*?"

The wings of the moth-girl emitted a faint susurrating shiver. Then they relaxed and closed above her sunken head. But she was still perched on one of the bosom-curves of the monster-killing Club where she must have looked to any smaller creature, to a thirsty louse for instance, searching for half a drop of sweat from a human hand, like an exhausted sea-mew resting on the crest of a sea-wave.

And her voice filtered down like a distillation of mist into that long and narrow crevasse where dwelt the club's consciousness.

"Is it true, O immortal one," she asked—and behold! it was brought about by her very fear of the gods that the voice of Pyraust, the moth-girl, gathered up as she spoke some of the rhythmical lost notes from the wailing of the earth over the rape of Persephone; and thus, while not too faint to be audible to the smallest louse, had in them that which caused even the pine-wood sap in the club of Herakles to stir and rise—"please, please tell me if it is true what I heard the Priest of Orpheus tell the Priestess of Pallas Athene: namely that on the confines of the country of the blameless Ethiopians there have now come back from the Kingdom of the Dead the First Man and the First Woman; and that the First Woman, whose name is Niobe, no longer weeps like a ceaseless torrent from an eternal rock; and that by her side once again is the first man, whose name is Phoroneus and who was the son of a Melian Nymph who came from an Ash-Grove, even as thou thyself, O immortal one, came from a Pine-Forest."

Now indeed had the moth-girl said the wrong thing! She had been taught from childhood about the Melian Nymphs and about their association with Ash-trees and there had been a family tradition among her own brown-moth ancestors that it had been by the special intercession of one particular Melian Nymph that the original pair of brown-moths had extricated themselves from the hidden parts of the Great Mother.

But what she had never been taught, or, if she had, what she could never keep in her head, was that the effect of every act and every word and every gesture of every living creature depends, not on the *nature* of what's done, spoken, or indicated, but on the *manner* of these performances.

And where this impulsive flutterer made her mistake was in speaking so carelessly about Ash-Trees and Pine-Trees that the natural implication was left upon the atmosphere that the only difference between them was that one was the haunt of Nymphs and the other of Lions.

But the savage beast with whose brains the Club of Herakles had sprinkled the pine-needles of the Nemean Wood had never made a more violent sign of fury than the heavy thud with which the Club struck the paving stones of that palace-porch or the harsh groan with which it bade the terrified little flutterer "get back to your Priest of Blasphemy and your Father of Lies!"

Out into the dawn flew in deadly silence Pyraust, the brown moth, while Myos, the black house-fly, spread his gauzy wings and with the tense buzzing sound that always, for all its low pitch, suggested the impetus of a classic messenger, flew in pursuit of her to the Temple of Athene.

It was at this moment that the cow-herd Tis stretched himself with a comfortable groan and rising to his feet lifted up first his bare right leg and then his bare left leg, supporting them against the base of the third pillar, while he fumbled for his sandals. He had been sleeping in his single garment, his shirt-tunic or "chiton", and he now surveyed his companion, the boy Nisos, who, asleep in a similar garment, though fashioned a little differently as befitted not only his fewer years but his nobler birth, had been so suddenly submerged in sleep that though the cords that bound his sandals to his ankles had been loosened and now trailed over the flag-stones, the sandals themselves remained on his feet.

Tis regarded the sleeping boy with friendly amusement for a moment. Then he shook him gently by the shoulder. "*That girl* will be down here in a moment," he said. "In fact I keep thinking I hear her step. Of course neither she nor Leipephile would worry about me if I were like you a son of Naubolos who claims to have more right to be King of Ithaca than Odysseus himself.

"But if I were your elder brother or your uncle that girl Arsinoë would still throw her witch-look on me just the same as she does on you. She hates us all, and not altogether without—God! master Silly-Boy! wake up for Hermes' sake! Tie your sandal-strings tight!" As he spoke the Cow-herd disentangled the boy's sandal from the cords of the mattress on which the lad had been sleeping and helped him to get his foot into it.

"Has Babba been making a noise?" enquired Nisos somewhat irritably. "The old lady ought to be ashamed of herself," he went on, "if she has been raising hell again just because her damned udders are too full. Didn't I hold on to my bladder when it was nigh to bursting yesterday when mother sent me to the Temple to see Stratonika and I had to wait till her morning chant was finished and she'd put off her garlands and black ribbons in the porch?

"How ridiculously different from one another women are, Tis! Who would ever have imagined that Stratonika was Leipephile's

Sister? It seems just simply crazy to me whenever I think about it. I can't help rather liking Leipephile myself. It's the way she smiles at you when you tease her; as much as to say: "of course, kid, I know perfectly well you're much cleverer than I am; and I'm a bit of an idiot; and I know that the great House of Naubolides is much grander than we Pheresides can ever claim to be; but yet," so her looks seems to say, "you and I, Nisos Naubolides, are born to understand each other. That's what the gods have willed that you and I should understand each other!"

The boy was now engaged in smoothing down his blue-black hair with a small ivory comb which he drew from an interior pocket of his "chiton" and the odd fancy crossed the patient mind of Tis that his own left eye upon which Nisos seemed to have concentrated his gaze had suddenly become a mirror, but a mirror that didn't interfere with his keeping both his own eyes firmly fixed on the boy's face. "It'll be your brother Agelaos she'll soon have to understand, if what Eurycleia told me the other day is true," muttered Tis carelessly.

"O I know all *that*," cried Nisos; "and Agelaos is as simple as Leipephile! It's Mummy and me who are the clever ones. You should hear us confabulating in the kitchen when she's stewing pears and how I say something about Leipephile and she says something about Agelaos and how we both laugh. Dad has no more idea than Agelaos how mother and me talk about them and what we say and how we laugh; but naturally"—here the boy gave the cow-herd a very searching and very quick look—"naturally it's different between *us*, Tis. You're the oldest friend I've got; and I'll never have another like you. However! We are what we are, Tis, old partner—you the perfect cow-herd and me Eurycleia's clever little House-help—and if dreams mean anything some very queer happenings are on the wind. Do you know what I was dreaming when you woke me up? No, no! I'll tell you later! There's Babba making that noise again! Don't let's wait here, Tis. I'll come out with you. I've got to see mother anyway before I help Leipephile with the old man's breakfast. So I'll come down the road with you to the Milking-Shed and then I'll go on to Aulion. I'd better run in at Druinos as I pass its gate. My mother and Leipephile's mother tell each other everything! Dad and my brother can't understand how everything they say to. each other is known all over the island.

"But what can you expect from two elderly well-to-do mothers' with trained servants and children as grown-up as Stratonika and Leipephile on the one hand and my brother Angelaos on the other, and with nothing to do but comment on what other people are doing and saying?

"I call it perfectly natural and right. Why shouldn't our mothers have their little pleasures when they are too old to make love? I don't like these Temple-chanters who blame Nosodea and my mother for exchanging tales about their husbands and children. I know well how stupid Dad and Agelaos are; and we all know what a funny old customer Damnos Pheresides is! who in the name of Aidoneus can say what goes on in that queer-shaped head?

"If I were Leipephile's mother I should certainly want to talk to *somebody* about my husband." The shrill boyish voice of Nisos Naubolides drifted away between the olive-trees till it was lost among the slaves' graves. Very soon both that youthful voice and the cow-herd's hoarse responses to it were lost in Babba's call to be milked.

Even the Sixth Pillar, whose unusual consciousness had been at once fortified and dulled by its bewildered ponderings upon those two deeply-engraved letters, that "U" and that "H", which had in the early times appeared on its base, could no longer hear a sound.

Little big-eyed Myos the house-fly, was gone; indeed he was at this moment waylaying in the porch of Athene's Temple in defiance of the Priest of Orpheus his pathetically frail acquaintance Pyraust, the brown moth. Thus the most intelligent consciousness left just then in the Porch of the Palace—for the five younger Pillars were even more lacking in response to anything outside their own substance than their venerable comrade the Sixth Pillar who at least had kept up an interest in the letters "U" and "H" for a few thousand years—was the half-burnt pine-wood Club of Herakles, whose heavy head and almost feminine bosom as they rested between those fragments of quartz while the movements of the man and boy were still causing vibrations through the substance of the flagstone, lost no opportunity of swaying consequentially, and pontifically, first to one side and then to the other of their narrow enclosure.

It was indeed with almost a sacerdotal alternation between east and west or left and right, and with a quaint blend of judicial finality and suspended fatalism, that the Club of Herakles acted the part of Guardian of the Gate that early Spring morning.

Thus it was with a shrewdly expectant acceptance of the worst rather than a mischievous enjoyment of what was happening at the moment that the Club listened to a light step descending the unseen stairs to the door behind the throne and watched the stealthy opening of this same door and the emergence therefrom of a plaintively wistful middle-aged woman who looked as if she would have more willingly reconciled herself to welcoming the last dawn that would ever reach this earth than the particular one which was now removing the kindly veil of darkness from the repetitive horror of life.

The Pillars in the corridor were by no means evenly placed. They were indeed so divergently and so erratically arranged that they resembled the sort of massive supports that might have been found in the crypt of some sea-king's palace beneath the floor of the ocean, the building of which had been disturbed by the movement of sea-monsters.

The expression in the woman's face as she made her way from the inner door to the entrance was only too familiar to all the dwellers in that house. It was indeed the expression of such an enduring quarrel with existence that there was not one among them who would not—whatever words he or she might utter with their lips—breathe a sigh of gratitude to the gods on her behalf if they heard of her death. "The poor thing has gone whither she longed to go!" would have been the instinctive feeling of them all.

As the woman now threaded her way to the entrance she glanced apprehensively at every pillar she encountered; and in the case of the second one and the fourth one she slipped cautiously round them, as if to make sure that nobody was watching her. She wore the sort of robe or "peplos" that by means of the way a certain fold was draped over the curve of one of her breasts left room for a secret pocket at that particular place where a pair of scissors, or a knife, or a dagger, could be quite comfortably and easily concealed.

What this forlorn creature carried hidden in the fold of her foreign-looking garment on this eventful morning was as a matter of fact known to none, not even to the Club of Herakles. It was a carefully sharpened carving-tool of the sort used by woodcarvers. But what increased the self-conscious caution of this secretive woman's movements was the awkward bundle she carried in her bare arms wrapped in a linen cloth.

Whatever this object may have been it agitated the forest nerves of the once root-inspired club; for the club was naturally, since its flesh was made of wood, hostile to every metallic object and it recognized at once that whatever the girl was carrying it was something made of bronze. Bronze or not bronze the woman kept pressing it tightly to the pit of her stomach, while every now and then she gave a sharp jerk with her bare shoulder when that carving-tool in the fold of her robe scraped against her soft skin through its covering.

Safely past the great club, whose judicial watchfulness changed to angry perturbation as it felt her passing, Arsinoë, the Trojan, whose father was Hector, and her mother a sister of that Dolon who had been slaughtered so unmercifully by Diomed so that his weapons and all he wore might be offered up by Odysseus as a pious offering to Athene, found herself among the graves of the slaves and among the olive-trees that bordered on the graves.

Safely past both graves and olives, and clearly keeping a definite purpose in her tense brain the Trojan captive directed her steps to an uncultivated tract of wild country, about a mile square, which was avoided by all the people of Ithaca.

This particular expanse of ground was unploughed and unsown; nor was it planted with fruit-bearing trees or with nut-bearing trees or with any grain or any flowers. A few very ancient oaks and ash-trees and poplars had grown there for ages and there were several reedy swamps where the mud had a brackish smell though the sea was more than a mile away and where there were strangely-stalked mosses that looked as if they had grown there along with antediluvian marsh-lichens which had been the food of creatures so monstrous that the mind shrinks from picturing them.

At any rate the natives of Ithaca had for unchronicled generations avoided this particular square mile. It had come to be known as Rima or Arima, though these musical syllables had no known connection with the mysterious tribe of a similar-sounding name to which reference is made in certain ancient poems; and it was avoided for a very definite and particular reason. It had, as a matter of fact, become the "Temenos", or consecrated shrine, of two fearful Beings who must have been worshipped as Deities in Ithaca long before the Golden Age of Kronos, and long before any dweller in the island had so much as heard of Zeus and his thunderbolts.

Not only was this weird expanse of haunted ground the "Temenos" or dedicated shrine of these two strange Beings, but it was the immemorial stage of an unending argument between them, a sort of phantom-ritual, not between two worshippers but between two objects of worship. They were both female Deities and what must have been in pre-historic days their unqualified hideousness had been blurred and clouded, and, if such a word can be used, be-ghosted, by the passing of time, as the most horribly shaped rocks can be overgrown by congenial funguses.

One was Eurybia, whose name means "far-flung force"; and the other was Echidna whose name simply means "the Serpent". Eurybia was the grandmother of Hecate; while Echidna was the mother of the Chimera and of the Hydra and of Cerberus, and also of the Lion of Nemea, not so very long since destroyed in its savage old age by the introspective Club of Herakles, whose repose between his two quartz pillows had been disturbed only an hour ago by this tragic captive concerned with nothing but her carving-tool and the mysterious bronze object wrapped so carefully in its linen cloth.

The shrine of the Grandmother of Hecate was on the lower level of this mile of unfertile land. Indeed it overlooked the most frightening portion of the haunted swamp where any imaginative intruder might well fancy that he caught shadows and reflections in the black water and among the swaying reeds of hovering ghosts that had drifted down the ages from an epoch in which mortal men by day as well as by night had to struggle with creatures whose limbs were not only deathly cold but had a saurian effluvium from centuries of reptilian life in salt-marshes, where terraqueous abortions of both sexes embraced and devoured one another. The shrine of the Mother of the Chimera was in a different position, although there was only a quarter of a mile between them.

This portion of that "holy ground" stood under a tall black rock of some primeval adamantine stone, at once much smoother and much darker than all the other geological strata in Ithaca. In substance as well as in appearance the "eidolon" of Echidna was completely different from the image of Eurybia. Neither of them possessed a realistic human shape, but each was a misty phantom, associated with a material and movable object. At close quarters Eurybia was nothing but a thick wooden stump; while Echidna "the Serpent" was a short but very massive pillar of clearly articulated white stones, each one of which contained, embedded in the texture of its substance, a noticeable array of fossils, many of which, though by no means all of them, had originally been shell-fish.

Above and around each of these two Images or Idols there swayed and wavered and hovered and moved and shook, sometimes growing thicker and sometimes lighter, a tremulous body of palpable vapour unmistakably resembling a female human shape. Both shapes not only grew darker and lighter, thicker and thinner according to the occasion but they also contracted and expanded in actual size.

There was, however, one very curious thing about them. The mist that composed them was entirely impervious to the wildest winds. The wind might flow from North, South, East or West, and blow so softly that it would scarcely stir a feather, or so violently that it would rock the pinnacles of a mountain or upheave the roots of a deep-grown forest: in neither case was its presence so much as visible, however closely you watched, by any effect it had upon these two superhuman phantoms of mist. They exchanged human speech in the language common to both Achaeans and Trojans; speech that could be heard and understood by any native of that island who entered this unconsecrated, this unholy, this unwalled, unguarded, undefended, unassailable tract of demonic ground.

Yes, any reckless child, any rebellious prowler, any philosophical tramp, any desperate bandit, any life-weary beggar, any obsessed youth in pursuit of his ideal vision, could cross at will the boundary of this weird spot. Especially could any daring novice in religion, anxious to obtain supernatural support for his own particular interpretation of the Mysteries of Orpheus or of the Mysteries of Eleusis come stealthily and humbly to a smooth lawn equidistant between these two Beings, or between the wavering pillars of vapour that represented them, and, as he listened to the wind-impervious, storm-immune, rain-indifferent, unbridled and unholy dialogue between them, either be upheld in his special vein of mystical revelation about the secrets of the cosmos or be driven in a wild reaction against every spiritual cult in the civilised world to the desperate madness of parricide or matricide or to some astounding incest or bestiality or perhaps even some unheard-of attempt to side-track or undermine the very fountain-spring of human sexual life and to pervert the unmistakable intentions of nature.

But the absorbed intensity of the daughter of Hector, whose

uncle Dolon was the son of Eumedes of Troy, was as unaffected by this undying dialogue of the dead as was the carving-tool she carried in that special fold of her garment which was the mark of the highest-born maidens of Ilium. She went straight into the centre of a grove of Ash-Trees, or Meliai, just as if she herself had been one of those Melian Nymphs born of the Great Mother at the first separation of Heaven from Earth, a grove of trees that grew on the eastern margin of the smooth lawn of delicate grass that lay midway between those two demonic pillars of cloud. Had Tis the cow-herd and Nisos the princely young house-help been following her at this moment they would certainly have stopped in horrified amazement at what they saw.

Both of them knew well as indeed did all the retainers of the royal House of Odysseus that the long-cherished divinely sacred arms of Achilles had been kept in the treasure-crypt beneath the palace ever since by the influence of the goddess Athene over merchant-sailors, they had reached Odysseus' island home.

Whether voyaging eastward or voyaging westward, they had been brought safe to Ithaca five years after his own miraculous return. But who would have believed that Arsinöe, the youngest niece of Dolon the Trojan spy, could have carried the divine art of carving to such a pitch that she could carve an Ash-Tree, devoid of branches though it was and standing erect in its death, into the actual shape and form, as he was when he lived, of Hector, son of Priam, husband of Andromache, defender of Ilium?

And where and how could the girl have learnt such a god-given gift? Had she strayed as a child, while following the chorus of the maidens of Troy in their Orphic worship and received secret lessons from some outlawed offspring of Hephaistos, the son of Zeus? But learn the great art to some purpose she had, and this grand figure of Hector himself, standing tall and stately in the heart of this Melian Grove, was the result.

And now upon this noble image, carved though it was in perishable wood rather than in immemorial marble, this sad, lost, helpless Trojan maid had hung all those Hephaestian fragments of divine workmanship upon which the rising sun was already beginning to pour its pure blood-sprinkled gold. Holding it high with both her hands, as if it were a goblet of the very nectar of the Olympians, Arsinöe now disentangled the horse-hair-nodding helmet from its covering of white linen and placed it on the Trojan hero's majestically moulded head.

Then at last carefully removing her carving-tool from that proud fold in her garment that marked her as having been a privileged attendant at Priam's Court, the Trojan girl set to work to suggest by a series of delicate scoopings and indentations the precise appearance of Hector's forehead—so un-Hellenic in its curious curves but so pitiably well-known to every dweller in Ilium—as its outlines, partly concealed and partly emphasized by the horse-hair helmet, emerged as if newly created to greet the glory of the sun's first rays which now pierced with a long stream of golden light that little group of ancient ash-trees.

The moment she had completed her final touches to the dead, whose figure was now entirely accoutred in the divine armour of Achilles, which, piece by golden piece, save only the world-renowned shield which had never reached Ithaca, she had brought from the palace to that ash-grove, at first doing this month by month, and later week by week, as her purpose in its prosperous secrecy gathered momentum, she wrapped the linen cloth about her carving-tool and without giving her finished work any final glance turned to retrace her steps.

Her face as she turned to go re-assumed that look of Cimmerian hopelessness which had never left it since the day when her companions who had been pointed out so implacably, one by one, by Eurycleia, as the girls who had given their maiden-heads to the Suitors, had met their death by hanging—"no clean death for such" Telemachus had declared with all a young man's righteous ferocity—and no graving-tool were it as powerful as the talons of the Erinyes themselves could have done for a human face what that event once for all had done, long ago as it was now, to the face of the youngest niece of Dolon.

But no sooner had she commenced her retreat over that square mile of mystery called "Arima", the boundary of which, as all the natives of Ithaca knew, Odysseus in his old age never cared to cross, than she was aware of a new sound, a sound entirely distinct from the wild and hoarse dialogue between those two pillars of cloud, to which she paid no more attention, perhaps less, than did the frogs in that haunted swamp.

But the sound she heard now was completely unusual and very startling in that ghostly place. It was the unmistakable cry of a wounded bird. She heard it long before the bird itself fell miserably to the ground at her feet and lay there helplessly fluttering. Quickly she bent down, seized it, and pressed it to her breast. This she did with no change of expression and with the same unmoved, unsmiling, unhappy, inscrutably fixed look.

But she knew what had happened, and she knew what bird this was; none other in fact than Heirax the Hawk, the messenger-friend of Nisos, the princely House-Helper. Heirax had been wounded in the air, either by an attack from some other bird, or by an arrow from a human bow, just as he was reaching the cliffs of Ithaca, and for the last few minutes he had been desperately flying forward in hectic jerks and feverish swoops, with the frantic hope of reaching the palace and of delivering to her friend Nisos the tremendous news he carried before loss of blood brought him down.

But his fatal day, or, as any native of the island would have put it, his predestined "Keer" had come. He felt himself falling, and impelled by the natural instinct of all dying creatures to seek a hiding-place, he deliberately swerved so as to fall in "Arima". It was only when quite close to the ground that he realized that he was destined to fall at the feet of the one single person belonging to the palace who was no friend of his friend Nisos. Leipephile was his best girl-friend and in his thoughts Heirax always pronounced that simple creature's name as if it lad been Leip-filly; thus totally avoiding the proper stress with Its accent on the "peph" that flippant second syllable.

Heirax's pronunciation made the name more dignified as

well as more appealing, though the sound of the word thus uttered would have made Agelaos, the girl's betrothed, want to treat him as alas! the hawk was going to be treated now.

Not for nothing had the Trojan girl always stayed awake while the rest of them, including the king's old nurse, nodded in weariness under the eternal divagations of their "much-enduring" lord. "Tell me, Heirax," whispered Arsinoë now: "what your news is and I will swear by any oath you choose that I will tell it to Nisos. If you tell me, I will carry you back to the palace where they have drugs that will strengthen your spirit, and ointments that will stop the blood, and potions that will heal the pain. But if you will not tell me . . ." And she pressed her knuckles against the bird's throat.

And Heirax the hawk said to himself; "It matters nothing whether I tell or refuse to tell. The news is bound to spread anyway. The only loss will be to Nisos and me. I shall lose the pleasure of telling him and he will lose the pleasure of being told by me." He shifted his position slightly against her left breast and opening his beak made the sounds that Nisos had taught him.

Nisos had been a good teacher for a Hawk, especially for one born on a small island and accustomed to rocks and shores and sands and caves and curving waves and tossing wisps of foam. So his words were clear as to their meaning; though they were ungrammatical and disconnected in their utterance.

"Zeus," he whistled—and at each sound drops of blood oozed from the wound in his side—"thunder lost . . .
                        peak of Gargaros . . .
. . . alone . . . Hera on Olympos . . .
        . . . alone . . .
Trojans rebuilding Troy in Italy . . .
. . . Rome . . . Seven Hills . . . Tartaros
               broken loose . . .
    Niobe weeps no more . . .
  . . . Chaos comes back . . .
                 Persephone

ATLANTIS

> ... leaves Aidoneus ...
> Prometheus escapes ...
> ... Cheiron free ...
> Helios conquers
> Apollo ...
> ... Atlas no longer
> ... the sky ...
> the Mysteries ... blown far and wide ...
> ... Typhon free ..."

Here there was a long pause; and in the interval the Trojan girl could hear the hoarse voices of those two Pillars of Cloud raised in an absorbed argument with each other. Eurybia was maintaining that what had happened was the overthrow of the Olympians by the Titans while Echidna was arguing that what was convulsing time and rocking space, and upheaving the Abyss till it was tilted as high as the Zodiacal Signs, was nothing more or less than the victory of the Eternal Feminine whether divine or human or diabolic or angelic or bestial or saurian or reptilian or earthly or aquatic or ethereal or fiery, over the male.

Then Heirax whistled: "Take me to Nisos or leave me to die in Arima!" Ever since she had heard the Hawk's astounding news an absolute change had approached Arsinoë's tragic face. It had not taken possession of it. It had only come near it. But it had come so near it that from now on to the end of her days at uneven intervals and for uncertain reasons there began to burst forth or rend forth or tear forth, or jet forth, or explode forth, a flame of exultation so formidable that anyone might have imagined that some fiery particle of the lost lightning of Zeus had by some mad chance got entangled in her hair giving to this already dangerous emotion of hers a supernatural power.

"And now I beseech you," Heirax implored her, opening and shutting his beak with a queer, shrill, scraping sound, "take me to . . ." But it was out of a dead throat that the name "Nisos" dissolved in the air; for without a word the girl had wrung the bird's neck.

ATLANTIS

But Heirax did have, for all his sudden end, a sort of tributary memorial set up in the scoriac floor of the Trojan girl's memory; for whenever afterwards she recalled her exultation at the image of Zeus robbed of his aerial weapons and compelled to look down from one of those peaks in Ida, so officially familiar to him as the divine Umpire, and to hear news therefrom, without the power to interfere, of the rising of a new Troy on those Seven Italian Hills, she always felt herself lightly toying, as in her heart she derided the Fathers of Gods and Men, with the swaying neck and dangling head of that small enemy of Ilium, so limp in her hands.

But she didn't toss that lump of blood-wet feathers either into Eurybia's swamp or Echidna's slaughter-cave. She carried it back to the feet of her tree-carved image of Hector and there as she curled it up, claws against beak and wings against belly, she murmured to it aloud: "I don't fancy the worms of Arima will bother with *you*: but you'll be eaten for all that! In this little matter, the friends of great Hector and the enemies of great Hector are the same. Eaten of worms are we all when we come to it: but at least we give birth to our own worms and are devoured by what we ourselves have engendered." It may have been that some dim little-girl memory of the funeral-rites of the man whose horse-hair-crest above the armour of Achilles seemed just then to stir in reciprocity, came into her mind at that moment; for as she stared at the bird on the ground and thought of the Son of Kronos on his Thunderless peak her triumphant mood relaxed a little. At any rate it relaxed enough to enable her to hear a thin little reedy voice like an infant's pipe played in a subterranean gallery.

"Aren't you ashamed," piped that thin voice, "to talk so loud that a person can't hear Echidna's answer to Eurybia? Is it nothing to you what has *caused* this terrible Pandemonium that is shaking the bowels of the universe, cracking the kernel of the cosmos, splitting the fundament of the crustaceous globe and disturbing every civilized and scholarly and sophisticated and weaponless worm who dwells below the vulgar and brutal surface of this blood-stained and desecrated earth?"

As Trojan maids, whether young or old, were addicted to become when crossed in any personal quest, Arsinöe became rude. "And who may you be?" she enquired.

"I happen to be," replied the unruffled worm, "what below the surface of the earth we call a philosopher. I pursue the purpose of all true philosophy which is to live happily without helmet or breast-plate or greaves or shield or sword or spear or claws or teeth or sting or poison. But the human race refuses to let us stay quietly underground. It digs us up. It impales us on fish-hooks.

"And this invasion of our right as individual souls to pursue truth in our own fashion began early in the history of this planet and is not confined to the cruel race of men. As serpents practise it upon toads, so do toads upon us. Contemptible little birds swallow us whole and we perish in their loathsome little stomachs.

"Primeval saurians from the aboriginal swamps delight in swallowing us and love to feel us wriggling to death in the fearful stench of their foul entrails. Are you not ashamed to bring your blood-shedding absurdities, your ridiculous feuds, your childish armour, and your murderous weapons into Arima, so that a person cannot even hear the drift of the metaphysical argument between Eurybia and Echidna and hearing it judge calmly for himself whether what is happening is the long-expected revolt, so welcome to us worms, of women against men, or is a revival of the ancient struggle between Kronos of the Golden Age and his 'Peace to all Beings' and the reign of these accursed Olympians with their infantile motto: 'The Devil take the Hindmost?' Are you not ashamed of yourself, you carver of dead trees?' Arsinöe touched carelessly with the tip of her right sandal Heirax's squeezed-up corpse that had the appearance, after the way she had handled it, of a feathered tortoise.

"Is it permitted," she enquired sarcastically, "to a humble carver of images who has not yet learnt that the earth belongs to those beneath it, to ask the name of the person who is addressing me?"

"I am the Worm of——" But the mysterious syllables "Arima" never reached her ears from the uplifted point of soft-wrinkled redness emerging from its crumpled collars of pink skin that diminished in tapering elasticity till they reached that prehensile projection: for she was off at a pace that was almost a run. "I must just go and see," she told herself, "what that little devil Nisos is up to now."

As she hurried away she took care to adjust the "Palace-of-Priam" fold neatly against her breast with the carving-tool wrapped tightly in the linen cloth she had used for the helmet. Not for one second had it occurred to her that, exquisitely as she had caught the curves of her hero's skull, the way she had armed him would certainly have made Hector's brother, the wanton Paris, smile; for that Trojan helmet by no means went well with the armour of Achilles while the absence of the famous Hephaistian shield hindered the separate pieces of the golden armour from producing their proper cumulative effect.

"Have you got a mug or a cup of any kind with you, Tis?" she asked boldly as she passed the open door of the shed where Babba's large, warm-blooded black-and-white body was being milked. "Come in, lady! Come in lady! Certainly I've got the best possible cup here for a beautiful maid like thy precious self!"

Thus speaking, and squeezing the final drop of milk from Babba's depleted udder, Tis gave the cow a friendly slap, followed by a vigorous propulsion towards the hay at the head of her stall, and without further delay proceeded to dip into the brimming pail between his knees a great battered silver ladle, which, as his only valuable possession in the world, he kept hidden in a secret place in that ramshackle shed.

"Here ye be, lady," he chuckled. "'Tain't every day old Tis has a fair lass to entertain in's own banquet-hall! 'Tisn't wine, as dost know of thyself, being as ye too, like Babba, must suckle offspring when the man and the hour be come; and it aint spiced with nard or thicked out with Pramnian cheese. But right good milk it be, warm from Babba's teats and properer for a maid like thee than any of the rosy!"

The Herdsman went on with his quaint compliments long after the Trojan captive had possessed herself of the ladle's gleaming handle and taken a satisfying sip of its warm contents. When she had restored to its owner the one and only heir-loom in his family except their name, for Tis's Father, grandfather, and great-grandfather, who all worked on their own farm at the other end of the island, were never known as anything but Daddy Tis, Grand-Pa Tis, and Old Tis, she begged this middle-aged youngest and simplest of the Tisses to tell her if he knew whether Nisos Naubolides had gone back to the palace.

Without the faintest hesitation—for what did this middle-aged youngest of the Tisses know about cosmogonic upheavals and Trojan second-births?—the herdsman informed her that the young princeling of the great House of Naubolides hadn't yet returned from visiting Aulion his ancestral home. "He said something," continued the innocent herdsman, "about running in to Druinos on his way back. My lady Pandea," he said, "loves a gossip with my lady Nosodea."

"But Master Tis," protested the Trojan girl, aware that there was an obscure shadow wavering across the path she was now travelling though keeping well out of her immediate reach and as unable to shake her new secret triumph as it would have been to touch the adamantine unhappiness of her former mood, "how do you explain this business of the Priest of Orpheus being able——"

But the girl stopped short. What was the use of trying to make a man like this see what she could or couldn't understand among the confused doings of these infernal Achaians? "One thing's clear," her thoughts ran on: "Telemachos was, is, and ever will be my most dangerous enemy here. He is a priest in Athene's temple; and suppose he heard rumours that I'd been seen at work in that grove of Ash-Trees within the confines of Arima, he might come himself and get hold of me, independently altogether of Odysseus, and treat me exactly in the same cruel way he treated those others at the killing of the Suitors."

The lonely Trojan woman stood like a statue between Tis, who was now wiping his silver ladle with fresh-plucked moss and Babba who was switching her tail in growing impatience to be out, in the sunshine, cropping grass. The girl's eyes were fixed upon empty space, while before a secret judgment-seat in her hidden soul each of the island-leaders connected with the Palace or the Temple appeared one by one.

She thought of the great statue of Themis, daughter of heaven and earth, and sister of Okeanos, which stood at the foot of the grassy slope leading up to the porch of the Temple. This goddess of humane Law and Order, and of the righteous customs and traditions of mankind, had been worshipped in Ilium as devoutly as she was worshipped here; and Arsinoë's chief links between her youthful happiness and her mature servitude were the many gods of Hellas that were worshipped by both races.

Once or twice when the moon was full she had even slipped out of the palace-porch, and stealing down to the Temple barefooted, so that no grass-stain on her sandals, or gossamer-seed caught in the knots of the threads that fastened them, would betray her daring to the sharp eyes of old Eurycleia, had gone so far as to pay a visit to the stone image of this Goddess of divided mankind and to kiss the earth at its base.

Of the parents of the two brothers Agelaos and Nisos whose names were Pandea and Krateros, she had always preferred Krateros; not only because as the head of the Naubolos family he was the ancestral rival of Odysseus and Telemachos but because his appearance always struck her as un-Hellenic and even a little Phoenician. Nosodea, the mother of the Priestess Stratonika and of Eurycleia's Maid, Leipephile, who was the betrothed of Agelaos, she disliked most of all, more even than the King's old nurse, Eurycleia herself, whose caprices she had to obey.

Exactly *why* she so hated Nosodea she felt now, as she mentally caused the woman to be dragged before her judgment-seat, that she could not quite make clear even to herself. "She's such a regular woman!" she found herself repeating; but she knew she was packing into the word "regular" several qualities that were by no means exclusively feminine.

ATLANTIS

Nosodea's husband, the father of the two girls, was a good deal older than his wife and was something of an enigma to the whole island. The adjective "geraios" meaning "old" was invariably added to his name by the whole neighbourhood; which in itself suggested, Arsinoë could not help thinking, that everybody felt the man to be different in some curious way from all his contemporaries.

And the odd thing was, the Trojan girl now told herself, while Babba fidgetted more and more irritably and Tis watched her with the expression with which when slaughtering an animal he waited for it to fall stunned after giving it a blow between the eyes, the odd thing was that for some inscrutable reason which completely baffled her she felt there was something in common between herself and Damnos Geraios and that if she could only get hold of the man when Nosodea was well out of the way she could form an alliance with him not only against his wife and two daughters but against the whole world!

"Well!" she sighed, almost as if she would have liked to spend the whole day thinking of all these people from the new background of her feelings, "I must be off, Master Tis! Thank you a thousand times for the milk!"

But it was at that moment that the Trojan woman received a startling shock. The herdsman suddenly lifted his muscular body from the tree-root that had been serving him as a milking-stool. He did not raise it to its full height, which at its best was nothing beyond a man's medium stature, but he raised it sufficiently to make it resemble a quadruped swaying about on its hind legs. He still held the silver ladle; and as if to assist himself in an agitating process of confused and difficult thought he grasped it tightly at both ends and drew it angrily up and down across his forehead like a glittering rod across a sullen and silent musical instrument.

While absorbed in this process he kept repeating in a series of harsh cries the words: "Lady! lady, lady! The dream! The dream! The dream!"

Arsinoë experienced a spasm of such nervous irritation at this impediment to her already over-delayed departure that it was with an effort she suppressed the impulse to leave the man to his fit, or whatever it was, that was now doubling him up, and just hurry off. But impulsive selfishness was as foreign to Arsinöe's introspective nature as was impulsive geniality.

"What dream are you talking about Master Tis? You really oughtn't to give people such shocks. You quite scared me, jumping up so suddenly like that. Can't you tell a person quietly, Master Tis, what's come over you?"

But Tis continued to totter like a quadruped on its hind-legs; while, though holding it with only one hand now, he scraped his forehead with the ladle.

But it was at this moment that Babba, drawn into the situation by an obscure feeling that her friend and protector was being unfairly scolded, and also, by a less obscure desire to be led where she could find juicier and more sap-filled nourishment than the dry hay which at present bristled with so many sharp stalks over the edge of her wooden bin, shuffled back to Tis's side and pressed her cold nose against the log from which he had just risen.

This instinctive bovine movement combined with the tone of rebuke in Arsinöe's voice brought Tis to himself and he began hurriedly to explain. "You see, lady," he almost blubbered, "great-grand-dad's, bit of land at the blasted end of this here rock of beggars and bastards was called, in them blessed days of old, *after*, if ye understand me, the home-stead of Aulion of the Naubolides and also after the home-stead of Druinos of the Pheresides; and we was taught by grand-dad, whose old dad taught he, that on the day when Aulion and Druinos, our poor old bit of rock-dust and grass-root being called, thee must understand, by the name of Auliodruinos came under one hand, *that* one hand would bring down forever, break-up and bust-up, for good and all, you understand the House of Odysseus! And it just then came into me head that last night I dreamed that Grand-Dad was once again talking to us same as 'un used to talk about this final confirmation and arbitration of They Above."

At this point Tis stopped, and a look of abysmal satisfaction overspread his countenance. It was already familiar to the captive from Ilium that the use of long-drawn-out proclamatory expressions such as "confirmation" and "arbitration" was in itself comforting to the agora-loving inhabitants of Hellas; so now that she saw that look on the herdsman's face she lost entirely her humanely feminine scruples about leaving this incredible simpleton alone with Babba. It was clear they understood each other. It was indeed not inconceivable that Babba herself derived vague images of rich green grass from words that sounded so rhetorically satisfying as "confirmation" and "arbitration".

With her pride in the news that the unburied Heirax had brought quite unimpaired, therefore, by any twinges of a humanely feminine conscience, the Trojan girl, with one of the rare smiles that few in Ithaca had ever seen on her face, indicated to times during that disturbed February night, whileTis that it was time for him to think less about his grandfather and more about his job. She was not greatly worried at being so late; for she felt pretty sure, such were her own secret good spirits, that the king's aged nurse would be too conscious of calamity on the wind to take her delay as more than a ripple of annoyance following a rolling wave of menacing premonition.

CHAPTER II

Four times during that disturbed February night, while the atmosphere in the palace-corridor grew tenser and tenser, and the Herculean club between its quartz-props grew more and more surly, and the fly Myos and the moth Pyraust were working themselves up to a fever of agitation, did the lonely old monarch rise from his bed and look out of his two windows. One of these faced due West, that is to say towards the opposite quarter of the sky from the one upon which the corridor of the six pillars opened. The other window of the king's bedroom faced due North.

It was the middle of night when he got out of bed for the fourth time; and this time he heard a certain thin, frail, feminine voice uttering a quavering, rasping, high-pitched appeal from the ancient oak opposite his window. This was a hollow oak-tree not only familiar to his own boyhood, but equally familiar to the boyhood of Laertes his father; and it was the abode or what almost might be called the second self of a Dryad.

His encounters with this ancient Oak-Sister had been rarer since his marriage. They had been interrupted of course by the Trojan war and his capture by Circe and Calypso, and had been only intermittently resumed since his wife had followed his parents into the shades and his son Telemachos had turned into a reserved, self-centred, philosophy-absorbed priest, serving Athene indeed, but serving her in a very different manner from the way he served her himself.

The voice he heard now as he leaned out of the window which looked due North was consequently not only a little querulous but a little injured. He was wearing his usual night-blanket or "claina" which save on the hottest nights he kept buckled round him by his broad body-belt or "zosteer"; so it wasn't from chilliness that the Dryad's voice struck him as having in its tone something so disturbing that it went beyond querulousness or hurt feelings. Laertes, his father, who had often talked to her out of this same window, used to call her by her name; a name she had received from a patroness of hers, one of the less well-known Graces, a Spartan Grace named Kleta, or "the one called for in time of need".

The Dryad Kleta was indeed a touchy, highly-strung, super-sensitive Nymph, whose chief pleasure was in what she persisted in calling her "garden": and if you wanted to bring down her anger upon you you had only to meddle with this obsession of hers. Kleta's garden in reality was simply and solely a wild strip of uncultivated woodland, not as rocky or swampy as the haunted "Arima", but, like it, belonging to no individual owner, and extending as far as the crest of an up-land ridge from which the wooded peak of the mountain known as Neriton was visible as well as the high rock above that Naiad's cave where on his return to slay the suitors Odysseus had been helped by Athene herself to hide his Phaiakian treasure.

The oak-tree from which this disturbing appeal reached him through the thick darkness was not only large enough and hollow enough to hide three or four old Dryads as emaciated as Kleta; but it was disfigured and deformed under its lowest branch, as well as above its largest branch, by two deeply-cut indentations, now almost filled up with mosses and small ferns, one of which, the lower one, having been made by the childish axe of Laertes and the other upper one by a similar childish tool wielded by himself.

As he leaned now out of that wooden aperture and murmured his response to that quavering voice he couldn't help thinking of the days when his mother had stopped him from interfering with Kleta's so-called "garden". What the old Nymph liked to do was to arrange every tree, every shrub, every flower, every clump of grass, every dead or living root, every wild fern, every spray of ivy, so as to make exquisite patterns and delicate arrangements, and even to design suggestions of god-like terraces, and the mystic purlieus or enchanted courts and secret vistas leading into divine sanctuaries where the smallest insects and the weakest worms could be safe at last from all those abominable injustices and cruel outrages, and all those stupid brutalities and careless mutilations that lack even the excuse of lust.

But it was not only of things like these that the aged Dryad Kleta constructed what she called her garden. What she really set herself to be was a protector and fulfiller of the intentions of her universal mother Gaia, the Earth. Kleta was in fact a sort of voluntary gardener of wild nature, planting and re-planting and trimming and cutting and watering and grafting and designing, as if she were a spirit-like impersonation of all the various maturing elements and an embodied shield-bearer against all the destructive ones.

ATLANTIS

Not an inch of Kleta's garden in the slow long passing of the years was neglected. That spartan grace who visiting Ithaca once every five-hundred years had noticed this young oak-tree with its entwining "hetaira", or devoted "companion", and had given the Dryad her own name, was well-satisfied with her protégée. If that portion of the island called Arima was dedicated to mystery and prophecy, the portion of it tended by Kleta was dedicated to the unruffled preservation of what is usually obliterated.

Kleta would arrange with absorbed contemplation and deeply pondered purpose all those little separate twigs and straws and tiny pieces of wood and fungus and fir-cone that lend themselves to some subtle extension of the power of Themis even over such chaotic realms of pure chance as are offered by the man-trodden and creature-trodden trails and tracks and paths in a wild island like Ithaca.

Anyone, whether human or more than human, who turns nature into a garden is liable to find an unbelievable number of very small things that have once been parts of other things but are now *entities on their own* such as bits of wood, bits of stalk, bits of fungus, bits of small snail-shells, bits of empty birds' eggs, bits of animals' hair, bits of birds' feathers, bits of broken sheaths of long-perished buds and shattered insect-shards, strewn remnants of withered lichen-clusters, and scattered fragments of acorns and berries and oak-apples that have survived in these lonely trails and tracks to be scurf upon the skin of one world and the chaos-stuff for the creation of another world.

It was especially the curious hieroglyphs and mysterious patterns which are the written messages from all the unnoticed things that die to make the dust out of which other things are born that fascinated the aged Dryad as she moved day by day about her wild garden.

It was because of her sensitiveness and touchiness with regard to her interpretations of Nature's intentions, and the odd uses to which Nature's smallest leavings and litterings can be put, that Kleta had often burst into fits of furious anger with the childish heroes of three generations of the Lords of Ithaca.

ATLANTIS

The first time he left his bed that February night he completely soothed the old Dryad. But by the fourth time he leaned on that great plank rather like a ship's rail, that crossed the opening into his bedroom at the top of a short ladder of thick pine-wood boards, he felt as if it were he himself, quite as much as the Dryad, who needed soothing.

This time he held a torch in his hand and had sandals on his feet, while Kleta, who was watching that illuminated window with trembling limbs and a troubled mouth could only stare in amazement at the figure that confronted her across that black gulf. Odysseus was anything but uncomely, anything but deformed or badly built, but it must be confessed that in the flickering blaze of his torch he presented a somewhat eccentric appearance at that moment.

He was not a tall man; and this fact which the famous Helen hadn't failed to notice made the massive breadth of his shoulders and the enormous span of his chest something that bordered on the fantastic and grotesque. Nobody's vision of him, arrested at first by these peculiarities, would be able all the same to dwell on them for long.

The startling proportions and unique grandeur of his head would inevitably dominate any enduring impression. He was very nearly totally bald; so there were no attractive curls to distract an onlooker's or even an interlocutor's attention from the peculiar majesty of his skull and of the way his eyes were set in it. His forehead itself was neither particularly high nor particularly low. Its breadth was its chief characteristic and next to its breadth the unusual distance between his eye-sockets.

This distance made it impossible for him to stare at any person with that kind of concentrated intensity which suggested that the object of the gaze had the power of giving him something that it was essential he should have, or of taking something from him that it was essential he should not lose.

In fact this breadth between his eye-sockets produced an effect that was at once sub-human and super-human. It gave him that look which certain large animals have of being completely oblivious to everything save their own immediate purpose. But it also gave him the look of a Titan or a Giant or even of a God from whom other mortals, whether male or female, had no claim for more individual notice or respect than swarms of gnats or midges.

His nose was neither curved like an eagle's beak nor protuberant as a boar's snout. It carried forward the straight line of his forehead and its character lay in its massive and bony breadth; for its nostrils were not especially wide nor did they twitch or contract and open with the abnormal sensitivity of horses or deer. Curiously enough it was not his majestic skull nor this weird breadth between his eyes that gave to the countenance of Odysseus its most familiar attribute.

Every person, whether male or female, in any group of people who encounter one another day by day, possesses some particular physical characteristic more realistically charged with that person's predominant effect upon others than any other attribute. In the case of the aged Odysseus this was his beard. If the wily old warrior had any special personal vanity or anything about his appearance upon which he himself especially concentrated it was his beard.

To get the effect that pleased him over this beard of his it had become necessary for him not only to trim it with the utmost care but to shave off or cut away all the hair on the portions of his face other than those that served him as a stage for this dramatic emphasis upon his beard.

As he now leaned out into that hollow sap-scented darkness holding his blazing torch, his beard was emphasized precisely in the way that satisfied this one queer streak of personal vanity in him. It was no wonder then that the old Dryad's appeal to him to come down those wooden steps, for they were much more than a ladder, and listen closely to what she wanted him to hear became an appeal that he felt to be irresistible, for in certain deep and narrow mole-runs in their nature the personal vanity of god-like men surpasses by a hundred-fold the natural vanity of women. But there was more in this than that. There was a queer psychic obsession in it; for once when, in middle manhood, and under the influence of this rather eccentric vanity of his, and of the method he had deliberately adopted for trimming it, his beard showed signs of taking the shape he desired for it, his mother Antikleia cried out to him when she caught sight of him emerging clean and fresh from a bath: "By the gods, boy, your beard is as pointed as the prow of a ship!" and, as it chanced, in flinging out this casual remark she proved she had read, as mothers sometimes, though not often, can read, what had hardly been known to himself, the hidden urge behind what he was doing to his face.

"O why is it," he groaned to himself, this wily old sacker of cities, and enslaver of their defenders' wives, "that we mortals have the power of re-creating our actual appearance with which we confront the sun and the moon? Animals and birds can't do it though they can rejoice in the change or lament over the change when it's done for them!"

If it had been some special competition of opposite odours during that February night, as they hovered round his home, some of them unspeakably exquisite, some of them revoltingly excremental, a few actually sepulchral, that swept his memory back at that moment to his mother's words about the way he trimmed his beard, he was still descending that wooden flight of stairs, when a gust of wind from the sea whirled away from above both himself and Kleta's oak a thick veil of mist, leaving in sight not only several zodiacal constellations, but among them, and yet not among them, such a shy, timid, lonely, brittle, shell-like crescent, that the idea of the Moon as she was before Artemis meddled with her, or Apollo meddled with the sun, whirled into his heavy skull.

This same gust of wind, not satisfied with making him aware that his disturbed sleep was connected with the fact that they were now in "noumenia" or the beginning of the month, brought from far-away, across rocks and deserts and forests and seas, in fact from the entrance to Hades itself a vision so strange that he paused in his descent, and holding his torch at arm's length, so that its flame shouldn't touch the protruding point of this same bowsprit-beard, shut both his deep-socketed, widely-separated eyes, and drew in his breath in such a gasping sigh that it was as if he were swallowing his own soul.

What that wind brought to him, as it revealed under those far-off stars that tiny crescent was nothing less than the glimpse he had in Hades of the ghost of Herakles himself, glaring round him like black night with his fingers on the string of his bow, while round about him whirled flocks upon flocks upon flocks of birds in feathered panic, their beaks and wings and claws indistinguishable as they circled.

But his vision of the former owner of the great club that nowadays was always so patiently waiting in the porch till its-hour came round again, was gone with the gust that brought it. The old man leapt to the earth from the final rung of that wooden flight of steps and tightening his belt about his middle and holding his torch so that neither its flame nor its smoke should impede his movements he hurried across the uneven ground to the hollow oak.

It was certainly a pitiful old face that looked out at him from that mouldering recess; but he had known it now for all the years since Penelope died; and though in its lines and wrinkles, and in its scooped out hollows where soft feminine flesh should be, and in its bony protuberances where beguiling girlish dimples should be, it was a ghastly enough mask of the ravaging power of time, it had the same strangely preoccupied look it always had.

It was a beautiful face—no! not "beautiful" exactly—say rather haunting with its own special kind of poignant wistfulness—and it wore a permanent expression that betrayed the Dryad's incurable inability to lose herself in any love or worship or devotion or absorbing affection that implied the sacrifice of the smallest fraction of that larger half of her conscious life that was given up to her struggle to be a tender nurse, not only to all the wild vegetation within her reach, but to the innumerable off-scourings of animal, vegetable and even mineral life about her, that seemed to her queer mind to be in need of a friend.

Arrived at the hollow oak the old king thrust the torch he carried into the ground, where its quiet flame, now that the gust of wind had subsided, burned as steadily as a large candle. "There's so much, Odysseus, to tell you," the Dryad began, "that I don't know where to start. Kleta-Charis, my name-mother, has been here: that's the chief thing I wanted to tell you. She was resting for the night in that cave of yours belonging to the Naiads where Athene helped you to hide your treasure when you returned to slay the suitors."

"And where, now, old lady," the king interrupted. "I am building my ship for my last voyage! But what did Kleta-Charis say? Don't 'ee be afraid to tell me, old friend. I know of myself from what I've been feeling all night that there's something new and strange on the wind; though whether from East or West the storm is coming, and whether Zeus or Poseidon is behind it I've not yet learnt.

"What I cannot understand is why my friend Athene hasn't come to tell me what has been happening tonight. In all my life until now she has always come to me at a great crisis. Is it so serious, do you suppose, Kleta-Dryad, that she has been summoned by the gods of Olympos to a grand council? Or has she gone to the East, whither the great gods were always accustomed to go at this time of year, to receive worship and reward worshippers among the blameless Ethiopians?"

"Sit down on this, my child," the lady of the oak leaned forward from her hiding-place and using both of her long emaciated arms spread out on the dark mosses and small ferns between them the skin of a recently dead wolf.

"Kleta-Charis," murmured the old Dryad in a low hoarse voice, and it was clear to her hearer that she spoke with an effort and with a grim determination to let him hear the worst at once, "Kleta-Charis told me that the great gods were at this hour in such extreme danger themselves that they had no time to think of the fate of their votaries and champions. She said that the whole of Tartaros has broken loose, and that in their first attempt to resist this upheaval, Zeus and Poseidon, blind with anger, raised up such a world-swallowing sea-wave that it swallowed the whole continent of Atlantis; and that the cities of Atlantis with all their populations had a now sunk into Hades, where, if Aidoneus reigns still—but does he, Odysseus, does he reign in Hades still?—he ought to be marshalling them in their due order and bringing their leaders and chieftains, and especially those among them who were unjust and cruel, before the judgment-seats of Rhadamanthus and Minos."

The old Dryad, having poured out all this in one breath save for a gasp at the word "Atlantis" and another at the word "Aidoneus", sank down on her knees in the inside of the hollow tree-trunk and rested her chin and her hands against the rough, powdery, thousand-year-old jaggedness of disintegration which for nearly a century had constituted the window-sill of the slowly dying oak which was in a sense her house, and in a sense herself.

She breathed heavily, but freely enough now, as she watched the effect of her words upon the massive, upturned, almost bald head beneath her, as he squatted cross-legged upon the wolf-skin, while his torch from its muddy socket in the wet moss threw a wavering beam of light upon his outstretched bowsprit-beard which at noon-day was like the solid silver of a graven image in a temple.

But the most silvery beard in that darkness, In spite of the crescent-moon and the stars and the torch, would have been reduced to a colour-levelling monotone by the encompassing gloom. He remained silent for a long moment. Then he said slowly: "My friend Athene is bound to appear soon. She will touch me with her immortal hand. She will counsel me with her divine wisdom."

After hearing this the dweller in the dying oak fell silent in her turn while far-away they both could catch the voice of some fortunate sea-bird that after losing itself inland fell to uttering repeated cries of relief when it caught once more the sound of waves breaking on the rocks.

"Athene will probably appear to me," began Odysseus again, "in the form of a young fisherman or goatherd when I go tomorrow, today I mean, to the cave of the Naiads where I'm building my ship. It was clever of me—eh, Kleta, old friend? —to go to a place like that which all the island regards as so sacred to the sea-powers that they daren't approach it? My difficulty, as I knew from the start, when I began working on the keel and the body of my ship, will be to collect enough sail-cloth to make a big enough main-sail.

"You, of course, old friend, always busy as you are with tending your wild garden, have no idea of the things we men have to consider, especially in matters of war and of ships. I've made up my mind to hoist sail again before I die. I'm not going to rot here alive till I'm eaten by worms. You tell me Zeus and Poseidon and Aidoneus have between them drowned the whole of Atlantis. *That* doesn't look to me as if the power of the gods were declining!

"Zeus, the Father of Athene, has often been influenced by her far-sighted wisdom; and when she visits me she will tell me how to propitiate the Father of men and gods. Even if Atlantis is at the bottom of the ocean, why should I be worried? Answer me *that*, name-child of the loveliest of the Graces! Couldn't I steer my ship, when once I've got her mainsail, over the graves of a hundred Atlantises?

"I tell you, old friend, I can't see what there is in this news to make me miserable. I just can't see! I feel at this moment as if I—— "

But he suddenly stopped; confounded by what he saw in the old face staring at him out of that hollow tree.

"What's the matter, Kleta-Dryad, old friend? For the sake of all the Olympians tell your child what's the matter?"

The Dryad uttered a choking sound in her throat that was like the sob of a sea-wave caught and imprisoned behind cruel rocks when it longs to leap and curve and curl and toss and crest and fume and foam and race over the ocean's surface. Then she said, speaking in a queer voice that seemed to come from the middle of her old bent spine and to force itself between her ribs and her withered breasts: "I can't hide it from you, my child;

ATLANTIS

I can't hide it from you! But what Kleta-Charis really came to tell me was that Keto herself, the most terrible of all sea-monsters, has been seen in your cave!

"Oh child of my soul think of it! Yes, Keto herself, sister of that awful Eurybia who along with Echidna haunts Arima over there, where only those of us who have lost their wits ever go; yes! Keto the sea-monster who plays the beast with old man Phorkys of all the old gods of the sea has been seen in your cave; and since she has been there not a Naiad dares to go near it; and Kleta-Charis told me that nothing would ever induce her or any of her sisters to visit the place again! O my child, my child! It's terrible to think of! What it will really be is a second Arima.

"Yes, Odysseus, a second 'Arima' whose threshold none of us will dare to cross. What are you doing? Where are you going, Odysseus? You're not forgetting there are two hours still before Dawn, are you? Where are you going, Odysseus? You frighten me when you pull your blanket round you like that!"

Her voice rose to a hoarse shriek. "Stop, Odysseus! Stop! I tell you there are two hours more of night before the dawn comes. You can't go *now*, my child! You can't go like that!"

The only reply he made to her frantic appeal, as he rose to his feet and wrapped his blanket more tightly round him, was to turn his face towards the East and stand absolutely still with his mouth open, his nostrils wide and quivering, and his breath drawn deeply inwards in long spasms of excited suction.

But when the troubled old creature went so far in her agitation as to clamber grotesquely if not indecently out of the hollow oak and seize him by the wrist, he did speak, and when he spoke he did so with a natural and easy calm entirely free from all intensity of locked-in emotion.

"I am only going to my room," he said, "to get some sleep, and I've not the least intention of going anywhere, Kleta, old friend, till I have had a good meal. Athene will no doubt either send me a message or come herself. I only hope she won't send Telemachos. Why is it, Kleta dear, that I find it so hard to feel at ease with Telemachos since his mother died? He's become so rigid and austere and pontifical; more of a priest than a son. The great goddess herself is free enough and natural enough with me. I can even fool her a bit now and again and make sport of the way she has treated me and challenge her to treat my son in the same way.

"And all this without her getting angry with me or my getting angry with her. Though she's an immortal Olympian, and I am very much of a too-human mortal man, the goddess and I understand each other perfectly. Nothing anyone said to make trouble between us about her telling Telemachos things she doesn't tell me would make me angry with her. She's the goddess who all my life has helped me; and I am the one from among the rulers of men she has chosen to aid and defend—and that's all there is between us.

"This business of priesthood and worship, and sanctity and calling upon the dead, and swallowing the smoke from mystic tripods, and eating the flesh of dead or of living gods, and drinking their blood, and bringing the dead to life by boiling their bones in magic cauldrons is something beyond me altogether and alien to me, and I cannot understand what has come over Telemachos since his mother died. He's become so silent and secretive and so wrapt up in all this priestly ritual, that I can't get a word out of him. He says he has no wish to be king of Ithaca and lord of the islands when I'm dead!

"Sometimes I think it's all due to this curst Priest of Orpheus. But that is hard to believe; for Telemachos from his infancy has seen the Maenads and Bacchantes of Dionysos without wanting to join them! He has seen the Mysteries of Demeter and Persephone without wanting to follow them into the Kingdom of Aidoneus. I tell you, Kleta, all the priests and prophets of the gods that I've known, and I've known many, are such as teach us rulers how to overcome our enemies and how to break down the gates of their cities and take their women captive.

"No, I can't understand it, Kleta old friend. Do you remember how the other day you asked me why I didn't go to the Agora over there and make a public oration calling upon the people to collect all the sail-cloth they could get hold of and bring it to me? There are thousands and thousands of pieces of it woven into the huts and hovels of slaves in our city and hanging idly in the chambers of our merchants, when they ought to be filled with all the winds of heaven and carrying good well-benched ships over all the waves of the ocean."

He picked up his torch and looked about him. The torch had begun to burn badly and its smoke had an unnatural smell because of the moisture rising from the wet ground into which it had been thrust; but as he brandished it in the air to quicken its flame this badly-smelling cloud of smoke drifted away towards the Temple of Athene.

The old king followed its departure with his eyes while his head remained turned to the West. Slowly that small cloud of evil-smelling vapour floated away over the Temple towards the Agora. With his imagination conjuring up his speech to the assembled people of Ithaca he followed that small cloud to the low walls of their compact little city and to the amphitheatre outside those walls, with its stone seats and wide stone platform, where the citizens of the whole island, if once gathered together in a popular "ekklesia", could be conveniently harangued.

Then turning once more to the troubled old Dryad who had taken to heart so bitterly this invasion of the Naiads' cave by the monster-wife of the oldest of the "Old Men of the Sea" he saw that she was weeping silently with her forehead pressed against her knuckles and her hands clinging tightly to that uneven edge of rottenness, so frayed and so fragile and so soft and crumbling that it looked as if it had ceased to be a substance and had become a momentarily objectified taste or smell, such as, together with the aged transparency sobbing in its midst, might vanish like a ghost at cock-crow.

As the king turned his back upon her and moved off towards the stair-way to his chamber he had the feeling that the bowed old creature were nibbling her own flesh as if it were a bread of phantom-sorrow made of the crumbling wood of an ancestral oak.

ATLANTIS

Back in his room, however, Odysseus behaved exactly as he had declared to his old friend he would behave. He loosened his belt, wrapt his blanket more evenly round him, and lay down on his bed, shutting his eyes so as to replace any sort of steady staring into darkness by an absolute blindness to the whole phenomena of the visible world.

Thus he remained, and no one but himself could possibly have told whether he were awake or asleep, till dawn was more than well advanced. In fact the sun was high above the horizon, and all the paths and vineyards and gardens and woods and desert-places were illuminated by full daylight when he rose from his bed and shouted for his ancient nurse.

It was indeed in magnificently pleasant sunshine that Odysseus found his circular bath of polished stone awaiting his appearance. Eurycleia had already seen to it that no fewer than eight great water-jugs of carefully varied temperature were arranged in order round that hollow circumference of polished stone.

From the surface of some of these jars the steam rose in clouds into the air, while, in other cases, ripples from newly dissolved circles of vanishing bubbles, all tinged with rainbow colours, proved from what clear fresh springs they had come. Here Eurycleia awaited him herself, and as, with the help of Leipephile and Arsinoë, the old nurse poured in alternation the cold and lukewarm and hot streams over him as he crouched and bent and straightened himself and moved this way and that, under the varying temperatures of those jars of water, his thoughts took shape and formulated themselves into a resolution to quicken to a much more rapid speed his preparations for hoisting sail once more and setting out to explore the world again.

"Yes," he thought, "I've given this pleasant routine of the beautiful seasons repeating themselves, and the beautiful days following the beautiful nights in beautiful succession as Themis the great Goddess of order under the will of Zeus decrees, its full opportunity to soothe this itching, fretting, chafing, gnawing, fermenting, biting, seething ache in my wicked old midriff!

"But this happy easy lazy time has not done it! The marrow in my bones howls and growls for the random odds of the old great Circus! I must, I must taste again the salty taste of real plotting and real planning and real deceiving and real achieving!"

In his massive, caustic, long-sighted, super-human and yet subhuman way Odysseus had acquired the power of what might be called a "postponement of thought" while a series of instinctive impulses directed his actions. This power which would certainly appear an odd one to most clever people, had not so much been forced upon him by the particular nature of his experiences as by the prevailing mood of his reactions to these experiences.

This power was not essentially a philosophical one, nor was it even a predominantly intellectual one. What it really might be called was the controlled release of that deep intimate rush of life which at special moments takes possession of us all with what feels as if it were a wild prophetic force under the direction of a calm calculating will.

While he gave himself up, therefore, to all the small physical movements which the process of being bathed by a commanding and rather cantankerous old woman, a beautiful, secretive, middle-aged woman, and a lovely but incredibly simple young woman, his whole nature was gathering itself together, not so much to follow a thought-out plan of action as to have his nervous, electric, magnetic soul kept, in intensely conscious reserve, just under his physical skin and ready for any event, a soul that was not necessarily composed of a single compact consciousness but retained the power of dividing itself at will.

It was indeed a very curious power that his soul possessed, of splitting itself up, if need were, into an array of square-headed conscious souls that still were Odysseus "pro tem", though they were Odysseus in multiplicity rather than Odysseus in unity!

By the time the old hero was seated on his simple throne in the great open dining-hall of the palace, to which hidden steps descended from the upper chambers, and had begun to break his fast with bowls of red wine thickened by various powdered nuts and sweetened by a particular kind of honey, while he accompanied this rich beverage, after pouring out a libation to Zeus, by devouring greedily—for this first meal of the day was a good deal later than usual—the particular portion of the backbone of a fatted hog which best pleased him, he was fairly at rest in his mind.

He knew more or less what he was going to do, and he left the details of the thing to chance and occasion. Never in the history, not only of Ithaca, but of all Hellas, had there been such a born opportunist as Odysseus was. He had always been a difficult one for women to mould to their will.

It was because her powerful personality took the line of indomitable independence that Penelope had suited him so well; and it was probably because she had brought up their only child to live his own life independently of each of them that as a mature man Telemachos was so reserved and self-centred.

On this particular day therefore the old king had already thrust clean out of his contemplated groove of action any visit to or visit from his ritual-absorbed offspring. What he had to do was to visit the Naiads' Cave and find out if Keto the Sea-Monster had meddled in any way with the building of his ship of escape. "How queer," he told himself as he swallowed his final bowl of enriched and thickened wine, "that I should think of my ship as a way of *escape*! Escape from what? Have I acquired a hatred for an honoured, peaceful, well-regulated life? Is it now again just as it was on the Isles of Circe and Calypso where women's love was my accursed chain?

"No, no! That's absurd. My wife is dead and has left none to take her place. What's wrong with me then? To reach home from those immortal bitches was to escape slavery. But now that I'm at home and at peace, in rich, untroubled luxury, with my son a devoted priest of my divine protector, now that I am free from all ills of mind and body and have no enemy that I couldn't destroy with a look, a step, a thrust, a blow, now that I'm within a bow-shot of the 'herm' of Themis, the Mistress of Order and Decency and Custom, and only a couple of bowshots from the Temple of the Daughter of Zeus, what's the matter with me that I can't rest by day or night till I've built my ship and hoisted my sail and am steering for an unknown horizon?

"Well, let's see," he was addressing the three women now, "what's been happening in my Cave of the Naiads. No! I'm not going to rush off, Nurse darling, in any mad hurry nor with unmoved bowels nor unrelieved bladder, and I hope to find you, and Leipephile and Arsinoë too, ready to give me as good a bath as this when I come back tonight; and I can tell you, my dears, I fully expect I may need it! But we shall see. Good luck to us all!"

All was dim in that long, low corridor, for the Sun was steadily mounting towards high noon and not until dawn tomorrow would there be any striking sign of the lord of light again, whether written in fire or written in blood. The Sixth Pillar was aware of a queer throbbing sensation under each of those grimly-scrawled letters upon its pediment as the king approached it and passed it, making straight for the Club of Herakles near the low arch leading into the olive-garden.

"O my! O my! O my! O my!" sighed the up-lifted arm of the solitary olive-shoot that had reared up between the flagstones of that ancient threshold; but when Odysseus stopped in front of the swollen-bosom'd club and taking it up with his left hand and transferring it to his right took a firm hold of it in its narrowest place, which was about three-quarters of its whole length if you measured from head to heel, he proceeded to carry it at right angles to his hip as a hunter carries a boar-spear when making his way through a thick forest.

By no unusual chance or casual accident, for they had been hovering over the rough ground of the slaves' graves, awaiting him for several hours, did Myos the house-fly and Pyraust the girl-moth settle upon the great weapon, as the old hero held it at this horizontal angle to his person, and secrete themselves, as best they could, in the deep life-crack of the club's conscious identity, where existed all the organic pulses of its mortal being.

They were both still huddled close together in this dynamic concealment and were still keeping up the metaphysical debate into which they delighted to throw the whole life-energy of their restless natures when Odysseus, after a rapid walk of four and a half miles, reached the sea-coast.

For a few moments the effect upon him of facing the sea was overwhelming. The purpose of his coming to where the waves broke was completely swept away by the waves themselves. In their breaking they took this purpose of his and tore it to tatters of lacy wisps and wind-tossed feathers and flying flurries of fleeting foam.

He had come to the same exact spot only a day or two ago when the waves were no wilder than they were today and the sun was no more dazzling; and yet the sight of this far-flung spray, of these gleaming sun-dazzlements hadn't swallowed up then in such a gasping whirlpool of sensation every plan and scheme he had been carefully formulating.

What was there about the sea today that made its effect upon him so much more overpowering than it had been that other time? In the intensity of this question, which his whole spirit seemed to be putting to some faraway heart of the cosmos, he grasped more tightly the club which he carried in his right hand.

Ah! how well the club knew that tightening of the fingers! "Not quite as strongly grasped," it thought, "as when Herakles heard the growl of that monstrous beast! But I know very well what my new wielder is worrying about now—what's in these roaring waves that wasn't in them before?

"*That's* what's sticking in his gullet, not the salt wings of the strangling wind nor the whirling spray. And I know what it is that's in them. I know what it is that's made them different. I know what it is that lurks behind these curving and cresting and breaking waves. It's nothing less than Keto the unspeakable, Keto from the abysmal chasm in the floor of the Atlantic, Keto by whom Phorkys the Old Man of the Sea begot Echidna the Ghost-Serpent of Arima, who, by her own son Orthos the brother of Cerberos, gave birth to the feline abortion that called itself a Lion whose brains I converted into good rich dung for the ferns and honeysuckle of the Nemean Forest!"

Thus murmured the club of Herakles in the hand of its new

master, while Myos the fly and Pyraust the moth hugged each other in the crack of his body where his soul was most active, and while Odysseus with an impatient effort turned his back on those gleaming waves and entered the cave.

Then it was that the club endeavoured, by barging against every sea-weed-covered wall and colliding with every gigantic shell-fish that extended its wrinkled curves and scaly convolutions and encrusted horns from every obtruding buttress and arch, to catch his new master's attention by creating a dying-away echo that could just out-reverberate the hoarse long-drawn roar of the retreating tide by repeating the syllables "Keto-Keto-Keto-Keto" over and over again.

At last they arrived—Odysseus and his vociferous weapon—to the palatial interior of the cave, where the roof was high and the walls smooth, and the pavement, by being lifted up well above shore-level was not only dry but free from all rocky or stony obstructions.

The central hall, so to speak, of this cavernous palace by the sea resembled a gigantic workshop under immortal jurisdiction —not the jurisdiction of Hephaistos the god of fire but of some antipodal God of the extreme opposite element, that of water, but nevertheless a great and divine artificer.

In the centre of this elevated floor, which was surrounded by several subsidiary caverns that Odysseus had converted into storehouses for the materials of ship-building, lay the unfinished hull of a well-formed sea-going ocean-ship.

When the old hero, with his still murmuring but now much less tightly held companion, reached this half-built ship, which had a most curious look in this ocean-temple, he swung round and faced the wide up-sloping approach by which he had come.

This incline, which, as he now gazed down its full length, had become an astonishingly steep ascent, grew narrower and narrower the nearer it got to the flying surf and wildly tossed spray of the breaking waves.

"What has become of all the Naiads?" the king asked himself, "who were wont to frequent this cave? Have they been frightened away by that Monster of the Deep, Keto, the mate of Phorkys, the Old Man of the Sea?"

The king looked calmly round, evidently deciding, as not only his Heraklean club was deciding, but as the fly and the moth in their hiding-place in the bosom of the club were still more anxiously deciding, that some appeal to the absent Naiads to whom the cave belonged was called for at this juncture. Had the club, however, and, still more had the insects in the bosom of the club, made the appeal that followed, it would no doubt have been a more tactful one, but at any rate the king's voice echoed mightily through the whole place.

"O divine Naiads, I know your lives are determined, even as the lives of your cousins the Dryads, by the lives of the Forests and the Fountains and the Groves and the Caverns which you deify by your dear presences but which you cannot survive, whereas the fifty daughters of Nereus remain undying and imperishable even as Keto herself, the monstrous wife of Phorkys, for the sea cannot cease to exist, any more than can the earth herself, mother of us all.

"But it was the great goddess Athene who met me here when I was brought home by the ship of the Phaiakians and she told me to pray to you and to worship you and to cry aloud to you whenever I came here to build my ship for myself. And thus I obey her; and through my weak old voice it is the great goddess herself who calls upon you, O heavenly Naiads, who calls upon you to tell why you have deserted this beautiful cave and whether the cave itself is soon to be destroyed under the wrath of Poseidon the Shaker of the Earth as he avenges himself on the monstrous—— "

He was interrupted by a clear young girlish voice which was certainly not that of any Nymph, whether an immortal Nereid or a more vulnerable Naiad, but was obviously the voice, as Odysseus and his Heraklean club and those other living consciousnesses within the club, felt at once, not only of a maid of human origin but of a maid who spoke with the native island accent.

"Go away, you horrid thing! Go away! Or I'll call the King!" The little girl had evidently been watching the approach of the wily old warrior and his war-experienced weapon; for she now sprang up from the deepest portion of the ship's stern, where this one man's dry-dock work had advanced furthest, and with outstretched arms and streaming hair began shaking her fists and staring with wide-open eyes at something at the waves' edge.

Odysseus swung round on his heel; but between what this island-maid beheld and the line of his vision there was some obstacle, the corner of a rock, or an enormous fossil jutting out from the wall, or perhaps only an extra-thick tuft of salt weed on the floor of the descent into the sea, that completely hindered his vision as he struggled to focus the object that was giving her this shock.

It was an intensely awkward moment; for it was clear that the advancing monster, if such it were, must have assumed that Odysseus could see it as clearly as did the maiden but was scared either by his own old age or out of respect for the power of the immortal sea-god from interfering.

"She thinks," said the club of Herakles to himself "that the king is so old he'll just remain quiet and still while she tears the girl to pieces and swallows her!"

This idea was so appalling to the great weapon that, inspired, as we all can be by sheer desperation, he made one surpassing effort and slipping out of the hero's hand fell with a crash upon the rocky floor.

And then, in stooping to pick him up, Odysseus saw Keto. Never had the shrewd old hero shown more self-control or more subtle and convoluted cunning than he showed now. With the club in his hand and held by the middle as hunters hold a short boar-spear he ran down the slope straight towards the creature who was already half-out of the water. Keto's face was that of a beautiful woman, though it had at that moment an expression of horrible lust, mingled with insatiable greed: but it was not her face but her hair that was the strangest thing about her.

Her hair was of an extremely weird tint and was so long that as it spread out over the wave that was carrying her forward it changed the colour of the wave to its own hue. It was doubtless due in part to the fact that the season being an exceptionally early spring, there was so much fresh green to be observed in every direction, together with such startling contrasts as the blue of the sky and the purple of the mountains, that this weird apparition of Keto's hair struck these three consciousnesses as it came nearer and nearer, with that appallingly beautiful face at the head of its advance, as something so absolutely ghastly in its reversion to a colour that could only be described as a manifestation of Death and Nothingness in the midst of Life and Joy, that each one of them felt the approach of something like a frozen paralysis.

Not one of the three, not the wise old king with his staggering burden of memories unequalled by any man who has ever lived upon earth, not the terrific club of the greatest killer of anti-human Pests who has come to the rescue of humanity, not the young girl in her fresh youth from the oldest and simplest of the farming homesteads, had ever in their life before been thus paralysed by all that was suggested in a mere colour, and that colour without horns or claws or teeth or sting—just simply the colour of hair!

But all three of them felt simultaneously that their fearful impressions from Keto's hair were connected with one single simple thing, with nothing more or less in fact than the dead leaves of one particular kind of tree—O so well known to them all!—that grew somehow round every one of their homes in this island.

Over and over again had all three of them felt some strange shudder over this particular colour; the Heraklean club rather less than the old man or the young girl, since *his* native home was really in the forest of Nemea, situated on the "epeiros", as the islanders called the mainland.

Like a flash that combined the deadly bolt of forked lightning with the more widely spread illumination of sheet-lightning, some peculiar horror for normal mortal senses seemed to lurk in the mysterious colour of this sea-monster's hair. Yes! the only parallel to it was the colour of the dead leaves of that one particular tree in autumn, especially when autumn came earlier in the year than usual, causing these dead leaves to be isolated from their fellows.

It wasn't a negative colour or the absence of anything. It was a positive colour, and it possessed its own absolutely special metallic gleam. The colour grey, contrasted with what this colour was, would have appeared a friendly and natural if rather a melancholy apparition. But this colour flung forth a metaphysical shock. It possessed a look as if Nothingness itself, the primordial and perhaps the ultimate *Non Est* had chosen to incarnate itself in visible appearance.

"You will see me again!" it seemed to say to the old king, to the young farm-girl, to the club that slew the Nemean Lion. And the club was fully aware of the fact that there was a special reason for its sharing the horror that now menaced the other two, the fact namely that the Nemean Lion whose brains it dashed out on the "epeiros" was actually, though belonging to the earth, an offspring of this monster of the deep.

Little did either the old man or the young girl guess that the forward rush with which they both followed the Heraklean weapon, as, straining itself forward till it almost flew out of the king's grasp, it rushed with blind defiance down that slippery slope straight towards the beautiful face in its terrible hair, had anything to do with the fact that the weapon the king carried knew so much more than they did of the creature they were encountering.

So terrific, however, was the shock of sheer panic that struck them all three when they came within reach of that swirling whirlpool of hair—the colour of the absolute void before there was any world at all—that fortunately for the two human ones it broke through, just as if it had really been a flash of metaphysical illumination, the natural barrier between the consciousness of the club of Herakles and the consciousness of the man and the girl, so that when, within a couple of yards of the wave's edge, they finally stopped, Odysseus was able to threaten that beautiful face in the midst of that abysmal hair with the knowledge possessed by the weapon of the son of Zeus and his mortal bride Alkmene.

"Beware, you evil mother of good daughters, you mother of the Graiai, born with white hair, of the Graiai, who still live in Kisthene, the cavern of rock-roses, where there is neither sun nor moon, and where no stars shine, and who have only one eye to see with, and only one tooth to eat with! Beware, I tell you, you demon-mother of the white-haired Graiai! If ever your face is seen again near this Cave of the Naiads I shall rob your daughters of both their one eye and their one tooth; for none knoweth the road to Kisthene of the Rock-Roses better than I, wanderer as I've been through both the world of the living and the world of the dead!"

Had Keto, the eldest daughter of the Sea, possessed, at the back of her swirling hair, now the very colour of that Nothingness into which everything shall return, possessed a foam-drop of the feeling resembling ours, she would have been softened in some infinitesimal measure by the poignant sight of those two pathetic human beings, the little farm-girl with slender outstretched arms and the broad-shouldered shepherd of the people, brandishing his old cracked root of a twisted pine disfigured by honeysuckle and brooding on the spilt brains of lions; but that drifting face remained as impassive as the exquisite convolutions of a cockle-shell; impassive and implacable, and still slowly advancing.

But it was at that moment that behind this intolerable sea-horror with its appalling beauty and its deadly hair there suddenly rose up a three-fold prong held aloft in a vast overshadowing muscular arm. "Stop, all of you! stop, I say!" boomed the god's terrific voice, as the outstretched trident was directed towards them.

With the sluicing and shelving roar of a hoarse, out-drawing, tidal retreat the whole volume of water, swallowing up Keto entirely as it went, rolled back about the tall and menacing torso of Poseidon. Recognizing his worst personal enemy in this insatiable avenger of the Kyklops Polyphemos and this passionate ally of the Trojans, Odysseus contented himself with shrugging his massive shoulders, with extending an imperative yet kindly hand to the young girl, with swinging the club in an almost humorous gesture of submitting to fate, and with walking, without another glance at the ship he was building, slowly forth from the Naiad's Cave by the nearest inland path; a retreat from action that was an unspeakable relief to both the fly and the moth.

"Were you on your way somewhere, child?" he asked the young girl in a friendly voice, still retaining her hand. "I'm herdsman Tis's youngest sister," the girl replied in a docile voice. "Grandfather sent me with a message to him. Grandfather told me to stop at the Naiad's Gave and see if it was true that you were building a ship. They say, down our way, that if you, my lord, sail from Ithaca, one of the Naubolides boys will be king in your place: but I tell them that's all silly nonsense."

The girl's obvious sincerity made Odysseus look more closely at her and he was struck by the oddity of her appearance. She had one of the plainest faces he had ever seen, and her stomach and torso were shapeless and graceless, but her legs were as beautifully formed as those of some incomparable dancer. "I'll take you to the house," he said. "Tis sleeps there and the women will find a place for you."

CHAPTER III

Never had Nisos Naubolides felt surer of himself or of his destiny than when, on this same morning of the old king's visit to the cave of the Naiads, he set out for the Temple of Athene. He had come straight from the presence of his mother Pandea whom he had found as he had expected, not in the Naubolides homestead of Aulion, but in the house called Druinos, where lived Nosodea, the mother of the two girls Leipephile and Stratonika, who was Pandea's best gossip, best scandal-monger, and best-loved friend.

The old Odysseus must have been still lying on his bed with his eyes closed after his nocturnal conversation with the Dryad Kleta when Nisos set out so full of confidence in himself and his future. As to Myos the fly and Pyraust the moth, they must already have discovered for the benefit of the Club of Herakles and of the inquisitive Olive-shoot which had sprung up near the club, some important news about the ambiguous activities of the Priest of Orpheus who had occupied the ante-chamber to the Temple, for they were now flying back in their return from the Temple.

At the foot of a long slope of carefully tended green grass that led away from the Temple in an Eastern direction there was an old roughly hewn ungainly statue—scarcely a statue at all for it was more like a low stone pillar or "herm", with the crude outlines of a clumsily carved feminine face just indicated at the top of it—not of Athene but of the Goddess Themis, the special guardian throughout all Hellas of law and order and justice and decent behaviour.

Nisos stopped in amazement in front of this image. He knew every curve and every hollow and every tinge of colour upon this ungainly block of stone. But behold! there was this morning a horrible great crack clear across it. It was a crack that reached from what might have been the figure's left shoulder to what might have been its right buttock. Nisos now examined the injured image with the utmost nicety from top to toe.

As he was doing this he suddenly paused with an excited gasping little cry, the sort of cry a young soldier might have uttered who had just discovered on the battlefield the severed head of his general.

It was not quite as startled a cry as that; but it was in the sa me category of shocked astonishment. What he had seen were unmistakable blood-marks at different places all over the stone's surface.

"*Whose blood?*" was the question that shot through the boy's mind. Down on his knees he sank and began scrabbling with both hands in the grass. Here his startled curiosity was more than rewarded. Again and again his fingers encountered certain curious horny objects, which, as he lifted them up into the sunlight that was now blazing down upon him from a cloudless sky, revealed themselves without doubt or question to be nothing less than broken finger-nails, enormously sharp and superhumanly long finger-nails, some of them thicker than others, but almost all, he soon noticed, bloody as well as broken. "*Whose blood?*" the boy desperately asked himself again.

His whole feeling towards these abnormally large finger-nails was an extremely queer one. It was indeed such a confused and complicated one that, clever as he was, the lad was completely non-plussed. What agitated him was not so much these large and bloody finger-nails in themselves as what they represented and the world of associations they brought with them.

"This must be," the boy told himself in one of his characteristic introspective mole-runs, as he automatically gathered those horrible fragments into a heap, "this must be what you feel when you go mad. Didn't Herakles go mad? Didn't Ajax go mad? I mean when they'd annoyed Zeus in some way? Perhaps I've annoyed Zeus in some way without meaning to, and what I feel now is the beginning of my punishment."

For the last year and a half Nisos had deliberately cultivated his tendency to elaborate his fancies and enlarge upon his feelings. He had done this ever since the day when, neither of them knowing that he was within hearing, he had overheard his mother say to his father, "Nisos will be a famous philosopher one day! Don't you see how introspective he is?" "Introspective is what I am!" he had henceforth always told himself.

And when other boys beat him at racing or jumping or throwing the discus, "I'll be a prophet," he told himself, "when you are all common soldiers!"

His face just then, while the blazing sunshine caught the five beads of perspiration on his forehead and behaved towards them with the same passionate intensity as it was at that moment displaying towards the whole Aegean Sea, had a very curious expression. At that heap of supernaturally large and inhumanly pointed finger-nails, all torn and bloody he felt he was in a dream, whence, though he knew it *was* a dream, he was unable to force himself to wake. "Heavens and Earth!" he thought. "Of course I know whose finger-nails those are! They're the 'Harpies, the Snatchers'! They must have some quarrel with Themis." He shut his eyes and with the back of his hand wiped those five miniature seas of sweat out of existence.

And then he remembered what he'd been taught about the Strophades or Isles of the Turning-Point, and how it was there that Themis compelled the fierce sons of the North Wind, brandishing their sharp swords to turn from their pursuit of these fatal females who had no weapon but their own snatching nails! And so this foul crack in the image of the goddess of Order was the gratitude of these infernal Harpies!

Well, well, well. He decided that it might be wiser not to tell his mother about this crack in the image of Themis, nor to ask her what he had better do about this little heap of finger-nails. "Cover them up with Babba's dung! Tis would say", he thought; and then he thought: "No! I *won't* be the one to tell mother. Those bloody nails give me the shivers!"

He did his best, as he left that desecrated image and made his way up the grassy slope towards the temple, to recover his self-esteem by remembering his mother's words about his being "so introspective". "Neither Daddy nor Agelaos," he told himself, "would have the cleverness to feel things like this as I feel them."

He was still nearly half a mile from the top of the slope where the first buildings began when he saw the two insects, so well known to him in the palace-porch, flying slowly towards him engaged in some absorbing argument between themselves. Yes, he was sure he knew them both. One was that pitifully nervous and weak-looking brown moth with fluttering wings. The other was that extremely self-centred house-fly with a calm collected manner, a black head and staring eyes.

And now if it were possible for him to enter into conversation with them, or at least into some sort of intelligent communication with them, he would gather all sorts of hints as to what this Orphic Priest, who called himself Enorches, was doing, and have something important to take back to his mother quite apart from those horrible finger-nails, concerning which he had decided to remain silent.

Yes, he was pretty sure he knew both these insects; but of course it was possible that the house-fly, with those transparent prismatic wings upon which it was always cleaning its rapidly moving feet, had two or three, or even four or five, brothers and sisters. It was also possible, though less likely, that the brown-winged, anxiously obsessed, sacrificially dedicated moth had a twin-sister who resembled her so closely in the eyes of gods and men that only a caterpillar could distinguish the one from the other.

Indeed if it were not for some multiple-footed, velvet-muffled relative, to whose cocoon-piercing, chrysalis-searching eyes no pair of winged creatures were exactly alike, how easily might the brown moth have been a nameless unidentified nomad, flitting over the earth's surface until she fell by her own propensity for self-sacrifice into some worse fate than becoming the obedient servant of the Priest of Orpheus.

Such a born Ambassador was Nisos that he had hardly caught sight of the two insects fluttering through the air towards him, so submerged in their metaphysical argument that they had no attention left for what they were doing or where they were going, than he stretched out his hands palms downward towards them and addressed them with his fondest and politest social salutation, a salutation that was only a little less respectful than the one he used, in his imagination, for kings and queens, and also, it must be admitted, for members however young of the ancient houses of the Naubolides of Aulion.

Having thus saluted them the youthful diplomatist uttered a deep sigh and ejaculated the gnomic syllables, "What a shame!" The subtle implication of this sympathetic groan was indeed, though few would have had the sensitivity to catch it, that the ignorant, vulgar, illiterate, brutal retainers of the Priest of Orpheus had clearly refused to allow the sophisticated homage of such noble insects to enter the inmost shrine, in spite of the fact that all the world owes honey to honey-bees, silk to silk-worms, pearls to oysters, and Tyrian dye to the lovely sea-shell, Porphura.

Seeing that he had succeeded in interrupting their dispute and that they were hesitating and flying in circles and hovering round his outstretched hands, the boy withdrew one arm, moved the other with a mute solicitation, and drawing in his breath with an instinctive movement of his whole frame that was in itself a crafty-imitation of a sub-human gesture, he made a peculiar humming sound between his palate and the back of his tongue.

All these things were done, all these signs were made, purely on the inspiration of the moment; but seeing them still hesitate and feeling in his open mouth and widened nostrils the morbid smell of the incense-heavy sacristy-dust they carried on their wings, he suddenly lifted the back of his hand to his mouth, licked it with his tongue, and stretched it forth again.

Ah! He was indeed a clever plenipotentiary. He had done it! Both the insects settled on the back of his hand which the moth desperately caressed with her wings and the house-fly began hurriedly to use as an ash-can for the dirt he scraped, first by the aid of one gauzy wing and then of another, from his exploring feet. Here indeed was the Ambassador's opportunity! He must convince himself that he had come from the kitchen of his mother Pandea, the wife of Krateros Naubolides, straight to this sacred half-mile of well-watered grass.

He must let that ominous crack in the image of Themis be blotted from his mind and that bloody heap of super-human claws vanish like an obscure dream. Here upon the back of his hand were two living creatures, each of them endowed with wings, who had come straight from this temple, borne forth upon a dusty wafture of incense-bearing smoke.

But how, in the name of Tartaros, was he to obtain from them the information he required? How on earth could he cross the gulf between his human consciousness and their insect-consciousness? How was he to enter into conversation with this brown moth and this house-fly now that he *had* persuaded them to settle upon the back of his hand? Nisos Naubolides never forgot to the end of his mortal days this crucial moment. He drew his arm a little inwards towards his ribs and hung his head, staring helplessly at the back of his hand where from the knuckle of his longest finger, which she evidently felt to be a wisely chosen observation-post, the brown moth was explaining to the black fly, who was cleaning his shoes on the knuckle of Nisos' finger, just how it was that with such unusual words and gestures the Priest of Orpheus had bidden her show her friend off the premises and see to it that he never returned.

What, in the name of their universal mother the earth, was he to do to break down this cruel wall of difference between his human senses and those of these two creatures?

And then suddenly, to the born diplomatist, the inspiration came! Of course there was only one thing to do, and that was the thing indicated by every vibratory law of tellurian politeness. He must pray to Pallas Athene!

No sooner had he decided upon this line of action which was obviously the most proper, the most natural, the most pious line for a diplomatic ambassador to a great goddess's temple to adopt, than he lifted up in his heart an intensely concentrated prayer to Athene, imploring her to reveal to him how to exchange thoughts and experiences with this moth and this fly.

It was soon clear to him that the goddess had heard him and had taken measures without delay to give him an answer to his prayer. Well must she know the limits of her power and not only its limits. She also must know the evil effect, so often precisely contrary to the desired effect, of manifesting her power in her own person. So to enlighten him as to the way moths and flies received and remembered their impressions she evidently brought it about that her most understanding worshipper in the vicinity should at this critical moment be descending that grassy slope.

This was an elderly virgin called Petraia who belonged to an island family into which in each generation for hundreds of years an old maid with Sibylline inspiration had been born. Petraia was not the prophetess for this particular generation but she was twin-sister to the woman who was. And the goddess knew well that there existed, as happens sometimes with twins, a mysterious thought-transference between Petraia and her sister, who had fled from the world to the sacred Arician Forest of the Italian King Latinus, where she had become a follower of the immortal Nymph Egeria who lived like an oracle in a hidden cave.

It was through her sister's association with this Italian Nymph that Petraia was able to keep the virgin-goddess whom she served in close contact with all that preceded the founding of the New Troy, destined, so the word went forth, to rule the world from its Seven Hills.

Nisos was thoroughly at home with Petraia who in his infancy had been his nurse as well as his mother's midwife, so that he at once accepted her appearance at this juncture as an authentic answer to his prayer. Without a moment's delay in one wild rush of excited words the boy poured out the whole of his story and explained his difficulty about the insects.

The slender and stately old lady surveyed him with whimsical scrutiny. "So you want to get the news from those two small prisoners of yours, do you? And you need an interpreter?"

"O Nurse, I'm thankful it's you!" gasped Nisos. "Mother wanted me to find out what's going on and I don't feel like telling her about what I've just seen down there"; and he gave his head a jerk in the down-hill direction. "Does the goddess, do you think, know all about *that*? Does she know they've left a lot of their disgusting nails or claws, or whatever they are, behind, and all bloody too? Why does she let such things happen, Nurse, and so near her Temple? Themis is cracked clean through—does she know *that*?—clean through, from shoulder to hip! Mother will have a fit when she hears. I'm not going to be the one to tell her, nurse. You bet your life I'm not! You know what she is when she hears things like that. She'll go rampaging off to Druinos to pour out everything to Nosodea; and there in his corner like a hunched-up toad you may depend old Damnos Geraios will be gloating over every word and thinking what new silliness he can invent for dear sweet simple Leipephile and what new imaginary wickedness for that idealistic fool Stratonika, so that she'll have to lacerate herself to the bone to purge it away! But tell me, nurse most sacred, nurse most precious, nurse most holy, does our great goddess, who sent you here in answer to my prayer, know about Themis?"

He looked searchingly at the virginal midwife as he asked this question. He knew well that his faith in the omnipotence of their goddess wasn't what it had been when he was five years old. He was nearly seventeen now, and in these last years he had had a great many very private and rather peculiar thoughts; but it would still have shocked an indestructible vein of piety in him to think that such things could happen as this horrible attack on the obelisk of Themis so near Athene's very judgment-seat, without her knowing anything about it!

Petraia smiled that reassuring familiar smile that had so often comforted him in his paroxysing panic lest the feathered bosom of aboriginal Night should swallow him up alive.

"Let's think of your insects first," Petraia said now, and she added: "Moths and Flies before Law and Order!" She added these words with that particular kind of domestic persiflage that is more annoying to a boy nearly seventeen than a slap in the face.

However, he obediently lifted the back of his hand closer to his eyes and stared at the moth and the fly so intently that he could see the delicate lacy fringes on the margins of the moth's brown wings and the metallic circles like polished adamant round the bulging eyes of the house-fly.

As Nisos stared at the insects it seemed to him that he could feel like a palpable wafture of nard-scented air the divine power of feminine virginity, a power that male youth always recognizes without knowing precisely what it is, pass from Petraia's hand to the nerves of his shoulder. It did, yes! it actually did, transform the quivering of those brown wings and the friction of those jet-black legs upon those gauzy wings into the expression of thoughts that a human being could follow. "So that's it!" he said to himself sharply and shrewdly.

And he was so afraid that just as a crib of some classic paragraph might be snatched from a school-boy before he had got the hang of it, that this preternatural translation of the sign-language of insects into the sound-language of men might be withdrawn before he got its full import that he began announcing to Petraia in a louder voice than he generally used and in a hurried and curiously jerky manner that what the insects had revealed to him was that there was a quarrel beginning, that might soon become a deep rift, between Zeus and Hera, the former being alone on the peak of Gargaros deprived, one rumour declares, of all his weapons, while the latter was almost equally alone on the summit of Olympos.

He further announced to Petraia that the effect of this quarrel upon the great goddess Athene was to force her to withdraw herself from taking any part in any public movement until the issue between Zeus and Hera became clearer or definitely resolved itself in one way or another.

"But at this point," so he explained to the old midwife, "while the moth understands that our goddess has left Ithaca altogether, the fly is sure she is still in the island, and probably still in the temple; but is unwilling to commit herself, or take any side, or make any definite move, till things are clearer than they are at present.

"Another thing the fly tells me, Nurse dear, which astonishes me a good deal, and to confess the truth gives me a funny feeling, indeed, if I were absolutely honest, as you used to teach me every Naubolides with our claim to the kingship ought to be, makes me shiver and shake is that Tartaros has broken loose, and that Typhon, the most terrible of all the Titans, has burst his bonds from beneath Etna and is again breathing fire and smoke against the gods.

"But you see, Nurse dear, what makes it so hard for me to tell you all they say is that they keep contradicting each other as if they were speaking as ambassadors from opposite camps. For instance what the fly says is that the real reason why our great goddess Athene has withdrawn 'pro-tem' into herself is that she is waiting to hear what Zeus will do if certain rumours that have reached her from Italy are correct, namely that at a special place in Italy where there are seven sacred hills the descendants of Aeneas the pious ally of Priam have already begun to build a new Troy.

"The moth, on the other hand, swears that Athene has gone to visit the blameless Ethiopians to find out for herself whether it is true that Persephone has quarrelled with Aidoneus and helped Teiresias to bring back from Hades the weeping Niobe, the First Woman, together with her husband Phoroneus, the First Man."

Long before the insects had ceased revealing their discoveries to the undulations of the knuckles of his now weakly and wearily extended hand, the inspiration proceeding from the virginity of the old maid who had nursed him ceased to give him the clue to the small creatures' sign-language.

He gazed helplessly at her, while a wave of tiredness and the feeling of being a hopeless fool engulfed him. "What do *you* make of it all, Nurse?" he murmured feebly.

"It is clear enough, Nisos," commented Petraia, "that a female moth and a male fly are bound to be on opposite sides in the great 'old battle'."

"What old battle, nurse darling?" enquired the boy, contemplating the insects on his knuckles with re-awakened interest.

"Between males and females, silly!" There fell a dead silence between them with the weight of a heavy stone: a silence that was broken at last by the old maid herself. Her voice rang out with something of the prophetic resonance that had belonged to that twin-sister of hers who was a neophyte of Egeria, the Nymph in the Cave in the Italian forest.

"Didn't I always tell you, forgetful child, how Apollo and Artemis persecuted Niobe, the First Woman, whose husband Phoroneus was the son of a Melian Nymph? Didn't I tell you how that pair of murderous deities—holy Athene guard me from them!—between whom and our great Goddess there has always been war since, like that dangerous Cyprian Aphrodite, they took the side of the Trojans and may the golden Sun, Helios, and the silver Moon, Selene, shake off such intruders!—didn't I tell you how that murderous pair killed the children of Niobe the first woman? And how they wouldn't even let their neighbours bury those beautiful maidens and heroic youths? Haven't I told you all that?

"And now this liar of a house-fly is trying to make out that our great goddess has lost herself in some kind of trance when the pillars of the world are shaking. O you male creatures, what infants you are! Children of women and nurselings of women, it is your mothers, your mothers, always your mothers, who are to blame! It is only from us, the unmarried ones, the childless ones, who have never known a man, that you ever hear the truth! That is what my sister always used to say. That is why she went to that forest of Aricia, which in Italy must be like the Nemean Forest in our main-land, and a little like our Arima too, only much bigger. Lucky, yea a thousand times lucky, are we in Ithaca to serve a Virgin Goddess!

"The mothers of men are the worst traitors to the cause of women. I tell you, boy, from the beginning of all things women have been betrayed, exploited, enslaved, insulted, perverted, depraved, debased, by men!"

Petraia drew breath at this point, while Nisos, feeling a little uneasy, since he still assumed it was in direct answer to his prayer that his old nurse had appeared on the scene, stared at the black fly on his knuckle with the vague idea of finding an excuse if not a justification for the wickedness of men in that big black head supported on those gauzy wings.

But the indignant old maid went on in mounting emotion, until her indictment soon became so detailed in its survey of the wrongs of women and so crushing in its denunciation of their corrupters, that all he could do was to rub his knee with his free hand while one method of defence followed another in mute succession through his bewildered brain.

"Petraia," he thought, "must have gone down to Hades like our King Odysseus for she can't have seen all these things happening round here." And then as his attention wandered a little from what he was hearing he became aware of an extremely unexpected and very curious experience. He found himself in fact whispering to the fly and being whispered to by the fly in a language of which he was absolutely ignorant. It was like a dream, though he was fully awake. The fly was a boy among flies as he himself was among people. And with this other boy he was now making fun of everything.

"But it's our great goddess—it *must* be——" he told himself, "who in answer to my prayer has arranged this meeting with Petraia and has helped me and the fly to make friends! She is a Divine Being, therefore she must herself understand the language and the thoughts of all the animals, birds, reptiles, insects and even plants, that walk and fly and creep and grow around her temple."

He had begun to call the fly "Kasi". "Kasi-kid," he said, "isn't this whole business just like a game of Blindman's Buff? Don't you think so, Kasi?"

The old midwife at his side went on with her arraignment of all males; but he kept his attention fixed on the fly, for it had become a deep joy to him to feel that they'd really made friends. "Kasi" was an abbreviation of the Hellenic word for brother and it was the old class-mate expression that all the younger boys of Ithaca had made use of between themselves in the Island's preparatory-school.

As for the fly, it was natural enough that since it had got older considerably faster than his new friend it was as gratified at being called "Kasi" as Nisos would have been if he had been treated like a young comrade by one of the heroes in the Trojan war.

"Blindman's Buff?" cried the Fly. "It's as if we were all buzzing round a new-dropt cow-turd of Tis's old Babba, all warm and steaming! But this lady-moth here keeps giving me a flap with her left wing to remind me that I promised to escort her home; so I'm afraid I must say 'cheire!' for we must do what the ladies tell us, is it not so?"

"It is indeed the sad truth, Kasi," admitted Nisos. "Ta-Ta! till the next time!" shrilled the Fly. But when the insects had commenced their flickering and wavering departure in such close colloquy that the all-seeing sun, whether ruled by an Olympian or a Titan or by nobody but his flaming self, couldn't decide whether to turn them into one darting jewel or into two darting jewels, Nisos found that Petraia had fallen silent and was regarding him with a look that was a palimpsest of different expressions. It had reproach in it. It had a grievance in it. It had mischievous amusement in it. It had a puzzled pity in it.

But in place of any sad, weary, resigned, disillusioned acceptance of fate it had a gravity that was faintly whimsical. "Those finger-nails that disgusted and disquieted you so, my dear," she remarked at last, "show me who cracked that image of Themis. And now listen to me, child; and lay to heart what I tell you; for I am not speaking only on my own authority. I am speaking to you, Nisos, you Babe that I took from your mother, as an unwedded mortal on behalf of an unwedded immortal, for I tell you, boy, that at this very moment I can feel her presence inspiring me and teaching me exactly what to say and exactly what not to say to you, Nisos, child," and Petraia's voice quivered with emotion, "the greatest event, and by far the best event, that has ever happened in the history of our terrible world is now happening.

"From the lowest depths of Tartaros to the highest peaks of Olympos a great revolt is in progress which if successful will change the world. But it is a revolt against Fate Itself, as well as against the Will of the All-Father, a will that always bows to Fate and then pretends to be what the All-Father Himself would instinctively will, which of course really and truly it *isn't*, only All-Father Zeus can't and daren't do what he'd like to do!

"Those who attacked that Figure of Themis were entirely justified in so doing. The Harpies, or 'Snatchers', as our enemies call them, are women like us, *like me*! They are women, and they are maids, and they are not only old maids, they are immortal maids! And they have joined the great revolt that began before dawn this night, this night that has now become day, the first day of the greatest event in the history of all days!

"Need your old nurse tell her babe what that event is? It is the Revolt of Women! Yes, of the Women-Slaves of the entire universe! Yes, Nisos, nothing less than that, the revolt of all Females in the cosmos against the tyranny of all Males in the cosmos! Themis, the goddess of Custom and Habit and Tradition, has always been unfair to us women, always trying to force us back into slavery to men whenever we've tried to escape. And, as with Themis, so with the Fates. They too are against us. They too want to hold us down to the laws, ways, manners, morals, usages, privileges, conventions, institutions, organizations, founded upon male stupidity and bigotry!

"But our maiden goddess will be on our side; yes! she will lead us! She—— " And then suddenly, after a terrifying pause, the boy heard Petraia utter a ghastly groan, followed by a horrible shriek. "She's gone, gone, gone, gone! She's left me! She's deserted me! Athene! Athene! Athene! Where art thou, Athene?"

Nisos looked in positive fear at the woman. Her whole countenance was convulsed, distorted, twisted awry; while her eyes, enlarged and deepened into the most beautiful and most terrible eyes Nisos had ever seen in his short life, gave him the feeling, as they turned on him, as if his whole nature were being summed up and weighed and analysed and judged by the central nerve of the entire universe!

"What's the matter, nurse?" he gasped in a low voice. At his question her gaze of terrible insight changed into one of contemptuous irritation.

"Oh, nothing, nothing, nothing, nothing! *Nothing's* 'the matter'! What *could* be 'the matter'? A person may be allowed, I take it, to change colour for a second when the goddess she has been serving for forty years begins inspiring her with the deepest secrets of life in one blob, one blur, one blot, one gobbet of prophetic truth; and then, just as a person's in the act of expressing it glides off, glides away, glides into thin air, glides back to her grove or her grotto or her shrine leaving the person, *leaving me,* to be nothing but the silly, speechless idiot I always have been!"

Petraia stopped speaking and covered her contorted face with her two hands, while the boy noticed how big the tears were that forced themselves between those thin fingers and ran down between those wrinkled knuckles as the tall figure swayed and shook with her dreadful sobs.

Nisos was staggered. All he felt was awe and wonder; awe in the presence of such human emotion, and wonder that so wise a goddess could treat a faithful servant so unkindly and ungratefully. If only Petraia had been less upset she would have remained in touch with her twin-sister who in Aricia was at that very moment struggling desperately to convey to her by vibrations of pure thought that in this cosmic revolt on behalf of women, though the Fates and the All-Father and Themis might be against them, they had on their side the terrible Avengers of Blood, the Erinyes, who, according to Egeria, the Nymph in the Cave, could bring with them to the battle the Graiai, the Gorgons, the Sirens, and even the Nymphs of the Hesperides!

Had the woman only possessed the power to visualize the scene at that moment in the cave of Egeria, where the twin-sister on her knees with her long bare arms outstretched and her face transformed by an ecstasy of worship was invoking all the Chthonian deities on behalf of Petraia herself, that crazed creature might have been checked in her bitter wrath. As it was, she left Nisos without a word more; and the boy heard her as she went off talking blasphemously to herself about her service of the great goddess and how on this day of days the goddess had deserted her.

"So my life is to repeat itself, is it?" the boy heard her mutter, as she went up the slope with the particular aberrations of her way of moving when she was excited, which might be described as a limp and a jerk followed by a hop, exaggerated to a ridiculous degree, "always to repeat itself, is it? And there's never, never, never, never to be anything the matter! What's the matter? O I'll go and see if anything's the matter! The matter with my knees perhaps as I pray to you! With my voice perhaps as I sing hymns to you! With the floor of your shrine perhaps, with the echo of your arches perhaps, with the smoke of your incense perhaps? Or could it possibly be, that what the matter is, that you aren't in your temple at all? Just somewhere else!"

Muttering and babbling in this blasphemous way Patraia stumbled up the slope towards the temple and vanished from his view among the many marble buildings that surrounded the central shrine. Left alone without the fly, or the moth, or the old midwife, or, for all he felt of her presence, the Goddess either, Nisos himself began slowly ascending the slope. Strange thoughts flitted through his head as placing one foot carefully and pensively in front of the other, and then the other in front of it, and then repeating the process, he mounted that grassy hill.

Since it was not the time for any particular celebration, or for the performance of any particular ritual, this ascent to the Temple and to its agglomeration of marble buildings, interspersed by the wooden houses of the priests and the still rougher and cruder hovels, mostly constructed of tattered sail-cloth and twisted withy-twigs of the slaves of the priests, was at that moment almost entirely deserted.

Surrounded therefore by an atmosphere of consecrated silence our young friend had one of those opportunities that come to us all at rare moments of really "collecting", as we have come to call it, his wandering thoughts; and, as often happened when he was alone, his mind journeyed into a cloudy realm composed of an entirely imaginary circle of things and people.

This circle, person by person, and background by background, was his future, that far-off future, into which by the help of what he felt so strongly within him, what to himself he always called his "cleverness", he was certain he would one day come.

Where many island children watching their companions being scolded for behaving badly would say to themselves: "*I am good, I am!*" Nisos would say to himself: "I am clever, *I* am!" and he had an absolute faith that, if he didn't die by a violent death, he would one day be the memorable figure of his epoch. He never defined, or tried to analyse precisely, of what the power within him which he called his "cleverness" consisted.

His mother always told her neighbour, the lady of Druinos, that it consisted of a gift for subtle flattery and of a genius for propitiating older and wiser people. But of his real secret ambition he never spoke to his mother. The only person who had the faintest inkling of what it was, for nothing would have induced him to talk to Petraia about it, was his friend Tis, the herdsman.

But what in his hidden heart he actually imagined himself becoming was an inspired prophet. If Petraia could be so upset by the idea of their goddess deserting her and not speaking through her as Apollo did through the oracular woman at Delphi and as the Nymph Egeria did through Petraia's twin-sister in Aricia, why shouldn't *he* become the voice of some Divine Being, and win respect and esteem for himself for all time by expounding that Being's philosophy?

He began to wonder what kind of divinity he would be most fitted to represent, and most happy in representing. And as he pondered on this important point he found himself staring at one particular blade of grass the top of which, the *point* as it were, of this brightly green dagger, had turned into a pale brown colour. The point had not shrivelled or crumpled in this transformation. It was still as smooth as the rest of that leaf of grass; but it was discoloured.

ATLANTIS

Something had bitten it or the excretion of some poisonous creature had sucked the life-blood from it; or, for all Nisos knew, this single grass-leaf with all the consciousness it possessed had uttered a curse against Zeus himself, the lord of high heaven, and had thus drawn upon itself an individual flash, especially adapted to a small object, of celestial lightning.

At first Nisos couldn't help associating this discoloured point with Petraia's unseemly outburst; but as he went on staring at it his secret dream about his own future on this island stirred within him.

"Yes, by Aidoneus," he thought, "I know what special kind of prophet I'll be, a kind that has never existed in the world before! I'll not be a prophet to the clever who are weak and timid and nervous like me. I'll be a prophet to the strong who have been hurt in some way. Yes, I'll be a prophet to the healthy and strong who are like this leaf of grass with a brown tip."

"Listen to me," I'll cry, "all you who are strong but yet are stupid; you who are hurt and hit without knowing why! Listen to me!" He stood still, imagining himself a man with a long flowing beard, taller than he was now, much more distinguished than he was now, and possessed of philosophical secrets known to no other sage in Hellas. He glanced casually up the slope in front of him. All those glittering marble buildings he knew so well were hidden by the grassy ridge at the top of the ascent and he noticed that Petraia had entirely vanished.

"She must be visiting Stratonika," he said to himself. "Yes," he thought, "I'll be a Prophet to the strong who've been hurt, and the healthy who've fallen sick! The half-dead ones, the tortured ones, the mad ones, the diseased ones have all got prophets; but strong, stupid, silly things, like this blade of grass with a brown tip, who just stares back at a person, think they don't want a prophet; but they do! O yes! you do, stupid grass, whatever you think! You wait till I'm older and cleverer and have a beard; and you'll soon see! It's the stupid things that need the clever prophets!"

Having decided on his future in general, Nisos now felt a need for beginning to practise the art of prophecy in a more special and particular manner; so he began plodding steadily on, with drops of sweat falling from his forehead and his eyes upon his sandals which were discoloured by pollen-dust and rabbit-dung.

Suddenly he turned his attention, drawn by an impulse for which he couldn't account, away from the ridge in front of him to a clump of trees on his extreme left; and he even began walking hurriedly towards it. The trees were only a portion of the group of natural objects that was now his objective. In the blazing sun and against all this greenery the many-coloured mound he was aiming for had almost a purple look.

Nisos knew the place well. It was of natural rather than artificial origin, formed by the intermingling of three separate things, a rather oddly scrawled rock, the stump of an oak, and the twisted root of an ash. Over this dusky excrescence there grew a mass of waving ferns and thick clumps of a specially dark moss; and as Nisos now advanced towards it its queer purpureal tint appeared to be spotted by blood-red patches which glowered like raw wounds in that burning sun.

Everyone who knew Ithaca knew this spot and it was locally called Lykophos or "Wolf's Light," a name which implied that faint grey light before dawn that was more suitable to eyes of wolves than of men. The Lykophos-Mound seemed especially prominent at this moment. Its queerly scrawled rock, its oak-stump, its ash-root, together with the sap-filled living energy of its ferns and moss and honeysuckle, and its minutely delicate early Spring flowers and their clambering foliage, accentuated just then something about it, some powerful atmospheric emanation, that always made it an object towards which certain living people and certain living creatures gravitated with magnetic or hypnotic attraction but from which others shrank away with instinctive dread.

Nisos himself was one of the former sort; but his friend Tis, the herdsman, though he used simpler words, had given the boy the impression that to him there were always shocking blood-drops oozing out of that rock; while, for all its ferns and mosses and small spring-flowers and spreading foliage, there were always raw skinless hollows between its hieroglyphic surfaces and its leaf-mould ledges that suggested festering wounds and pus-exuding sores.

Among our other friends from the porch of the palace the black house-fly was repelled much in the same way as Tis. What the fly felt every time it flew near the Lykophos-Mound was an aching void in the pit of its stomach; as if some poisonous-looking meat-cover of brassy gauze had suddenly been precipitated out of the air to surround every half-crumb of edible farinaceousness and every half-drop of absorbable stickiness in the entire world.

It was however quite calmly and thoughtfully, and yet rather doggedly, for he was anxious to pick up for his extremely human Mummy a few fragments of more ordinary, more domestic, more everyday news than had recently been bewildering him from so many thaumaturgical if not supernatural directions, that our young friend was approaching the Lykophos-Mound, when he heard in the air above his head the strangest combination of startling, terrifying, and unbelievable sounds that he'd ever heard in his life.

And as, trembling with pure terror, he looked up, he saw a sight that froze his blood. What he saw gave him the impression that he was in the midst of a nightmare and that if he burst into a wild cry himself, these *other* cries, together with the incredible shapes that were descending from out of the air, would cease and dissolve and sink away, shaken into nothingness by his mother's approach as she answered his frantic screams.

But not for nothing had he been brought up by a mother like Pandea and a nurse like Petraia. Not for nothing had he listened as intently as that wicked old toad of a grandfather, Damnos Geraios himself, to the tales exchanged between his mother and her grand gossip, the mother of Leipephile and Stratonika. Above all it hadn't been for nothing that he had done housework for the aged lady who had been the nurse of three generations of royalty. As, half-petrified with terror, he gazed upward at what he saw, these two wide-winged female Horrors, uttering these appalling screeches as they flapped down towards the Lykophos-Mound in the half-circle of a raven-like swoop upon their prey, he knew at once who they were. One was an Erinys, one of the Avengers of Blood or Furies, and the other was a Gorgon.

Talking about it later with the old palace-nurse he came to the conclusion that the particular Erinys who made this attack must have been Allekto, whose name means "the never-ending" and that the Gorgon who tried to help her in this attack was Euryale whose name means "the wide sea".

But at the actual moment he had this appalling experience he only knew that without question one of them was most certainly an "Erinys" or "Fury" and the other was most certainly a Gorgon. The pair were clearly much too absorbed in catching their victim off-guard to notice Nisos at all. In fact they behaved as if he were a short, branchless tree, devoid of all sensibility save of a passive vegetative kind.

He was not, however, so paralysed with terror that he couldn't stagger to the trunk of the nearest spruce-fir; from which vantage-point, and clinging to this friendly tree with both his arms, he recovered a sufficient amount of "cleverness" to begin to take careful and detailed note of this whole amazing event. Amazing it certainly was: so much so that even the tree he was so desperately clutching, with some childish idea of taking refuge from the enemies of the gods with the daughters of the earth, displayed an unmistakable sign of being troubled in its quietude; for it exuded such a large drop of sticky tar that it tickled a nerve in the boy's smooth cheek. But in spite of his trembling legs and the tickling in his cheek he didn't fail to notice that the whole being of this pursuing Fury, whom he later discovered to be Allekto, "the never-ending", was so lost, diffused, absorbed, mania-mazed and blood-crazed, in its mad punishment-lust that though at this moment she was flying, the wings she flew with were feathered with the smoke of burning carrion, while from her mouth there issued, along with a stream of poisonous saliva, such a horrible alternation of bellowing and barking and such an appalling mixture of the stench of decomposition with the stench of excremental filth that the boy, though his stomach was empty, was unable to resist the motion of vomiting; and no! never for one moment did he fail to notice that everything about her had simply become one single rushing wind of all-devouring, all-consuming vengeance.

The creature whom Allekto was half-carrying through the air with her was also a female Being, and although it was not till later that Nisos learnt that she must have been Euryale or a daughter of "the wide sea", and in fact that she was a progeny of the sea monster Keto himself, he already knew, from her tusks like those of a wild pig, and her claws of brass, and the serpents that were a living portion of her flesh and blood, and above all from that unspeakable and utterly indescribable look in her eyes that made it impossible for any other living child of the earth or of the heavens to face her glance without at least the risk of being frozen into stone with sheer terror, that she was one of the Gorgons, an immortal sister of the mortal Medusa.

While absorbed in his contemplation of these two monsters, who were now hovering round and round the Lykophos-Mound, Nisos had not yet noticed the most important person of all in this cosmic-comic burlesque show, namely the Being whom these two monsters were preparing to attack. She, he found out later, was none other than Atropos, the smallest, but at the same time the wisest and the oldest, of the three Fates, or the "Moirai", those who can, when so they wish, decide the Destiny of every man and every woman born into the world.

Young Nisos Naubolides must have had something in him of the spirit of Odysseus, though, in place of being related to the king, his father Krateros and his brother Agelaos were the only living rivals of the old hero as claimants for the kingship. But the boy certainly displayed something beyond his boasted "cleverness" when, in order to find out what really was the object of this mad attack by the Erinys and the Gorgon, he made a run to another small fir-tree-trunk and clung tightly to it.

Yes! There she was, Atropos herself, the unturning, unbending, unwavering, unrelenting, implacable Decider of mortal destinies! As Nisos saw her, *she saw him,* and for an incredible moment this "clever" boy who had just made up his mind to be the prophet to the strong, looked into the eyes of Fate, into the eyes of her who could decide the Destiny of any man and any woman born into this world. Yes, they looked each other full in the face.

Atropos was under a spruce-fir just as Nisos was; but she was seated beneath hers, while he was clinging to his. As he looked at her now Nisos realized that the flesh and blood of which she was made was neither the normal flesh and blood of mortals nor what he had always been taught to believe was the immortal flesh of the gods with its veins full of ichor, that divine liquid more like the sap of imperishable vegetation than the raw red stomach-turning juice that mortals call blood.

No, the boy realized as he gazed at her that the mystery of her being was far deeper than anything he had been taught to attribute to her or to her sisters. In fact the aura that hovered round her and the spirit that emanated from her were so transporting to him that the frightful noise kept up above his head by the barking and bellowing of the Fury and the still more terrifying sound, resembling a series of viscous and glutinous thunderclaps following one another like a procession of sea-blown bubbles and finally bursting as they broke into the air, made by the Gorgon, became no more than hens cackling in a yard.

Yes, the material out of which Atropos was made was clearly as different from the ichor-nourished substance of the Olympians as it was from the horn-like material of the bodies of the Erinys and Gorgon. Nor was it made of that vaporous stuff, only a little thicker than mist or spray such as composed those phantom-like forms who eternally harangued each other in Arima. No; the truth is that the longer Nisos Naubolides looked into the eyes of Fate and the longer Fate looked into the eyes of Nisos Naubolides the more clearly did the latter realize that the imperishable frame of Atropos, this "one who could not be turned", was made of a substance drawn from a level of existence outside both time and space, though cunningly adapted to play its part in each of them.

But the boy proved how "clever" he was by imbibing like an inexhaustible draught of timeless experience much more at that moment than the mere physical nature of the oldest of the Fates; for there came over him in a trance that was more than a trance the surprising knowledge—and this, though again and again he blundered hopelessly in trying to describe it in words, was really with him to the day of his death—that Atropos helps us in the creation of our individual fate by an infinitely long series of what some would call nothing but blind, stupid, dull, dreamy, moon-struck "brown studies", many of which take place inside the walls of houses, and others when we are moving about on our ordinary errands outside.

In these interruptions of our ordinary consciousness we fall into a brainless, idea-less moment of dull abstraction in which we cease to think of anything in particular but just stare blindly and dully at some particular physical object, no matter what, that happens to be there at the moment. This object, in itself of no particular interest, and never selected for its real purpose is merely an object to stare at, lean upon, rest against and use as a trance-background, or brown-study foreground, or, if you like, like a shoal beneath a stranded consciousness, or a reef of brainless abstraction, wherein we simply escape for a moment from the trouble of being a conscious creature at all.

Nisos showed how born he was to be an interpreter if not a prophet by his complete acceptance—as from the trunk of *his* spruce-fir he faced the Mistress of Fate as she leaned against the trunk of *her* spruce-fir—of the revelation that our individual destiny is made up of an accumulation of brainless, uninspired, brown-study moments of abstraction wherein we cease to be organic living creatures and almost become inanimates, almost become things of wood and stone and clay and dust and earth, almost become what we were before we were intelligent or instinctive creatures: almost—but not quite!

For, as our young friend looked Atropos in the face, there was permitted to him what is permitted to few among us mortals during our lifetime, namely the realization of what actually happens to us when we fall, as we all do, into these day-dreams. At that moment, as Nisos Naubolides now knew well, all over the surface of the earth there were living creatures, many of them men, women, and children, many of them horses, cattle, lions, wolves, foxes, wild asses and tame pigs, sheep and goats, rats and mice, who were standing or crouching, lying or sitting in one of these brooding trances when dazed and dreaming, we are asleep and yet not asleep.

For Nisos at this moment almost all the inhabitants of the earth, at least such as were not included in his school-geography-books, were "blameless Ethiopians"; and what he conjured up at that instant over the entire face of the earth's surface were millions of men no different from those he knew so well, no different from the king and the king's son, no different from his own father, Krateros Naubolides, or from the old man, Damnos Geraios, or from his own familiar bosom-crony, Tis, the herdsman from the other end of Ithaca, all of whom, as they went about their affairs, fell now and again into these day dreams of fate where, asleep and yet not asleep, they created without knowing it their future destiny.

And as he looked into the eyes of Atropos he seemed to become the blood-brother, the "Kasi", or school-camerado, of all these day-dreamers, till their dream was his dream, and without any "pomposizing," or processioning in the manner of Hermes, he became aware that with this whole great multitude, including not only his fellow-men but all creatures upon the earth, he was, without knowing it, living a double life, in fact two quite separate lives, one in this world and one in some other world.

"Why it's just as if," he said to himself, "I was in one of those dreams when I *know* I'm dreaming, and *could*, if I wanted to, wake up, quite naturally, easily, and without any particular effort, rather than go on dreaming."

He was beginning to feel almost reassured, when suddenly he received an extremely unpleasant and thoroughly disconcerting shock. He beheld those two hovering Horrors make a downward swoop towards the Spruce-Fir against which Atropos was leaning. It was a shock that gave him a very disagreeable sensation, a sensation as if his heart-beats, his pulses, his quick-drawn breaths had been pounded into one single blood-dripping welter, and that this welter of automatic physical functionings might at any moment absorb the attention of his whole conscious being.

"What on earth can be going on in her head," he thought, "to give me such a feeling?" And then without warning, and still under the power of her eyes his entire mind became concentrated upon the old Odysseus. "I'm not going to endure," he thought, "no! not one day longer, this wretched plot that father and Agelaos and the rest of them are working up against the old man. Arsinöe's with them of course. That's only natural since she's a Trojan. But none of the rest of us are Trojans! What's come into us, what's come over us, that we're so against the old man?"

The unpleasant sensation he had just been through of feeling as if the beating of his heart, the flicker of his eyelids, the throb of his pulses, the breath of his lungs, had got mixed together in one raw palpitating bubble of blood-streaked eruption, now began, as Nisos disentangled himself from this reeking blood-sweating mass, to take its due proportion in his mind as he connected it with the drowsy passivity of his body, and not only of *his* body, but of all the bodies of all the human and sub-human creatures as they pause in their work or in their play, in their hunting or in their fighting, to forget themselves in day-dreams and trances.

And it was then that Nisos realized that not only heroes and kings and prophets and soothsayers but all living things are subject to an unseen, unfelt, unrecognized fate, and that it is this fate whose current flows, above or below, it matters not which, the heart-beats and pulse-beats of the lives of us all.

And the boy finally realized that there are points in our lives that we ourselves think of as turning points, but which, under the eyes of Atropos, the one with whom is no turning, are in reality only the fulfilment of our inherent destiny.

The boy had hardly reached this conclusion when the threatened attack began. The Erinys and the Gorgon descended with a sickening stench from their foul throats, with a horrible hissing from their bosom serpents, with an excremental vapour from their festering flesh and putrid scales, and with a screaming and a barking that silenced every bird and every wind.

It had nothing to do with the eyes of Atropos, for they had left him perforce—the instinctive impulse with which the boy now flung himself into the midst of that terrible struggle. The final issue may not have been in doubt; but Nisos was too young, and, just then too wild with desperate courage and too dazed by supernatural shocks to think of anything but his physical contact with that pair of Horrors and with their serpents and their stench and the sounds they made and with their appalling strength.

One comfort he had as he fought on, gasping and sweating, to free that oldest of all the beneficent powers in the world from those two demons, and that was nothing less than her own faint though very clear voice, encouraging him.

Another comfort he had was the uninterrupted humming of small insects round the Lykophos-Mound. These little creatures seemed quite oblivious of what was going on. Up and down across the surface of the rock they flew, dodging one another with quivering antennae and hovering wings; while first one, and then another, snatched a sip of Nectar from between petals of flowers so delicate that from their disturbed rims rose no sounds audible to human ears; though to lesser insects no doubt they sounded with the rain-drop clarity of tiny bells.

But what gave the boy a strength beyond his years was not only the fact that the oldest of all the goddesses was calling upon him to aid her, but that, although her voice was as faint as the remote sound of the sea-wind in a sea-shell, it was a voice with the most far-reaching echo he had ever heard.

For the echo of the voice of Atropos was no ordinary echo. It was a special and peculiar one, and it responded to every syllable that the old creature uttered; for through the substances of all the material elements of which the Island of Ithaca was composed this small faint echo of the oldest of the Fates could pass. Through substances that seemed bent on resisting its passing this echo easily and naturally passed. The old Fate's voice went forth first; and then the echo followed it like a faithful disciple doing the will of its master. Passing through everything that resisted them they went on; till they reached the yawning void where all echoes cease.

And the echo of the voice of Atropos had the peculiarity of entering into all the substances that carried it forward, as well as using them to help it on its way towards the ultimate void. The echo entered now into the fluttering insects who were sucking the Nectar from those tiny flowers. It entered into the burning sun above those three immortals and above this one mortal just as it entered into the heart of the Lykophos-Mound.

The curious thing was that the boy accompanied his final terrific effort with his human hands and feet against the two monsters by a low-murmured, very rapidly enunciated, rational argument, defending his own and his mother's friendly attitude towards the old king of Ithaca compared with the hostile one of his father Krateros and his brother Agelaos.

It was indeed only when he reached the culmination of this rapidly murmured, rational, and almost legal argument, with which he was punctuating, so to speak, his violent physical struggles, that he suddenly discovered that the battle had been won and that the Fury and the Gorgon had vanished. In his relief at this consummation, just when the throes of the struggle had become more than he could bear, the boy lost consciousness.

When he recovered he found that Atropos also was gone and that it required so much effort to leave the Lykophos-Mound and to drag himself up the rest of the hill that all that had passed grew steadily more blurred and more indistinct. One thing alone limned itself clearly on his mind, like a reflected image in water amid a crowd of globular bubbles, and that was some reference made, either by himself or by the oldest of the Fates, to a certain woven stuff.

This stuff he kept visualizing; but the shock to his nerves of what he had been through had made him completely forget its name. He remembered that the whole matter of this stuff had to do with some difficulty in procuring it and some difficulty with regard to its fabrication. He could see its colour. He could sense the feel of its substance, but its name and its use, though both of these had been familiar to him from his infancy, he had completely forgotten.

The shock he had received from the sight of those two monstrous creatures had left a queer blackness, a gaping, yawning, bleeding chasm in the compact body of his natural and orderly memories.

"I am myself," he kept repeating as he climbed the hill. "Nisos is Nisos; and Nisos is clever; and Nisos is going to be the prophet of those who are strong and healthy but who have been hit in some way—hit as I am now!—and who need a prophet rather different from former prophets."

And then in a flash it all came back to him and the gap in his memory was filled. "Othonia" was the word; and sail-cloth was the stuff. Atropos had told him—so he had had it from the Mouth of Necessity Itself—that Zeus, alone on the summit of Mount Gargaros, deprived of his thunder-bolts and separated from Hera his Queen, had decided to unite all the will-power and wisdom he possessed with the will-power and wisdom possessed by Themis, the goddess of what was orderly and seemly, and with whatever Atropos herself, the oldest of the Fates, she who *was* Fate Itself, decided might be for the best.

And what was "for the best", here and now in Ithaca, was that Odysseus their lord and king should hoist sail again and depart for the Isles of the Blessed whither Menelaos, the brother of Agamemnon, had already sailed.

So *that* was it! And the little black spot in his rattled brain was no more than "othonia", a rag of sail-cloth, a woven wisp of crumpled weed, which had been completely obliterated, swept forth, cast away, blotted out from his terrestrial brain by the stench of those loathsome immortals! Othonia! Othonia! Othonia! Sails! Sails! Sails! *Sails* for whatever ship Odysseus can build, Sails for whatever crew Odysseus can find, to carry him on his last voyage across the sea!

It was in this first blush of his relief at the recovery of his memory that Nisos Naubolides suddenly felt himself seized by the wrist. He had been so absorbed in his thoughts that he had not noticed the man approaching him; but there at his side was the mysterious Priest of Orpheus. "*COME!*" was all the man said.

Nisos, who felt that if he could only avoid looking at the fellow's face he could cope with him perfectly, tried to pull his arm away. But this he found he couldn't do. And how queer it was that he couldn't look at him! Only an hour ago he had looked into the face of Euryale, the Gorgon, without being turned to stone. In the eyes of Fate Itself he had been finding comfort; but not with a secretive, intrusive wretch who wasn't even a priest of Dionysus, or of Demeter, or of Persephone or of the authentic Mysteries of Eleusis, but only of these new-fangled, sanctimonious, priest-invented, fabulous Mysteries, of an Orpheus who himself was more of a fantastic poet than a hero or demigod, he felt entirely paralysed.

So here was he, Nisos Naubolides, the favoured one of the oldest of the Fates, one who was fated to use his cleverness, when he became a man, to grand prophetic effect, here was he, for some mad, mystical, demoniac reason, unable even to glance at the face of this crafty intruder! "Well," the boy said to himself, "I know I heard old Damnos Geraios, Leipephile's grand-dad, tell mother once that there were certain papyri which absorb certain pigments and others that cannot absorb them. So I suppose my particular kind of 'cleverness', though it may have Fate Itself on its side, would be entirely wasted on this man."

ATLANTIS

By this time the man in question had conducted him to a sinister-looking square building, *"Go in there and learn reverence!"* was all he said as he pushed him in and barred the door behind him.

Nisos was so relieved at being liberated from the man's touch, and from the nearness of a face he felt he couldn't bring himself even to glance at, that the first thing he did was to clap his hands. "Well!" he said to himself, "as long as I don't have *that* filthy sod hanging around, I don't care what happens!"

What had happened was indeed a curious experience for a young prince of the House of Naubolides. He found himself enclosed in an extremely small and absolutely square cell that was nakedly bare from the centre of its ceiling to the centre of its floor. Ceiling, walls, floor, were all of the same stone and this stone was of a most unusual colour. He tried in vain to think of any object he knew that was of this peculiar colour. The nearest he could get to it was a thunder-cloud he had once seen when he was very little reflected in a muddle of rain-water near the cow-sheds of his home.

He stood on one leg for a second which was a custom of his when dumbfounded. But he soon brought his foot down again and remained with his heels together and his eyes fixed on things far beyond the queer-coloured walls that surrounded him.

The point he was considering now was simply this. Why should his natural awe and pious dread in the presence of the oldest of the Fates have produced in him no shrinking at all but on the contrary an indignant protectiveness and an unbounded respect, while the mere touch of this Priest of Orpheus, not to speak of the appalling disgust roused by the thought of seeing his face, made him shiver all over? Without having to separate either of his heels again, remove either of his feet from that weirdly coloured stone floor, Nisos decided that what really made the difference was that Atropos, like the Goddess Athene, had been well known to him from babyhood. His cradle so to speak had been rocked to the rhythm of the Three Fates and to the Rhythm of Athene's name. He didn't put it to himself in those exact words; but that was the substance of what he now thought.

But there was more in it than that. There was something else that was much harder to put into words, whether only to clear it up for himself, or to explain it, if he had to explain it later, to his mother. The oldest of the Fates was in reality much more like himself than this terrible priest of *none knew what*. She fought for her friends as he did. She felt pity for that poor old Zeus left lonely on the peak of Gargaros without his thunder-bolts, just as, if he ever thought of the All-Father at all, he would have felt pity himself.

And the same with Pallas Athene. She was one for telling huge palpable lies. And he had to do that himself. *That* was necessary in life's ups and downs. He had to do it every day! When he became the Prophet of the strong and healthy who have been hurt and hit in some way, he would show them the importance of being clever! But when this Priest talked of reverence it was clear he meant something quite different from proper piety.

Did these "Orphic Mysteries" which this weird new kind of Priest celebrated mean some blasphemous and horrible change in the proper manner of worship? Once again Nisos lifted up his right foot and stood on one leg thinking hard, like a young sand-piper pretending to be a heron.

"This must be," he said to himself, "one of those moments in the life of a clever prophet when he has to think about thinking. What the teachers at School say is always: 'Think, Nisos! Think, Kasi! Think, Agelaos!' But if you're going to be a prophet—you've got to do more than think. Any fool can think. You've got to think about thinking."

Finding however that the position in which a person thinks about thinking has an appreciable effect on his thought Nisos returned his right foot to that queerly-coloured floor with some violence. "We can't think properly about thinking," he thought, "without bringing in ourselves. Atropos has to be Fate unswerving or she cannot think. Athene has to be the natural daughter of Zeus' brain or *she* cannot think. Was this new kind of priest not thinking of himself at all but, busy in the establishment of some Secret Society, or Holy Cause, or Community Conspiracy, compared with whose dark and inhuman and impersonal purpose, he himself, the man Enorches, was as nothing?

"When I think," the embryo prophet now told himself, "I think like Athene and like Atropos and like the old Odysseus, from myself outwards. But I have a revolting suspicion that, when this horrible Orpheus-man thinks, he thinks towards himself inwards."

It may have been partly due to the queerly-coloured stonework of this square cell, but our young friend's mind at this point turned, as if automatically, to an interior vision of those two letters carved upon the oldest Pillar in the Porch of the Palace. He felt, as he thought of those letters, as if they were engraved upon the substance of his own soul.

"From now on," he told himself, "I shall dodge, avoid, and undermine in every way I possibly can, these infernal 'Mysteries of Orpheus'." Having decided this point the youthful challenger looked round him more carefully than he had done before. Yes, this chamber into which that man had thrust him was certainly a naked one! It was as if he were imprisoned inside a hard, square, semi-precious stone: a stone that, *with him inside*, might have been worn by some tremendous titanic giant, a giant as big as Atlas who was reported to hold up the sky.

The boy had been thinking too hard, thinking with a cleverness that had become a strain. His nerves now began to behave as if they might in a little while make the sound of *popping*, after the manner of certain seed-pods. In pure nervousness he began to do funny things. He went up to the wall directly under a little square hole, that let in all the light the place had, and began to scrabble at it with his nails; at nothing in particular, just at the wall.

But this silliness was brought to an end by his wondering if it were possible that there might be—but this was probably only a little less silly—any scratches on these walls that resembled that "U" and that "H" on the base of the Pillar in the Palace-Porch. "Apparently," he thought, as he looked carefully about him, "to escape in soul from a Priest of Orpheus is easier than to escape in body!"

But he set himself the task of examining his prison in the manner in which he fancied his old friend, Myos the fly, would have examined it if *he* had been the one to show scant reverence to Orpheus. In his nervous excitement Nisos almost laughed aloud when he imagined Pyraust, the moth-girl, asking Myos to tell her who Orpheus was, and the fly describing him to the moth as the first original spider.

But he now meticulously examined every one of these four walls dutifully thanking as he did so the sky-god Ouranos, Zeus' grandfather, for the light that came from a small half-a-foot-square window near the top of one of them. He was growing nervous again now. With his birthday in sight, for he would be seventeen in a few days, he felt he must hurry up with his mental development if he were to be recognized by the whole Island as the Prophet to the strong by the time his brother, duly married to Leipephile Pheresides, had inherited their father's claim to be king in succession to Odysseus or even—here he looked round in real apprehension now; for where, in the name of Zeus, was the door through which he'd been thrust into this place?—even *instead of* Odysseus!

"Oh popoi!" he groaned. "Was there ever such a fool as I am? Of course it's to stop Odysseus from hoisting sail like a real king and to keep him petering out in his palace till he dies of idleness, or what Mummy calls 'malakia' or some such word, that Dad and Agelaos have been hiding up for years all the 'othonia' or sail-cloth they can get hold of!

"If ever," Nisos thought, "there has been a fool in Ithaca I am that fool!" But he had no sooner "given himself to the crows", as the island saying had it, as the greatest fool among all the "kasis" or class-mates of his age from coast to coast, than he suddenly become certain he *had* caught sight of the Pillar's "U" and "H".

Madly he rushed towards those scratches and pressed against them with both his bare hands. By Zeus, the Pillar *had* saved him! A great stone in the wall moved outwards, fell silently on a bed of moss outside, and lay there motionless. In the sun that stone took to itself a completely different colour from the one that had characterized it within those walls.

It struck the boy, as he jumped upon it, and jumped away from it, and ran off free, that that heavy stone looked as if it were drinking in, in that one second, enough air and sun to give it a new colour for a thousand years!

CHAPTER IV

A few days after the momentous encounter between the oldest but far the most powerful of the Three Fates and the boy Nisos who had now reached the age of seventeen, the hero Odysseus awoke in the grey "wolf-light" of the pre-dawn, and, with nothing on but his blanket, his sandals, and his broad ox-hide belt, scrambled down the ladder and shuffled across the intervening space to the Dryad's hollow tree.

It must be confessed that on this occasion the old king was the awakener of the old Dryad, and not the other way round. It gave Odysseus indeed something of a shock when, in that pallid "wolf-light", with one hand on the soft-crumbling edge of the phantom-grey orifice, he peeped down upon the crumpled heap of faded substances, patches of linen, pieces of cloth, bits of bone, fragments of withered flesh, tangled twists of lichen-coloured female hair, in fact all the accessories and visible appendages of what might well have been an aged human female's bed, including the old lady herself reposing within it.

The patches of linen and cloth were so pitiably the kind of objects that a wandering female beggar would have picked up in her capricious travels that Odysseus drew back with that sort of instinctive reluctance to disconcert a sleeping female that any male householder might feel who finds such an one slumbering in one of his out-houses.

But, along with this feeling, another and a very different one came over him as once more he thrust his bowsprit beard and his massive almost bald skull over the edge of that crumbling orifice.

This was a much more intimate and personal feeling, though sex and sex-shyness entered into it. It was indeed the sort of self-restrained courtesy on the relations between the sexes such as Odysseus had learnt as a child from his mother, Anticleia, the sophisticated daughter of the crafty and mischievously magnanimous Autolycus. In an island-palace such as theirs, crowded with alien visitors from half the coasts of Hellas, some kind of calculated refinement in ordinary personal contact was essential; and it was the dignified reserve of such well-brought-up behaviour that the old man felt he had outraged by peering down upon this sleeping old woman, as she lay half-naked amid her long-accumulated bits of human finery like some moribund forest-fungus that had just managed to survive the winter.

"I must wake the old creature somehow," he thought, "for if I'm to carry through this touchy business of appealing to the people in open 'agora' I *must* find out more about these strangers from Thebes who've got the daughter of Teiresias in their keeping, and the Dryad is the only one who can help me."

He turned his pointed beard to the West without getting any inspiration. Then he turned it to the East and despatched across all the forests and mountains and seas and swamps and deserts that separated him from the land of the blameless Ethopians what he felt to be the swiftest kind of prayer. "What actually is it that I have done," he asked himself, "to vex her as much as this?" And he drew a sigh that really came without any pretence from the very bottom of his being, "I've prayed to her as if my prayer were a wave, a wave that *must* bring her back. Yes, I've sent a wave to the Eastern edge of the world! It's a wave of the sea I've sent; only it's not merely making a furrow of sea-water; it's making a furrow of earth-mould, a furrow of broken branches, a furrow through all the forests of the Mainland till the Mainland itself reaches the edge of the earth!"

The old man's pointed beard seemed to follow his thought as if it possessed the power of transforming itself into the wave its owner was imagining. "But what sort of thing is the edge of the earth," Odysseus wondered; "and do the blameless Ethiopians peep over that edge as I peeped just now at the sleep of the Dryad?"

As he pondered on this, he saw in his mind a terrific chasm of absolute darkness along the fringe of which hung suspended gigantic smoke-blackened shapeless rocks, beneath which there was nothing but a hollow bottomless abyss. And then it seemed to the king, as he imagined himself lying on his stomach on one of these blackened rocks and staring down into the abyss, that he saw the sun coming up out of that unspeakable gulf.

"Do the blameless Ethiopians," he wondered, "ever fall over that frightful edge?" He imagined the great goddess who was his friend, standing there in all her divine beauty, with the terrible Aegis-shield on her arm, its magic tassels dark with the darkness of the gulf of Erebos, while from her breastplate glared forth upon all who dared approach her the dreadful head of Medusa, the dead Gorgon, with the still living hair of its twining serpents feeding on the obscure mystery of its human fate.

Standing motionless the old man gazed for a long moment over that imaginary world's edge. "She would be with me if she could," he murmured aloud; and then shrugged his shoulders. "The gods with me or the gods against me," he thought, "I shall do what I shall do; and what will come of it will be what will come of it!"

He then swung round but instead of leaning against the uneven edge of crumbling and rotten wood and peering down at the sleeping old creature as he had done at first, he now proceeded to call upon her by name; thus giving her an opportunity to arrange her appearance a little before presenting herself. There was enough light to catch her expression fully and clearly when, after a couple of minutes delay, she appeared at the entrance to her hollow tree.

"What—is—it?" she groaned hoarsely. "Has Krateros Naubolides attacked the Palace?"

The old king smiled under cover of his beard. "Not yet, my friend, not *quite* yet. But no doubt if the Palace doesn't take precautions and take them quickly too he *will* attack us before we know where we are. And *that*, my dear old friend, is precisely why I have come to disturb you so early. I feel ashamed of myself for breaking up your dream but there's something I'm very anxious to know, and you are the only mortal or immortal, the only Nymph of land or sea, who can help me to attain this knowledge."

Never in all his days had the crafty old wanderer seen such a look of unmitigated beatitude as rushed into the haggard face of Dryad! "O my dear child!" she cried, "I never thought the Olympians would give me a chance to"—Here the ancient creature had to struggle grimly with a rush of up-surging sobs—"to help the son of Laertes at a real crisis in his life. And I never would have presumed to push myself forward, whatever knowledge I might happen to have, without some sign, some invitation, some request, at least some permission, some opportunity, some door ajar. But now that you yourself have spoken, my dear lord, and have as the Persians say, stretched out your sceptre towards me, I can tell you all I know."

"Tell me, old friend, tell me quick; so that I can act at once. It has become fatally clear to me at last, though it took many days to make me believe it, that my wise goddess and ever-faithful protectress must have hurried away in anger and contempt from our wretched and ignoble quarrels and from this 'complicated world-crisis' as our more pompous contemporaries will love to call it, though of course, as you and I know well, if every battle between Gods and Titans is a 'world-crisis' our poor old world has never been free from one. Yes, it is natural enough that she should do what our great Olympians have always done at a crisis, gone off; gone off to recover her faith in the natural piety of humanity by enjoying for a while the innocent worship of these guileless races. And so, my dear friend, I'll put to you without further delay, the question I should have implored our great Goddess to answer. It is this.

"I have been assured by Eurycleia that the maiden Eione who has lately come to serve in our household, and who is, she herself declared, when I found her in the Gave of the Naiads, a sister of our excellent herdsman Tis, has revealed in recent conversations the discovery of an extremely important secret.

"It was to reveal this discovery to her faithful brother Tis that Eione came here from the opposite end of Ithaca. Eurycleia indeed assures me that Moros, who is Eione's grandfather and also the grandfather of our faithful Tis, has discovered that there is a formidable pair of foreigners, calling themselves Zenios and Okyrhöe, who have occupied for several years—nobody seems to know exactly for how long—a lonely and desolate farm-house on the extreme sea-verge of a rocky headland that has been deserted for generations and left to fall into ruin. There are springs of fresh water in that lonely place, there are remains of several walls and even the remnants of a few wooden fences but the ground that was once protected by these things has been so blighted by sea-winds that it is doubtful if any grain would grow there now; and, if it did, it is certain its chance of its surviving the depredations of beasts and birds would be small.

"But grand-dad Moros swore to Eione—you're listening to me, aren't you, old friend?—that this queer foreign couple came here from Thebes after the death of Cadmus and that they brought with them enough treasure to keep them for a hundred years. And grand-dad Moros declares further that he has spoken with both Zenios and Okyrhöe and has learnt from them that they have under their protection in their half-ruined dwelling a young maiden who is the living daughter of the great prophet Teiresias.

"Eione's grand-dad swears he has been told by this couple, who have several times welcomed him to a lavish meal in their lonely refuge, whose local name is Ornax, that this young daughter of Teiresias, who has inherited from her father a startling amount of his prophetic inspiration, declares that if Odysseus does not sail from Ithaca this Spring on his last voyage he will die miserably in his bed, yes! in his bed in his ancient palace, of an ignoble disease flung upon him out of the deep sea by his deadly enemy Poseidon. Unlike other youthful prophets this young girl has never once contradicted, never once altered by a single breath, this terrible prediction. Her protectors Zenios and Okyrhöe swore to old Moros again and again, so Eione tells Eurycleia, that if ever Teiresias' daughter whose name, it seems is Pontopereia, came here, with this prophecy of hers, she would inevitably convince us all of its truth."

The aged Dryad gave two or three jerky hops forward till she stood on a heap of last year's dead oak-leaves. Here she became more erect than Odysseus had ever seen her; and raising her withered arms above her head she began clasping and unclasping her gnarled fingers tightly round the back of her neck.

"O my child, my child," she murmured. "Say the words, only say the words, and I will help you to the limit of my power and—and——" Here the old lady broke off, under the strength of her emotion. "—— and beyond the limit!" she added in a gasping whisper.

"You mean, my dear friend," said Odysseus quietly, "that by the laws of decency and order that the world owes to Themis and to which Zeus himself bows, it would be improper for you, a mortal Nymph, to help me, a mortal man, before I had prayed and implored you to do so?"

The Dryad nodded furiously. "And we are further," he went on, "since both of us are doomed to die, we are further obligated by the ineluctable courtesies of the cosmos to accept whatever comes of such an appeal for help made by a mortal man to a mortal Nymph? Isn't that so, old friend?"

And once more the Dryad nodded; but this time resignedly rather than passionately.

"Well then, old sweetheart," the crafty hero concluded, "I

do most earnestly beg your help in this difficult situation, but unluckily"—and it would have been clear enough to Penelope, had it been she who was just then listening to the old king, that this heroic courtesy in face of the unregulated chaos of life was extremely unpalatable to the old creature to whom it was offered—" it looks to me as if, since I am a man who cannot escape death, by reason of my association with the body of my mother, and since you are not one of these immortal nymphs of fountain and grove and cave and river but like myself are doomed to old age, it seems that even working together we shall find it no easy task to get out of this appalling dilemma: but easy or hard, I *will* lay it before you, old friend, exactly as it is."

He made a sign with his hand towards a large mossy stone a few paces to the North of her decayed and crumbling tree-trunk; and here they both sat down. "I understand from Eurycleia," he went on, "and she of course gets all her knowledge of the tricks of our enemies from"—but catching a look on his companion's face that he knew only too well, Odysseus interrupted his appeal for help and his tale of difficulties by reminding the Dryad that the aged Eurycleia was being assisted in the palace by the boy Nisos who was the younger son of Krateros Naubolides, the chief enemy of their House, as well as by the simple-minded maiden Leipephile who was betrothed to Krateros' elder son.

"You see, old friend, we over-praised warriors of the last war before the last, are reduced, when our hoards of golden loot are exhausted, to living upon our native acres with very scanty attendants and upon pretty meagre fare, and if among these attendants there are some like the girl Arsinoë, who are captives of our bow and our spear, most of them are no different from the ordinary retainers of any well-do-do landowner."

What he had seen in his old friend's face that led him into reminding her of all this was a dark-scaled shadow of coiling jealousy that at the mention of Eurycleia's name rose like the crest of a venomous tree-toad into the Dryad's eyes.

But he hurried on now, speaking much faster, and clearly

hoping by the mere rush of his words to drive back this moribund demon into its hiding-place amid the rotting roots of ancient hate.

"What I've decided to do now, my friend, is what I've been planning in the marrow of my bones for many and many a day; yes! you can guess what I mean. I've decided to call such an assembly of the men of Ithaca as there has not been for twenty years! To this assembly held in the agora, just as was the one about which they've so often told me when Telemachos made his great speech—and it's ironical to think how absolutely impossible it is even to imagine his making a speech like that today—I've decided to appeal in person on behalf of my desire to hoist sail for the last time. I've decided to implore the people to help me finish the ship I've begun in the Gave of the Naiads. I've decided to implore them to furnish me with all the sail-cloth I need.

"And with this sail-cloth I shall hoist upon a mighty mast such a sail as has never been seen before upon any sea."

They were seated so close to each other on that mossy stone that each of them was conscious of the smell of the other's skin. The skin of Odysseus smelt in the nostrils of the old Dryad like a particular kind of sea-weed she was always especially anxious to keep from encroaching upon one of her favourite rock-pools where an uncultivated tract of land to the north of her dying oak-tree bordered on the sea.

The skin of the Dryad on the contrary smelt in the nostrils of the old king like an especially rare and fragrant fungus that grew out of the bark of the most ancient stumps of long dead trees.

Neither of the two old friends suffered the least distress from this vivid consciousness of the smell of the other's skin. In fact a very curious phenomenon was the result of this mutual awareness, a sensuous result and a psychic result, and a result which gave each of them a peculiar pleasure. The fact is that from now on they would both enjoy summoning back at will, from, below their most sacred and secret shrines of intimately erotic "pot-pourri", the separate smells of their separate skins fused together in one delicately united smell which was neither that of sea-weed nor of fungus but rather of those divine rock-roses of the land of the Graiai, the land that is called Kisthene, and that lies beyond Okeanos.

It was the Dryad and not the King who was the first to break the enchantment that had begun to wrap these two old friends round and about in its fatal folds as if with the invisible mantle of Urania, the heavenly Muse. "And now tell me, child of Laertes, what it is that in my crumbling corruption and my deciduous decomposition, I can do to help you fulfil your daring plan? Tell me, tell me, only tell me; and you'll soon see what an old Nymph, even if she is destined unlike the Naiads and the Nereids, to perish utterly, can do to help you!"

"Well, it is like this, old friend," and the cunning Wanderer gave her one swift sidelong glance out of his deep-sunken, glaucous-green, totally unreliable, wholly unconquerable eyes, and then, as he went on speaking, fixed his gaze on a small group of trees that was, as he well knew by this time, directly between the rock where they now sat and the little walled capitol-city of the island, "though it has been, of course, for years and even centuries, the custom with us for none but warriors, or at least none but grown-up males, to address the people's assembly in the 'agora', this custom has of late grown less strict.

"Indeed in our life-time, as you, old friend, will remember, these assemblies of our traditional city-life have not only been open to all our people, but have been subjected to all manner of natural and even domestic interruptions. Now do you catch, my dear, what I am driving at? What I want to do is to get hold of this daughter of Teiresias and have her brought here under the good influence of young Eione and my faithful Tis, not to speak of young Nisos, who naturally enough, as happens in most Hellenic families, takes the opposite side to that of his elder brother in our civil strife; I mean of course, in this case, in the struggle between our House of Laertes and their House of Naubolides. Once have her safely here on the scene and I am confident she will exert such an influence on our side that my opponents will be completely vanquished. I'm perfectly well aware of the almost imbecile stupidity of Krateros 'eldest son, our young Nisos' brother and of the equally helpless imbecility of the daughter of Nosodea who is betrothed to him. Our danger does not lie with *them*; though the House of Naubolides as represented by these simple old-fashioned Princes has actually, as all our islanders know, older and better claims to sovereignty than has our House of Laertes.

"No! No! the danger lies in an entirely different direction. It lies in the machinations and infernal cunning of this Priest of Orpheus who, by reason of our instinctive Hellenic weakness for mysticism and the occult, can lead us astray in any devilish direction he likes. It was only by the purest accident and by the boy's sudden remembrance of that signature of the son of Hephaistos on the Pillar in our corridor that young Nisos was saved the other day from Hades alone knows what fate at the hands of this bloody-minded priest.

"And so, my dear," Odysseus concluded, "the great problem for me now is how I'm to get hold of this thrice-precious little prophetic maid, Pontopereia, and transport her here. I know this Ornax place, this lonely promontory by the sea. But what about this Zenios and Okyrhöe? Heaven knows who *they* may be! Probably they are Thebans who claim descent from Kadmos himself, and possess magic powers beyond anything we've ever heard of!

"Well, old friend, there is my appeal to you—clear and definite enough but most damnably difficult. However! I know what tree is the king of all trees, and I know what Nymph is the empress of all wildernesses, and since she rules by turning the wilderness into a garden—well, there we are!"

He turned his head away from the group of trees that led to the North and let his gaze rest on the Dryad at his side. Few old women in any forest have answered an old man's questioning gaze with a more radiant look.

"I surely *can* give you advice in this matter, thou brave son of a brave father, and I'll do so without delay! It is not of course by any wisdom of my own, that chance has given me my opportunity of jumping into your boat and of snatching thus boldly at the rudder. It is due entirely, as you can guess, to my goddess-friend Kleta, loveliest of the Graces.

"But listen, precious child of Laertes; listen and store away my words in the depths of your great bald skull! You know the place where our city-walls descend most steeply from the 'agora' to the harbour? And you know where there's a second pair of walls at that steepest place that lead down between the rocks in a wider bend, though they too finally arrive at the harbour, only by a more circuitous route?"

Odysseus, who was listening intently, gravely nodded. "People don't often nowadays go to the harbour by that roundabout way; for, though the shorter street is terribly steep, it's only in bad weather that it's really dangerous to man or beast. In fact so few people ever do go down to the harbour by the circular route of which I'm now speaking that there are places in it where those sweet-scented, bitter-tasting plants grow—your mother probably taught you their ancient name; but I only remember what Penelope used to call them when you first brought her here as your bride. Not a pretty name at all *she* used to call them!"

Again the king gravely nodded.

"Well, my child," went on the aged Dryad, "just at the point where this roundabout way leaves the straight one there is an unwalled road, narrower than a street, but more frequented than an ordinary mountain-track, which leads to the summit of that ridge of rocks which your mother always maintained the farmers up there called "Cuckooor Throne" or "Kokkys-Thronax", but for which your father Laertes had a grander name that I've forgotten. But never mind the name! What I have to tell you now, my dear, is more important than the name of any ridge of rocks. The folk who dwell up here, when you get to the top, are almost all small farmers. Their houses, however, are large and look very comfortable from the outside.

"But you know that rocky ridge I'm talking about better than I do; so it's silly to go on describing it to you. Anyhow, among the farm-houses up there—and part of this ridge must be nearly as high as Neritos—there's a farm-house called Agdos where lives in complete loneliness a middle-aged farm-labourer of the name of Zeuks. This Zeuks has, as you can imagine, been so laughed at and so teased because of the resemblance of his name to that of Zeus, the supreme Ruler of gods and men, that he has become extremely eccentric and will only plough and sow and dig ditches and plant roots and prune trees for those among the farmers up there who use his name respectfully and never laugh at him because of it.

"In all these matters of words and letters, Odysseus my dear, I am as ignorant as this poor Zeuks, but I have the intelligence to know that if a farmer wants to get work from a hired man who isn't a slave he's got to treat him with respect."

The winner of the arms of Achilles once more nodded in grave acquiescence; but in his heart he thought: "When I hoist sail again I shall need no tying to the mast to keep me from the Isle of the Sirens!"

"It was," continued the old Dryad, "because of his hatred of being laughed at, that Zeuks began to leave the island on short fishing excursions on board a small schooner called 'the Starling', and it was on these excursions, upon which he was entirely alone, that he enlarged, so to speak, the nature of his booty or loot and took to indulging in a little cautious piracy.

"For several years it was the prevailing idea among the farmers of Kokkys-Thronax that their whimsical neighbour Zeuks had discovered not only a particularly profitable sand-bank for fishing, but a particularly profitable market for his fish. The barns of Zeuks' solitary homestead seemed to grow, autumn by autumn, fuller of the well-salted meats most necessary for the nourishment of strong men, and, spring by spring, of the honeyed sweet-meats most savoured at the festivals by women and children.

"But now, listen carefully to me, thou son of my lord Laertes. On the high ridge up there for three successive nights a great mist came out of the sea. This was long before your marriage with Penelope and she knew no more about the thing than you do yourself. It was your mother who knew all; and it was your mother who told me all. When those three nights were over—and you must understand, Odysseus, that it was then the identical time of year that we have reached today—very strange stories began to spread far and wide over our island. It was rumoured that during the three days when the unusual sea-mist covered that high ridge this unaccountable farm-labourer Zeuks had actually succeeded in bringing across the sea from Crete or Naxos,—Naxos I *think* it was, but I'm completely ignorant of everything outside what I call my 'garden' and how it could have been that a crazy one like this farm-labourer who wouldn't labour if you didn't treat him like the son of a prince, could do what no hero has ever done I cannot explain—succeeded I say in bringing across the sea and to that very ridge above our harbour, a living pair of immortal, super-magical, demogorgonic horses, Pegasos, born of the blood of Medusa and born with wings, and Arion, born of Demeter by the semen of Poseidon, and born white as the whitest dawn but with a mane black as the blackest midnight.

"But why do you turn your head away, Odysseus? And why do you sigh with that weary, cynical, bitter sigh? Is the whole subject full of infinite weariness to your mind? Is it so riddled and perforated with what a realistic shepherd of the people like yourself probably regards as romantic rubbish?

"But I *will* stop, Odysseus dear, if you feel that anyone who takes seriously such crazy local rumours cannot possibly be a real practical help to you in bringing Pontopereia the daughter of Teiresias here to influence the decisions of our Assembly."

The hurt feelings in the old lady's face were so vivid, and evidently must have risen from such a deep level of her whole being, that Odysseus looked at her in amazement. Since Penelope's death his amorous propensities had been only aroused by his memories, and as these were almost entirely concerned with immortals, who by reason of having no blood in them except the liquid known as "ichor", which has such a distinct cousinship with chlorophyll, the eternal greenness in vegetation, the physical effects of emotion upon flesh and blood had rarely attracted his attention; and when he noticed them at all, for he was as self-centred as a diamond, it was with so little disturbance of his own emotions that they were less to him than rain-drops on his bowsprit beard.

"What on earth's the matter, old friend?" he enquired. "Of course I want your help, want it very much indeed, want it especially at this juncture when I've *got* to get hold of Teiresias' daughter but can't think of any way of doing it, except by crossing the island on my own feet and carrying the girl off, like a warm bundle over my shoulder!

"But you are a wise lady, a friend of my parents, and, I daresay, of my grand-parents too, and you know all that is rumoured from skin to skin, to say nothing of mouth to mouth, from this damned Ornax promontory to the top of this confounded 'Cuckoo-Throne' where the Agdos-place of your precious old Zeuks must be hiding those heavenly horses in his pig-sties till he can find somebody to buy them! Who but a wise girl like you, my dearest friend, could possibly have told me that there was a shy old farm-labourer, with a homestead named Agdos perched on the top of Kokkys-Thronax, or whatever it was mother called it, who had got the winged Pegasos and the black-maned Arion hidden in some creaky shed or ruined stick-house up there until he hears of a travelling merchant rich enough, and by the gods daring enough, to make him an offer? Aye! But isn't it more likely that Pegasos and Arion will hoof this poor old Zeuks into the sea, and carry their purchaser to the Moon to sell *him*, than that an imaginary Phoenician trader will offer to buy the winged offspring of the Gorgon and the black-maned by-blow of Poseidon's rape of the mother of us all?

"But listen, my dear," he went on; for with all his adamantine, mortised-and-tenoned, indurated, inveterate, homogeneous, impregnable, bowsprit-bearded egoism, the son of Laertes was born crudely kind and had acquired an almost supernatural discretion; and he could see that any off-hand sailorish jocularity which diminished the gravity of the startling facts the Dryad had disclosed was ill-suited to the tempo of the occasion. "It is clear that as in what you call your 'garden' you have worked at fulfilling the inscrutable intentions of our mother the earth, under whatever name she likes best to be invoked, so you have been permitted a most rare communion with every living creature, mortal or immortal, finned, furred, feathered, scaled, naked as a serpent, disembodied as a mist, such as ever has been, ever is, or ever could be associated with the surface of this rocky island.

"And when, as at thishour, inthepresenceofthemostdangerous, crucial, important, and fatal conjunction of the Zodiacal Signs of my destiny upon earth, you my parents' oldest friend, you the world-famous Dryad of the oldest oak in Hellas, take upon yourself the piloting of my boat through the earth-waves of mould and sand and gravel and clay, the only offering I have wherewith to thank you, Kleta-Dryad, is the cry of gratitude in my whereheart: 'vox et praeterea nihil!' as Petraia the Midwife always says, in the language of their New Troy, about her twin-sister's Nymph in that Italian cave."

He was silent, his eyes fixed steadily upon her face, his ten fingers, with the intention no doubt, in true Odyssean style, of simulating calm, resisting the natural human tendency to clasp and unclasp themselves under the pressure of agitating and anxious thought, tugging at the fastenings of his broad belt, while he even went so far as to indulge in the motion of a long shiver.

Then he straightened himself. "Well!" he muttered: "I must have a good bath and a mighty meal and a lordly action of the bowels; and I must get hold of Nisos, and, if I can do it without scaring any of them, discuss with him and with Tis and Eione at what hour we'd better make our visit to Ornax; and whether, we'd better assume, and I fancy Eione will be our best advisor on *that* point, that these mysterious strangers, Zenios and Okyrhöe, have come to Ithaca from Thebes and belong to the House of Kadmos, and that they have been within their legal right according to our Hellenic tradition in possessing themselves of the person of Pontopereia, the daughter of Teiresias.

"But you are the only one, I swear to you, Kleta darling, who have given me the true clue to my fate at this supreme crisis in my turbulent life; add thus while the Sun, once more Helios Hyperion, freed forever from the yoke of Apollo, looks down upon me, and the Moon, once more the virgin Selene, freed forever from the yoke of Artemis, looks down upon me, as, in this stick-house of a stable for immortal horses, I carry on my haggling with Zeuks—not with Zeus on the top of Gargaros in Ida, but with Zeuks on the top of Kokkys-Thronax in Ithaca—what I shall have in my heart will be neither the tricks of Zenios of Ornax, nor the wiles of Zeuks of Agdos, but the wisdom of the Dryad whose garden was the cradle of Odysseus."

With these words the crafty hero did what even his father had never done—if Laertes *was* his father rather than that "Father of Lies", the great Hermes himself—he flung his arms about the old creature's neck and kissed her with such dexterity that the protruding point of his bowsprit beard rested tenderly upon the curve of her left shoulder.

He never knew, nor did any of his household ever know, far less any of the city-dwellers between the walls, or any vineyard-owners outside the walls, what the old Dryad did when in silence he had released her, in silence had turned his back upon her, in silence had re-mounted the steps to his bedroom; but the scattered offscourings of dismembered vegetation, the sheddings from dead leaves, the tiny bits of dead sticks, the half-stripped feathers, the empty husks of grass-seed, the pale straw-heads of withered stalks, not to mention the almost invisible insects for whom these minute objects were as stately avenues of cyclopean ruins, in fact all the unconsidered and unrecorded things that in their infinite multitude made up her "garden", accepted the opinion of a small black slug who assured its neighbour, a still smaller beetle, that the gods had turned their Dryad, as they had once turned Niobe, the ancestress of the human race, into a fountain of tears.

But the sun mounted up, steadily and ever more steadily, into the heavens, until he reached a point when the phantom moon that floated opposite to his rising, seemed to be drifting so aimlessly in a sky which was incapable of doing justice to more than one great luminary at the same time, that she looked as if nothing could hold her back from sliding down in an utter dive of helplessness into whatever element of complete extinction awaited such as sank and sank and sank, till they reached the nadir of the universe.

None of the three women, however, who poured first cold, then tepid, then pleasantly warm water, over the king in his bath, had the faintest resemblance in her mood just then to the moon in her vanishing. They were all indeed, although each in her different manner, far too intensely interested in the problem with which Odysseus had just confronted them to think of anything else. This was the question as to what special treasure or treasures he and Nisos had better take with them to Kokkys-Thronax if they were to be in any sort of secure position in bargaining with this madman, Zeuks.

Bargain with the fellow it was clear they had to; and from what the Dryad had said it was also clear that he was likely to prove an extremely shrewd bargainer. It did cross the cunning old hero's mind that it might be possible to take a band of men up there, surround this homestead called Agdos, and carry off that immortal pair of horses by force; but the more he thought of such a violent and arbitrary way of going to work the less he liked it.

His one fixed idea, the one final purpose of all this planning and scheming was to hoist sail once more. What in every bone of his body, what in every pulse of his blood, what in every centre of his complicated nerves, he longed for was simply to sail again into the unknown. He couldn't explain this urge, even to himself. It was deeper than any ordinary desire or intention.

His old friend the Dryad could have explained it to him. It was an obsession, like the migratory passion in birds and fish and insects and even in the spawn of eels!

In his old age it had become the final impulse of his energy, of his sex, of his fight for life, of his deepest secretive struggle, of his struggle, not so much to obey a destiny imposed upon by fate, as to create his own destiny. All he wanted now was to hoist sail once more; and, when he had hoisted sail, *to sail*! It was not that he cared greatly *whither* he sailed, or to what end; but since he knew more about the coasts of the "blameless Ethiopians",— for such was the name he had been brought up to use for the dwellers on *both extremities* of the earth—to the East than to the West, it must be to the "blameless Ethiopians" of the *West* that he would sail.

Yes, he would sail West. And if to touch the limits of the earth in that direction and to reach the "blameless Ethiopians" who dwelt at those limits, that is to say where the Sun, who could travel a thousand times faster than any other living thing, was wont to rise, after traversing, swifter than the wind, the lower regions beneath the earth, was his destiny he would fulfil it.

Odysseus was impelled all the more strongly to make the supreme voyage of his life a voyage towards the West, because, if these late wild rumours told the truth, the whole of the continent of Atlantis had been sunk to the bottom of the sea. From his childhood he had been hearing tales of this mysterious continent, and now to learn that it had been forever submerged, in fact that it existed no longer, made the sort of impression on his peculiar mind, a mind at once obstinately and implacably adventurous, and yet craftily empirical and practical, such as a high-spirited boy would receive who suddenly learnt that what he had been taught were stars floating in space were really tiny holes in the arch of a colossal dome; an impression of which the practical effect was to strengthen his decision that at all cost this ultimate voyage of his must be to the West.

"I shall sail," he told himself, "*over* the waves *under* which lies Atlantis!"

And it was extraordinarily exciting to the peculiar temperament of this insatiable adventurer to think of reaching some unknown archipelago of islands, on the Western side, that is to say the *further side*, of a sunk continent.

Such were the old wanderer's thoughts as the three women

gave him his bath in the upper chamber. While he was eating his breakfast, however, not only the three women to whom he was accustomed were called for consultation, but the little new-comer Eione was also brought in. It became indeed, before it ended, this breakfast of Odysseus on the morning of his encounter with Zeuks, what might be called a Council of State, for our young friend Nisos, now past his seventeenth birthday, stood proudly and demurely at the foot of the table from whose silver plates and flagons and salvers the well-browned, savoury-smelling hogsflesh and the barley-bread and the creamy milk and the fragrant red wine were soon, it was clear to all, putting the old hero into an especially good mood.

Among the women it was Leipephile who, for all her simplicity, watched the king of Ithaca with the most anxious expression. She could not quite understand her own feelings in the matter, but she had learnt enough from the teasing replies of Nisos and from certain rough and casual words dropped here and there by Tis to make her feel that the expedition which was now being planned had something at the back of it that was inimical to Agelaos her betrothed, something that not only her own mother Nosodea but Agelaos' mother Pandea would most certainly regard with serious concern and alarm.

As for the Trojan girl, or rather the Trojan woman, her bewildered resentment bred from years of captivity and always seething in her veins was now assuming, as it had never done before, a definite personal apprehension. They were discussing what particular treasure had better be brought up from the subterranean vaults beneath the palace and it naturally entered the Trojan prisoner's head that some golden object from the world-famous arms of Achilles that by the secret aid of Athene had been awarded to Odysseus instead of to the more daring, more fool-hardy, and far more powerful Ajax, might occur to the crafty old king as a more tempting exchange for the winged Gorgonian steed and the black-maned abortion of the great Mother than any vase or goblet or jug or cup among the rare gifts brought by Odysseus from the palace of Alcinous, the father of that young Nausikaa who had fixed upon the wanderer the first-love of a romantic maiden.

This armour of Achilles, as the Trojan captive well knew, had been brought to Ithaca in one of the ships of Menelaos long before the winner of it had himself got home: and what if it now occurred to Eurycleia his aged nurse, if not to the old king himself, to descend to that secretest chamber of all in the caves beneath the palace only to find it empty? Arsinoë had never been greatly worried at the thought of anybody finding her graven image of Hector, now so glittering in the armour of his slayer, within the haunted purlieus of Arima, since she knew that where abode those two terrible Phantasms, Eurybia the sister of the monstrous Keto, and Echidna, Keto's daughter, and where Odysseus himself never dared to go, it was unlikely that anyone, even if they risked it, would reveal to a soul where they had been or what they had seen there.

But to descend to that lowest of all the treasure-caves beneath the palace with the idea of finding something wherewith to bargain with this crazy Zeuks, *that* was quite a possible move. But even if the old man or this handsome boy-pet of Eurycleia's *did* find that chamber empty, was it likely that anyone would accuse her? Who would guess she had learnt the art of carving? Who would suppose she had ever lived closely enough to Hector to recall his features so well as to be able to carve them?

The aged Eurycleia was the only one during that quaintly palatial and yet so wholly domestic council of war to guess the meaning of the gloomy prognostication lowering in the frowning brow of Agelaos' simple betrothed, or to puzzle over the furtive glances now at the king, now at Nisos, now at Tis, by which were revealed the nervous apprehensions of Arsinoë. The final issue of the discussion had probably been foreseen all along by the shrewd old nurse, who was, though she would have vigorously denied it, quite as "polumetis", or full of the wisdom that wrestles with life's realities, as was Odysseus himself.

It was in fact decided that Nisos should carry over his shoulder in a capacious sack, as he followed closely behind Odysseus, three precious objects, a golden Tripod, a golden Mixing-Bowl, and a golden Flagon. The two first of these came from the Phaeacian palace; while the third had been brought to Ithaca by Anticleia, the mother of Odysseus; and it was a marriage-gift to her from her own father Autolycos who all his days had been a great collector of such treasures. Wherever he went he found them; and whenever he found them he saw to it that they were not left behind when he moved on.

And now that these royal domestic female advisers had concluded their deliberations, while their chief was still devouring his meat and drinking his wine, it can easily be imagined in what high spirits our young friend Nisos was when he set off, brimfull of every kind of ambition to follow his aged hero and king on the first really official adventure, as you might put it, of his life.

Odysseus explained at the start to his excited follower that he had decided to avoid both the Temple and the City in approaching the homestead of Zeuks; so that their progress was less rapid than it would have been had they followed the various main thoroughfares.

Odysseus carried no weapon except our old acquaintance the club of Herakles, while Nisos, walking with a rhythmic swing of his whole body, balanced on his shoulders an enormous sack, to which, first on the right hand and then on the left, he kept lifting a hand, or, sometimes it might be, only a few fingers, to steady the thing's weight under the shocks of the way.

The first thing they both realized when they crossed the border of Zeuks' farm was the fact that for all the precautions they had taken to reach the place un-heralded there was already quite a gathering of Zeuks' neighbours, small farmers with their wives and children, clearly collected there to get the thrill of an immensely grotesque and wildly comic, if not a shockingly startling, encounter.

Odysseus quickly understood that the half had not been told him of the fantastic personality he was now to meet for the first time. Into his mind, and indeed into the mind of his youthful attendant too, as they now both looked round at the faces about them, there entered the suspicion that this little crowd of men, women, and children, gathered on this level expanse of rough grass with lichen-covered rocks and a sprinkling of spring flowers, was anticipating an extremely dramatic scene, but was prepared to feel no particular sympathy for either side.

Evidently something beyond all ordinary events was going to happen, for the children kept whispering to one another, while the younger among them lifted puzzled and rather frightened eyes to the faces of their mothers; and indeed it was plain that what everybody expected was that their old, weak, deserted, and poverty-stricken king was now going to be completely out-matched, out-witted, and rendered helpless if not ridiculous, by this famous country-side clown whom none of their richest farmers could tame. "They are all thinking," Nisos told himself, "that the old man must be in his dotage if he fancies he can cope with such a crazy rebel against all established authority as this weird creature Zeuks.

"And everybody here must feel," the boy's thoughts ran on, "that the moment the king really sinks into the helpless silliness of old age, the House of Naubolides will assert its claim to rule; and to rule not only Ithaca but all the neighbouring islands as well."

For a moment, as he rested his heavy sack upon a rock and automatically jerked his body so that the knife in the leather belt which his mother had given him on the day he was seventeen might fall into the precise place most convenient for clutching it at any sudden necessity, he felt a shiver of family-pride rushing through him, and of thankfulness to the Fates, the oldest of whom he had so recently defended, that he was different from the farmers' boys of his own age in this crowd whose eyes he could see were fixed on him, he hoped with envy, though in one case he fancied he caught a couple of them laughing at him.

But if the king's armour-bearer, or more strictly his currency-bearer, for it was purely in preparation for a shrewd piece of trading that the boy carried that heavy sack, had his own private thoughts created by the general atmosphere around him, the old hero was not without his own sharp-edged reactions to this highly-charged occasion. What he, from old experience of the moods of flexible-susceptible human beings, suddenly felt now was a complete surprise to himself. He felt that his own encounter with this queer personage who had the audacity, as well as the subtle cunning, to steal, by the aid of heaven knows what irresistible spell, the actual winged horse sprung from the blood of Medusa was not the sole cause of the crowd's excitement.

He couldn't help noticing that in place of staring eagerly and excitedly in the direction of the outbuildings and barns of the homestead called Agdos, the eyes of most of the people assembled here kept turning to the circuitous upland track by which he and Nisos had reached this flat expanse of level grass and evenly strewn gravel, just as if they expected a considerable rear-guard of well-armed soldiers to be following him!

"Surely they cannot," he thought, "really imagine that I've got a body-guard of Ithacan warriors ready, like those who arose from the sowing of the dragon's teeth, to fight to the death wherever I lead them!"

But he quickly gave this mental question a physical rebuff with his broad shoulders, sharp-projecting chin and massive skull; and was prepared as he used to be, day following day, twenty years ago, for whatever ambush of his enemies was to burst out from round the next corner.

Odysseus had full need to be thus prepared, for in another second an enmity greater than any searching tentacle of Scylla or any whirling suction of Charybdis revealed itself to them all.

From the very same path by which the old king and the boy Nisos had just reached this spot came a hurrying figure of whose identity neither of them had any doubt. It was Enorches, the priest of Orpheus!

A curious shudder of supernatural awe ran through that whole crowd. The younger children clung to their mothers' hands and garments whilst the men bit their lips, tightened their belts, and looked anxiously at one another. Nobody turned to the well-roofed sheds of Agdos, whence the mocking clown who called himself Zeuks was awaiting his turn on that typically Hellenic stage, which seemed, as was always happening in the midst of those eternally contesting islands and cities and races and cults and political parties, to have been called into existence, for some malicious purpose of its own, at that particular moment, by some invisible master of ceremonies.

At first glance Nisos simply could not resist the childish impulse of pure panic which caused him to heave up his sack once more on his shoulders and retreat before that advancing figure till he was a few paces to the rear of Odysseus, though he kept his head sufficiently to restrain himself from crouching, precious bundle and all, actually behind those broad shoulders.

As he watched Enorches advance straight towards them, evidently prepared to speak face to face with Ithaca's king, it was only by an intense effort that he forced himself to do what even his encounter with the oldest and most powerful of the Fates had not enabled him to do, namely look the man in the face.

But the boy did manage to do this; and no action in all the years of his life was destined to be more momentous, and this purely in its effect upon himself, than his action in this case. And Nisos not only looked straight into Enorches' face. He quite deliberately forced his mind into its fullest, clearest consciousness as he did so; though the effort he had to make to do it was an extreme one, almost as if he had to embrace a boy or a girl with whom he was in love but whose body was hung with glittering sharp-edged and even pointed ornaments that hurt him as he pressed them with his arms and hands and naked skin.

But what, beneath that dazzling sky and burning sun did he make out of the face of the Priest of Orpheus? Well! The dominant features of it were its eyes and mouth. Nisos felt as if the visage into which he was now looking lacked forehead, ears, cheeks, and nose, lacked everything in fact but eyes and mouth; eyes to seek out its prey, and mouth to swallow it when found.

In that blazing noon and because of something demoniacal about the whirlpool-like suction of that mouth, Nisos felt as if this appalling Being had no forehead or nose, or ears, or chin, or even neck! Enorches was, he felt, literally all eyes and mouth, like certain fish, certain serpents, certain birds, and certain insects.

As he gazed in fascinated horror at this Priest of the Mysteries the creature moved—the boy could hardly think of the man as a human person—a few steps nearer to the old king. In making this move Enorches naturally came nearer to Nisos also, who felt such a shiver of terror, that, lugging his great sack along the ground, for having once faced that visage he couldn't take his eyes off it, even to lift up his bundle, he found himself in a position whence his magnetized stare of terror inevitably included Odysseus also.

And then to his astonishment the old king, taking no more notice of Enorches than if he'd been an over-officious retainer in a crowded court, turned to him himself. "Don't you think, Nisos Naubolides," the old man said, "that it might be a good idea when we come back with the daughter of Teiresias to make use of this level expanse in place of the traditional "agora"? Do you get what I mean, my lad?

"It strikes me somehow as a freer and less formal place, and being further from the city and further away from the city-walls it seems to me to be less under the influence of conventional rules, and more likely to be friendly to new and daring schemes, such as my wish to sail Westward, beyond the Pillars of Herakles and the Atlas Mountains, over the unknown waves that now, as we hear, hide the sunken continent of Atlantis. What are you staring at, boy? What's come over you? This is only the Orpheus fellow, you know, come to beg me no doubt not to begin giving away my treasures until he has had his share for the Mysteries.

"How did he find out, the rogue, about this madman Zeuks having ensorcerized Pegasos and Arion? Well—we needn't ask *that*. These Priests find out everything. The winds and waves themselves whisper to them, and the babies in arms babble to them, of the intentions of destiny.

"But isn't this an agreeable spot for a grand assembly? Isn't this just the very sort of place where orators are moved to speak freely and where true shepherds of the people can naturally draw inspiration out of the air? I was a fool, Nisos Naubolides, not to think of this place. I warrant it was the old associations of our "agora" up there stopped me from thinking sooner of a real grand appeal to our people. This will be the exactly right place for Teiresias' daughter to invoke the Olympians and propitiate the Fates.

"I feel like speaking to them now, only there aren't enough of them at the moment; and these, as you see, dear lad, are just the farmers' families round here. But what a place to inspire anyone! Look at these men and women, so lusty and well-fed! And what handsome-coloured cloth they're wearing! Do they weave these garments themselves nowadays do you suppose? How interested Penelope would be could she see how richly purplish in this noon-sun and under this cloudless sky gleams that excellent mingling of sepia and violet!

"And do you see how that noble Fir-tree up there stretches a horizontal branch from its very heart towards that other tree — I can't quite make out what tree *it* is — down there against the blue water of the bay? O yes! And when I come to address the assembly here — I tell you, my boy, it'll be like that very first assembly ever held in Ithaca, about which I used to hear from my mother before I was your age.

"Heavens! I'll make them sit up. Hermes! But I'll make them acclaim *you*, my dear lad, above your stupid brother, to rule in my place when I have hoisted sail. By Olympos yes! you shall look down past all these farmers in their richly-dyed cloth at that divine tree yearning to exchange its sap with that great pine; and as you see the sails of those fishing-boats on those blue waves you'll think of your old king looking down through the water of an unknown sea at the sunken palaces of Atlantis!

"Yes! By the 'aegis' of the Son of Kronos which is now the 'aegis' of Pallas Athene! when once, with the help of Pegasos and Arion, we've got Teiresias' daughter here, we will drag enough sail-cloth out of them to carry me to the shores of the unknown West! By the Olympians, yes! Why should this rustic father of yours, why should this stupid brother of yours, not be forced to give up their place to you, my dear boy? It worked before in this island, that sort of change; and it can be brought about again. O! if I could only get all the men of Ithaca assembled here I would know how to persuade them! Haven't I seen——"

He was interrupted by a wild rush of all the crowd round them towards the sheds and barns of the homestead "whose name", as they had heard so often that day, "was Agdos". Enorches himself followed the crowd, passing both Odysseus and Nisos without a word: and there, before them all, walking, each of them on his four legs, quietly, obediently, tamely, patiently, came the winged dark-skinned horse, Pegasos, and the much smaller whitish-grey horse, with a sweeping black mane, known far less widely through Argos and all the mainland, but known well in the islands nearest to Ithaca, under the name of Arion.

Yes, quietly, gently, obediently, those two imperishable and immortal creatures walked forth from their stable towards Odysseus; while Nisos, who soon had his great sack of treasures, heavy as a king's ransom as they were, hoisted on his shoulders, opened his mouth and breathed in gasps while he awaited what would happen. Arid there, sometimes behind his immortal captives, and sometimes beside them, and sometimes even before them, was Zeuks himself!

Zeuks was a man of middle height according to ordinary human measurement; but among his other peculiarities he possessed an astonishingly natural power of appearing to be taller or shorter according to the convenience, as you might put it, of the particular occasion. It was as if the occasion itself became a sorcerer who called up, out of the abyss of the uncreated, exactly the right puppet-homunculus that the trick required.

Evidently what was required at this moment by the inevitable situation was to get these unusual creatures safely, quietly, and in docile subjection, into the immediate presence of the king of Ithaca. Meanwhile within that unclosable, unhealable, impenetrable, almost invisible crack, that extended down the whole length of the Club of Herakles, an intense argument was going on between Myos the fly and Pyraust the moth.

They had not been caught asleep, these two members of the royal household of Ithaca. In fact they had both been awakened by the stir in every inhabited portion of the palace, even before Odysseus had to end his emotional talk with the old Dryad which was the chief cause of his being where he was now.

Tis had been the first to disturb them. He had gone earlier than usual to milk Babba, for he wanted to get the pail of fresh milk safely into the palace before he drove the cow to a fresh strip of pasture, well the other side of the haunted Arima, upon whose devilish soil nothing would have induced him to tread. Then Arsinoë had flicked and flapped with one of the last scraps of a particular Pelasgian veil that she had surreptitiously extracted from Eurycleia's private treasure-box but took care to use before the old lady got up.

It was only after this event that she used a piece of the common stuff which the old nurse was wont to dole out for dealing with the dust which in both corridor and hall gathered with special heaviness owing to the nature of the rocky substances out of which Ithaca's royal cave had been originally and primevally dug.

It was indeed of dust that the two insects were arguing in their accustomed hiding-place within that warm perambulating retreat. Dust played as large a part in their life as wind and rain played in the life of the king of Ithaca; and so, while Enorches was striving to cast whatever devilish spell he fancied would be most effective against the creations of the blood of Medusa and the horse-play of Poseidon, the fly Myos was explaining to the moth Pyraust that every grain of dust was an actual world and that it was foolish to philosophize about the universe until you stopped talking about Etna being flung upon Typhon and talked about Arsinoë disturbing worlds with her duster.

Meanwhile Nisos also, like his newly-made student-pal or Kasi-kid, was philosophizing after his fashion. What struck him, as this dancing Zeuks led his magnetized captives towards them, was the smooth-sliding manner in which each separate event or incident or occurrence, whether it was of cosmogonic importance, or was of the faintest and most attenuated significance, a mere ripple, you might say, crossing the surface of the oceanic time-mirror of life, was accepted by Odysseus with the same unalterable equanimity.

Here was the winged horse Pegasos, born of the blood of the Gorgon, and here was the black-maned Arion, born of Demeter herself when she took the form of a mare to escape Poseidon; and dancing round these Divine Abortions was the queer individual who had the power of hypnotizing any equivocal creation who crossed his path and yet was no Bellerephon or Perseus or cast at all in the heroic mould; and here, beside them, surveying these lusty apparitions with the eye of an executioner was the Priest of the immemorial Mysteries who looked as if there were nothing in sight he would not gladly offer up to his chthonian divinities.

And yet what was this amazing old king pointing out to him now—to him whom he had recently been considering as his successor in the kingship over the heads of a father and elder brother—but some casually noted aesthetic point about the contrasting beauty of a certain massive tower of greyish-yellow stone, to the North-East of where they stood and rising from a corner of the city wall, and a glittering roof of white marble to their North-West belonging to the Temple of Athene, pictorial elements that justified still further, the old man explained, the idea of this particular spot as a new assembly place.

"Don't let me ever forget," the boy prayed in his heart, though to no particular deity, "the calm he shows at a moment like this!" And it really was, this time, without any thought of it being "clever" of him to notice such things that Nisos followed up his secret prayer by telling himself that though those weirdly startling wings rising from the shoulders of that submissive great horse, and that black mane sweeping the ground belonging to the other animal, were striking phenomena of creative nature's power, it was really a more striking thing that a king who lived alone in his palace with his old nurse and a couple of maids should be so completely equal to occasions like this.

Was it, Nisos asked himself, that that great massive skull possessed an imperviousness to shocks denied to other human craniums? Well, anyway that bowsprit-like and carefully trimmed beard accentuated the quality of the man's self-possession. And Nisos decided that when once *his* beard began to grow he would treat it with exquisite care. "A prophet," he told, himself, "can clearly hide a great many natural feelings behind a well-managed beard, and if he can hide them, cannot he rule them, cannot he force them to obey him, as this horse with wings and this other with a trailing black mane have been forced to obey this madman Zeuks?"

CHAPTER V

It was with the utmost interest that Nisos watched Zeuks and tried his best to weigh him up and get to the bottom of him. The impression he first got of this eccentric farm-labourer was that he was of middle height, of middle age, and of middle social estimation. He noted how essentially Achaean he was in every detail, in dress, in manner and in general appearance; not Pelasgian, or Dorian, or Ionian but an evenly balanced middle-of-the-road Achaean, moderate in all the imponderables, in tribal habits as well as personal reactions, and conveying, wherever he went, beneath the whole paraphernalia of his comic humours an impression of dispassionate calm; a calm that was not merely temperamental, like the coolness of Odysseus, but was the deliberately arrived-at attitude of a definite metaphysical philosophy.

Watching Zeuks carefully Nisos decided that it was this unobtrusive mediocrity that enhanced to such a startling degree the peculiar features of his countenance, features for which it would be difficult to find a more accurate epithet than bulbous. Bulbous they were, and bulbous they remained, under all the contortions and distortions of his remarkable physiognomy.

Every single one of the man's features was so to say swollen by the inordinate pressure within it of the particular purpose for which the creativeness of nature had designed it. The forehead of Zeuks seemed bursting with its overpowering plethora of thought. His nose seemed bursting with its abounding zest for smelling. His mouth with its full lips, its strong white teeth, its grandly sensuous curves, seemed to have been created by the insatiable palate and indefatigable tongue within it, a couple that were united in conjugal understanding, the palate as the female to the tongue as the male, for the tasting and enjoying of almost everything that could possibly, conceivably, indeterminably be tasted and enjoyed.

But his eyes,—"What is it in this man's eyes," thought Nisos, "that makes me feel so nice and warm?"—his eyes were surrounded by a thousand wrinkles and creases and rufflings of the ruddy skin round them, creases that seemed so infinitely tickled by what you had just said, or were just going to say, or simply by the way you were the self that *could* say such things, that merely to watch their response to you and your remarks gave you a delicious sense of having found your place in the world, a place which, the more you said, or the more entirely you put yourself behind what you said, would grow hourly, daily, monthly, yearly more agreeable to yourself, if not to all concerned!

But it was the eyes themselves, apart from those friendly and rampageously benevolent wrinkles, that were made to encourage everybody they approached to enjoy the world and to enjoy being the person who was thus enjoying it.

Zeuks' eyes were in fact so deeply set in his bulbous head that Nisos got the feeling that they receded into a mass of substance which they themselves, in their immense zest for life, were everlastingly creating afresh behind that mediocre skull with its pair of eternally recessive holes.

ATLANTIS

Nisos couldn't then—he put it down at first to the glare of the noonday sun, but he changed his mind later on—catch the exact colour of Zeuks' eyes; but for that very reason he decided they were probably hazel. It was indeed, all considered, an extremely complicated moment in our clever young friend's life. He might be seventeen and he might be the one destined by fate to become the prophet to the strong rather than to the weak, but it began to invade his mind, as he stood there, leaning on his heavy sack, which in its turn rested on a lichen-covered rock, that because a hero had won in his time almost miraculous victories and had used incredible physical strength and still more incredible mental cunning to win the victories, it did not mean that to the end of his days such an one would inevitably be the centre of every dramatic human situation that could possibly arise.

It was exactly noon on this desirable level expanse, with the homestead of Zeuks overlooking it to the East, and that high corner of the City-Wall and that gleam of the Temple's marble roof out-topping it to the West, exactly noon on the very spot selected by the old king as the perfect site for an assembly of the people that would be swayed by his eloquence.

Well! here was Zeuks, coming dancing out of his ramshackle shed and leading, yes, actually leading, the immortal creatures they had come to buy!

The well-dressed crowd of prosperous farmer-families seemed puzzled as to where to turn to get some hint of the manner in which they ought to receive the thousand-years wonder of this smuggling into their home of these Divine Beasts. Were they to get it from Zeuks or from their king?

Alas! from neither! The Personage who was destined to direct their feelings was none other than Enorches, the Priest of Orpheus! Yes, to the absolute amazement of the seventeen-year-old "prophet to the strong", there was not a family there, not a man or a woman there, not even a child, who did not excitedly turn to greet Enorches.

It is true there was one little toddler of about two-and-a-half who stretched out a plump arm towards the Club of Herakles, no doubt being attracted by the roundly twisted curves of that formidable bosom, in the cracked interior of which Myos the Fly was still expounding to Pyraust the Moth the metaphysical philosophy of dust and how every grain of it was a world.

But apart from the child who admired the Club and the two insects who were inside the Club, the whole of that excited assembly of well-to-do farmers with their wives and children instinctively divided itself into two parties, the largest of which gathered closely round Enorches and displayed evident hostility to Zeuks, while the other advanced with irresistible curiosity towards Zeuks and his Divine Beasts, constantly looking back, however, as they did so, the women glancing apprehensively over their shoulders, and the children alternately stumbling as they turned to stare at Enorches, or clinging to their mothers' belts and pressing their faces against their garments.

Not a soul among that whole company made any move towards or away from their old king, though Nisos did notice two of the men whispering together with furtive glances at himself and his great sack.

"They're saying to each other," he thought with a faint shiver: "We'll take *that* off him before they get away from here!"

Meanwhile Odysseus, having gravely turned his pointed beard to the North, the West, the South and the East, and having instructed Nisos to remain close to his side—"No! no! my boy, much nearer than that! In fact you'd better put a finger into my belt, if you can balance that thing on your shoulder with one hand"—advanced slowly straight towards the swaying and dancing Zeuks.

Neither the word "swaying" nor the word "dancing" accurately describes the sinuous movements with which this queer creature hypnotized those two animals. As in every other aspect of this singular person's character, if you had never seen him before it was necessary for the understanding of his peculiar nature to catch not only the general expression of his face but at least a few of its special expressions; and among these it was especially important to note what his expression was when he experienced an access of respect and reverence for anyone or anything he suddenly encountered.

Nisos had the wit to realize quickly enough, when Odysseus had greeted Zeuks and was conversing with him, that what those little, searching, deep-set eyes, peering out from the receding depths of what seemed an eternally replenished background, expressed just then was a mixture of deeply affectionate respect and humorous amusement.

And it was further evident to Nisos that this singular person's profound respect for the king was increased, not diminished, by the fact that he found the old hero so infinitely entertaining. It was also evident that Odysseus felt absolutely at ease with Zeuks and entirely natural in dealing with him. Indeed he continued to be so direct, so objective, so practical in his handling of him that it was difficult for Nisos to see what there was about such shrewd and downright and matter-of-fact business relations that could excite not only ribald laughter but hugely humorous enjoyment.

But it was quite evident to Nisos that either the old king enjoyed being laughed at, or, and this is what seemed to the boy the more probable, that he had been so toughened by all his experiences of the ways of the world, that his self-created thick skin and his long-practised straight-to-the-point opportunism had made him as impervious to humour as he was impervious to love!

Nisos inserted a second finger into the king's belt, the longest finger he had. In some queer fashion the old man's imperviousness to everything but the one single desire to sail away, to sail over the sunken towers of Atlantis into the Unknown West, touched the boy to the heart. It was a purpose he could understand. It had something about it that resembled his own fixed intention to become, when once he had grown a pointed beard, a Prophet to the Strong.

Let the rollicking humour of Zeuks bubble and bubble from what springs it would! Let it burble up against the old hero's face pebbles as hard as balls of brimstone! There'd be one friend for the old adventurer who'd be as tough and impervious as himself! Yes, imperviousness was what the future "prophet to the strong" felt he must struggle to win.

But fate had other moves to make; and there were several farmers there who, although with homesteads on the same ridge as farm-labourer Zeuks, and although they had come out to see the farm up there at high noon, were in part self-pitying puppets moved by fingers other than their own, and yet were in part also living creators of the future of Ithaca.

Enorches had already begun to scream angrily at Zeuks before Nisos, with his right hand supporting the treasure-sack balanced to a nicety at the back of his head and with two fingers thrust deep into the belt of Odysseus, had even realized that he himself, and the deserted old king, and the winged Horse, and the black-maned Horse, and Zeuks and the Priest of Orpheus were in a random knot together, with the flabbergasted but still fascinated crowd hemming them in on all sides and surging round them.

"It's no good your grinning and chuckling at me, thief, robber, pirate, serf!" cried Enorches. "It's no good your fancying that a wretch like you, the lowest of the low, the basest of the base, born to be the slave of those who rightly and properly by the laws of Themis and Zeus and Eros and Dionysos and the Inspired Singer Orpheus rule the entire world, can make a covenant with a king to put in his keeping this mad Spawn of the Gorgon and this By-Blow of Poseidon and Demeter!

"Did you think, Dung of the Earth, did you suppose, Turd of the World, that the Stars in their Courses would fight for a blob, a shred, a foul pellet, a filthy crumb, a drop of cuckoo-spit, a clipping of toe-nail, like you? There are many who rule us. There are many who strive to rule us. There are many who once ruled us. Erebos and Tartaros are full of such as once lorded it over us! And where are they now?

"Don't you understand sod of sods, don't you comprehend, dreg of dregs, that what you've been given hands and feet for by the beautiful ones, the creative ones, the powerful ones, the one's eternally to be worshipped, is the privilege, dung of dungs, blob of blobs, squit of squit, curd of curd, scurf of scurf, flake of flake, chip of chips, drop of drop, sweat of sweat, the privilege to serve your betters, and yet here you are actually daring to decamp with demigods!

"Yes! to steal, to kidnap, to imprison in your wretched pigsty these two sacred creatures, the feathers of whose wings and the hairs of whose manes you are unworthy to kiss! Release them, I command you! Hand them over to me, the god-appointed guardian of the holiest of holy mysteries!

Though Athene may have fled to her shrine among the Ethiopians, I have not fled; and where I am there will always be a sanctuary for any offspring of the ever-living gods, however far blasphemy and sacrilege and atheism may spread their savagery! Give up these holy creatures I say! Yield them over to me now and I will see that you escape the punishment you deserve! But refuse and it will fall upon you! Harken unto me all ye that are here, devoted worshippers of the most high Gods! Have you not heard—has it not been revealed to you——"

It was at this point that Enorches, whose very name had been given him at his birth because of the enormity of his testicles, and who had been called ere now by fellow-priests "the well-hung brother" proved his manhood by leaping forward with a spring and scrambling up upon one of the rocks with which Odysseus's new-found "agora" was sprinkled and by bursting into a ringing oration.

"Our whole Hellenic way of life," he cried, "is in danger my friends, and we're not alive enough to what's going on to do anything to save it! We haven't even cleared our minds of all the childish poetry our mothers and nurses put into our heads to stop us piddling on the floor, or upsetting the pot on the fire, or cutting off the tail of the dog, or giving the hen's best chicks to the cat! We have been too shallow and stupid, my friends, in our whole attitude to religion!

"We have accepted like babies all our mothers told us about the Twelve Olympians, about Zeus, Hera, Poseidon, Demeter, Apollon, Artemis, Hermes, Aphrodite, Hephaistos, Ares, Themis, and our own Athene.

"But, my friends, all this is sheer childishness, and what it leads to is exactly what has happened in the case of this worthless pirate, this low-born thief, this dung-heap rapscallion, this off-scouring of the city's brothels who calls himself Zeuks so that he may blaspheme the more, so that he may make a mock at our Father in Heaven, and, worse still, put to scorn our Father's Sister and Mate, the great Queen of Heaven, Hera herself!

"What none of you are grown up enough to understand, though I've been explaining this very thing for the last ten years, is that by certain new, certain occult, certain mystical, certain sanctified, certain divinely inspired revelations, drawn at length and explained at last from the most sacred and precious oracle that we of pure Hellenic birth can boast, an oracle do I say? an inheritance, a birth-right, a talisman, an enchantment, a divine and celestial Word, by means of which our enemies are inevitably defeated and our intentions are inevitably fulfilled, we know that we've arrived at a point in our development where Eros and Dionysos appear in their true light. Does anyone here on this fair platform, looking down on the rich harbour of our island-home, realize the full significance, the concerted value, the abysmally-charged import of the birthright of which I speak?

"Has anyone here been so freed of late from our mothers' lullabies and war-tales as to know what I mean when I say that our way of life in Hellas has been saved only just in time from its final extinction by recent interpretations of the prophecies of our unique poet and singer, Orpheus?"

At this point in the midst of the resounding oration of Enorches there suddenly occurred the sort of movement of relaxation in that well-to-do careless crowd which suggests an articulate admission that the subject of a speech is totally beyond the intelligence of its listeners but that the personality of the speaker, and the fervour of his arguments, not to mention the dramatic situation in which he is taking so dominant a part, are all conducive to the said listeners' settling down to listen in self-satisfied pleasure as if they'd been suddenly transported to an agreeable theatre.

ATLANTIS

What pleased our young friend Nisos in all this, especially when he noticed that both the two portions of this unconventional hill-top assembly, the part of it that had been so fascinated by Zeuks and his unusual horses as to feel definitely hostile to Enorches, and the part of it that remained under his spell, had both relaxed, was the fact that Zeuks himself had suddenly taken the initiative with Odysseus, and had advanced close up to him, trailing the long thin leather straps by which he drew the two horses after him, and that the two were now engaged, under the very nose of the excited orator in what looked like a very harmonious and mutually satisfactory bargain.

Meanwhile the speaker was approaching the culminating points of his speech, which were entirely concerned with the Mysteries.

"What is revealed to us in the Orphic Mysteries," he was saying, "is the inner truth, the ultimate quintessence, of our whole Hellenic life. This essence, this quintessence, my dear friends, floats like an exhalation through every moment of our existence. Whither and Whence does it float? *That* is no simple question; for it is fed by a thousand ineffable imponderables!

"Mystery it is, and mystery it pursues. From mystery it ascends and in mystery it is engulfed. As the heat of this thrice-sacred noon dissolves in those blue waves down there, so there is a sweetly-dissolving high noon in the life of all of us Achaians towards which we are moving even as I speak; and I swear to you, brothers and sisters of this Isle of Ithaca, that it is only in the celebration of the Orphic Mysteries that you, men and women of Hellas, can rise to your full spiritual stature and rejoice in your full divine inheritance!"

Enorches was clairvoyant enough to grow aware at this point that his large audience were enjoying his speech delivered from that jagged little rock in precisely the spirit he cared least of all for it to be enjoyed, that is to say, as a theatrical performance, and he allowed his arms to sink to his side and his voice to die away.

But he didn't come down immediately from his little rock.

He looked round him with a quite special expression, the expression of a creature with the beak of a bird of prey and the body of a serpent, a creature who has bitten its prey in half, and swallowed half of it, but still feels unsatisfied.

And it happened to be just at that very moment that Pyraust, the girl-moth, implored her boy-friend, Myos the House-Fly, to remove his powerful front legs from the particular one of her languidly trailing wings which it was always easiest for her to straighten out first when she had decided to spread both her wings in flight.

"I *know* he's calling for me to go to him," she explained, "and when he's calling so strongly it hurts me, yes it hurts me very much, not to be able to go to him! So lift up your front legs, my beautiful one, I beseech you! They are so strong and so gloriously black; and O! how weak my poor trembling brown wings seem in comparison with them! But lift them up now, I beg you!"

But the fly remained obstinate. "In a second; all in good time, all in due course!" he buzzed. "But while we are together I do so want to settle once for all this one single point. Surely you do admit, my sweet one, you can't help it, that in the smallest atom of dust, just as in the smallest grain of sand, there is a whole world of reality. Never mind all this noisy speaking and shouting! It's about shams and shows; not about reality at all!"

Thus speaking Myos pressed his two front legs, so black, so shining, and so extremely strong, more firmly than ever upon the quivering wing of the girl-moth. "But look who's here!" he added presently; and, again, after another pause: "Aren't you glad, my Crumb of Crumbs, that I didn't let you go when he first began bawling out his blathering bluster? Why! you'd have bumped into her! And I can tell you, my leaf of longing, my flying feather of dainty fancy, if you had bumped into her it would have been the end of you!"

The brown moth ceased struggling. The fly removed his leg from her wing. They both settled themselves down as comfortably as they were able in those narrow quarters where they were only about six inches below the powerful fingers of the king of Ithaca as he went on bargaining with Zeuks. Neither Zeuks nor he paid the faintest attention to the torrent of rhetoric from the lichen-covered rock, a torrent which, as soon as the speaker realized what newcomer it was who had now appeared among them, recommenced with redoubled vigour. For the personage who had burst in upon that extemporized "ecclesia" was in fact no other than Petraia, the old-maid midwife; and it was a Petraia worked up to a considerable degree of professional indignation, not to speak of virginal vituperation.

She advanced at a pace which could only be described by the vulgar expression "at a run". She forced her way straight through the crowd till she reached a family group whose members were pushing against each other to get as close as they could to Pegasos and Arion.

Here she singled out a woman, obviously about as far advanced in pregnancy as it is possible to be and, clutching her by the only portion of her person which was not already pre-empted by three other children in addition to the small creature as yet undelivered, she dragged her away protesting loudly, a protest shared by so many of her brood that her carrying off by Petraia caused quite a little convulsion and a sort of counter-eddy in the stream of people who surrounded those two supernatural beasts.

As she dragged the woman towards the farm-house which was nearest to Zeuks' domain they passed so close to the club of Herakles that Myos and Pyraust could clearly catch what Patraia was saying, and she was saying a great deal.

"A self-respecting woman like you," she was complaining, "ought to be wiser than to be so interested in these playthings of men! All that these silly boy-men want are more and more playthings! What they don't realize is the true meaning of this great news that is now spreading through the entire world. They don't realize, these silly boys, that during a few recent weeks there has been a revolution in Nature herself! Nature herself has decided to assert herself at last. And *this* means, *can* mean, *does* mean, and *will* mean only one thing! And that one thing is this: Women from now on are no longer subject to men.

"And it means more than that. It means that women are not only from now on freed from the yoke of men, but that men are from now on subject to women, and must learn, if they don't want to witness the death and perishing of the entire human race, to subject themselves to their mothers and wives and daughters.

"From now on men must learn that their highest worship is their worship of women and that this worship is called *Uranian* because it resembles the inspiration of the Heavenly Muse!"

All this while Petraia never ceased dragging her pregnant captive towards the Bed of Delivery, the Bed which everyone present at that stupendous scene was forced by her ringing declaration to behold as the only holy and thrice-blessed Bed to be desired by all! The unfortunate or divinely fortunate woman in whom the shock of this outrageous publicity had already started the suspended pains of labour was imploring the three children who were clinging to her to let her go, as well as imploring Petraia not to drag her so fast; and so shrill was the desperate falsetto clamour of their combined voices that the man of the family following uncomfortably behind was unable to succeed in his attempt to appear to be absorbed with interest in a particular white sail on the horizon of the bay.

Just before passing out of sight Petraia called the man to the woman's side, and, as the two of them with their children vanished from sight, she herself swung round once more and uttered, in a tone more piercing than any she had yet used, her final defiance.

"News has just reached me," she cried, "from my sister, who serves the Nymph Egeria, in the land of the King of the Latins where the Trojans have founded a new Troy, that Persephone herself has escaped from the Kingdom of Death and has begun to hasten across the face of the earth to find her mother Demeter! When these two meet, so has the Nymph Egeria told my sister, the world's new age of the real rule of women will begin!

ATLANTIS

"And then it will be that men will sink back once more into what was their position when the world began, that is to say into complete inferiority to women; so that from that moment onwards their proper use and value and status in the world will be as it was in the Golden Age under the Rule of Kronos; that is to say as merely the breeding animals that we women use at our free will and pleasure, so that we can bear a sufficient number of girl-children who will in their turn become the rulers of the earth!"

With this final cry of defiance Petraia was gone; but Nisos, whose diplomatic caution, not to speak of his vivid personal fear of the fellow, had made him keep his eyes on Enorches who had remained silent on his rock during Petraia's outburst, now found himself unable to resist a shiver of panic when he saw the Orphic priest solemnly, pontifically, and with awe-inspiring intensity, lift up his right arm and point with extended fingers, as if uttering a devastating malediction, towards a particular point upon the horizon of the noonday blueness of the sea.

"Listen to me, O people of Ithaca!" he cried, "and be not deceived by an excited creature who knows no more of what has really begun to happen in the world than a feeble-winged moth!"

At this point it was no more concealed from Nisos than it was concealed from the Moth herself or indeed from her friend the Fly, that a thought-wave of some sort had been passing, consciously or unconsciously, in its gloating religiosity and its bitter belligerency between the Orphic priest and the two insects within the split bosom of the club of Herakles, one of them the priest's natural sacrificial victim and the other his natural biter, stinger, teaser, poisoner, tormentor, scavenger, devourer, and final exterminator.

"That little grey spot on our horizon," he cried, "is only one of thousands of islands in Greek waters! To it and from it, through all our bays and estuaries and harbours and river-mouths, the word is now being carried from promontory to promontory that the true Rulers of the world have at last come into their own and henceforth will prove themselves supreme. You all, O beloved sheep without a shepherd, know well in your hearts of whom I speak! I speak of that immortal pair of Deities destined by fate before the foundation of the world to be its ultimate masters. Need I say, my precious and dedicated people, some of whom are destined to be transformed and transported by the one, and some of whom are destined to be transfigured and redeemed by the other, that I speak of *Love* and *Drink*, of Eros and Dionysos! Between these immortal ones is a miraculous communion, a holy understanding, in the divine mystery of which each leads *to*, each mingles *with*, each is swallowed up *by* the other: Love in Intoxication, and Intoxication in Love!

"It has been revealed to us at last that all this childish domination of the inhabitants of the earth by the twelve Olympians has been infantile play-acting; and that the time has come for the real rulers of the universe to be recognized by us all for what they are and what we their subjects are.

"This was, O people of Ithaca, this was, O people of Hellas, whether you are Achaeans or Pelasgians, this was the meaning of the Songs of Orpheus! Orpheus and his Priests have, from the beginning of History, alone known that the true divinities behind Zeus and Poseidon and Aidoneus, the true divinities behind Hera and Demeter and Athene and Aphrodite have always been the same, that is to say Eros and Dionysos!

"The Mysteries of Eleusis have always in their unutterable essence, of which we may not even yet reveal the true nature, been identical with the Mysteries of Orpheus. Come then, O people of Ithaca and of all the sacred Isles, come then, and acknowledge the truth that only in the sacred ecstasy of Eros and Dionysos, that is to say of Love and Drink, is the Secret behind life revealed and the Secret behind death shown to be identical with it!

"This is the reason, let me now announce to you, my friends, why Aphrodite has been imprisoned by Hephaistos in the Island of Cyprus, and why Prometheus has been imprisoned by Dionysos where Atlas holds up the sky. What is happening now to our world, what is shaking the pillars of the earth, what is rocking the walls of Erebos, what is ransacking the recesses of Tartaros, is that Eros is shaking off the childish notion that Aphrodite is his mother, and is now showing that, as he once caused the aboriginal night to be impregnated by the whirling elements of Chaos, so today he is making Okeanos enlarge his boundaries both to the West and to the East and making the sun and the moon throw off the rule of the children of Leto! Come then, O people of Ithaca! Follow the Sun and the Moon! Shake off these bow-and-arrow tyrants, Apollo and Artemis! Throw down the altars and idols of the gods of Olympus, and worship none but the two Supreme Mysteries of the Universe, Eros the Mystery of Love and Dionysos the Mystery of Ecstasy!

"Worship these alone; and Eros will give you the only clue to the inexhaustible joy of life, and Dionysos will give you the only redemption from the inexhaustible misery of life!"

It was at that moment, as the voice of Enorches died down, that Nisos recalled a curious little event that had occurred just before he set out that morning with Odysseus. Carrying the heavy load with which he had started, his head held high and his right hand raised to keep the balance of the great sack which was swaying on his shoulder, he had been too excited to give much thought to those he was leaving.

In her natural feeling for her betrothed, the elder son of Krateros Naubolides, Leipephile had turned aside while the king's old Nurse was waving them goodbye.

Naturally enough also the Trojan maid Arsinoë had turned aside from watching them depart. But Eione, the little sister of Tis, had followed them. Yes, she had followed them as far as the last Olive-Tree in the palace garden.

Here, as she waved her farewell, the wind from the bay, which they were facing as they went off, blew a loose fold of her garment so shamelessly clear from her perfectly formed thighs that unwilling to give an impression of immodesty and at the same time reluctant to stop waving to them till they were out of sight she went on waving with one hand while with bent head and floating hair she re-folded her garment about her limbs with the other hand; and it was the simple and direct childishness with which she accomplished this double task of waving with one hand and controlling her rebellious clothes with the other that so particularly touched Nisos and became for him a kind of visual symbol or dramatic emblem of the charm of the eternal feminine.

He had been rather slow to recognize the peculiar quality of Eione's charm, owing to the fact that there was nothing in her plain and simple face to correspond with the unusual loveliness and grace of her figure, but now that he was setting off on this historic expedition the whole quality of her personality invaded him.

He wasn't a conceited fool. He wasn't so fanatically hostile to this sinister Priest of the Mysteries as not to admit to himself that what filled his mind at that moment with this plain-faced, exquisitely moulded young girl was what the fellow was saying about Eros. He had never heard till now of the primordial cosmology, so to speak, of the Mysteries, and there was something about the thought of shaking off the familiar personalities of the Olympians and concentrating upon the idea that the primeval origin of all things was Eros, that appealed to him extremely.

He had always tried to think of himself as born to grow into a mysterious prophet, and the notion of such a prophet having a love-affair with some dedicated female was peculiarly appealing to him. Nor at this moment as the echoes of Enorches' voice died away among the rocks and caves of his native island, did it seem a negligible stroke of fate on his behalf—perhaps showing the hand of Atropos herself, to whom he had been of some service—that the female to be associated with his career should be the youthful sister of his faithful old friend, Tis.

In any case the Spinners of our human destiny did not give Nisos at this moment any further time for romantic thoughts about the youthful Eione with her homely face and her exquisite limbs, for he was called to the king's side by an imperative summons.

He obeyed with alacrity; and he found at once as he placed his treasure-bearing sack at the feet of the two protagonists that the transaction had been, with satisfaction to them both, brought to a successful conclusion.

Odysseus was obviously in the particular mood into which he never rose or sank except when things fell out almost exactly as he had hoped, and yet without any exhausting effort on his part. His great square head seemed more like a fleshless skull now that he'd got what he wanted than when he was still fighting for it. His chin was so relaxed and at ease that his beard had the look of the bowsprit of a vessel that has reached a halcyon sea of undisturbed calm, with the Sirens in the form of friendly birds clinging contentedly to the rigging.

As for Zeuks, he turned his head slowly towards Odysseus, then slowly towards the Priest of Orpheus who had now rushed between them, shooting himself down from the lichen-covered rostrum of his eloquence like a fleshly arrow from an hieratic bow.

"*Eros!*" cried Zeuks with the inconceivable gusto of a guest at a delicious private banquet who has just tasted what to him is the renewal of a long series of forgotten delights, enjoyed long ago and far away. "*Eros!* Why it's wonderful to realize at last that we can freely embrace our divine boy as a grown-up independent Deity, acting on his own without any woman's help!" And as if to prove his delight Zeuks started singing:

> "Ha! Ha! Ha!
> Hee! Hee! Hee!
> Smell, taste, listen!
> Touch and see!
> Touch, see, listen!
> Taste every juice!
> Embrace Aidoneus!
> And you won't fear Zeus!"

Nisos felt such a burning atmospheric fire-ball of protection whirling round his head from Zeuks' deep-set humorous eye-holes that he actually dared to make a faint flicker of an ugly face of impudent defiance at the Priest of Orpheus: and when he turned to see how Odysseus was responding to the encounter between these two formidable ones he experienced an agreeable shock; for Odysseus was, as a matter of fact, making much the same sort of grimace as he was making himself, only it was made in accordance with the hero's age, dignity, and heroic past. The old king indeed scrupled not to nod several times with his great massive head in the direction of Zeuks, as much as to say: "I am entirely of your opinion, O most excellent dealer in immortal horse-flesh! And as for this noisy rhetorician, he hides, as his type usually do, his only spadeful of good turf under bushels of mystical bad hay."

Obviously aware that their presence, combined with the special quality of their unusual nature, had much to do with this unseemly contention, both the winged Pegasos and the black-maned ivory-coloured Arion now began to use all their animal powers, four legs, their muscular shoulders, their nervous haunches, their arching necks, even the flashing wings of the one and the sweeping mane of the other, to thrust their way into the very centre of the contest.

This put the torch to the pyre. The fury of the Priest of Orpheus broke all bounds. "*What?*" he shouted, projecting his carrion-crow physiognomy so close to the king's impassive skull that it really did cross Nisos' mind to wonder what would happen if the man's vulturine beak were actually to snatch a gobbet of bleeding flesh from the throat beneath that proud ship's bow.

"Have you been dreaming," was what the Priest had the gall to mutter to the King, "in the decrepit vanity of your degenerate flesh to which in the solitude of its ancestral cave an outworn Olympian, herself a refugee in Ethiopia, has granted a retreat wherein your moribund body can decompose at leisure; have you, I say, been dreaming that the present-day inhabitants of Ithaca, only a few among whom can even remember the lies and tricks and multiple disguises and devices, for which in days before their parents were born, you won for a year or two some kind of a melodramatic notoriety, will stand by quiescent while you terminate Tyrian transactions with dung-heap pirates, and hand over treasures which properly belong to the people of this island to do with as they wish? Give me these two horses, this moment, you Zeuks, if that is the ridiculous appellation put on you by some former clown in mischievous blasphemy or cringing sycophancy towards the tottering Thunderer we call Zeus whose very thunderbolts have fallen once more into the hands of that one-eyed race of Cyclopean Giants from whom he originally stole them; yes! yes! give me these horses this moment!

"They shall remain in the sacred stables and in the consecrated meadows of the celebrants and hierophants of the Mysteries! They shall be made joyful by Eros, the Lord of Divine Lust, and shall be redeemed from the service of men by Dionysos the Lord of oblivious ecstasy!"

Thus speaking Enorches snatched at the bridle of Pegasos with one hand and at the bridle of Arion with the other, evidently hoping that the power of his personality, and the authority of his manner, and the occult magnetism of his touch would produce the required vibration of super-human force in sufficient accumulation to enable him to carry them off to those usurped purlieus of Athene's shrine which he had now appropriated as his own. But the event turned out otherwise.

Never had Nisos felt prouder of the old hero than he did at that moment: never had he felt more utterly resolved that no insurrection against him by the House of Naubolides, even with his own dad, Krateros, and his own brother, the betrothed of Leipephile, as its leaders, should ever meddle with the old warrior's authority!

In a flash, in the flickering of an eyelash, in the curve of a single ripple on the halcyon sea outside the bay, Odysseus had made use of the Club of Herakles as if it were a battering-ram and had administered to the Priest such a blow in his belly that the man went over in a perfect summersault, legs and arms in the air, and lost all his breath for a moment when he struck the ground. Next, with a series of rapid gestures and commands, so calmly and quietly made that he might have been seated in his hall at the end of the pillared corridor, Odysseus got Nisos and the treasure, still in its great sack, on the broad shoulders of Pegasos, and Zeuks himself, shaken by terrific amusement, lodged on the immortal creature's rump, and finally, just as his enemy, having regained breath was scrambling to his feet, he got himself, the club in his hand, and within it the Moth and the Fly clinging desperately together, balanced somehow upon the black-maned Arion.

All would have been well and they would have escaped in royal style, leaving the Priest of the Mysteries confounded, if it had not been that at this moment of all moments the old everlasting competitive instinct was aroused in the black-maned horse, progeny of the semen of Poseidon when Demeter played the mare, an instinct to show that a horse born of the coupling of Land and Sea could be faster, though it never left the earth, than one with wings so wide that their shadows stretched further than any bow could shoot and whose parentage was the spilling of Gorgonian blood!

With this natural but luckless urge propelling him the horse Arion started off with a bound before the old king, being a poor horseman since the isle was too rocky and mountainous to breed horses, had properly settled himself on its back; with the result that the old man, feeling himself to be slipping, tugged violently at the bridle, causing the creature to rear up on its hind legs.

Here was Enorches' chance, and "the well-hung one", as his fellow mystagogues called him, who was now beside himself with blind fury, seized Pegasos by his nearest wing, and Arion by the nearest portion of his flowing mane, and with a mighty wrench and a superhuman tearing and rending, of which the maddest follower of Dionysos would have been proud, pulled out a whole quarter of that flowing mane by the roots and the whole of the left wing of the Flying Horse by its roots, screaming, as he did so, in a voice that seemed to whirl like a sea-vulture round their heads in strident circles: "By all that's beyond our knowledge, and beyond our powers of knowledge, I curse you both!"

But they were no ordinary mortal horses these two; and after a quick exchange of equine-heart to equine-heart commentary on the situation with their heads touching, disregarding the Priest of Orpheus as completely as if he were an inanimate reproduction of the male organ that had simultaneously come to life and become inebriated, but whose antics were of no interest to creatures of their immortal breed, they leapt forward on their dedicated journey.

Thus it was that in spite of the abundant mixture of ichor and blood which dripped from the two horses' injured sides, and in spite of the insecure seat and bad horsemanship of the aged king, and in spite of the weight of the sack of treasure and its uneasy balancing by so young a rider as Nisos, and in spite of the fooling and jesting of Zeuks, who astraddle on Pegasos' rump, began murmuring a bawdy Bœotian ditty at the expense of the defeated priest, it was long before the sun showed any sign of sinking that this unusual group of living souls reached the rocky harbour-town of Reithron Paipalöenton. The laziest loiterers round the water-front of this town must have realized as they saw them, if they had not done so before, that something had happened, in the heaven, or in the earth, or in Erebos beneath the earth, that had materially altered the normal adjustment of the celestial and terrestial order, causing the most weird concatenations of persons and things.

Here they saw, for instance, these Reithron spectators of their harbour's routine, two mysteriously unusual horses, both dripping with blood, one of them with a single useless wing of many cubits length and a bleeding hole where its fellow had been and the other with a ghastly raw place where half of its sweeping black mane had been plucked out from its neck, so that its skin, though naturally of a greyish tinge, showed like white ivory blotched with blood, while riding upon one of these creatures was the most famous of all the heroes of the Trojan War save the swift-footed Achilles, and riding on the other, with a handsome boy in front of him, was a figure of comedy so extravagant that he might have been the tipsy Silenos himself, fresh from following Dionysos across the world!

And if the philosophic observers of Reithron Paipalöenton were struck by the outward appearance of our travellers, what about the Moth and Fly within the life-crack of the Heraklean Club?

"Are we still ourselves, Pyraust, my sweet friend?" enquired Myos, the house-fly, of his bewildered companion, while the west wind rushed wildly past them and the waves broke under the hooves of their two steeds, as they followed the jagged coast-line of that long and narrow island from one extremity to the other; but there was a tense moment of speechlessness within the bosom of the club of Herakles until after several convulsive and deep-drawn shivers the brown moth collected strength enough to reply.

"*You* are yourself, O imperturbable invertebrate! But, alas for me! I haven't got the courage, nor the personality, to follow my own purposes and go my own way—O how wild this wind is! It would blow me into the forest if I were out in it; or if it were from the East I'd be drowned in the sea!—no! I haven't got the strength of will to live my own life for myself in my own way; and even now my conscience is all worried because I didn't go to help the Priest when he was surrounded by enemies! How brave he was to stand up for himself against them all and not even be afraid of tearing the feathers out of one of them and the hairs out of the other!

"O the poor, lonely, holy, heavenly man! O the wildly-loving, desperate man! O the great, erotic champion of blind, beautiful, abandoned drunken passion! O divine intoxicator! O the blessed inspirer of eternal hatred carried to a point beyond all understanding! How could I have borne to see a Priest of the Love of very Love and the Hate of very Hate frustrated in the ecstatic piety of his revenge, just when his beautiful anger had become a devouring Worm that could not be destroyed and a consuming Flame that could not be put out?

"I was a wretched disciple not to fly over to him, a miserable hand-maid not to whisper to him with my fluttering wings how much I admired him, how deeply I venerated his mighty, his majestic, his mysterious anger!"

The house-fly, who had listened to this outburst with troubled concentration, was now turning the subject over and over in his great heavy black head. At last he hummed: "I am afraid, my dear Pyraust, that I can't quite follow your reasoning—but, heavens! how right you are about this terrible wind! I almost feel as if our living protector, this immortal club of Herakles, must soon be blown out of the king's hand!——

"That priest of yours certainly was beside himself with anger; that much I cannot deny: and when men are like that, whatever it may be that has roused their fury, they are all alike. They fall into a fit of abandoned rage and every kind of reason vanishes.

"But have you noticed, Pyraust, my pretty one, how this great weapon in which we're travelling so fast, yes! this club of Herakles itself and nothing less, has been for some time, as we have been whirling along this infernal coast, conversing with the rocky ground itself, yes! actually with the very ground against which the eight hooves of our bearers have been striking, and very often striking fiery sparks?

"Have you noticed *this* queer fact, O soft-hearted one?"

Both the insects were quiet for a minute listening intently. Then Pyraust murmured in rapt admiration: "Yes, Myos most clever, Myos most discerning, Myos most sage, you are perfectly right! Our thrice-blest travelling shrine *is* talking to somebody or something. How marvellous of you to have found that out! I suppose we could scarcely dare—eh, my wise one?—to speak to our sacred Sanctuary and ask point-blank—no! I fear that would be too rude and impertinent! What do *you* feel?

"*Could* we dare?"—and the brown moth turned to the black fly the yearning of her whole quivering being. Again they were silent, listening to the wind whirling past them as they huddled together in the deepest shadow they could find in that narrow refuge.

"Why can't we listen to them without asking leave?" whispered the moth a moment later.

The fly made no answer. But his dark and corrugated countenance contorted itself into creases that could have been naturally interpreted as the tension of a profoundly scientific brain interrogating and interpreting Nature according to an elaborately technical process of his own invention.

"He's talking to our Sixth Pillar," he whispered at last—"O! O! how nice and out of the glare it is now! Do you know how *that* comes about, Pyraust?"

The moth shook her head; while her eyes opened wider still in dumb amazement that there should exist in the world anyone as wise as her friend the fly.

"The cause of this particular obscuration of dazzlement," announced that philosopher with the shrill certainty of a successful scientist, "is simply a human hand. Yes, whenever the old king who is holding the weapon that is our travelling equipage changes the position of his fingers, owing probably, but we can't be perfectly certain on that point, to some faint feeling of cramp, there occurs an over-powering alteration in the nature of our environment."

The moth bowed her small head and folded her silky wings in a paroxysm of passionate humility before such insight. But the sound of a very curious humming and drumming now presented itself to the startled attention of both of them.

"Do you hear *that*, my beautiful one?" enquired the fly.

"I most certainly do," replied the moth. "Can you explain this also? Has *this* any connection with the way our ancient king holds his club of Hercules?"

Very gravely did the fly consider this simple question; and then he said, speaking very slowly: "My own feeling is that this curious sound has no connection at all with our heroic old king, or with the way he is holding the weapon which at this moment is our hiding-place.

No, precious one; my feeling is that this sound has to do with a conversation that is actually going on now, between the weapon which is our most blessed vehicle and the ground itself, including all the rocks and pebbles and even the very grains of sand, over which these astonishing horses are carrying us all on their backs."

The brown moth uncurled her silky wings a little and stretched out her tiny legs with an even less noticeable movement. Then with one of her antennae she touched the precise centre of her friend's heavy forehead and after having done so she licked the spot she had touched; and then instead of withdrawing her tongue and curling it up she made vague motions with it in the air as if inscribing upon that most elusive of all elements her unspeakable reverence for the wisdom of the fly.

Since it was the black-maned son of Poseidon, by the Earth-Mother in her disguise as a Mare, who was leading this singular cortège, and since Odysseus, who was holding Arion's bridle-reins, along with the club of Herakles, at outstretched arm's length, was, of all the warriors of that age, owing to the rockiness of Ithaca, the least acquainted with horses, it was natural that, quite apart from the dazzlement of the burning afternoon sun and the aridity of the rocks and sands and shelving stretches of bituminous gravel and shingly marl over which those eight unusual hooves clattered, there should be several abrupt arrests in their advance, and not a few perilous debouchings from the simpler direction indicated by commonsense.

But something or other, either the imperturbable spirit of the old king or the resolution of both the horses, kept them going. The bloody wound in Arion's shoulder made by the rape of half his mane did not seem to unsettle his mind; nor did the stream of bantering railleries addressed to the badly injured Pegasos by the incorrigible Zeuks diminish that godlike creature's speed.

And the pace they were going seemed to accelerate the scientific conclusions of the alert Fly. "No, by Aidoneus!" he suddenly cried; "No! my precious Pyraust! I was right in calling that weird sound we hear all the time a conversation or colloquy; but I made a mistake as to the identity of one of the interlocutors to whose dramatic secrets we have been listening.

"I took it for a simple dialogue between our Heraklean Club and the curving sea-banks of our sacred isle. But do you know who it is with whom our House of "Rest in Motion" is conversing?"

The brown Moth fluttered the feathery points of both her wings and allowed the proboscean sucker at the tip of her tongue to make a receptive gesture. "Yes?" she whispered, "yes? O I can't wait to hear!"

"It's none other," announced the triumphant Fly, "than our old Sixth Pillar in the Corridor at home! So I really am a Discoverer! Eh? What?"

The astounded Moth could only feel herself grow an infinitesimal portion of an inch smaller.

"What," she murmured, "does our Protector say to the Pillar? Isn't there a danger that the startling news of our being carried to the other end of the island by Pegasos and Arion may give the Pillar such a shock that its marble frame will split open, as that image of Themis did when the Harpies attacked it with their nails?"

But the Fly, after licking the sensitized tip of each of its front legs and after drying these delicate members on its transparent wings, made use of them with exquisite care and chivalrous nicety as dainty brushes to remove any feathery film that might be obstructing the hearing of the brown Moth, and ordered her to give herself up to listening and not to forget all that the Pillar itself had taught them about the universal language of matter in use even by its minutest particles.

"Don't 'ee forget, dear Pyraust," he added, "how when we began our study of the alphabet of matter we learnt how much more important the sensations that certain words convey to us are than the precise nature of the words used or the number of syllables they contain.

"Above all, my dear girl, don't forget what the Olive-Shoot always tells us, how in the science of language it is a combination of assonance and alliteration that conveys the idea; and thus it is only in poetry that the real secret of what is happening is revealed."

They were both silent, listening intently; and it is clear that the club of Herakles, now held tight in the old hero's hand, must have been putting some very crucial questions to the Sixth Pillar; and it struck both our listening insects, not to speak of the club itself, that it was really a masterpiece of technical triumph this invention of the "Son of Hephaistos", whoever he was, who divulged the open secret of the long-hidden language, whereby the four elements, earth and air and fire and water, could hold converse together.

At this moment Pyraust and Myos had not to wait a second before they could hear it, the clear unmistakable voice, so familiar to them in that old corridor of their royal cave, of the Sixth Pillar.

"No," came the voice. "There is not a word, not a sign from Pallas Athene. It is universally accepted that she is in one of her shrines among the blameless Ethiopians; but how long she will remain there or what particular thing it was that roused her wrath against us all in Hellas, nobody has the faintest idea.

"As to the other gods, news has come that the rumour was true which declared that Typhon, the most powerful and monstrous and terrifying of all the titanic brood of the Great Mother, Typhon whom Zeus only just managed to overcome by means of the thunder and lightning given him by that weird Cyclopean race of one-eyed half-gods, to which Polyphemus belonged, Typhon who was buried under Etna, had truly and indeed broken loose from his dungeon.

"It is said he is now confronted by Herakles himself, Herakles the son of Zeus, and has been stopped by Herakles from advancing more than a few miles from the fiery crater out of which he has burst.

"There is no need for you, O great Club of Herakles, who have lived with us so long, and whom we of the palace-corridor have come to regard as one of ourselves, to feel hurt that it is not yourself who are now in the strong hand of Herakles as he holds back this monstrous Demigod from destroying the whole population of Italy and Greece and from advancing upon Asia and Africa.

ATLANTIS

"They say that the Three Fates have long ago decided that it is only by the metal iron that Typhon can be defeated and they further tell me that Hephaistos has now forged for Herakles out of iron a weapon as deadly if not as shapely and supple as you are yourself! If you ask me what has happened to great Hermes, the cunning messenger of Zeus, and the subtle intermediary between men and gods and between the living and the dead, I can only tell you what *my* messengers tell me; and as you know *my* messengers are the fiery, aqueous, aerial, terrestrial, magnetic quiverings through the elements that are swifter than the feet of Hermes or the wings of Iris, the murmur, that is to say, of element to element, and, where the earth is concerned, the whisper of rock to rock, and of grain of sand to grain of sand!

"And from these I have learnt the startling news that Father Zeus is no longer served by Hermes the Messenger; but on the contrary that Hermes has gone back to his birth-place in Mount Kyllene, whither his mother, Maia, the loveliest of the Pleiades, is still drawn down from the sky by the poets who worship her; so that she, along with her son's music, shall enable countless generations of unborn men and women to embrace the dark spaces of life's dubious experience with pleasure instead of pain!

"You, old corridor-companion, keep on telling me about this devilish priest of Orpheus with his mad incantations and his mania for Eros. Well, my friend, let me now tell you what I hear about this young Eros of the Mysteries. I hear he has recently mutilated himself so that he can make love to both sexes and be loved by both.

"My messengers are obscure as to the precise harm—if harm it is that he has done to himself; but that he has done something very serious to himself they do most strongly affirm, assuring me that the old Eros that gods and men have known until this hour is no more; and that a new and different Eros has taken his place. The elements also tell me that the goddess Aphrodite after being unfaithful to him with both mortals and immortals for so long has now fallen in love again with her crippled lord, Hephaistos, and is struggling to keep him to herself with every art she knows and all this in the Island of Lemnos!

"As to the Father of the Olympians, the great son of Kronos himself, the elements tell me that he is still on Mount Gargaros, but without his thunder and lightning which have been taken back by that same Cyclopean race from whom he originally received them. What makes it worse for this poor Thunderer, deprived of thunder, is that not only has his own son Hermes deserted him, but his other messenger and emissary, Iris, the Rainbow, has been entirely pre-empted, appropriated, and taken possession of, by Hera, the Queen of Heaven, who is now left alone on the summit of Olympos, with only a handful of frightened attendants, and surrounded by the empty palaces and the deserted pleasure-halls of the once-crowded City of the Gods.

"Under these conditions, as you may easily imagine, O great lion-slaying Nemean Club, to still possess a messenger like Iris is an indescribable relief, and you may be sure that Queen Hera makes the most of it, and despatches the luckless Iris on the most difficult quests. For example I happen to know that at this very moment this youthful immortal is wandering through the uttermost lands of the blameless Ethiopians searching for Pallas Athene.

"You ask me what I learn from the elements about Hermes since he no longer serves the Father of Gods and Men? Well, old companion of so many years, you who along with me have seen so many strange faces in our corridor to the palace of the king, what I have gathered from over-hearing these communications between the elements, which of course simply means the contact of air with water, water with fire, fire with earth, is so startling that I myself have difficulty in believing it. But what I've learnt I'll tell you at once, old friend, if my voice still reaches you, as your un-winged Pegasos and your un-maned Arion whirl you to the end of the isle; and it is this.

"All the spirits of all the mortals who ever lived on earth have defied Aidoneus; and, following the ghost of Teiresias, have broken loose from Hades and are wandering at large over the whole earth. It is now Persephone who is searching for her mother, searching frantically, searching desperately for her, through all their familiar abodes, through all their ancient haunts, by every public way, along every well-known river.

"Hast thou seen my mother?" is her cry. "Hast thou seen a stately woman with a mantle over her head and a staff in her hand?"

"But the most astonishing part of the news the elements have brought me is this. By the advice of Hermes, who it appears has been down to Hades to find the mysterious and awful Aidoneus who carried off Persephone and made her swallow those honey-sweet seeds of the fatal pomegranate, this dark ruler of a deserted Hades has summoned his brother Poseidon to meet him at the utmost limit of the West where the Titan Atlas, as a punishment for opposing Zeus, holds up the sky.

"Here Aidoneus and Poseidon together may be able to persuade the Son of Kronos to join them in leaving Olympos to Hera and in restoring and building up again the shattered order of the world; in forcing the ghosts of the dead back to Hades, the Titans back to their punishment in Tartaros, and with the help of Atropos, the oldest of the Fates, getting both Eros and Dionysos under such complete control that the entire——"

It was at this crucial moment that the two insects within the bosom of the club of Herakles had to clutch each other in sheer panic. The whole cortège had stopped with a terrific jerk. There was a ghastly sound of eight equine hooves scraping against some flinty floor of rock.

In the stress of this shock the two wounded animals, Pegasos still bleeding where his lost wing had been torn out, and Arion still switching and bleeding where he had lost half his mane, drew up side by side. Odysseus as he slid down to the ground, not without a certain grim satisfaction, shifted his grasp from the reins to the bridle of Arion, while Nisos, leaving to Zeuks all real responsibility for the wounded Pegasos, pushed the treasure-sack as well as he could to the part of the creature's back that was still unhurt.

ATLANTIS

As for Zeuks, he set himself to make a timely use of the healing properties of human saliva. He spat exhaustively upon the raw place in the creature's side from which the wing had been plucked, and when he had finished doing this he proceeded to blow upon the glittering bubbles of his own spittle until the whole surface of the creature's side was as iridescent as if the luckless Iris herself, exhausted by her pursuit of Athene among the blameless Ethiopians, had dissolved in fatigue upon his back.

Nisos glanced quickly round to see if the old King were using *his* spittle as balm for Arion's shoulder from which Enorches had torn at least half of that flowing mane; but in place of anything of that sort Odysseus was leaning his own elbow upon Arion's back together with the Nemean Club while he investigated the cause of this abrupt halt of their divine steeds.

Nisos had only to follow the tilt forward of the old king's beard to share his discovery, and they both faced the interrupter of their ride with cautious wonder. It was at a wild, shaggy, goat-legged, goat-horned, and yet human-shaped figure lying fast asleep in the shadow of a great rock that the old man and the boy now gazed in astonishment.

And then Nisos suddenly realized that there was another figure in their path, and one with which he was already acquainted. This second figure was nobody else but the eldest of the Three Fates, the powerful Atropos herself.

Then once more the boy faced her, the same frail woman, resting her back just as she had done before against the trunk of a spruce-fir that grew upon the very rock beneath which the sleeping Goat-foot lay. Unlike this goat-horned, goat-legged figure, however, the little old woman with her back to the tree was wide-awake; nor did the tree against which she was resting break the glare of the afternoon sun for her in the manner in which the rock did for the Being below her.

"O! I never thought——"" gasped Nisos the moment he met the eyes of this little old woman.

"No, you never thought, my boy, did you, that you and old Atropos would meet again so soon! In truth I never expected it myself. You see," she went on, keeping her eyes fixed on the boy and completely disregarding both Odysseus and Zeuks, "we Fates are not—I wish indeed we were!—the sole arbiters of destiny in this mad world. It was, for example, only in very vague shape that we Three foresaw all that's happening upon the earth today.

"But when this confusion ends, for confusion by its inherent nature cannot last, neither we three, nor the goddess Themis, whose image the Harpies broke, no, nor even the great Son of crooked-counselling Kronos, himself, will be the only arbiters of what happens. There will still remain, my dear boy, those two great Powers, and I am not talking of Eros or Dionysos, whom we all, plants and trees and beasts and birds, and fishes and reptiles and worms and insects and men and gods must obey, Necessity and Chance."

The eyes of Atropos seemed to hold behind them, when she had done speaking, so much more than the half-named body of a little, fleshless, shrivelled, skinny old woman, that Nisos continued to stare in petrified awe into their singular depths.

The sensation they gave him was that the sky above Ithaca and indeed above all the isles in all the bays and seas and straits and gulfs of the land of the Achaeans, together with the interiorly receding depths of all that land itself, the depths, in fact, of all the various solid elements that composed the rocks and sand and earth and soil of which that land was composed, had that pair of eyes *as their eyes*, and were even now, those remotenesses of sky beyond limit, and those staggering recessions of terrestrial matter beyond limit, gazing at him in a positively ghastly intensity while they informed him that the real deciders of his fate and of the fate of the old hero at his side, and of the fate of Eione, the ideal loveliness of whose perfect form had been for him the living background of the whole of this wild ride, were not the Fates nor the Gods nor the sublime obstinacy and cunning of Odysseus, but, as Atropos herself had just admitted, the inescapable pressure of pitiless Necessity and the motiveless antics of causeless Chance.

ATLANTIS

The tension, as they thus met once again, between the heart of Nisos and the eyes of Atropos was however soon brought to an end by an abrupt awakening movement in the goat-legged and goat-horned Personage lying in the shadow of that rock. He didn't wake quickly. He awoke slowly. But no sooner had he lifted a hand, not even to scratch his head but to grope with lecherous fingers amid the foliations of grey lichen that covered the base of the rock than an astonishing thing happened; and what was queerest about this thing was that it was felt by everybody and that it was inescapable.

Both the animals quite evidently felt it. Odysseus felt it. Nisos felt it. And Zeuks felt it. The fragile old figure beneath the spruce-fir on the top of the rock must at that moment have been occultly, covertly, and peremptorily summoned to some other significant parting of the ways for persons in whose destiny she was interested; for she promptly took advantage of this opportune distraction, and gathering her flimsy garments about her scrambled down from the rock and disappeared among the trees to sea-ward.

Nisos was amazed at what had begun to happen to him the very first moment that this goat-legged sleeper opened his eyes. He had been so hypnotized into a sort of philosophic acceptance of things he could only half follow, that, when he found himself shaking from head to foot in extreme panic-terror, but without the faintest notion of why the sudden fear had come upon him, he felt as if he were going mad. Was some appalling danger threatening them all, including the animals who had brought them here? And had the oldest and strongest of the Spinners of Destiny come to warn them, and had now gone to ward off from them the approaching danger?

Nisos felt certain he was not more affected by this sudden and inexplicable panic than were his companions. He could see that the horses were trembling; and indeed he experienced in the teeth of this weird terror a proud satisfaction that his own right arm which, while he was holding his colloquy with Atropos, he had kept stretched out, had not loosened or lessened the pressure of the hand with which he was supporting the great treasure-sack, propt on the back of Pegasos.

And it was clear to him that the wits of Odysseus were not in any more danger of being lost in this mysterious panic than his own. The old king calmly advanced towards the recumbent goat-man, dragging Arion with him. Nisos noticed too that he held the bridle with his left hand while he advanced, and that he gripped the Heraklean club firmly with his right.

"Hail to you," the old king said, "whoever you may be—whether immortal or mortal, whether god or man! And I pray you, if you are a god, to pardon us for disturbing your noon-sleep before natural termination. I am Odysseus and I have come with Nisos Naubolides and with our good friend Zeuks to do honour to the daughter of the great dead Prophet Teiresias whom many-voiced Rumour declares has been brought from Thebes to a dwelling here, hard by the sea. If, therefore, whether you are a god or a man, you will assist us in finding this House, I, Odysseus, son of Laertes, will of my free heart, give you whatever your soul desires of the treasure we carry with us."

The prostrate goat-man heard him to the end without stirring. Then he made a very quick movement. He rolled the greenish-black eye-balls of the enormous whites of his nymph-ravishing eyes, and without changing his position, or relaxing his clutch upon the lichen-tuft he was fondling, he took in everything. In fact from the look in those exploring eyes he did more than take in everything. You could have said he devoured, drank up, and erotically possessed everything; not only the old warrior with his bowsprit beard and full-bosomed club advancing upon him, but the half-winged Pegasos, the half-maned Arion, the grave, slender boy Nisos, and every bulge in the choreographic blur which the blazing sun created out of the bucolic features of Zeuks—except the great sack of treasure, across which those rolling eyes flitted without offering it the faintest attention.

Then the old king spoke again: "Are you prepared to show us the way to the house by the sea, whither these Thebans, if such they are, have brought the daughter of Teiresias?"

The goat-horned, goat-legged one suddenly leapt to his feet and with a rough and rude gesture pushed past Odysseus and seizing Zeuks by his elbows stared offensively and yet in some queer way possessively and almost paternally into his face. Over the wounded back of Pegasos, which, though still tender to the touch and not by any means healed, had been considerably soothed by its owner's spittle, it was still possible for Nisos to see Zeuks' expression, and it was an amazement to him to remark how quietly, and yet with a sort of comical expectation of more dramatic revelations to follow, he took the gross, yet almost cajoling stare of this horned and hairy Being.

"You are!—you are! And yet you *cannot* be!" blurted out the puzzled and bewildered God-Beast; and Nisos never forgot the mixture of earthy roguery, rustic guile, spontaneous magical power, along with the professional horned-ram propitiation of a cunning old shepherd, in the goat-legged creature's tone.

But the capturer and dominator of Pegasos and Arion, the man who was more than a match for the Priest of the Mysteries, was once again completely master of the situation. With an easy assumption of authority—and yet our clever young Nisos didn't miss the shade of something that resembled a curious spasm of play-acting in his tone—Zeuks freed himself from the God-Beast's hold and turned to Odysseus.

"We are in the presence, O King," he blurted out with an irresponsible chuckle, while the goat-horned creature leaned his chin upon the head of Pegasos and began whispering in one of the flying horse's nervous and twitching ears, "of none other than the great god Pan himself. For some curious reason that I cannot explain to you, O king, this great and most benevolent deity has, ever since he first appeared to me on my farm, confused me with a lad he knew on the farm of farmer Dryops, whose favourite Nymph was Erikepaia, though we ignorant farm-labourers persisted in calling her Dryope or Dryopea, but who rejoiced to share Pan's bed in the moss and ferns of this farmer Dryops' Arcadian inheritance.

"Unlike the jealous and tyrannical Dryops, whose despotic arms

Erikepaia joyfully exchanged for those of this famous god who fills the udders of Arcadian cattle with the richest milk and the hives of Arcadian bees with the sweetest honey, I have been proud, though she *was* loved by this kindly god, to have myself loved the lovely Erikepaia long and loyally, and long after she grew too old for a god's embraces I loved her. I loved her when she grew old with the oak of her adoption, which she and I together dug up from that Arcadian valley and planted here, here by the side of this rock, here where thou, O great Pan, whether thou knewest it or not, wast sleeping a moment ago.

"Her oak has fallen into dust and Erikepaia with it; but never once did the Nymph who had been loved by Pan or the farmer, my poor self, who loved the Nymph that had been loved by Pan, ever think of him save with true worship."

It was only when Zeuks had finished speaking that the last thing anyone of them expected happened.

The goat-legged Being swung away from Pegasos and approached Odysseus. Then with a movement so swift and yet so gentle that Nisos imagined he was lifting the hero's hand to his lips as a sign that he would himself be his guide to the house of the fugitives from Thebes he bit the king's hand with such sudden and vicious force that the old man dropped his club to the ground.

In an instant the god was upon the back of Arion, who with mildly startled up-tossed head tore his bridle from Odysseus, and, while what was left of his beautiful black mane was tossed across his rider's lean, goat-hairy shanks, set off at a gallop in the direction from which they had all just come; but as he rode away, the god of milk and butter and honey looked back over his shoulder at Nisos, as if deliberately wishing to include him also among the victims of his mischievous and shameless amorousness.

"Pegasos has told me," he cried, "that you've left at the palace a sweet little shepherdess called Eione who is just made to delight my simple taste. She'll suit me better, I fancy, than any prophetic daughter of Teiresias!"

Horse and rider, they were soon out of sight; but the shrewd

Zeuks had not missed a swift instinctive move towards Pegasos made by Nisos the moment the goat-horned one flung out that word: "Eione".

"No, no, my dear boy!" he cried sharply. "'Twould be crazy to try to catch them! And what could you do if you did catch them? All the while I lodged—and in this very place—with Erikepaia, she never once told me of any occasion during the time she was loved by Pan when he made her jealous of a mortal maid."

He turned to Odysseus with a look of whimsical appeal, which, though it had something at once gravely conspiring and gaily mischievous, contained also an immediate and extremely practical warning. And then, while he kept one hand in kindly restraint on the boy's shoulder, he boldly laid the other on the Club of Herakles which the king, having picked it up from the ground, had carefully balanced, too absorbed to give it more than a secondary place in his mind, on the unwounded portion of the back of Pegasos.

"Our young friend here, O great king," protested Zeuks; "is impatient for our return so that he can protect his girl from the advances of this amorous goat-foot; but I tell him that, though, we can wound these immortal creatures and even draw ichor from their veins till they are too weak to move, we cannot plunge them as they can plunge us into that vast company of spirits beyond counting, such as have lately, the rumour runs, broken loose from Hades—into the company of those who can only fly like the flight of birds where no birds are and can only cry like the echoes of voices where no voices are, until the end of time."

"Let us, O great Master," begged Nisos, who for all Zeuks' words could not help vividly visualizing the white soft body of Eione helplessly yielded up to those lean hairy shanks and to those gross bristly lips of the immortal Goat-foot, "pray desperately to Atropos that fate may conquer both necessity and chance and bring us quick, quick, quick, to that House by the Sea whence without delay we can return home! O dear master,

O great king, this, I swear, is what Pegasos wants, for I can feel him trembling and quivering under our hands!"

All the while the boy was making this appeal he was working hard with both his hands to get the great sack of treasure nearer the horse's tail and further away from its shoulders.

"But, my friends," groaned Odysseus, raising his bowsprit beard and drawing in his breath towards the four quarters of the horizon one by one. "How, in the name of Pallas Athene, are we to know in what direction this accurst place lies? If only we could hear the sea; *that* would be a surer help than any praying to any goddess of fate."

For a moment they were all three silent. Then the two men became aware of unrestrained sobs breaking from the throat of Nisos. And for another moment, however intently they listened, that was the only sound.

Suddenly Odysseus murmured, as if thinking aloud: "I have felt *this* happen before, once, twice, three times before! There may be nothing in it; but, on the other hand, it may be—We must doubt everything—*including doubt*. Yes, *there*! There it is again! So be it. I can only try." He lifted the club an inch or two, held it very lightly, and waited again. He held it as if he were testing its weight. He held it so that in its whole length it was removed from contact with the back of Pegasos. Then, still holding it lightly with his right hand, but grasping the horse's bridle with his left, he began walking rapidly straight past the rock and into what looked like the thickest part of the fir-forest that completely surrounded them. Nisos, lifting his head now, thought silently: "He is making the club lead us! O Atropos, let us get back in time to save her!" The path by which they had come had vanished; and now indeed there was no path at all. But Odysseus led them forward without the faintest hesitation, nor was there any hesitation in the manner in which Pegasos followed, the treasure-sack propt on his rump, and Nisos keeping it from falling, while Zeuks with a large fern in his hand followed close behind, driving the flies from the raw on the horse's back whence Enorches had wrenched the wing.

ATLANTIS

Thus they steadily advanced, weaving their way in and out among the closely-growing fir-trees, and every now and then ascending and descending some small eminence usually of a circular shape and not unfrequently crowned with incredibly ancient stones of a kind totally different from any the island itself supplied, and in some cases, Nisos noticed as they passed, engraved with hieroglyphs not one letter of which he could recognize as Achaean or Hellenic.

And as they went on it was still the club of Herakles who led them; and Nisos often wondered whether he himself or Zeuks could have possibly caught, just through the palm of their hand, that subtle, illusive, delicate quiver, like the faint ripple of water seeking its level, by which the club conveyed its intimation of direction to the hand that had blinded Polyphemos.

Meanwhile within his "life-crack", as to himself the club called their refuge, the silky wings of Pyraust, the brown moth, were fluttering with a desperate desire to fly homewards in the track of Arion and Pan.

"You shan't! You shan't! You shan't!" shrilled the black fly in its highest-pitched voice. "I'd perish before I'd let you do anything so crazy! Don't you see, you sweet, delectable, adorable, little fool, that the trees are already throwing long shadows, and didn't you notice that on the crest of that last little hill we crossed the tree-trunks had a golden glow on their bark?"

The lovely little moth hurried to retort to this in an ironic assumption of pitiful weakness and naive innocence that not only made the fly feel a complete fool but removed from his proud heart every drop of that sweet metheglin of male superiority with which he had been intoxicating himself as he pictured their flight home together side by side in the "Wolf-Light" of the early dawn.

"Oh I know, I know," cried the brown moth, "how lazy and luxurious it is of me to think of flying in the dark. But O it's so nice, though I know it's naughty of me to enjoy such a thing, to feel the great big strong black night holding me up on every side and whispering to me all the time: 'Lean on me and you'll be absolutely safe! Spread out your beautiful wings under me and you'll see how soon you'll learn to swim with me, ride with me, float with me, yes! you darling little moth, till I fill every nerve beneath your skin, and every pore in your skin, and every cavity in your lovely and trembling form with my calm and cool support!'

"Thus whispers the black night; and nobody can ever know," continued the subtle and teasing moth, "all that the darkness of night means to me!"

The fly gave such a jerk of metaphysical excitement at this speech that the club's consciousness of a shock in the "life-crack" of his honeysuckle-twisted or ivy-twisted bosom very nearly disturbed the whole piloting of their cortège.

"Why then, O most lovely and bewitching of self-deceivers, do you always try so desperately to burn yourself to death in any flame of light?"

The beautiful moth's answer to this piece of logic had, however, to be postponed; for it was at that very second that they arrived at the end of the wood. There, before them, lay the salt waves with their islands and ships and rocky reefs and wide-stretching curving bays. And there, beyond all these, in far-away, vision-fulfilling, story-ending, mystery-resolving, resting-places for the imagination, the eyes of those three human beings were led further and yet further, to the vast horizons of the encircling sea.

And the great Club of Herakles ceased its rudder-like quiverings as impelled by an irresistible impulse Odysseus lifted the great weapon high above his head and shook it in the air as if he, a man among men, were taking it on himself to challenge that golden sun-path which, originating behind him, was now flowing across the darkening waters!

Yes! and to challenge the divine ether itself he lifted it up, the ether under which the sea-spaces before him extended beyond the ships, beyond the islands, beyond the main-land, beyond those far-away Asiatic mountains, on the Eastern verge of the world, where from the image of Niobe, the mother of mankind, fell no longer that ceaseless torrent of tears, and finally to challenge the very trident of Poseidon himself as he strove to dominate the multitudinous waves.

The two men, the now one-winged horse, the Heraklean club, the two insects, and our young friend Nisos, they were all silent; they were all gazing in front of them. What they saw as they gazed was the ruin of a building so colossal in its pre-historic enormity that the first impression Nisos had of it was that it ought to have sunk down by its own weight thousands of years ago to the very centre of the earth.

But what else did the boy see that made him even forget, as he looked, Eione's danger from the shaggy lasciviousness of the Goat-foot from Arcadia? He distinctly saw, erect on a huge flat stone under a cyclopean arch, the figure of a young girl, a young girl of about the same age as Eione, though she may have been a little taller, and it seemed to him as if, with an outstretched arm, that figure was waving to him; not to the others, but to him — to him alone.

CHAPTER VI

"But you don't answer my question, Pontopereia. Why do you keep climbing the tower and looking inland like that? You're not up to some game with any of these farm-boys round here, are you? I've always told you I wouldn't stand for that sort of thing; so you'd better not begin it.

"I don't mean that you're not to climb the tower, child; so you needn't put on that sulky look. I know you like looking out over the bay and counting the sails and watching for foreign ships. I like doing that myself. Yes I'm always ready to play our old game of pretending we're waiting for the King of the Blameless Ethiopians; and that when his ship shows itself it will have a black sail, so that we shall know it.

"No, no! You're not to slip off like that without a word! You're much too fond of doing that; and I've noticed it's grown on you as a regular habit these Spring days. Of course I know all young girls get Spring-Fever. I used to get it myself. In fact, old as I am, I do still. The wily old Earth-Mother herself must have had it, or something uncommonly like it, when she left her daughter alone with those daffodil-pickers, a proper temptation for the King of Hades. Daffodil-pickers! She had to swallow a few Pomegranate-seeds before she learnt how close lie the borders of Heaven and Hell!

"But you weren't looking seaward, or counting ships, or pretending to be waiting for a black sail. You were staring at those fir-trees and at all those half-bare oaks and at that open clearing on the top of the ridge, where on fine days we can see the Rock of the Nymph of Dryops.

"Have you got into that crazy head of yours that just because I let Eione take you up there when this Moon was young you'll see that same chit of a dairy-wench waiting for you in the same place now this Moon is old?

"O yes! and another thing, Pontopereia, while I've got you to myself; for I don't know what Zenios would do if he heard of this little new game of yours. Don't you ever again—yes, you may well steal into the shadow of that Bust of Kadmos!—but you *must* listen to me now, though I can see how white your cheeks have gone and how those clumsy great legs of yours are shivering and shaking!—Don't you ever again, my girl, go into Zenios' underground treasury! I expect you've so often heard me laugh at the old fool about his pride and his miserliness and about all that nonsense of his being the rightful heir to the throne of Thebes, that you've begun to fancy you can play any of your wild-girl games upon the old stick-in-the-mud.

"But I can assure you, my fine girl, that though you may be a prophet's daughter, and though you may even have prophetic visions of your own, there's one thing you *can't* do, and that is meddle with Zenios' treasure-shelves! Why, my dear crazy child, if he found me—yes, *me*, my very, very self!—fumbling and fidgetting, and flopping, and flouncing from shelf to shelf in that treasury of his there'd be a rumpus that would bring Omphos, Kissos, and Sykos up from the fields!

"And do you think he'd put up with a child like you flibbertigibbetting down there? I don't like to try even to think of what he might do—yes! do to you and do to me too for not looking after you better!—for I've seen him in these furious moods, which is something you, my good child, have never seen, and I can assure you if you *had* seen him in one of them you'd never again take that silver key from its hook in his bedroom, never again go down those steps to that door."

It was clear that Pontopereia would be obedient. But it was absolutely certain also that had the inscrutable Atropos met the eyes of this lovely guardian of a clumsy girl at this particular second the woman's exultation over her victory would have sunk to the vanishing point.

"Where is Zenios? Is he coming home to supper?" enquired Pontopereia when she had recovered herself.

"O yes," replied Okyrhöe, glancing at the reflection of them both in the big polished shield hanging on the wall over their heads, the shield which Zenios always swore had belonged to Kadmos himself, "he'll be back all right for supper. In fact he's got to meet that funny old man Moros, your friend Eione's father or grandfather. I forget which it is! But he's a quaint old fellow; and he certainly knows how to flatter. Zenios thinks highly of him since he's ready to listen without end to endless talk about the great House of Kadmos, whence it came, and whither——"

"Whither it'll go when you and I have escaped from it!" interrupted Pontopereia; and though the girl's eyes were fixed on the arched entrance to the room where they were talking, an entrance which in some incredible antiquity, had been carved out of ten yards of solid rock, Okyrhöe's eyes were still absorbed in the reflection of the two of them in that great polished shield. And so intense was the power of concentration with which Okyrhöe's self-interest had endowed her vision that it seemed to her a quite natural yielding to a quite natural impulse when she allowed the young girl to steal from her side and slip away in silence through that low deeply-cut arch into the open air, while she watched herself arrange her hair, arrange the veil that covered her hair, arrange what covered the veil that covered her hair, and, as she did so, permitted herself luxuriously and voluptuously to lie back in her chair and to tell herself, for the thousandth and one time, the thrilling story of her life up to date and all its drastic moves and dramatic crises.

It must have been her feminine suspicion that Pontopereia had taken advantage of Zenios' troublesome mania for being flattered to start an amorous affair with some farmer's son of the neighbourhood, or even to exalt this new friendship with Eione into a romantic attachment, that set her own mind running so recklessly upon her own youth.

Anyway she let herself recall the time when, being younger than Pontopereia was today, she had been a fellow-attendant along with Arsinoë among the crowd of spirited young girls from every part of the mainland at the court of King Priam in Ilium.

Her inspiration for these memories came from her own beautiful face; and as at this moment, with Zenios walking to meet his aged flatterer and Pontopereia remorsefully pretending to be looking for a black sail on water that was already too dark to reveal any sail, and with Nemertes, the stalwart mother of their three faithful servants, Omphos, Kissos, and Sykos, yes, with Nemertes, she told herself, now at work in the kitchen preparing a plentiful meal for the three lads and a no less plentiful, but rather more elegant one for Zenios and herself, there was no immediate necessity to leave this shield-mirror, she allowed the motions of her fingers, about her head, her hair, and her perfect throat, to follow the arbitrary motions of her memory.

And she remembered how her crafty mother from Crete, who had made her change her name from Genetyllis to Okyrhoë, had warned her against making friends with a wild strange girl at the same court whom everyone but the girl herself knew to be a bastard daughter of Hector.

But with Arsinöe she had insisted on making friends; and had proved her wisdom in this when the crash came and the city was taken, for she succeeded in making Andromache, Hector's widow, believe that it was she, and not Arsinöe, who had the right to call Hector father, and she had betrayed Arsinöe into the hands of Phoenician merchants bound for Ithaca, and while clinging herself to the ill-starred Andromache, she had succeeded at last in becoming the wife of the miser Zenios, and in aiding him in his flight from Thebes in company with Pontopereia.

It had only been when Zenios in his craving for masculine society had begun to exercise his hospitable influence on the susceptible Moros that Okyrhöe learnt that Arsinöe like herself was a refugee in Ithaca; and although this piece of news had at first been a considerable shock to Okyrhöe, she was now, as she airily, though by no means absent-mindedly, practised various expressions in profile, in three-quarters-face, and in full face, telling herself a fine story as to what she would do if by any strange chance she found herself confronting once again her old acquaintance, Arsinöe, the daughter of Hector the son of Priam. . . .

"Okyrhöe! what do you think? Who do you suppose——"

The beautiful lady rose and swung round from her shield-mirror like an indignant sea-mew from the crest of a wave.

The shock of seeing Pontopereia so quickly again and in such an unaccountable whirl of excitement was as irritating as it was startling. The girl had left her at her shield-mirror. The girl now found her at her shield-mirror. There was something annoying in being thus caught practising seductive expressions and the effective manipulation of dramatic drapery.

"How often must I tell you, Pontopereia, that I won't have you calling me Okyrhce! You must call me Mother."

"But you are not——" the girl began; but seeing real anger in the woman's face she hurriedly broke off. "The King of Ithaca has come, mother! He's come with a heap of golden treasure to buy me from you and take me away with him!"

The excitement of Pontopereia was so overwhelming that it

seemed to have loosened her hair, enlarged her breasts, increased her height, and transformed her whole being to such an extent that her figure seemed to fill the arched passage that led out into the air. As a growing girl the daughter of Teiresias was at the opposite pole of girlhood from the young Eione: for, while this latter's face was plain and homely, her limbs were these of a perfect dancer; but while Pontopereia's limbs were thick, heavy, awkward and unwieldy, her face was moulded with exquisite delicacy as if for the perfect expression of pure inspiration. It was a face that lent itself to be possessed by a power that, even as you watched it, seemed able to change human flesh and blood into some rarer essence, as though air, water, and fire had joined in revolt against the heavier and more substantial fourth element with which they are normally associated.

But though Okyrhöe had already recovered her composure and was now arranging her drapery round her shoulders with the absolute poise of a complete balance of personal being, as she begged the excited girl to tell her how large a bodyguard Odysseus had brought with him, and as she shifted her position from side to side in attempts to see if any of the royal attendants were visible between the outlet from this sequestered chamber and the curves of the sand-dunes descending to the edge of the sea, it was clear to Pontopereia that she had not yet decided upon her line of action.

"May I go and bring them in, Mother? And then may I run and tell Zenios who's come, and bring him back before he's gone too far? The only danger is that if I do catch up with him—you know what he is, Mother!—he very likely will just come back alone and send me on—miles and miles on very likely!—to tell old Moros that the king has suddenly come to supper and if *he* comes too there'll be one too many!"

The daughter of Teiresias certainly revealed her insight into Okyrhöe's nature by assuming that when the lovely lady finally decided in what direction her own chief private interests lay she wouldn't waste a second in making up her mind what she wanted done.

But what a girl of her age, however great her prophetic inspiration, naturally couldn't know, was the enormous though imponderable part played in the lives of all grown-up women by that curious sixth sense that can only be clumsily and crudely defined by the words *social instinct* Nor could she know that this same "social instinct" resembles pure animal instinct much closer than it resembles anything rational or logical, and, as such, depends to a large extent on sight, sound, taste, smell and touch.

"Can he possibly remember me?" Okyrhöe thought. Then, having dismissed that idea as out of the question—"Never mind," she said to herself, "whether he does or not, I remember *him* perfectly well; and I remember that with him, where women are concerned, there are only two things, either simple lust, or simple affection. *That* being so——" And her train of thought concluded with obscene images.

Meanwhile Pontopereia was wondering about the bloodstained ichor dripping from the left side of the one-winged horse, wondering about the implacably-pointed beard of Odysseus, pondering on the deeply cracked bosom of the club of Herakles, pondering on the jests and jokes and jibes and jabbering conjurations of the jiggering-juggering Zeuks, and finally seeing again the ever-vigilant Nisos with the gods alone knew what sort of precious treasure done up in a sack that reeked of mysterious far-away harbours.

But Okyrhöe had already had time to make up her mind. Like the smoke of a burning arsenal her astounding decision filled the room and went eddying forth in spiral circles over the whole of Ornax and over the dark waters of the whole bay.

"What I've got to do is to leave Nemertes to look after Zenios, take Pontopereia with me—by the gods if they want *her* they shall have us both!—go with them to the palace of Odysseus; and, once there, having got rid of the old man's old nurse, try my hand at being a combination of Kalypso and Penelope; and, as long as Athene leaves me in peace, *that*'ll be pretty easy!"

"No, child," she commanded in the strong firm tone of a born feminine ruler, "No, child, I'll come with you to welcome them. Oh no! I can't possibly spare you to run after Zenios. Let him meet old Moros and bring him back. Nemertes must prepare a really royal meal and when Omphos, Kissos, and Sykos have washed and changed their clothes and had their own supper, they must wait at table! So come on, child, we must tell Nemertes what's in store for her. It's lucky we killed that old boar-pig last week; aye! What a piece of luck *that* is! Nemertes must have enough meat in the larder for three Odysseuses! Well, come along my dear!"

It is certain that the primeval dining-hall of Ornax had never seen such a satisfying feast as the one with which, only a few hours later, the three gratified guests along with their entertainers were delighting their souls.

What added an unexpected and quite special interest to this improvised banquet was the fact that, along with old Moros, Zenios had brought back to Ornax none other than Petraia's sister who after a distressing scene with the Latin Nymph Egeria had embarked frantically for home; and by the aid of a real and not pretended black sail had been brought to this very coast.

To the complete surprise of their hostess the heart and soul of the whole dinner was Zeuks. Nor was it only Okyrhöe who was astonished at the way this plain rustic Achaean dominated the situation and entertained them all. Nisos was amazed at what he saw and heard. Zenios though he condescended to chuckle now and again, was obviously more interested in a flask of a special kind of wine that Moros had brought for him than in anything else; but the fact that the first Master that Ornax had had for a thousand years, had had indeed since men and Titans were almost indistinguishable in their hostility to the gods, was so abnormally thick-skinned, so self-centred, so toweringly conventional, did undoubtedly contribute to the banquet's success.

Zenios was indeed so magnificently stupid as to take it for granted that his being of the same blood as the famous Kadmos and possessing that potentate's Shield, Drinking-Horn, and Sceptre in the shape of a Thyrsus, were circumstances that did so much honour to any guest that chance might send him that no more was required.

And no more *was* required. Zenios' guests were the luckiest of guests. They were left to entertain themselves. Nor was the fact of Zenios being such an obsessed collector of objects made of gold detrimental to what might be called the pleasant negativeness of his hospitality. His visitors obscurely thought of themselves—so completely did the mania of the born collector dominate the atmosphere of his table—as if they too were rare and precious and had been brought there for that reason.

Nor was this feeling contradicted by the nature of the locality. Ornax was literally a House of Ruins; but it was not itself a ruin. It had come to be created out of a physical acme of desperate isolation in combination with a psychic acme of impervious conceit. But it had been created by a woman; and thus the newly arisen House of Ornax had advantages, qualities, amenities and conveniences, beyond most of the Kings' Houses in Hellas.

In the first place it was divided into five essential structures; the Mirror Room, where hung the Shield of Kadmos; the sleeping Chambers with little stone-passages and wooden doors connecting them; the Dining-Hall, prepared for the reception of about twenty guests with no less than three "guest-thrones", as well as the permanent host-throne, ensconced in which the greatest of Collectors enjoyed his meat, his wine, and an experimental variety of baked bread and sweet-meat condiments on every night of the year; the underground treasure-chamber, entered by descending quite a long flight of stone steps, at the bottom of which was a low-arched chamber entirely surrounded by extensive shelves scooped out of solid rock and crowded with all manner of ancient vessels and platters and bowls and goblets, things that were by no means all Theban, far less all connected with Kadmos, but things that had been got together by Xenios himself, in his double role as an acquisitive collector and an implacable miser.

And finally there was the kitchen. This was so large, so

ancient, so monumental, that a visitor's first thought would be that only a goddess could possibly preside over such a place.

Quite apart from her creation of this ideal abode for herself and Zenios, Okyrhöe had made sure that outside the great Kitchen there was a House of Shelter for Nemertes and her sons. And it was within the entrance to this annexe that a little private chamber had been constructed for Pontopereia and for her alone.

Okyrhöe had wisely decided, when the three of them first took possession of this long-deserted House by the Sea, that the best part for herself to play was the double one of Zenios' wife and the bastard daughter of Hector; for this was a role that left her entirely independent and free at any moment to leave both Zenios and Pontopereia for any other human "stepping-stone to higher things" that Fate or Chance might provide. Absolute freedom for herself had been the guiding principle of all her actions since she first heard of Ornax. She had heard of the place from a Tyrian pirate.

And she had scarcely heard of it before she persuaded Zenios to secure the services not only of the man and his ship but of the man's sister Nemertes, the murder of whose builder-husband she contrived on their way, for it can be imagined how soon she made the ship's master her accomplice; and indeed the man was well advised by his sister to weigh anchor and clear off while the going was good.

Old Moros had never seen in all his days on earth anything so memorable as what he saw at this banquet. He was a kind-hearted man, however. Kind-heartedness had indeed been his chief handicap in life. He always found it difficult not to identify his feelings with the feelings of every person, man, woman or child, whom he came across. Each personality old Moros encountered impinged upon the personality of old Moros more than in her ordinary, rough-and-ready rules for human existence Nature had altogether allowed for. Thus while he watched the famous King Odysseus with awe and reverence, and stole as many infatuated glances as he dared at their enthralling hostess, he couldn't help again and again and again, casting a sympathetic, protective, and even paternal look at the newly-landed sister of Petraia, who sat by his side, while their far-sighted hostess was thinking, "I must keep those two together till Moros gets so concerned about her that he fetches a cart to carry her home." For the obvious truth was that Petraia's sister was pregnant.

How far gone was her pregnancy old Moros was not experienced enough in the child-bearing of ladies to have the least idea; but he saw enough for his habitual sympathy to beset him. Most tenderly he warded off the excess of wine offered the woman by the tallest of the three sons of Nemertes. All the three were attired in some exquisitely-washed white stuff that somehow gave old Moros the feeling that he was surrounded by male Sirens in the depths of the sea, who were always wanting to refill both his own and his neighbour's wine-cup, the neighbour for whose sake, so as to keep her repeated refusals from being observed, for luckily the wine did not incommode his own stomach, he succeeded in keeping their two glasses on his side of her plate.

"For the third time!" cried Zeuks, rising to his feet and striking the black bull's horn, rimmed with massive silver, from which he was drinking, against the golden goblet that had been so carefully chosen by Okyrhöe for Odysseus, "I call upon you all to join with me in defeating the ultimate design of this Monster, Enorches, who has dared to wrench half the life from these two celestial Horses!

"What is it I heard you say in your heart just now, great king, that you want us all to do? I'll tell you! I'll tell you! I'll tell you now, and I'll tell you once and for all!

"Yes, yes! You can look at me with that everlasting look of yours, which says to the entire universe 'Stop this business of acceptance as if there were no such thing as choice. Come! come! Do something about it!' That's what your pointed beard, sticking out like the sword of a sword-fish is forever saying: 'For the sake of all the gods in the sky do something about it!'

"But when we ordinary people want 'to do something about it, we simply don't know what to try to do!' Listen, therefore,

ATLANTIS

O great king, to the word of one of the humblest of your subjects, and stick your beard into me when I go wrong in what I say!

"What we all want in our hearts, men and women alike, is a peaceful and at the same time an active life. There are too many prophets and oracles too, who always tell us to crown some king, to obey some law, to follow some hero, to embrace some system, to accept some philosophy, to invade some country, to sack some city!

"Well then, O great King, well then, dear Lords and Ladies, what happens? We burn that city, we over-run that country, we change our name, our language, our manners, our dress, our habits. But what is the result? Are we any happier? Not a bit of it! Are we any richer? Not by a farthing! Are we any wiser? Ask our wives and children! Are we honester, nobler, braver, kinder, tenderer, more sympathetic, more long-suffering, more enduring, more unconquerable, more impregnable? *We are not!*

"And yet we have invaded Persia, sacked Ecbatana, gutted Syracuse, burnt Troy! And yet we have accepted the philosophy of Parmenides. We have offered sacrifice to the God of Israel. We have bowed our heads in the Temple of Baal. We have given our maidens to Pan and our boys to Moloch. And are we the happier for it? Are we the wiser for it?

"Not a jot! Our eyes still weep salt tears! Our slaves still sweat blood! Our women still bear abortions! Our grapes are still sour! Our hives still lack honey! Our figs still lack sweetness! Our fountains are still slow to run, and our streams still sink in the same sand and dry in the same desert!

"What therefore is the word for the unenlightened and the sign for the uninspired? What is the clue for the lost in the wilderness; and the secret of recovery for the heavy of heart? Is it what Enorches calls the Mystery of Love that will save us? Is it the holy ecstasy of Dionysos that will set us straight in the path of happiness?

"Never on your life, great King! Never on your lives, my lovely companions! The only thing that can set us on the path of happiness is to create carvers of joy in our own secret selves and moulders of delight in our own hidden souls. And we must do it by the countering and confounding of the most extreme contradictions.

"We can't do it, I tell you, by trying to mingle these opposites in confused conglomeration! No! we must keep our lives in natural advances and retreats, in ebb and flow, in up and down, in pull devil and pull tailor, till the end of the only round we know in this crazy planetary game! Shall I tell you O great King, shall I tell you most sweet and beautiful ladies, what, in spite of this Priest of Orpheus with his Eros and his Dionysus, is the real secret of the whole of life, of the whole of experience, of the whole of existence, of the whole of everything?

"I mean of course the secret of it for each and every one of us? I mean the ultimate word that eventually, when we have all been dead for a hundred-thousand years, will still describe the idea, the feeling, the emotion for every single consciousness possessed of what we call life? I have decided to announce to you tonight a word of my own which at least expresses one aspect of the complicated meaning that some magic word must eventually possess, when in a hundred-thousand years it is invented. My poor word is a common and an extremely simple word. It is—do not smile, most grave King!

"Yes! I will boldly utter it!—It is the word 'Prokleesis'. And now I must struggle to make clear some of the beautiful, terrible, stirring, satisfying, comforting, restoring, consoling, redeeming, creating meanings that I have put into this natural and simple word, *Prokleesis!* For I do here and now, O great King! I do here and now, most lovely ladies! I do here and now, Moros my old friend, Nisos my young friend, and you three, heroic sons of the lady Nemertes, who is the friend of all of us, as indeed this banquet, which is the grandest banquet I have ever enjoyed, proves up to the hilt, I do here and now proclaim, to all living creatures in all the innumerable worlds, that for each and every one of us, whether human, super-human, or sub-human, whether male or female, whether old or young, that the word *Prokleesis* whose simplest meaning is a 'defiance' or 'challenge' is the best clue to life we can have!

"Yes, *Prokleesis* is the word. We must 'challenge' life from our childhood to our old age! We must 'defy' life to quench our spirit and to beat us down! We must 'challenge' it, whatever it may be, to a fight to the finish! Don't you see, O great King, don't you see, my sweet friends, how the crafty and wicked Enorches is really advocating an escape into death in place of a battle with life? His Eros and his Dionysos are both different names for the same plunge into the same Nothingness.

"One is a plunge into it by way of love, and the other by way of drink. Whatever else to be alive upon earth, or above earth, or under earth, may mean to those who are landed in it or sunk in it or confronted by it, it is clear that it means a challenge to a battle! O my friends, my friends, we have not got the secret of life, I mean the secret of our *experience of life for ourselves*, till we've defied it to make us cry,' Hold! Enough!' This challenge, this 'Prokleesis,' is *the secret of life for us*.

"As to what the secret of life is *for life itself*, who can answer such a question? We can only answer for ourselves. The animals and birds and fishes can only answer *for themselves*. Whatever it is that calls itself the cause of life, or imagines itself to be the cause of life, or is supposed to be the cause of life by the tribal tradition of this race or that race, or by the geographical tradition of Northern or Southern life, or of Eastern or Western life, or Middle-Eastern life, or of life at the bottom of the ocean, or of life among the Gods in the sky, or of life among the Titans in Tartaros, or of life among the ghosts of Hades—if Ghosts *have* any life and if there are any ghosts left there now; for the story runs that they have all escaped, even as this wise lady here has come back to her own from the Latin cavern of the Nymph Egeria!

"No, we have not the faintest idea as to how this world of colour and form, and of solid and watery and airy and fiery substance ever appeared before us or ever inspired its favourite champions with the overpowering suggestion that we ourselves are nothing but transitory and dreamlike portions of its evanescent mirage!

"Let us suppose that at this very moment there suddenly

crowded into this beautiful dining-hall twenty murderous pirates, from an unknown land beyond Ultima Thule, and carrying ropes woven of a breakable hemp! And let us imagine these pirates bind each of us, men and women alike, with their ropes, and deliberately begin chopping us to bits with their sharp knives! Gall up such a scene, O great King, thou who hast known in thy vast travels worse scenes than this! Call up such a scene, sweet ladies! Gall up such a scene, brave men!

"Now be absolutely honest with yourselves, every one of you here and tell yourselves, not aloud to the rest of us, but in silence, each heart to heart alone, exactly how you would feel as you watched what was going on and saw your own turn coming nearer and nearer, and heard the shrieks and groans of each particular victim."

As Zeuks spoke in this way it was very clear what the feelings of Omphos and Kissos and Sykos would have been under the conditions he described as from behind the chair of Zenios they listened with awestruck attention. It was also clear that the three young men's interest in what Zeuks was saying displeased their mistress Okyrhöe; for she promptly gave them a peremptory signal to go and help their mother in the kitchen; but as they discreetly followed one another out of the hall they received from Zeuks just as if they had been relatives of Zenios, and not servants at all, an extremely friendly and fraternal smile of recognizance.

Zenios himself, still absorbed in what remained on his large antique Babylonian plate, evidently considered that this drunken babbling horse-stealing bastard from a remote farm at the other end of the island whose future destiny even Atropos, unless the old lady had Anangke, or Necessity at one elbow, and Tyche, or Chance, at the other, would have been puzzled to predict, though he might propitiate a poverty-stricken king like Odysseus by his antics, was not the sort of person to interest a rich frequenter of the Bazaars and Markets of Thebes!

But Zeuks had not failed to notice that although the old King was too absorbed in his own thoughts to pay much attention to what was going on round him, there had come a moment, the same moment no doubt when the speaker had caught that response in the faces of the three sons of Nemertes, at which the old hero's pointed beard had suddenly jerked itself up in an automatic call to battle.

It was as if the bones of his jaw had answered a physiological summons independently of his mind. And this automatic jerk of the well-trimmed beard of the blinder of Polyphemus in some profoundly subtle way so completely satisfied the kidnapper of Pegasos that he suddenly became, at least in the eyes of Nisos who was watching him carefully a completely different person.

That curious appearance of being unnaturally bloated, as if his outer skin, like a leather bottle whereof the contents had become, by reason of some sort of spiritual fermentation, too powerful to be contained in such a prison had been replaced by a singular toughening, at least that is what appeared to have occurred, of the actual flesh of his face; and the result of this was to make the expression of his face harder, firmer, and though no less humorous, much more formidable in the nature of its humour.

Nisos noticed, something else too, though if he'd tried to describe it to his brother or his parents or even to his friend Tis, he would probably have become tongue-tied and might even have retreated into that quite special silence which we associate with idiots; but what he would have wanted to explain about this more powerful humour in Zeuks' expressive countenance was that in its inherent nature it was not proud or vain or conceited, nor did it, like almost all so-called "prophets" and "thinkers", shut all doors but the one it came in by, and close all windows but the one it looked out of!

By this time all their eyes were fixed upon Zeuks. The large platter upon which Zenios had been concentrating was now as empty as if that insatiable collector of every possible species of plate that the artists among men have ever carved and moulded in precious metal had licked it clean that night of every stain it had acquired while the blameless Ethiopians of the Sun's

Rising carried it beneath the earth to the blameless Ethiopians of the Sun's Setting!

Odysseus himself had allowed his wandering mind to return to the immediate situation; and he was now watching Zeuks with the sort of steady, quiet, amused, contemplative interest that the master of a Circus of performing animals would display in the unexpected arrival of a caravan of freshly-caught creatures from the Mountains of the Moon.

As for Okyrhöe, she had very quickly decided that Zeuks was a person who had to be treated on completely different lines from any of the other original personalities she had hitherto succeeded in dominating.

"I must take him," she told herself, "by a direct attack. It would be no good to try to get round him."

Old Moros was watching Zeuks very much as Tis would have done. Indeed Nisos, as he glanced at him to see how he received this unexpected oration from a plain farmer from Cuckoo-Hill, was struck by the almost exact parallel in the old man's features to the way Tis would open his mouth wider and wider as his wonder increased at the eloquence to which he was listening.

"He can't follow a word," Nisos told himself. "It's the man's power of stringing the words together that strikes him as the marvel!"

As for the fugitive from the Cave of Egeria, Nisos was still young enough to feel an intense discomfort every time she caught his attention, a discomfort which so far he had managed to ward off by repeating mechanically a little prayer to Hera about birth that Petraia had taught him in his childhood; but since by this time he had come to regard Zeuks as his fellow-adventurer and even had begun to tell himself an extremely romantic story of their more and more intimate association as in the wake of their heroic king they would trace in the unrevealing face of the waters the grave of lost Atlantis, it annoyed him to notice that whenever the pregnant woman looked at Zeuks she gave a queer kind of involuntary shudder, as if something about this startling apparition of a neatly-attired farmer of middle height, moderate good looks, and respectfully conventional manner, abandoning himself to an obscure thaumaturgic incantation for the redemption of the world, gave her a weird shock and made her feel that she must escape such a spectacle or her pains might begin without warning.

Nisos himself as he leant forward with his elbows on the wine-spilt-board, dug the fingers of his right hand into a new loaf from Nemertes' oven, while in his left hand he clutched tightly a small gourd. Little trickles of wine kept dripping from this latter object every time in his excitement he turned it upside-down; while fragments of sweet-smelling crust fell with almost equal frequency as he squeezed the loaf. The boy was in a queer mood; for although the immediate hoof-beat of each galloping moment of time thudded rough-shod, as you might say, over the fore-front of his consciousness, behind it there kept humming and drumming a troubled comparison, of which he felt heartily ashamed, and yet in which he was unable to stop indulging, a comparison between the daughter of Teiresias, who kept meeting his eyes and who was clearly studying him with interest, and his friend Eione, the youngest sister of Tis, the vision of whose exquisite limbs as she bent to re-arrange the folds of her dress had grown all the more vivid to him since his disturbing encounter with the goat-foot Pan.

But Eione's childish features were unquestionably plain and homely; whereas, as he was now at such close quarters with Pontopereia he could dwell for steadily increasing spaces of time upon her beautiful and subtly intellectual face.

Ironically enough those two troublesome hamperers of the well-governed order of Themis, namely Tyche and Anangke, or chance and necessity, prevented him, though it was only by means of the very edge of the supper-board from noting how totally devoid of lightness and grace were the awkward limbs with which Nature in the reckless scattering of her bounty had burdened the daughter of Teiresias.

Had the competent and capable Nemertes not been busy in her kitchen preparing a culminating dish of sweet-meats it is quite possible that she would have reacted to the words and behaviour of Zeuks in a manner that would have come nearer to the heart of the utterer than any of the rest.

As to Odysseus himself, that wily old hero had made it a rule long ago never to waste his energy in redundant reactions. He accepted the message of Zeuks at its purely practical and pragmatic face-value: and since only certain portions of it could fall in with his own purpose, his calm empirical mind had enough to do in isolating these from the rest without getting excited about anything else.

The moment he entered Okyrhöe's dining-hall, the shrewd old king saw that it was she and not the collector of images who was responsible for the transformation of the aboriginal Ornax into a contemporary palace far more luxurious than his own; and in his diplomatic brain there began to take shape, as he cast glance after glance at the changing expressions, the lively gestures, the rapid decisive commands, of the lady of the house, the embryo idea that if the soothsaying daughter of a dead prophet was likely to help the advancement of his adventure, this formidable woman, if by any possible compulsion or enticement he could sweep her into his scheme, might turn out an even more effective aid. He hadn't relinquished his faithful Heraklean club when he crossed the threshold of this complicated group of palatial erections. In fact from where he now sat, while the lady's airy revelations of her life in the city of Kadmos were interrupted by Zeuks' reverberating "prokleesis", he could see the familiar curves of his queer-looking weapon propped against the elbow of a small stone-seat cut in the wall, a seat that would be far too narrow for any contemporary hips, whether male or female.

No smile came to his lips as he realized the direction his thoughts were on the verge of taking, as in spite of himself he listened to Zeuks' description of the in-rush of the murderous crowd of imaginary pirates and projected himself, for the push of his practical imagination could hardly be described in any other way, into breaking his bonds, scattering the bodies of his enemies, and grasping his club by the middle!

But if Zeuks' outburst of "prokleesis" had made even the paramour of the Daughter of the Sun jerk up his trim beard, it can be well understood how it made the two insects inside it jump and cry out. With them, however, the situation was just opposite to what it had been earlier that day; for now it was the fly who was keen to leave their shelter and the moth who was all for restraining him.

"But, Pyraust darling, I *must* find out whether the King is sweating under his beard! I know him so well that I know that *that* is the great sign. If there's a drop of perspiration under his beard you may depend on it that he's going to do something serious and do it soon. Please don't hold me so tight, my sweet friend. I swear I won't go further than that fold of his chiton. Once there I can crawl perfectly well between a few grey hairs, and soon discover what I want to know.

"It'll only be like a microscopic thicket, and you know how good I am at threading my way through olive-branches and rose-bushes! Oh, I'll find the least drop of sweat if there is one to be found! You see he's still got that old nurse, Eurycleia, though she must be over a hundred years old, and you may depend on that old lady keeping him clean. You bet your life, my pretty one, I couldn't settle on Zeuks' chiton—you must remember, darling, that we house-flies are extremely sensitive to smells.

"We're not like carrion-flies or dung-flies who live on filth and naturally seek it out!—no! I couldn't settle on Zeuks' chiton, though he's a self-respecting, decently washed and well-dressed farmer, without being overpowered by the smell of his skin. But Eurycleia uses, though he's old now, the same unguents and essences that she used for him when he was a child; so that you needn't be afraid, dear heart, that your crazy Myos will faint from the old man's stench, and slip down under the fellow's shirt and be no more seen!

"Whatever happens, I can assure you, sweetest of Pyrausts, that I shall return safely to this heavenly shelter in the bosom of our Heraklean Club.

"No? You won't let go? You won't let me risk it? All right, I'm not going to break loose by force. So if you won't let me go, you won't let me go; and that's the end of it. Of course some would say I'm taking the opportunity of your prohibition to escape doing what I'm really scared stiff of doing.

"But I know *you* don't think like this; and yours is the only opinion I really value. As I have often confessed to you, there have been occasions in my peaceful life when I have had pleasure with exactly twenty-seven female flies. This I have never concealed from you. But when it becomes—— ""

It was at this point that the Moth—who so many times had heard her friend quote the well-known lines from Beelzebelle, the Sappho of Flies, that begin:

"airy-fairy-flickit-with-Mary" and ends:
"wagatail-wispy-with-honeymoon-Jane",

that there had been moments when she felt that if he didn't stop before one, two, three more ticks of the clock she would rush straight into the nearest fire—beat a tattoo with her free wing upon the wall of their retreat of so decisive a character that the fly yielded in every sense.

He left the topic of female flies. He gave up his exploration of the neck of Odysseus for a drop of perspiration. And he replied to the unspoken question that was behind all the moth had been saying, by assuring her that even if there had been no drop of sweat under the king's beard, and even if they all had to sleep where they were that night, they would without question be making their departure, if not by "Lykophos" or "Wolf's-light", certainly by the first streak of red in the sky. . . .

By this time Zeuks had reached the climax of his singular outburst. He was still on his feet; but he was standing in a manner in which we can be absolutely certain no Grecian orator had ever stood before while addressing a crowd. One foot was on his chair and the other on the floor.

This sounds harmless and conventional enough; but it only does so because we have not yet realized that owing to Zeuks' lack of height and his chair's antique height, his upraised knee was on a level with his chin. Nor was this all; for Zeuks' incurable indifference to the decencies of human dignity combined with his flagrant and absolutely unashamed fondness for his own physical person from head to foot, resulted in a very quaint issue: for seeing his knee so extremely near his mouth, much nearer than human knees generally are to human lips he clutched it with his two hands and digging his chin into it and pressing his clenched teeth against it he began muttering and murmuring *through* his teeth, for his teeth being tightly clenched he wasn't biting his knee, a strange rhapsody of self-enjoyment.

To all but one of the company then present this curious chant of ecstatic self-possession was inarticulate; but to the club of Herakles it was not only wholly audible but wholly intelligible.

"At last," said the Club to himself, "I hear the language uttered, which, if I were the ruler of the world, I would cause to be the language of the world!"

What the club heard as articulate speech could not be set down in the syllables of any tongue that was spoken then on the surface of the earth or has been spoken since; but it consisted of a groaningly murmured, thickly muttered, grindingly hoarse, creakingly wooden, scrapingly rocky, clangingly metallic, and also, naturally enough considering that our friend was rhapsodizing into the hardness of his own knee, a satisfyingly onomatopaeic paean.

The drift of what Zeuks was chanting had undoubtedly to do with that same "prokleesis" whose secret he had tried to interpret; only this was an attempt to turn his own body into a drum or trumpet or clarionet, or whatever it might be, that like some vocal sea-shell or land-shell transformed the heavy material sounds of rock against rock, root against root, earth-mass against earth-mass, sea-sand against sea-sand, through which the sixth Pillar from its fixed abode in that old corridor at home was able to communicate with the club of Herakles.

"Enorches"—Zeuks chanted at last, in a deep, rich, resonant voice, lifting his head from his knee and clasping that symbol of

eternal supplication with the fingers of both his hands—
"Enorches is the unhappiest man on earth! Anyone who understood to the full the real nature of the unhappiness of Enorches would die of pity. But this much, my friends, it is permitted to me to tell you; and tell it you I must since the knowledge of it is of the very essence of the supreme 'prokleesis' you are making with me, or if you prefer, I am making with you, here tonight.

"Enorches is deliberately lying when he says that Eros and Dionysos together redeem the world. He implies that they do this, one or the other of them, or both together, as the salvation of mankind, by means of mystical love or mystical intoxication. He implies they do it so utterly and completely that ordinary self-control, ordinary kindness, ordinary decency, ordinary honesty, ordinary courtesy, ordinary generosity, are rendered totally and wholly unimportant when these two mystical ecstasies are at work; and that it is in fact as an alternative to the good, the true, and the beautiful, that these celestial manias and heavenly drugs fill the entire stage and obsess the whole nature of man's consciousness.

"Now the diabolical lie beneath all this is the implicit assumption that we love to the point of ecstasy and drink to the point of ecstasy in order that life shall go on in the universe indefinitely and without end. Now the real secret purpose and the real secret motive actuating Enorches is the extreme opposite of this.

"What he really hates with a hatred that is co-existent with his uttermost being and with the uttermost being of what he hates is nothing less than *Life itself*. His praise of Eros and Dionysos, that is to say his glorification of Love and Intoxication as Substitutes for all other forms of Worship, is really a grand and supreme indulgence in deliberate lying. The one secret aim and the one final intention of this crafty Priest of Orpheus is to destroy all Life utterly and forever!

"In the depths of his own being he is so scooped-out by despair, so bled white by abysmal unhappiness that he has only one desire left, the desire that life once and for all and in every place under the sun and moon, and upon and within and below the earth, should be destroyed and brought to an end forever!

"Yes, what this Priest of the Mysteries aims at is that there shall no longer be any Mystery—in other words that there should no longer be any *life*. What he recognizes as the uttermost reality of his own destructive and negative nature is a fathomless, yawning void, an open mouth, a gulf, an abysmal hole; and this in-sucking shaft leads not to any kind of Being, but to that nameless opposite of all existence that can only be called Not-Being.

"Here, therefore, down in the depths of this priest's nature, is something much deeper and much nearer an absolute than Death; for Death, after all, implies that something has lived or it could not have died; but in this man's nature, when we go down to the very depths of it, we find *that* which can in reality have no 'nature' of any sort at all, for it is Nothingness Itself.

"Yes! What this self-styled Priest of Orpheus really feels, in his absolute and abysmal despair, is that it would have been infinitely better if there had never been any Life at all. But since life *has* appeared, what this Priest of the Mysteries would wish to see happen would be for the whole miserable mass of it to plunge headlong down and vanish in the Nothingness out of which it ought never to have emerged!"

While Zeuks let himself go in this sweeping diatribe they all watched him carefully in their different ways—Odysseus watched him as a steersman in dubious weather watches a distant horizon. Nisos watched him as an amorist might watch the eyes of one girl through the transparent body of another. The pregnant woman watched him as if he were a cock crowing on a dungheap. Old Moros watched him as if he were a dog going too close to a trap that ought long ago to have been sprung. Zenios watched him as if he were an itinerant musician, spoiling an opportunity for a good stroke of business.

Okyrhöe watched him, thinking: "I must make them stay and I must give *him* something to lie on in the Mirror-Room." Pontoporeia watched him, thinking: "Yes, I agree with this absurd 'prokleesis' up to a point; but he doesn't make it personal enough, for it ought to be some way, some mood, some turn of the mind, some twist of the reason, that would help you when you wanted to make friends with a person."

And finally, while the club of Herakles, still leaning against the elbow of that narrow seat cut out of the pre-historic wall, watched him, thinking: "how annoying if he starts a vibration that brings me crashing down!" Zeuks felt as if an irresistible unseen power compelled him to fling back his head and to gaze out into the darkness through a half-open door; and though the lights about him made the darkness outside absolute, the same power that compelled him to lift his head forced him to treat that darkness as if it were the whole vast immeasurable bulk of the massed material of the thick-ribbed earth, ridge upon ridge, hill upon hill, mountain upon mountain, towering up in its enormity to a toppling height, high above the encircling ocean that encompasses all, forced him to treat it as if it were this, and at the same time forced him to plunge into it and with his soul gathered together to break through it, to cleave it, to wrench his way through it, until he reached a certain particular spot on the earth's surface.

What particular spot? Ah! That's the point! "That's what has been"—and it was Zeuks himself who flung this jaggedly-splintered shaft of rending interjection into the thick bulk of that darkness—"What has been led up to in all this"—for the spot he was being forced to visit was nothing less than a stone shed near-by with a massively-closed iron-barred door in which Pegasos had been imprisoned ever since Odysseus released him.

In this shed, tied by the neck, Pegasos was at that moment groaning piteously and twisting his head from side to side; for the rope that tied him crossed and re-crossed and chafed abominably that raw part of his shoulder from which the wing had been torn and from which even yet dark drops of blood, mingled with ichor, were trickling down.

Slowly therefore now, in spite of all the eyes that were upon him, Zeuks rose, and deliberately crossing the hall to the open door through which that unknown force had just drawn his soul into the palpable darkness, he resolutely, but still slowly and very quietly, left the company and went out. Once outside and alone in the air it was not nearly so dark, and it didn't take him long to discover the stone shed where in the haste of their arrival Pegasos had been tied up. It was still necessary, however, to get some kind of torch or lantern; and with this in view he made his way, led by the smell of the fragrant smoke to where Nemertes was already drying, after having cleaned and washed with the exquisite care and nicety exacted by Zenios of all who touched his possessions, the vast array of plates and dishes used at tonight's supper.

She certainly was a shrewd and intelligent woman, this mother of Omphos, Kissos, and Sykos; and now when Zeuks entered her domain to get a light so as to deal with Pegasos, and found her directing her three sons in the complicated task of piling up and putting away all this precious crockery, he was conscious of being delivered, merely by drawing her attention to his situation, from a whole load of tiresome responsibility.

She told him at once to fetch Pegasos out of that cold and dark shed and to bring him into the kitchen; and when he obeyed her and they had tied this mutilated and one-winged creature, who had once flown above the turrets of Arabia and the domes of China and the pyramids of Egypt and had distended its quivering nostrils in its flight to catch the enchanted odours that are wafted down on certain human midnights from the ghostly valleys of the moon, to one of the shadowy meat-hooks that broke the flickering fire-lit surface of those friendly walls, it was easy to see from the immortal animal's grateful eyes as they were turned first to one and then to another till they finally rested on the woman herself, that the prospect of a night behind the cyclopean pre-historic walls of Ornax after his windy lodging on the outskirts of Cuckoo-Hill was now wholly congenial to him.

Nemertes hesitated not to take entire possession of Zeuks at once and to tell him exactly what he had better do if he wished his one night in Ornax to be really a pleasant one.

"You will have to sleep in the porch of the Chamber of the Mirror so as to be a guard for the sleep of the Mistress. This will be the sleeping arrangement with which nothing must interfere; but if you, my Lord Zeuks, and you, my Lord Pegasos, agree to accept this arrangement, it is in my power to give *you*"—and she turned to Zeuks—"and *you*"—and she stroked the great free beautiful useless unhurt wing of her animal-visitor which now trailed across a third of the floor," the peacefullest sleep you've ever had in your lives."

"Give us this?" enquired Zeuks in his most cheerful and humorous intonation.

"How will you give us this?" asked Pegasos with his appealing eyes.

And the woman answered by immediate action. She went to a great brazen receptacle in a corner of the kitchen and scooped up two handfuls of oats which she forthwith presented to the winged horse, who reverently swallowed them. Then she lifted the lid of a substantial chest made of sycamore wood from the main-land and brought out a small loaf. This she deliberately broke into four pieces, one big piece and three small pieces; and handing one of the small pieces to each of her sons who straightway began munching and masticating it with intense satisfaction, she gave the large piece to Zeuks who promptly kissed it and crammed it into his mouth, but allowed half of it to remain in one cheek, and half of it in the other, un-chewed and un-swallowed.

It was at this point that Zeuks noticed a hurried whispered conversation going on between Omphos, Kissos, and Sykos; and before he had made up his mind whether to ignore what he perceived or to boldly ask them what was the matter, Omphos, the eldest of the three, crossed the kitchen with obvious nervousness, while Pegasos, answering this respectful courtesy with equal consideration, did his best to move his unhurt wing out of the young man's way.

When Omphos reached Zeuks he stood in front of him like an earnest-minded school-boy summoned for an oral examination;

and Nemertes couldn't help noting how quaint it was to see the two cheeks of this examiner of young men bulging so auspiciously for his own future enjoyment but rendering him practically inarticulate before an academic questioner.

But the question asked by Omphos was a simple one. "Could you tell us, my Lord Zeuks, exactly what you thought of when you say we must still practise 'prokleesis' though we were soon going to be cut to pieces by those pirates?"

What Zeuks desired to do at this point was first to use his tongue to push both halves of that delicious little loaf into one bulging cheek, and then with that same tongue to discourse so eloquently on the practice of "prokleesis" when you were watching people tortured or when you were being tortured yourself, that not only Omphos but his sympathetic brothers and possibly even their wise mother would decide to try how it worked in the ordinary vexations of every day.

But all he could blurt out at the moment was: "Of course nobody can bear more than a certain amount of pain; and if you're watching its infliction on others there comes a point when you break out or go raving mad; but nothing helps anyone to endure what *can* be endured more than forcing yourself to feel in the way 'prokleesis' makes you feel: for when you feel like this it isn't the cruel enemy or executioner or torturer or murderer you are defying; it is Life itself!

"And what are you defying Life to do? You are defying Life to make you stop fighting Life! You are defying Life to make you worship Death! You are defying Life to make you lose yourself in those Half-Deaths of mystical ecstasy, such as Enorches praises; he who this very day plucked out the wing that was the twin of this!"

Zeuks' whole figure looked absurdly un-heroic and un-prophetic as with his mouth full of half-munched bread he pulled out from under his belt a corner of his shirt and used it to dab up a small trickle of blood-stained ichor that was at the moment feeling its cautious way along the spine of the Flying Horse in evident fear of ending its career as a living stream in a pool on the kitchen-floor.

ATLANTIS

It is doubtful whether even the most perspicacious ghost among those who were rumoured to have recently escaped from the under-world under the guidance of Pontopereia's father, had such an one passed through Ornax, would have been drawn to Zeuks as a person naturally provocative of spiritual attention.

But whatever an enlightened fugitive in the train of Teiresias might have thought of this short, vulgarly-attired individual, with his thumbs in his belt, who now proceeded to rub his bleached and bloated physiognomy, making as he did so a grotesque purring sound in his gullet, against the arched neck of the wounded offspring of the Gorgon's blood, Zeuks himself had not experienced a more delicious sensation of well-being since the days when he lived so contentedly with the cast-off paramour of the goat-footed Pan.

The bread he was masticating was proving so delicious and he kept turning it round and round in his mouth so long that when he finally did gulp it down it was simply saliva that he swallowed, only faintly tinctured with a lingering taste of wheaten bread. But it conveyed to every cell, tissue, nerve, fibre, gland and sense-centre in his whole body all the long air-nourished, sun-perforated, dew-quickened, rain-soaked experiences that had filled with more than physical richness each grain of wheat that made up Nemertes' precious flour.

Zeuks felt sure as he rubbed his head against the neck of Pegasos that the animal was feeling from its digesting of those oats exactly what he was feeling himself from his long-munched bread. It was therefore something of a shock to him when he heard the voice of young Nisos addressing him from the doorway and saw the others all turn round to greet the excited boy.

Nisos brought the news that Odysseus had decided to start for home extremely early; actually, in fact, before that faint grey light that preludes the rising of the sun and in Ithaca was called "Lykophos" or "Wolf's Light". Between the three sons of Nemertes, as Nisos made his announcement, a swift glance of pleasure and surprise had passed; and it was clear to both Zeuks and the boy that whatever the feeling of Nemertes might be, as far as Omphos,

Kissos and Sykos were concerned the fact that this visit was to end before dawn was an indescribable relief.

But Nemertes looked grave. Carefully brushing off from her clothes the smallest wisp of straw from the oats-bin and the least little wheat-bread crumb from the loaf she had just divided, she beckoned Nisos to her side. "Just a moment, my Lord Zeuks, if you don't mind," she said, and taking Nisos gently by the arm led him, avoiding the switching and quivering feathers of Pegasos' extended wing, for the animal evidently realized that a move of some sort was in the air, to a shadowy recess behind her cooking-stove.

"You are a good and faithful servant to your king, or I couldn't talk so straight to you," she said in a low voice. "But you're not the only loyal adherent in the world, any more than Odysseus is the only true and honest master. Now I beg you to follow me very carefully, my young friend, in what I'm going to say. My sons are too simple-minded and too uncultivated in their intellects to get the full force of what I want to say; but you have had a good education in the best school in this island even if you've never been on the main-land, and so I'll talk to you as I would to my husband, the Builder of Towns, who went to a school in Crete. My place in life from now on, you must understand, is to serve Okyrhöe, who at the moment, though I shan't be surprised if she eventually becomes the partner of a god, when no doubt she will herself release me from my service, who is, I say, at the moment the wife of this man Zenios who declares himself to be of the House of Kadmos.

"But the point, my dear Nisos, that I should find hard to make my sons understand is this. When at the death of my husband, the Builder of Towns, I undertook, largely for the sake of my sons, so that we could all continue together, the service of Okyrhöe, I swore to serve her faithfully and I swore it by the gods, especially by the great Themis, the goddess of Order and Justice.

"Now my three sons hate Okyrhöe; nor can I blame them for this. To Zenios they feel nothing at all; neither love nor hate, neither consideration nor contempt. They are, however, quite prepared to go on working for him, feeling that by so doing they are serving their mother. You follow what I mean? When I am faithful to Okyrhöe it is not for her sake, but the sake of the great goddess of Order and Justice and Right, by whom I swore. Now I will tell you something else. And this, Nisos my lad, is a serious warning, If my mistress bids me make up a bed for him over there"—and she nodded towards Zeuks—"at the entrance to the Chamber of the Mirror where she always sleeps herself, he would be wise to make some excuse. Let him tell her, for instance, that he never undresses and goes to bed before an early start like this. In fact he'd better tell her—— "

She was interrupted by a wild, excited, high-pitched, youthful voice from the other end of that spacious kitchen; and at once they instinctively moved apart, and quite separately advanced to meet the girl, who was Pontopereia herself.

"I've come," she was saying, and it was to every living person in that steamy, shadowy, fire-lit place that she addressed herself. "I've come to tell you that what I've been praying to the gods for a whole year might happen has now happened. The spirit of my father Teiresias has come upon me and the prophetic power of Teiresias has taken possession of me, and I feel flooded by what I know, and I feel afloat on what I understand, and I feel afire with what I have grasped, and if you don't enter into my meaning and catch the spirit of my revelation I swear to you that something dreadful will happen, and happen soon, and happen to all of us! So listen! listen! listen! and don't move, any of you here, till I've told you what I know!"

"Say what you've got to say, child; and say it quietly and say it quickly. We are all listening."

These words were not spoken by Nemertes who had approached nearest to the excited young girl and had even laid a firm and calming hand on one of her gesticulating arms. They were spoken by Zeuks, who, coming alongside of Nemertes as a massive and sturdy barge might come alongside of a sailing-ship, laid his hand upon Nemertes' shoulder and did so in such an affectionate and genial a way that no sensible or kindly person could possibly have taken offence; nor indeed could anyone, who in the position of Nisos and Nemertes' three sons had been destined to be spectators of this encounter, have denied that the combined magnetism of two such friendly and massive personalities was the very thing to calm the girl's excited nerves.

But was it the thing best calculated to bring to birth from this virgin frame a prophetic message from the world of spirits, or at any rate from a world beyond the reach of our normal sensations? Evidently to Nisos it was not, for he began pacing up and down with a frown of nervous apprehension. What he measured with his anxious steps was a limited stretch of the stone floor of that ancient chamber, a floor that may well have belonged, like the stone walls of the place, to some prehistoric god of silence, for there was a curious absence of every kind of echo to the human voice and of every kind of resonance from the human tread.

But as he paced nervously up and down, avoiding the now motionless feathers of Pegasos' prostrate wing, he couldn't help glancing now and again at the almost pathetic contrast between the illuminated beauty of Pontopereia's face and the clumsy heaviness of her limbs and indeed of her whole body from the waist down.

"What is prompting me," he thought, "to be so absurdly critical as to demand that a girl should be this or that before I can let myself fall in love with her, or think of her in my mind as my particular choice? Well! that's how I am," he concluded, "and there's no use making a fuss about it! I only pray that that accurst Goat-foot has encountered Enorches and made such a Dionysian raid upon that scoundrel's oldest wine that by this time he can't distinguish a young virgin from an old midwife."

Meanwhile Pontopereia was announcing in a tone whose prophetic intensity was no less assured, though it was calmer than when she first entered the kitchen, that if they wished their ride to be a success they must not wait till morning; no! not even if by morning they meant an hour before "Wolf-Light". On the contrary they must start at once; and if they felt sleepy they must console themselves by thinking how sweet it would be to lay their heads on their own pillows when they got home!

As far as Nisos could judge from the acquiescent pose of Zeuks' neat and pliant figure, for the face of the advocate of "Prokleesis" was turned towards Pontopereia, the man seemed prepared to do whatever she proposed; and it was a surprise to the boy when in the silence that followed her declaration Zeuks swung round and exchanged a rapid series of signals and significant signs with Pegasos, an exchange in which the horse's trailing wing played less of a part than its quivering ears, and the man's expressive hands less of a part than his thrust-out and sucked-in thick lips.

"Do you really think they'll get Odysseus to agree to such a thing at such an hour?" Nemertes remarked to Nisos when Zeuks followed Pontopereia out of the kitchen. "But though I'm only an old woman in an old kitchen and no prophetess I would advise you, sonny, to slip off, now you have the chance, and see our Master, yes! see Zenios himself, whom you're sure to find in his treasure-room at the bottom of that flight of stairs—you saw those stairs, didn't you, laddie, as you went into the dining-hall?—for what I fancy your old king has forgotten, and what I'm certain this queer fellow Zeuks has forgotten, is that great sack of treasure you unloaded up there in the porch. It *was* treasure, wasn't it? I saw, by the way you lifted it, how heavy it was; and I also saw, for we old women notice things like that, that when Zenios came back with Moros the first thing he did was to get the old man to help him trundle that sack of yours down those stairs. He has a queer sort of mind, has our master Zenios; and though I don't suggest for a second that he intends to rob anyone of whatever that sack contains, I know him by this time well enough to know that if six hours or even four hours are allowed by destiny to pass over a neighbourhood where our Master and any precious treasure are to be found, at the end of those hours, and generally long before they end, the master of whom we are speaking and the treasure of which we are speaking will have been brought into physical contact as if by the use of a magnet."

Nisos looked at the old lady in admiration. "By the gods," he cried, "I'd completely forgotten that curst sack! Why! You're a soothsayer too, though you do work in this old kitchen! I certainly *will* do just what you say, and see what's happened to that great golden mixing-bowl! I can tell your master, anyway, *something* about it—though whether the old king got it from his queen's father or whether Alkinoos gave it him in the land of the Phaeakeans I forget at this moment; but if I see it and touch it I daresay I'll remember what Eurycleia told me about it! Old as she is, *her* memory never fails her! Yes, I'll go straight down those steps and talk to Zenios!

"O I do thank you, lady, for putting it into my head! What I expect has been in our old king's mind all along is some sort of an idea, though it seems horrid to say so,"—at this point Nisos lowered his voice; not so much in order that his hearer's three sons shouldn't hear, as from an instinctive courtesy—proof, thought Nemertes, as she listened to him, of how well he'd been brought up—"some sort of an idea," he threw out in a hurried whisper as he rushed off—"of paying some sort of ransom or tribute for Pontopereia!"

As Nisos hastened to the northern edge of the pre-historic semicircle of stone ruins that these unscrupulous explorers from Kadmean Thebes had modernized and made habitable, he said to himself: "Tribute? Ransom? I wonder I didn't say 'Offering'. What of course it will really be, if the old king leaves that treasure behind without a word, will be buying the girl from him as we buy slaves in the market."

It was when he was feeling his way down those steps, and though it was quite dark he could see a light between door and doorpost at the foot of the stairs, that he stopped short, with one foot on the third and the other on the fourth step, and the extended fingers of his left hand spread out against the wall, for he had a sudden inspiration. "I'll suggest to Odysseus," he thought, "that I ought to visit Tis's home along with old Moros, now I'm so near, and that it might be a good thing if I went into the Naiads' Cave on my way back to see if the ship-keel is still as it was."

Meanwhile if Nemertes could have observed what was going on in her master's chamber at the bottom of that staircase she would have felt, well! not, as people say, "completely justified", for Nemertes had seen too much of the treacheries of life ever to feel precisely that, but she would have felt that she had not been far wrong in her knowledge of the ways of her master, as a collector of pre-historic treasures.

Long before Nisos had begun to make his way down those steps Zenios had been sitting on a low, rough, oblong couch of fir-planks covered with several layers of sheep-skins, a couch which in his lonely moods he preferred to any other. He was holding in his hands the heaviest and most precious of that sack's marvels. This was an unusually large Mixing-Bowl; the sort of Mixing-Bowl that among the more civilized Achaean tribes was generally known as a "Depas".

This particular "Depas" was an enormous one. It had a flat stand at its base and a circular handle on each side of its circumference and it was made of solid gold. It was in fact made of gold so heavy, so massive, and so purged of every kind of alloy, that as Zenios caressed it it gave him the feeling that it was something so totally different from all other things in the world and so absolutely divided from all other things in the world that when he gave himself up wholly and entirely to the pure sensation of this feel of it, he himself became isolated from everything else on earth. The handling of real gold, massive gold, pure gold, solid gold, had become the one positive lust, the one supreme indulgence, the one ecstatic cult, the one ultimate paradise of Zenios' existence; and when he did so, as he was doing now, he grew so identified with the precious thing he held, that with no effort other than passive surrender to bliss he became what, save for a few blameless Ethiopeans both in the extreme East and in the extreme West, a man seldom becomes, namely a motionless orb of convulsed sunlight, or even starlight, for whom the mere alternation of inbreathing and outbreathing is not only a sufficient satisfaction for one life, but a sufficient satisfaction to justify an infinite series of lives.

But meanwhile, very cautiously, and inch by inch, Nisos was descending the stairs towards this absorbed gold-worshipper. Now the approach of the aboriginal wild creatures in the forests of the earth towards one another has been from the beginning the cause of innumerable invisible vibrations across various expanses of earth and air and such primeval vibrations, whether of attraction or repulsion, or of pure warning, have never completely vanished from the human scene all the way down the ages.

It must have been some such vibration, and of pure warning too, that caused young Nisos, before he had reached the fourth step in his stealthy descent towards that chink of light between door and door-post, to change his mind completely, and, avoiding with exquisite care the least shiver of disturbing sound, to ascend those steps twice as quickly as he had descended them, and, once clear of that quarter of the restored ruins of Ornax, to set off as fast as possible to find Odysseus.

Even Zeuks would not have been able to interpret for the benefit of any other person seated on that broad back all the thoughts of Pegasos as the two of them waited patiently for their start from Ornax on their homeward journey. The whole thing is conjectural of course, but it does seem unlikely that an immortal creature however wounded could feel quite as agitated, as did Okyrhöe for example, when she discovered that she was really going to perch herself on the still bleeding back of a one-winged unflying flier, "with this low peasant", as she told herself "who out of vulgar blasphemy calls himself Zeuks", in front of her, "and this silly old King-Hero who won't be able to see more of me than my back", behind her.

The whole thing was a surprise and a shock to this beautiful designer of elaborate schemes; for the last thing she expected was to have to make her plunge into the innermost circle of Odysseus' life without the least preparation, indeed with what might almost be called a "hippodromic" leap. However! If she had to do it she had to do it, and with a courage and recklessness that would have drawn from her cautious slow-moving husband a very straight look, she rushed to one of the innermost chests in the furthest corner of her Mirror-Room and dragged forth from it a garment that Zenios had never known she had bought, for she had managed the transaction in secret with a Phoenician Merchant during a mighty purchase of golden cups.

No sooner now had she dragged out this garment and wrapped her lovely body in it than in a flash all her annoyance disappeared! It was exactly suited to the occasion. Nothing on earth could have answered this unexpected situation better. Even though the immortal creature she rode on was wet with ichor and blood, and even though "with this on" the old hero could not even see how shapely her back was, the effect of her face looking forth from that feathery cloud of heavenly whiteness was beyond what even she herself had ever dreamed of!

She walked up and down in front of Kadmos' Mirror-Shield. She arranged herself, with this wonderful thing about her, first on a couch, then on a chair, then on the couch again, and once more on a chair. Okyrhöe had never in her whole life felt so inspired by her own beauty. And the remarkable thing about it was that her head, her critical, fastidious, detached, acquisitive, unscrupulous head, remained absolutely clear and cold.

Dramatizing herself and gesturing and posing in front of that shield of Kadmos there was absolutely nothing in the consciousness of Okyrhöe that had the faintest resemblance to the self-adoration, the self-intoxication, the self-worship of the unfortunate Narcissus. Okyrhöe's mind was as cold and hard and ruthless as one of those short sharp Latin swords that the Nymph Egeria in her Italian cave would know more about than any Achaean woman.

Okyrhöe used her beauty purely, solely, and simply as a weapon. She fought with her beauty as if it were a sword. She sacked cities with her beauty. She dried up deep seas with her beauty. She blighted harvests, she devastated vineyards, she up-rooted forests with it. She was prepared to blacken shining stars and to put out burning suns with her beauty. Beauty for her was something wherewith to carve out empires or to drown continents.

The cloak she had extracted from the Phoenician's most sacred and secret caravan was made of the white skin of a huge prehistoric animal called a Podandrikon whose peculiarity was that round its waist it had shining scales and round its neck it had thick white feathers. Wrapped in the Podandrikon's skin the completely reassured Okyrhöe told herself with one last glance at the Shield of Kadmos that if this fond and foolish old king thought he would ever sail from Ithaca again he was mad.

With the face the gods had given her and in the cloak she had discovered for herself she would rule all Argos and all Boeotia and all Hellas from this old fool's rock-cave island palace! Thus thought Okyrhöe.

But the oldest of the Fates, as it used to be said at any special pinch concerning the goddess Athene, who now was so wrought up—and who can blame her—by the blind folly of her own people in the face of all this cosmic confusion that she had taken refuge with the blameless Ethiopians, "took other counsel". Yes, Atropos, the weakest, the oldest, but the wisest of the Moirai, or Fates, came, invisibly rushing, as she always did, to the crisis-spot and prompted Odysseus to make one of his own decisions independently of everyone. And such a decision he made; and it was so wholly material and practical, and so absolutely free from any general theory about the matter at issue, from any logical sequence of reasoning about the problem at stake, from any principle of action, from any "mystique" of action, from any philosophic metaphysic of action, that it could hardly be described as a decision at all.

Of course in his past there had been occasions, there *had* to be occasions, when he was forced to act according to some practical plan of action, when in fact to act at all implied a plan of action; but this was different, and the truth was that Odysseus behaved now like a skilful carpenter who has already taken the measure of the adjustments, of the shaping, the trimming, the nailing, the thickening, the thinning, the rounding off, the hammering, the polishing, which in this particular case he would be forced to employ.

Those who knew him intimately however—and of these there were perhaps now living only two persons, namely his nurse Eurycleia, whose extreme old age interfered with the expression of what she knew, and the goddess Athene, who had her own ethnological undertakings independent of any individual man or woman—would have been in a position to explain to us that there had been in this extraordinary man's life certain far-off but quite definite, concrete and material projects to the realization of which the whole complicated organism of his formidable identity was basically aimed.

Of these vast projects, like huge islands on immeasurable horizons, Eurycleia would probably have pointed to the taking of Troy, while Pallas Athene might conceivably have named the immense but misty and cloudy notion, like an old and battered world-sailor's fantasy, that at present loomed in the darkly-brooding background of his consciousness, the notion of sailing Westward, far past the Pillars of Herakles and the place where Atlas holds up the Sky, past even the shores of Ultima Thule where exiled Kronos awaits the day of his awakening, the notion in fact of steering his ship over the very waves of the very sea under which lie the drowned towers and temples and domes and palaces and streets of the sunken continent of Atlantis.

But what Odysseus decided upon now as his most prudent line of action was to accept Okyrhöe's astonishing offer to share with Zeuks and himself the wounded back of Pegasos on condition that her tender maternal arms should firmly encircle the awkwardly-moulded form of the prophetic orphan Pontopereia.

He was in fact wily enough to decide then and there to use to the limit the obviously possessive power of this beautiful woman so as to make sure that no sudden, wild, girlish impulse such as might very well spring up in a daughter of Teiresias should deprive him of her as an aid to the baffling of his enemies and the furtherance of his sailing.

"Oh, I'm so glad," cried this same eager girlish prophet, when she found Zeuks alone with Pegasos waiting for Okyrhöe and the old king, "to have a chance to ask you what you really meant by your terrifying story of those horrible pirates putting ropes round us all and deliberately chopping us to death one by one. I couldn't bear to see it done to anybody, however much I hated them; and it's certain I couldn't bear it myself. I should just go shrieking-mad, and struggle wildly and bang about till I was killed or killed somebody else!"

The girl's directness and simplicity had its effect. The expression upon the face of Zeuks would have suggested to anyone who had the particular kind of penetration that the great Theban prophet seems to have been not quite able to pass on to his progeny, that within the bloated mask of humorous relish for every conceivable aspect of human existence and of animal sensation that was Zeuks' nature there had been suddenly roused from sleep a small active insect-like second nature that was a drastically honest commentator upon all the man's impressions and was a pitiless exposure of all his own self-deceptions and all his own exaggerations and all his own boastings.

"I'll tell you the whole thing, my dear Pontopereia," Zeuks blurted out hurriedly. "I was glorying, you see, in my own mind over this idea of mine which I call Prokleesis or 'defiance'. I'm proud of this idea, which has become very important to me and which is something I'm constantly trying to practise. But I'm a terrible one for seeing everything as comic and I suddenly saw my own life-method, my own life-philosophy, my own private and special defiance of life as a comic thing; and I thought: 'How can I show up this prokleesis of mine as I love to show up all those other philosophic cure-alls that aim at dispending with Themis, treating old Auntie Atropos as a doting hag, discounting Necessity, and putting Chance to shame as a negligible wanton?'

"And I decided that the only way I could do this was by imagining a situation in which only a very few heroic human souls, and they probably already half-crazy, could possibly practise my philosophy of 'prokleesis', or defiance of the whole of existence, and so I conjured up the picture of those murderous pirates on the brink of chopping us all to death one after another, as much as to say: 'Well! If you can defy life while watching your best friends chopped to bits and waiting your own turn, you have to be something more than a clowning antic like me, whose head's been turned by a good idea!'"

The kidnapper of Pegasos with his hand on that Gorgonian Wonder's solitary wing must have drained at that second the ambrosial dregs of true philosophic glory, for the awkward figure of the daughter of Teiresias hunched itself into a shapeless heap of girlish admiration before the knees that had bent so faithfully all those years serving the aged Nymph deserted by Pan.

When Okyrhöe in the Podandrikon's incomparable skin, and with her bold hand on Odysseus' shoulder, finally appeared, it was evident that neither her own loveliness nor the unique wonder wrapped round her had made the old hero forget his Heraklean club.

"We shall be off in a moment, pretty creature," murmured the fly to the moth from the deep life-crack in that self-conscious weapon, "and then we'll soon find out how far the great god Pan has been able to go with young Eione."

"It's all very well for you to say that," replied the moth, "but I wish you hadn't gone to sleep while the Sixth Pillar was talking to the club just now; for the Pillar had heard about our mid-wife's sister having quarrelled with her Egeria, and being now with old Moros, at the home of Tis and Eione, and being on the point of having a child."

"How you beautiful girls," jeered the teasing fly, "do adore thinking of the results of love-making! What interests *me* is whether the great god Pan will be able to go to the limit with young Eione."

The moth stared vaguely out of the belly of the club into the surrounding darkness. "Yes, I wonder," she pondered, "whether Eione is old enough to have a child."

CHAPTER VII

It was a riderless Arion who met the four of them, that is to say the two women, Okyrhöe and Pontopereia, mounted between the two men, Zeuks and Odysseus, when they arrived at the palace-porch and dismounted from the wounded back of Pegasos at the entrance to the Corridor of the Pillars. There was still a little more of that weird before-dawn light called Lykophos to be got through ere the sun rose, for neither Pegasos' wounded shoulder nor his heavily-trailing solitary wing had interfered with the speed of his stride; and the darkness had only just broken when they got home.

The faithful Tis, however, was awaiting them, though since he had fastened Arion by a rope long enough to permit the animal to graze on the weeds in the Slaves' Burial-ground it was clear he was ready to wait patiently for some time. But it was from Arion's obvious restlessness and excited expectancy, to be seen in every turn of his finely-moulded head and every arching of his proud though mutilated neck, that Tis, who knew the instincts of animals as well as Odysseus knew the instincts of men, had guessed that some mysterious vibration existing between these two semi-godlike creatures had already begun to inform Arion of the near arrival of Pegasos.

When they actually did meet, their re-encounter would have delighted Nisos, and he would have observed with relief that each of them had now ceased to leave on the ground any trail of blood-stained ichor. The immediate witnesses of the scene however were too taken up with their own affairs to notice the condition of the pair of animals who were led off by Tis. He led them quite quietly and naturally to a shed adjoining the one devoted to Babba.

Babba herself, whose private affairs were less absorbing than those of any of the persons dismounting from the back of Pegasos, instantaneously thrust her horns through the wooden partition separating the two horses from herself, and then, hurriedly withdrawing these finely curved objects from the neat apertures they had made, proceeded to arrange her beautifully flapping ears so as to catch every faintest overtone and undertone of the thoughts and feelings that these unusual visitors exchanged between themselves.

But satisfactory as it was to an amiable and easy-going cow like Babba to have the distraction, though she could only understand half of what she heard, of listening to something that did at least make her forget the passing discomfort of waiting with full udders the time of her milking, it was a mild satisfaction compared with the pleasure Okyrhöe derived from talking to Arsinöe. The woman listened to every word Arsinöe uttered, to every sigh Arsinöe sighed. Nor was there any shade of seduction, whether frightening or reassuring, whether cajoling or propitiating, that she did not practise on her sister-handmaid from Priam's court.

She had Arsinöe just now entirely to herself, for Odysseus had gone off with Zeuks to present that unusual cattle-dealer, as a queer specimen of an island farmer, to their old family-nurse, Eurycleia. Time and place and circumstance therefore all played into Okyrhöe's hands and she threw such a thrilling intensity into what she was doing that she would have taken Arsinöe completely by storm if the latter had not possessed her own secret loyalties: but even these were troubled and shaken; for the girl accepted without question—being all the while herself the hero's child—the grotesque lie that Okyrhöe was a daughter of Hector. "You have the very look of his eyes!" Arsinöe cried. As a matter of fact even while she was uttering this ridiculous cry, and very largely because of the honest vehemence with which she uttered it, this impassioned carver of the features she had idealized from childhood, in complete ignorance of her blood-relationship to their possessor, not only revealed their outlines in her own face but imagined she found them where in reality there wasn't a trace of them.

To meet a sister-member of that girlish band of devoted hero-worshippers from Ilium was in itself an event that brought with it almost unbearable emotion, but to meet a woman who called Hector father loosened, as we say, Arsinoë's knees and melted her reserved heart. It was therefore in the sobs of her compatriot upon her beautiful bosom, a bosom no longer entirely concealed under the skin of the Podandrikon, a creature whose name, owing to its association with some mysterious oriental court-fashion, must always, so its wearer had explained to Zeuks as on their ride the night-wind whistled through it, be pronounced with the stress on the syllable "dand", that Okyrhöe won her first victory in the palace of the king of Ithaca.

It must, however, be allowed that in the bold invader's second encounter with the defenders of this pillared rock-cave the victory was on the other side. The old Eurycleia, who had looked after the wounds, and recognized the scars, and protected the eccentricities, and cured the manias, of three generations, saw through the mask worn so becomingly by this beautiful adventuress at the first glance.

To every point Okyrhöe brought forward the old lady opposed a plain blunt doubt of its essential veracity.

"My rule has always been," she declared at one point, "to obtain the word of a prophet or a teacher known through the whole of Hellas for proof of a family's claim to be connected with this or that hero of the days of our grandparents; and I have never myself accepted the word of a ghost. Odysseus undoubtedly does believe that he met the ghost of Teiresias beyond the brink of Okeanos and made the ghost drink of the blood of the animal he was sacrificing. Moreover I know that Odysseus feels sure that he himself and none other went down into the Underworld ruled over by Aidoneus the brother of Zeus and Poseidon. Indeed everyone who lives near our dear Odysseus has heard him tell stories about the ghosts of the famous heroes and heroines that he encountered in that Kingdom of the Dead.

"But I have seen so much of life in my time, young lady, and if you'll let me cry,' Go away!' or 'erre! erre!' to the bad omen, so much of death too, that when I hear people tell me that they are connected with the family of Peleus or Theseus or

Kadmos or Priam my feeling is simply this: if you have this noble blood in your veins your friends may be the better for it and your enemies the worse for it, but for you yourself life will be the same to you as it is to the rest of us, and death will be no longer in coming, nor kinder in the way in which it comes, than it is to the rest of us; for as my grandmother used to say, and she goes back further than your precious Kadmos, 'the nearer to the First Man the stronger the hand; the nearer to the Last Man the shrewder the head!'

"Thus although it was with her sweetest and most cajoling smile that Okyrhöe bowed herself out of the presence of the king's nurse, her thoughts, as she got the Trojan captive to introduce her to Leipephile, the betrothed of Nisos' brother, and then persuaded that same Arsinöe to take her to a well-cushioned chamber in a low-roofed passage behind the royal throne in the dining-hall, where Pontopereia was talking eagerly to young Eione, were nothing less than murderous.

"O you wait, you wait, you wait, you wait! you croaking and creaking corpse! It won't be you who'll choose the death you'll die. It'll be your meek and obedient Okyrhöe; and it won't be the prettiest death in the world either; I can tell you that."

Meanwhile, hidden away in that chamber at the end of that low-roofed passage between the great dining-hall and the subterranean kitchens and sculleries, where the meals were prepared and washed up and where the floral wreaths and the symbols and all the ritualistic paraphernalia for festival days were kept, Tis's little sister Eione was recounting to Pontopereia her escape from the amorous attentions of the god Pan.

"But didn't you feel," Pontopereia had just dared to suggest, "so spell-bound under his touch that you longed to yield to him?"

The two young girls were sitting cross-legged on opposite piles of Cyprian cushions. Eione was seated on cushions whose. prevailing colour was pale green, and Pontopereia on cushions whose prevailing colour was purple. Eione looked gravely and intently into her friend's eyes.

"No, my dear," she replied, "you'll probably laugh at me as absurdly ignorant, but to tell you the honest truth —"

"You mean you've never really been made love to?"

Eione neither reddened nor stammered. She just frowned and rubbed the sole of one of her sandals with two of her knuckles as if the unravelling of this difficult question required her whole mental concentration.

"I'm not sure whether I have or not," she said simply. "A boy who lives near us pressed me once very tight against him, when neither of us had much on, and I felt something—the thing they all have, I suppose, that makes them men—pounding and throbbing and beating against me like a stick with the pulse of a heart. But it didn't make me want him to do anything; and it didn't frighten me or disturb me. I just noticed it; that's all, and wondered what I'd feel if he did anything else, and whether I ought to help him to do anything else. And then somebody came—and that was all."

Pontopereia gave the purple cushion beneath her a mighty tug with both her hands so that it rose up like a wave between her thighs. "No," she said. "I can't call that quite enough; and to tell you the truth, my sweet one, I've never myself got as far as that—I mean in real life, if you understand. What I've always done, since I was O! so little, is to tell myself stories of love-making when I'm alone in bed. Sometimes I wake up in the night—you know?—feeling very amorous and then I tell myself, O such weird and funny stories—not very nice stories always, I'm afraid! It depends on what I'm feeling that particular night. But do tell me, my Sweet, what you did when Arcadian Pan laid hands on you. And first, do tell me this. Did his thin hairy legs and goat's feet give you the shivers?"

At this point, to Pontopereia's complete astonishment, Eione burst out laughing. "Shivers?" she cried. "I should say not! I like goats very much. Goats are my favourite beasts, just as Crows are my favourite birds, and blue dragon-flies my favourite insects and eels my favourite fish! I begged Arcadian Pan to let me stroke his thin. hairy legs and it wasn't he who made me sit on his queer knees, it was I myself who made him take me on them. And I kept making him lift up his goat-feet so that I could see them quite close and touch them, like I like touching the feet of real goats! Then I made him let me clean his goat's horns for him and polish them till they were lovely and smooth. Then I got him to teach me to make some real proper sounds with his pipe—yes! I played some real notes on Arcadian Pan's own flute!

"Yes, as I'm telling you, Ponty darling, everything between us was just as I liked it to be, in fact as I made it be. The truth is I never knew that great gods—for he *is* a great god, isn't he, Arcadian Pan?—ever let a person treat them, well! certainly not an ordinary farm-girl like me treat them, as he let me treat him!"

Pontopereia pulled out the uppermost one of her purple cushions from between her legs, and spreading it on her knees thumped it with her fists into smoothness.

"But what happened then, my dear? You aren't suggesting, are you, that having made friends with this astonishing Being in such a simple way you were separated from him by a mistake?"

Eione looked at her with a vague careless, idle, good-natured, but entirely childish and innocent look.

"I wish indeed, Ponty dear," she said, slowly, "that you could explain to me what happened for it's all so totally beyond my comprehension that I've been living in a sort of trance of confusion ever since. It's only your coming that's brought me back into my own real self again. Yes, on my soul! I've never had such queer feelings. It's just as if I'd been turned into somebody else; and somebody whose whole life goes by, without any move of her own, just as if she were a figure in another person's dream! I know it sounds all vague and sleepy and funny; but I swear to you, Ponty darling, it's true. Do you think I've fallen in love with Arcadian Pan? Ordinary girls like me *can* fall in love with an immortal god can't they? There's nothing impossible about it is there?

"Anyway, Ponty darling, I don't quite know what has happened to me and that's what's made me decide that, come what may, I *must* stick close to Arcadian Pan for a few more spring days and see what comes of it! One important thing has already come of it and that is our curiously complete agreement over this great cosmic Revolution. Mind you, some of us Island people still talk of the 'Minoan' or 'Cretan' revolution and others still talk of the 'Argive' revolution; but the only revolution that Arcadian Pan and I talk of is what we have come to call the 'Cosmic' Revolution, by which we mean a rustic pastoral revolution against a cruel, despotic, wicked, undemocratic, hieratic, privileged tyrannical Order of the Citizens of great Cities, which we — rustic shepherds and shepherdesses from the country — have joined together to break up forever!"

"But what will you put in its place?" enquired Pontopereia, giving her purple cushion a final caress with both her hands; hands which it must be confessed were not, like those of Eione, the hands of a born dancer.

"Anarchy! Anarchy! Anarchy!" cried the younger girl. "Don't you see, Ponty darling, this revolution of ours, which is really a revolution of the older gods against the newer gods, of the great old giant-gods, animal-gods, dragon-gods, serpent-gods, and, above all, women-gods, for the older times were *matriarchal times*, and women, *not* men, however heroic such men might be, ruled Heaven and Earth, since at the Beginning of things it was Gaia, our real old mother the earth, who gave birth to Ouranos, this holy heaven of hermeneutical humbug, that priests make so much of, and not the other way round! Isn't that a spry word, 'hermeneutical'? He taught me that!

"Yes! the thing that has thrown Arcadian Pan and me together has nothing really to do with his 'taking me', as he tells me they call it in the Arcadian sheep-folds, or his treating me as wives are treated, and it has nothing to do with my feelings, one way or the other.

"What Arcadian Pan feels drawn to do, as far as his treatment of a plain ignorant girl like me is concerned, is to keep his hands off me and the thing that male creatures carry about with them

ATLANTIS

out of me, until what you might call 'the ice' is broken between us; but, to break this 'ice'—which is of course my shyness and nervousness and pride and independence, and also, you needn't smile, my dear! my ignorance—the great thing is for Arcadian Pan and me, and don't 'ee ever think, Ponty my precious, that I don't know what an honour it is for a stupid little kid like me to go about with a great immortal god, especially one with the beautifully-thin hairy legs and the firmly-planted goat-feet of my favourite of all animals!—the great thing, I say, is for Arcadian Pan and me to have the same idea of a proper 'Cosmic Revolution' and the same idea of the kind of Anarchy we must set up in place of this confounded hieratic 'order'.

"What the old Dryad advised—and she told us that though her name 'Kleta' was given her by one of the Graces she was not displeased to bear a name that resembled Keto, the fair-cheeked sea-monster who became the wife of Phorkys, one of those honest 'old Men of the Sea' who *cannot*—and isn't *that* a significant thing in itself?—tell a lie about anything.

"That's what I said this morning to Arcadian Pan, and O! it pleased him so: and though he swore he couldn't be as honest as all that, being a shepherd busy with ewes and nanny-goats and rams, and as a player on the flute for country-girls to follow and as the cause of those sudden, nameless, deep, strange, inexplicable, mysterious, obsessing, panic-terrors which take possession of mortal men and make them scurry and scamper away like rats out of a barn, he liked honesty, he said. And so I told him that the 'old men of the sea,' that is to say the old gods of the sea, were the only 'honest' gods in the world because they lived in water, and water I told him is the one element in the world that *cannot*, in its inherent nature, play dramatic tricks upon us." "What about ships at sea?" thought Pontopereia; but she held her peace; and Eione went on. "Well! we shall want all the help we can get from the outspoken honesty of water if we are to make headway against Zeus, Poseidon, and Aidoneus, each of the three of them a superb master of lies! Yes, what Arcadian Pan and I feel is that these three Sons of Kronos are now trying to combine together, since one is the Ruler of the Sky, one of the Sea, and the other of whatever dark and dreadful world it is that lies beneath the Earth; and that what we revolutionists and rebels have to do is enlist against Zeus and Poseidon and Aidoneus all the subnormal and abnormal and supernormal creatures we can collect together!

"These three most powerful rulers among the Olympians have joined together to suppress with violence and magical force every rebel that is opposed to them and opposed to all the great Olympians who support them!

"Do you realize, Ponty dear, that fresh news has just reached this appalling priest Enorches from his fellow-priests of the Mysteries at Eleusis, informing him that Herakles, who has been guarding Mount Etna to keep that fire-breathing monster Typhon from breaking out, has been persuaded by Dionysos to yield himself up to an orgy of drink; and that while this has been going on, Eros, who had been chained with golden chains by Hephaistos or by some 'Son of Hephaistos', like the one who carved the letters 'U. H.' on the base of the pillar here, yes! chained to the arm of Aphrodite's throne in Cyprus, has broken his bonds and joined Dionysos, and together they have succeeded in throwing Herakles into what amounts to a mad trance of ecstasy, in which condition he has become so completely irresponsible that the monster Typhon has got entirely loose, has left Italy and Sicily altogether, and has gone, fire-breathing, ravaging, rampaging, to where, above the Garden of Hesperides, the Titan Atlas, whose punishment from the Olympians it has been to hold up the sky, is threatening to leave his job? What do you think of all this, Ponty dear? Arcadian Pan and I think that his departure will neither mean the end of the sky nor the end of the earth, but the end of the superiority of the sky over the earth.

"You see, Ponty dear, the garden of the Hesperides lies at the western verge of the entire world where the divine streams of Okeanos encircle the earth, and where once used to be—malediction on those who submerged it! is what Arcadian Pan and I say now—the beautiful sheep-grazed meadows of Lost Atlantis.

I took Arcadian Pan to the oak-tree of the King's old Dryad who was such a friend of Laertes in *his* time, and the Dryad revealed to him certain secrets of the Future of which he, although an immortal, had heard nothing; 'I am about to die', the Dryad said to us, 'or I shouldn't know these things myself.' And it was after our talk with the Dryad that *we decided to intercept Typhon*."

Pontopereia's blank amazement at these astonishing words made her whirl the purple cushion in the air before sitting down on it with a thud.

"You—and Arcadian Pan," she gasped, "intercepting that fire-breathing monster!" As she stared dumbfounded at her young friend, she became aware that the childish innocence in Eione's expression had suddenly changed to something else; and at this point she realized that between herself and this new Eione there was a blank space she couldn't bridge. "How weird," she said to herself, "are the ways by which two minds touch each other and dodge each other!"

And indeed it struck Pontopereia now as if they were the gestures of a complete stranger, when Eione suddenly stood up, opened her mouth as if to speak, but, in place of speaking, yawned, put the back of her left hand with careless indifference against her mouth, and, when her yawn was finished, with a half-smile, as if just waking from a pleasant dream in which she and Arcadian Pan might have been riding Typhon like an obedient horse, stretched both her shapely arms with clenched fists high above her straw-coloured head.

"You see, Ponty dear," she said emphatically as she let her arms fall to her sides. "Not only has this Echidna of Arima borne children to Typhon but the dragon, Ladon, who guards the apples of the Hesperides, is her brother; and there is a good chance that when Poseidon and Aidoneus come on the scene we shall have got Prometheus himself to stand up to them."

Pontopereia looked past her friend into far-receding space. She suddenly felt sad and lonely. Had this rash young girl, without in the least comprehending what was happening to her, fallen in love with Arcadian Pan? Was all that rather hurried and very startling and yet not completely satisfactory account of these great cosmic events an outward and visible sign of a much more personal feeling? Was it actually possible that a simple country girl like this should be subject to vibrations of emotion belonging to a superhuman conflict between Gods and Titans?

Pontopereia experienced just then a very perceptible sense of humiliation. When she had hastened their departure from Ornax she had felt without doubt the spirit of her father descend upon her and the inspiration of her father possess her soul, and she had exulted so much in this and felt so proud of it that it had seemed to her, as she bowed down in intellectual response before the gnomic humility of Zeuks, that her place in the struggle of life was with the great seers and the illumined soothsayers and not with ordinary women and girls.

But in this rough, earthy, primitive, uncomfortable rock-palace of the royal house of Ithaca she felt reduced in stature and importance. Her prophetic power seemed to have deserted her. While she had been listening to what Eione had told her of this news from the priests of Eleusis about the monster Typhon escaping from under Aetna and thundering over sea and land, till he reached the Garden of the Hesperides and the place where Atlas holds up the sky as his punishment, she felt as if without a definite inspiration from her father she had no place in these events and no power of her own to obtain such a place.

She even began to feel a doubt in her mind whether the beautiful and formidable Okyrhöe herself would be able to deal with this rock-hewn palace to which she had insisted on being brought.

With an intellectual candour that went further than the emotional simplicity of her friend she decided that the prophetic power within her must depend on the special atmosphere of particular places. "I don't believe," she told herself, "it will sweep me away at all here. Well, if I'm not destined, after all, to be a prophetess, *I'm not*, and that's all there is to be said! *But I wish Nisos was here.*"

This frank admission, so nakedly expressed, was a great relief to her; she felt as if in the midst of putting on the ritualistic robes for the worship of one of the greater Olympians she had suddenly snatched the things off and thrown them on the floor and rushing out into the open air danced on the grass the first dancing-steps she had learnt as a child.

Meanwhile since Nisos' brother had carried away the other virginal attendant it was natural that the two woman who had known Ilium and the Court of King Priam should drift off together. As may be imagined with one like Okyrhöe to deal with, it did not take Arsinöe very long to discover that this lovely creature who put on the skin of the fabulous "Podandrikon" to accompany her to the haunted area of Arima and who seemed to find that to talk about the importance of accentuating the syllable "dand" in this harsh word was the best way of keeping their Trojan emotion in its place, had the same will as herself to thwart, frustrate and bring to a disastrous and contemptible end, the one single aim of the old age of Odysseus, his desire to sail across the sunken towers of Atlantis into the Unknown West.

Over their bowed feminine heads as they moved through Arima, defying the dark influences of that sinister region, there moaned and wailed, just as over the drowned temples of Atlantis Odysseus might have heard his ship's rigging respond to the wind, the eternally monotonous dialogue between Echidna the mother of the Hound of Hell, and Eurybia the grandmother of Hekate.

But when, in the golden afternoon light, Okyrhöe was led by her new ally into the very presence of what looked like the absolute reality of the fully-armed Hector himself, her nerves did for an instant, for all their superhuman control, break into a choking gasp. For not only were Hector's lineaments represented in exact correspondence to the living truth but there was something about the curves of his broad low forehead that exactly resembled the shape of Arsinöe's head. She recovered quickly however; and they were returning in a deliberately loitering fashion; for Arsinöe had begun to explain to the visitor that Odysseus grew irritable if he had to speak to guests or even to catch sight of guests while dinner was preparing though she admitted that the old hero had come by this time to look upon his unaristocratic companion, Zeuks, as an intimate; but the two women's leisureliness at this moment received a shock that was as disturbing as it was startling.

By a grotesque piece of ill-luck they encountered the old Dryad Kleta; an encounter which brought them both down with a disagreeable jolt to the very things in Odysseus' life that they would have preferred to ignore just then, that is to say to the human pathos of his present situation, as an extremely old man without a wife, or a daughter, or a grand-daughter, whose only son had become an austere, inhuman, unsympathetic recluse and a devotee of some contemplative cult, about which, save that it had nothing to do with Dionysos or Eros, and was in no favour with Enorches, it was very hard to get any information.

The old Dryad stood in front of them for a perceptible number of pulse-beats, staring at them as if they were trespassers and intruders of an extremely suspicious kind; not necessarily outsiders to be crushed as we crush black-beetles but entities to beware of and to be guarded against.

The old lady already knew Arsinoë by sight and was fully aware she was Trojan; and her first thought was that Okyrhöe must have just arrived by sea from the same part of the country. It may be believed she did not miss the royal eccentricity of the fabulous Podandrikon skin; and her mind began vaguely flapping like an aged phantom albatross from one to another of all the far-off harbours of which she had ever heard, leaving, as it flew, a feather caught in the sea-weed of one promontory and a splash of white dropping upon the rocks of another.

"Take notice, proud visitor," she murmured, and then, with a quick glance at Arsinoë, "but you've been warned already, that we have to guard our renowned Odysseus from every agitating shock until the moment comes when he has got his ship ready to hoist sail and to sail away whither none of us will ever know! But sail he must and sail he will—away—away—away; and our duty now is to make everything as easy for him as we can until that heaven-appointed moment. Therefore, proud one, from far off, the best thing I can say to you is to bid you go—go quickly—go quietly—go at once! If you came by sea, find a ship and be off!

"There are ships sailing from this side of our island and there are ships sailing from the other side of our island. You wouldn't be here if you hadn't gold to pay your way. Well, stranger, find a ship and pay the master of that ship to take you to the harbour nearest the place where you would be!"

Okyrhöe made an effort to look more than humanly lovely and her features had certainly never been as goddess-like as at that moment. The sun was still overhead, though his tremendous arsenal of refulgence had sunk sufficiently from the Zenith to pour itself into every curve and cranny of Okyrhöe's countenance.

There are faces that cannot endure exposure of this kind, but Okyrhöe's face could endure anything. Indeed it looked to Arsinöe as she glanced at her companion that the intense emotion in the old Dryad's voice stirred up in the beautiful wearer of the Podandrikon skin a quivering vibration of self-assertion that rushed like a sea-breath touched by fire through nerves and veins and muscles and fibres and cells.

But if this rush of abnormal magnetism affected the recipient of the old Dryad's words, it also affected the Dryad herself. It did more than affect her. Leaving them helplessly standing there— and where she left them they remained; for nothing else at that moment seemed possible—she rushed wildly, blindly, desperately into the centre of Arima. Midway between the two figures of Eurybia and Echidna she paused for a moment, staring at them both like one deprived of speech by reason of the intensity of the feeling that possessed her. Then she cried out in a resonant voice that rang from end to end of that haunted enclosure, "Goddesses! Goddesses! Goddesses! Goddesses! worshipped for fifty thousand years in Argos and Ionia and Crete and Achaia and Lakedaimon! There is a battle going on that will never be repeated if it is not won now!

"It is a battle to restore to us women the ruling position we held at the beginning of things! In the reign of Kronos we held it—and *that* age was the Age of Gold. But it is Zeus the son of Kronos who has taken it from us, partly by his thunderbolts and partly by the cunning and strength of his two sons, Hermes and Herakles. Goddesses! My goddesses! You who have been worshipped in Ithaca for fifty-thousand years, harken unto me now!

"Persephone, the Queen of Hades, has left her Lord Aidoneus, and is now roaming the world seeking for her mother Demeter. But Hermes, that cunning one, has gone to both Aidoneus and Poseidon, yes! both to the Lord of Hades and the Lord of the Sea, and has brought them to the Garden of the Hesperides near the place where Atlas, as a punishment from Zeus, holds up the sky. And from there the three Olympian brothers, Zeus, Lord of the Sky, Poseidon Lord of the Sea, and Aidoneus, Lord of the Underworld, have resolved to resist this attempt of us women, led by Persephone, to seize again the universal rule and power that we once possessed. The great Olympian goddesses are wavering and have hidden themselves away. Athene has gone to Ethiopia.

"Hera is still alone on Olympos, but in a state of distraction. She has sent Iris to Ethiopia with frantic messages to Athene to return! But Iris seems unable to discover where Athene is hiding. Dionysos and Eros together are doing what Aphrodite cannot do; for Hephaistos has caught *her* in Lemnos and is keeping her a prisoner there.

"But Dionysos and Eros have between them ensorcerized the powerful Herakles and laid him low with Desire and Drink, so that Typhon breathing fire and up-rooting mountains can now drag forth Briareos from Tartaros this time for the dethroning, not the throning of Zeus! O great Echidna, Mother of the Sphinx, the Chimera, the Hydra and the Nemean Lion, help us now! O great Eurybia, grandmother of Hekate and daughter of Gaia the Earth and Pontos the Sea, help us now!

"And harken unto me, ye two, for I have great news! Arcadian Pan himself, yes! Pan with the beautiful horns and the hairy legs of a real living goat, has revolted against his time-serving, treacherous, cunning, thieving, lying begetter, Hermes, and is now, even now, leading by their bridles those two godlike horses Pegasos and Arion, so cruelly mutilated by Enorches the Priest of the Mysteries.

"And why, O great Goddesses, is he leading them? He is leading them with the idea of offering them to you Eurybia, of wide rule, daughter of Gaia and Pontos! He is leading them with the idea of offering them to you Echidna, daughter of Phorkys and Keto! He is leading them with the idea of being himself their rider and your guide and helping you to intercept Typhon in his fire-breathing course from Sicily to the Garden of the Hesperides, and make use of him, as huntresses make use of savage dogs, to defeat the Son of Kronos even though he is supported by Aidoneus, the Lord of the Dead, and Poseidon the Lord of the Sea.

"And then, when this resounding victory is won, this victory to which Atropos the oldest of the Fates who is a woman like ourselves will contribute her aid, we shall welcome completely to our side the wavering Hera and the wandering—""

She was interrupted by a long, melodious, vibrant, tremulous note of music which was so penetrating and far-reaching that it was impossible not to receive it into your inmost identity like a perfect draught of wine. Without any other declaration, or sign, or warning, or announcement, the two godlike horses entered that haunted enclosure, Arcadian Pan repeating from the flute he pressed to his bearded mouth that same meltingly sweet note over and over and over and over.

Pan himself was mounted on Pegasos, and the young girl Eione on Arion; and she certainly seemed to be riding Arion easily and naturally and as if entirely at her own volition.

"Lady Okyrhöe!" cried Eione, as they came even with the two women; and into this salutation the young girl threw exactly the right note of respect and courtesy.

As Eione later discussed what they managed to achieve with Arcadian Pan—for it was remarkable how quickly she felt completely at ease with the goat-foot god—they agreed that it was peculiarly and specially lucky for the success of their scheme that in former times, so rumour said, Echidna had been embraced by the monster Typhon and not only so, but, as one story declared, had given birth by him to the Hydra of Lerna, if not to the famous victim of the club of Herakles, the Nemean Lion itself! But whatever were the feelings, mortal or immortal, of the riders upon those divine horses, the impression they produced upon the two women was noticeable.

Never to the end of her days did Arsinoë forget what she then beheld. Okyrhöe took it all more lightly, for her whole life had been such a tissue of murderous tensions and such a chain of deep-plotted explosions that for life's events to jerk and bleed and jitter and squeal as you dragged them clinging to your scraping harrow over the rough and smooth of fate seemed natural enough.

But apparently those two strange Beings, Eurybia and Echidna who for years and years and years had sighed obscurely, darkly, obstinately, and in a sort of ghastly antiphonic ritual at each other in horrible isolation across the dedicated unholiness of their island Arima, now found themselves bound to move, just as if Atropos herself were in person directing the operation; and there was something about their having to move after so long that was almost geological, giving the impression that the places from which they moved were left raw and in some way not only bloody and excremental but scoriae, volcanic, and like what is left when an avalanche moves.

Echidna instinctively selected Pegasos as her horse and Pan as her companion, while Eurybia slid easily and inevitably upon the back of Arion. Each of these formidable goddesses, however, had the good sense to allow her fellow-rider to hold the bridle-reins of the particular animal she rode; so that as Okyrhöe the pretended daughter of Hector saw them pass that hero's carved image, and as Arsinoë, his real daughter, saw the hoof of one of the horses fling a clod of mud against the figure she had broken her heart to carve and bruised her flesh to arm, it was upon Eione and Pan that their attention was fixed rather than upon the two goddesses; and as they listened to that exquisitely magnetic flute-note from the pipe of Pan dying away in the distance long after both horses with their four riders had disappeared, the drift of their separate moods opened between them like a yawning gulf, the mood of the wearer of that weird Podandrikon growing as tense as the mood of a general in the midst of the bloodiest part of a battle, while the mood of the daughter of Hector fell into that sadness, proud and bitter and rejecting all sympathy, which had become her prevailing attitude to life.

Had the girl possessed any real friend, had Nisos, for instance, not been so much younger, or Leipephile not so extremely simple, she might have been drawn out of this embittered isolation, for it was so long after the Trojan War that the ancient rancours in most ordinary minds were beginning to lose their edge, if not to wear out. If only Eurycleia hadn't been so old it might have been different; but of all people an ancient family-nurse, and one who had nursed, as Eurycleia had, three generations of the same breed, would be the last to have any sensitized imagination left over for sympathetic consideration of the feelings of an alien.

It wasn't until those heart-breakingly sweet notes—or rather the last long-drawn-out unequalled note—of Pan's flute had died away that either Arsinoë or Okyrhöe gave a thought to the old Dryad who was the prime instigator of this disturbing event.

When they did turn to her it was simultaneously and with an equal feeling of something like real awe. "Let us help you home to your oak, Dryad," whispered Okyrhöe; and if Nisos had heard that whisper, to which Arsinoë added a less articulate murmur, he would have had a thrill of real pride at being a native of a Grecian isle rather than of a Trojan or a Theban plain, for clearly so great is the power of a Greek Nymph even in her extreme old age that formidable foreigners are subdued before her.

As they approached the skeleton oak-tree on the bark of which flourished a special kind of rich green moss, as if the tree were already horizontal rather than perpendicular, the Dryad's supporters both recognized that it was possible to look through the interstices of the bark into the interior wood of the tree which was split into long splintery filaments between which there were already oozing out and crumbling upon the lichen-covered ground certain thick masses of a reddish-brown substance which was the clotted heart-stuff or dust-resolved liver, or conglomerated entrail-matter, of that fast-perishing old tree.

Suddenly the Dryad stood dead-still between them, and laid one withered hand on the sleeve of Okyrhöe and one on the sleeve of Arsinöe.

"Give my farewell to Odysseus, you two. My name-mother is one of the Graces and just at this moment I felt her passing over me, warning me of my end. Zeus, it seems has got one last thunder-bolt left, a very little one, but large enough to dispose of my oak and me. Lest either of you should feel the shock of my destruction, it is important that you should hasten away. Don't stop running till you reach the entrance to the Hall of the Pillars. There you will be safe. Fare ye well. Let my memory be forgotten!"

So intense was the tone of her words that although all was silent round them Okyrhöe snatched at Arsinöe's hand and together they fled like a pair of panic-stricken pigeons. They did not stop running till they reached the entrance to the corridor of the Pillars; and then, when they did stop at last with their hands still clasped tight, each of them could hear clearly the beating of her own heart as well as that of her companion. In fact as they stood there in a sort of trance there arose from the pair of them a kind of mathematical and mechanical and wholly impersonal heart-beating, which went on till, in one single blinding flash of lightning, followed by a rolling clap of thunder, the Nymph and the oak-tree, and the stretch of ground where the oak-tree's roots had been, were reduced simultaneously to black ashes.

"What I don't understand, dear nurse," Odysseus was saying at that moment, as together with his new friend Zeuks he watched Eurycleia's face as he explained his ideas for the calling of the whole people together to listen to his plan for sailing across the drowned continent Atlantis. "What I don't understand is your objection to my telling the people exactly what I intend

ATLANTIS

to do. Why shouldn't I tell them, Nurse darling? I shall say that what I want for my sailing is the most necessary thing of all—namely 'othonia' or sail-cloth.

"And I'll call upon them all, upon the whole people of Ithaca to collect sail-cloth for me. What can Krateros Naubolides do to stop the people, my own people of Ithaca, that were my father's people before me, from collecting enough 'othonia' or sail-cloth for my purpose? And then, you see, Nurse darling, if they begin making the excuse that it's wrong for me, Odysseus the son of Laertes, to leave the rule of this Island to others, I've got this brilliant, eloquent, inspired young daughter of Teiresias to help me with them. Don't you see, Nurse, how she'll make all the difference at this open 'agora' and meeting-place of our people? I'll call on her, as we used to call on all those prophets of old; and, girl though she is, she'll do the trick for us, Nurse, my honey! Now do, for the sake of all the gods tell me what's weighing on your dear mind, for I know *something* is! Are you afraid that secretive scoundrel Enorches has got some new trick up his sleeve, some dirty, crafty, clever trick that I've never thought of, that he will play on me at the last moment?"

Eurycleia gazed intently at him, frowning. Then she suddenly shifted in her seat and stared out of the window. Then she addressed herself to Zeuks. "Did you hear anything, Master?" "I certainly did!" Zeuks answered; and in his turn addressed the King.

"I expect you must have heard it too, my Lord? It didn't sound as ordinary thunder does at this time of the year either! Something's going on."

The old Nurse rose, not without difficulty, and confronted the two men from her full height, one hand resting on the arm of her chair. Her stark gaunt figure towered imposingly over them in the afternoon sunlight which was now pouring into the chamber.

"I think you are right, Master Zeuks," she said quietly. "If I'm not greatly mistaken that wasn't ordinary lightning or ordinary thunder. That was a thunderbolt from—— ""

It was then that there came a hurried step outside Eurycleia's chamber and with all her simple impulsiveness Leipephile burst in.

The tall beautiful stupid girl was panting like a hunted animal. "What on earth is it?" asked the old Nurse. "What's happened? Was that a thunderbolt?"

"They're in the Porch," stammered Leipephile, recovering her breath with difficulty.

"Who are in the Porch?" cried the Nurse. "For the god's sake tell us what's happened, girl!"

"The strange lady in that funny cloak and Arsinöe."

"Well—why shouldn't they be in the Porch? Are they hurt? What's happened?"

"They say that Zeus has thrown a thunderbolt from Mount Gargaros, where he is looking down on the Garden of the Hesperides and on Atlas holding up the sky, and on Poseidon coming up out of the Sea; and on Aidoneus coming up out of Hades. They've just met the old Dryad——"" Here Odysseus interrupted her. "Met Kleta the Dryad, do you say, girl? What on earth was she doing all that way from her tree?"

"It is the Dryad *and* her tree, O king," replied the betrothed of Nisos' brother; and she spoke with less timidity and shyness now that she was delivering, or being delivered of, her chief news. "Yes, both the Dryad and her tree together, that the Son of Kronos has destroyed with a thunderbolt. The Dryad told them that the thunderbolt he was going to use was a little one and the last he had where he then was. But they told me to tell you that they know why the son of Kronos was angry with the Dryad." At this point Leipephile paused in her tale and surveyed her audience with the self-satisfied expression that implies the presence of news in the wind that can't be blurted out in a few words, and can't possibly be divined or guessed at, even by the cleverest listener. Her three hearers, not missing this expression, patiently imitated Eurycleia who had now resumed her seat at the table.

"It was," Leipephile went on, with obviously deep satisfaction at having such an important tale to relate to headquarters, "it was the goat-foot god Pan who began it all by consorting with the girl Eione—though I don't think he meddled with her maidenhead. The god Pan and the girl Eione were riding on Pegasos and Arion. And when the Dryad saw this she persuaded the goddesses Eurybia and Echidna who have for so long ruled over that place—" and Leipephile made a vague gesture with her hand in the general direction of Arima—"that place—you know—where everybody's scared of going—and what the Dryad told them to do was this. She told them, that is she told Eurybia and Echidna and Eione and Pan, all four mounted on Pegasos and Arion, to intercept the Monster Typhon and by a little bribing and petting and cozening and cosseting and coaxing—and a few terrifying threats too perhaps!—to make use of him as a savage hunting-dog; and, thus well-prepared for any event, to approach the Garden of the Hesperides."

There was a long silence when the girl had finished. Then Odysseus enquired: "Could you tell me, dear child, could any of you tell me, do you think, where the daughter of Teiresias has got to this afternoon while all these unexpected events have been occurring?" Leipephile stared at him with her mouth open, while Eurycleia and Zeuks exchanged a look by which the former said to the latter:

"Here's a typical monarch! Having made all this fuss to get hold of this damned girl, he now has let her escape!" while the latter said to the former: "We had better find out exactly from the woman in that weird cloak what kind of trouble this Pontopereia has fallen into on a fine afternoon."

But before they ceased to look at each other there were more light steps outside the door and Pontopereia herself appeared.

"Where's Eione?" she asked; and then seeing Odysseus she added: "Pardon me, great King, but they told me down there such a mad story that I had to come and see for myself! They said Eione had gone off with the goat-foot god and with two mysterious goddesses who for twenty years or more have been arguing together in a haunted place near here you call Arima."

"They seem to have told you the truth, child," replied

Odysseus. "But now that you're here the best thing you and I can do is to arrange a definite plan of campaign for ourselves at the 'agora' tomorrow. So sit you down here and have a sip of my wine. This is our Eurycleia. Yes, give her one of those cups you like using best yourself, Nurse."

Unlike many men of genius, whether in thought or in action, Odysseus was always vividly aware of the feelings of women; and he now glanced from Pontopereia to Leipephile and back again to Pontopereia.

"This lady," he explained to the latter, "is the betrothed of our young friend Nisos' elder brother, who, quite naturally, takes the side of their father Krateros Naubolides in our little island-feud. The pleasantest thing for you, my dear child"—he was addressing Leipephile now—"will be to have a quiet supper by yourself tonight and to go to bed early; for in this way you'll escape being torn between your loyalty to us and your affection for our opponents."

The tall simple girl didn't appear to object in the very least to being thus lightly dismissed from so momentous a Council of War; and after a nod from Eurycleia had confirmed the king's word, and after the kindly-natured Zeuks had muttered something about her being sure not to forget to have a good supper, she went off at once.

Then at last the party round the old Nurse gathered closely together to plan, as Odysseus had declared it was essential they should do, the general outline of his appeal to the people. But Odysseus had still got at the back of his consciousness a rooted feeling that there was something in Eurycleia's mind with regard to all that had happened and all that was happening which it was important for him to know.

But it was not until he and Zeuks had mapped out pretty definitely their plan of campaign for to-morrow's meeting in the "agora", and had decided to send the heralds at early dawn round the whole island to announce it, that in a single hurriedly pronounced word the old Nurse revealed what it was. Telemachos! Yes, it was his son; his son, who like a wooden dagger, with a handle at one end and a point at the other end, had got himself caught fast in the consciousness of the old nurse. Yes, it was the "eidolon" of his son Telemachos she had in her mind, teasing and perplexing her with misgivings of every sort.

It must have been approaching the hour for supper when Odysseus discovered what Eurycleia had in her mind. "One thing seems certain," he said, "and that is that this appalling Enorches hasn't made the faintest, no! not the very faintest impression on him! What *does* he think of that retreat of his, which this devil of a priest has certainly curtailed to pretty small quarters?"

"Another thing seems certain too," added the old Nurse; and going to the door at the back of her room she opened it and called down the passage. Then with the servant who answered her call she held a brief conversation, in the middle of which, telling the girl to wait a moment, she returned to Odysseus. "It seems certain to me," she told him gravely, "that your son really must, for all his philosophizing, feel lonely sometimes and want to get a glimpse of his Dad. I know I want to get a glimpse of *him*; and I think the Lady Penelope would feel that old Nurse Eurycleia ought to have this wish gratified. Do you mind if I send somebody—Tis, if he's about just now—to bid him come to supper tonight? There'll be *as it is* two women-guests and only one man-guest, so he will make up the table; and you at the head and your own Nurse at the foot will behold the board complete. So may I send Tis or somebody to bid him to come?"

Across Odysseus' countenance flapped like the wings of a black crow a momentary shadow of serious discomfort; but he had the strength to blot it out so completely that it was as if it had never been there. He nodded with the crushing acceptance and finality of Zeus. "Send anyone you wish and tell them in the Kitchen to prepare supper for two men and two women in addition to thee and me."

The old lady went back to the waiting serving-girl with this message. "She says Tis is there and she will tell him to go," she reported to the King on her return; and so it was settled, and that very evening Telemachos came. Nor among those sitting round the table in the throne-room at the end of the corridor of Pillars was there one who regretted this sudden resolve of the old Nurse to see her last Infant of the House as a noble-looking middle-aged man of fifty, sitting side by side with Zeuks, and opposite Okyrhöe and Pontopereia.

And the best of it was that the routine of custom in that royal dwelling made the whole thing easy. For the people in the Kitchen were always wont to bring the dishes up to a table just behind the royal throne and leave them there: from which position Leipephile and Arsinöe and Tis himself carried them round and then stood behind the throne of Odysseus while all the guests ate and drank at their leisure.

As might have been expected Okyrhöe was deeply impressed by the handsomeness and dignity of Telemachos; and as for Pontopereia she couldn't resist permitting a passionate prayer to Athene to embody itself in words in her mind: a prayer that if she should be called upon to utter words of prophetic insight in the presence of this silent, austere, good-looking man, with such broad-shoulders and such an intensely abstracted look on his stern face, she might be true to herself, true to her inspiration, and true to the great goddess who would use her as a reed through which to pour forth the rhythmic waves of her message to the world.

Their meal that night was indeed only half through when, constrained by a sudden urge whose origin was wholly obscure to her, Pontopereia asked Telemachos a plain direct unequivocal question.

"What would you say, My Lord Telemachos, was the real heart of your teaching? I mean the sort of thing you would have to explain to any student of philosophy, whether a boy or a girl, who wished to be considered as your proper disciple?"

Telemachos glanced quickly and a little uneasily at his father as if to assure himself that the old man would not mind his launching out upon such a topic at such a time; but as he received no warning against it, and, in place of that, saw something resembling the flicker of a benevolent smile cross his progenitor's face, he addressed himself to Pontopereia with sincere pleasure.

And the truth was that the longer she listened to him the more did Pontopereia feel drawn to the man and thankful she had risked her question. "He's lonely;" she told herself, "he's lonely and unhappy. He's invented this philosophy of his to fill a void. His philosophy is his kingdom, his wife, his children, his weapons, his ships, his ploughs, his horses, his granaries." And indeed his words, when he spoke, almost humorously fulfilled her prediction.

"I would tell this imaginary disciple of mine, lady," he said, "to make philosophy a substitute for every kind of success he can possibly want—no! more than a substitute, a fulfilment! I would say: 'What do you really want from life?' You've probably never asked yourself! Few of us do when we're young. But anyone who has watched you will know you've wanted the satisfaction of your hunger, your thirst, your lust, your hunting spirit, your fighting spirit, your collecting mania, your athletic mania, your building mania, your passion to be beautiful, to be a great artist, to be desired by many. Well, and what have you already attained in regard to this desire of yours? You've got the rudiments, the embryonic beginnings of all of them. You've got a body and a soul. You are a human being. You are living on the earth with the ocean around the earth, and the sun and the moon above the earth, and the stars above the sun and the moon, and the eternal ether above the stars.

"Well! consider your situation. You are a separate individual. You are a lonely individual. And though you may have got parents and brothers and sisters your happiness depends upon your own feelings for life, not upon their feelings for life nor upon their feelings for you. Well! you are surrounded by things that are made of the four elements, made of earth, made of fire, made of water, made of air. Very good. You have the power of embracing these things: of seizing upon them and embracing them so closely that you become one with each one of them.

"But these things, although like yourself they are separate and individual, are made up, just as you are yourself, of the four elements. Very well then! It is clear that when you, a human being, embrace the earth, you are embracing something made of the same material that you are made of. That is to say that a person made of air, water, earth, fire, is embracing other objects or entities or beings, also made of earth, fire, water, air. Thus with your mind and all your senses, thus with your body and all your soul you become one with the whole earth and with the ocean that surrounds the earth, one with the sun and moon, and one with the stars, and one with the immeasurable divine ether that surrounds the stars. Your body and your soul by this embrace become one with the body and the soul of the divine ether and with all that it surrounds. Earth, ocean, sun, moon, stars, ether, they are now one living thing; and to this one living thing, you, a separate living thing, are now joined in an inseparable embrace.

"You, and these things, now become one, have now become a larger one, an immeasurable one, but you still have the power in yourself, the terrific inexhaustible power in yourself, to work upon; to influence, to direct, to drive, to move this New Enormity, this vast new world, this world which you have created by embracing what you have embraced. In one sense therefore you have thus created a new world by joining the old world. Yes, you have created a new earth and ocean and sun and moon and a new immeasurable divine ether.

"Nor do you stop with this; for you go on working upon, and driving, and forcing, and moving, and directing, and re-creating, this immeasurable earth-ocean-sun-moon-ether, moulding it nearer and nearer to the secret desire of your heart; that is to say moulding this newly created earth-ocean-sun-moon-ether, and compelling it to obey your will.

"Now you may naturally say that you are only one of the innumerable separate individual lives who are working and willing and re-creating and re-moulding this existent one or super-one made of earth-ocean-sun-moon-stars and immeasurable depths of divine ether; and you will be perfectly right in saying this. You *are* only one of the many wills who are driving this earth-ocean-sun-moon-stars and immeasurable depths of ether forward upon its way. *Its way whither?*

"Ah! that is the impenetrable secret of which you are yourself a living part and a partial creator. You, a secret agent, have an obscure purpose in your mind; and so have your innumerable fellow-agents driving the universe *on its way*; but on its way *to what* —ah! *that* remains an impenetrable secret!"

Having completed his discourse Telemachos gave Pontopereia a hurried smile and a friendly but rather stiff little bow and once again, as at the beginning of his words, turned his head and glanced hurriedly and a little apprehensively at his father. Pontopereia missed nothing of these two motions; and from the nature of his smile, and from the quality of that respectful little obeisance addressed to herself, she clearly took in, as it can be believed the sharp-witted Okyrhöe did also, more of the man's own essential character than was revealed in the vague and obscure method of philosophizing he had been at such pains to advocate.

Telemachos had his father's massive, clear-cut, majestic, and severe cast of features. Where the general outline of their faces differed, apart from the fact that the old hero had a beard while his son was clean-shaved, was that Odysseus's features were rugged and rock-like while Telemachos's were like smoothly polished marble. Of the two of them, the son was the handsomer, the father the more easy-going, humorous and informal.

As you looked at the two of them you could see the effect of the fact that the father's life had been passed, and was still being passed, in a constant and lively stream of contact with friends and enemies, while the son's was now being divided between solitary walks along the edge of the sea and meditations in a small chamber surrounded by deep recesses full of parchment-rolls, either inscribed by the careful fingers and the exquisitely prepared pigments of ancient Sumeria, or by the less careful and much more daring imagination of the artists of Crete.

ATLANTIS

Telemachos could have devoted the closing periods of his discourse to an eloquent analysis of the nature of the cosmos, and of the part played in that nature by the four elements, as well as by the souls of the living entities, who are, as he explained, urging and driving and steering forward the whole body of life, and he probably would have done so, had he not suddenly felt in the depths of his being an inexpressible longing to escape from the whole business; not only from the urging and driving and stirring, not only from the desperate willing and the heroic share, if only an infinitesimal share, in the creation of the future, but from the things in themselves; yes! from the ancient earth herself, mother of us all, from the sun and the moon and the stars and from the divine ether;—from it all, from it all, from it all!

Yes, at that moment with everything that was deepest in his nature he wanted to escape from the whole struggle of life. Life from the start had been to him more of an effort than a pleasure. The fact of his childhood and boyhood having been passed in the absence of his father and in the invasion of their rock-palace by those insolent suitors had inflicted a bruise, a discoloration, upon his whole nature from which it had never entirely recovered.

Something about the gesture with which he now put both his elbows on the table and rested his forehead on his hands was in no wise missed by Okyrhöe, who was not at all anxious that this meal, so luckily, dexterously, and crucially arranged, if only by pure chance, should break up without certain definite advantages for herself having been established.

"What," she enquired suddenly of Telemachos, "is your feeling about this curious ride of Eione with Arcadian Pan on the backs of Pegasos and Arion, and carrying with them Echidna and Eurybia? The whole idea of it, they tell me, was of the old Dryad's urging and it seems that she and her oak-tree have together paid the penalty. But why Zeus should have been angry if the object of the ride was to intercept Typhon I fail to see. Your father has explained—haven't you, my King?— what an event in the history of Ithaca it is, this departure from Arima, well! from our whole island, of these two strange Beings.

ATLANTIS

"But what, I confess, puzzles me still, my Lord Telemachos, is this; and upon this I would like to hear your opinion. Are we to assume from the fact that Arcadian Pan and the girl Eione have gone off together that between this sweet-natured young creature and the goat-foot god there is, from now on, an authentic love-affair?

"Under ordinary conditions I am not inquisitive; and I know your father, our venerated King here, would not wish any of us to ask impertinent questions in these personal matters; but this is a most extraordinary and unusual expedition including not only Arcadian Pan but two powerful goddesses, one of them Eurybia, daughter of Gaia and Pontos and sister of Phorkys and of Nereus, and the other Echidna, who is said to have given birth to the Hydra of Lerna by this very same Typhon whom they are intending to waylay.

"In the first place, my Lord Telemachos, what puzzles me is that the ancient Dame of whom I caught a glimpse just now, and with whom I had the honour of a brief conversation when your revered Father took me into her presence, I am speaking of course of your old family-nurse, should have allowed a girl as young as Eione to go off on this wild adventure alone with Arcadian Pan and those two terrifying Goddesses who no doubt ruled over Ithaca and Achaea and Argos and Boeotia and Lakedaimon in the primeval far-away times before our mother the Earth gave birth to the Gods or the Titans or even to the mortal or immortal nymphs.

"In Thebes where my youth was spent a girl as young as Eione would still be in the care of her parents. Are your customs in this Island of Ithaca completely different from those on the mainland?"

There was a general silence. With what was quite clearly the faintest possible flickering of a smile at the left corner of his crafty mouth and with what was a definite movement of his beard in the direction of the Corridor of the Pillars, Odysseus saved his son, whom these significant questions had obviously embarrassed a good deal, from having to be the interpreter of local custom, by making use of the most primitive and also the most royal of all forms of summons.

Loudly, vigorously, and several times, he clapped his hands. Had he been a King in Jerusalem, or a Pharaoh in Egypt, he could not have clapped his hands with quicker effect. All the four guests present at that table, Telemachos, Zeuks, Okyrhöe, Pontopereia; not to speak of the attendants, including Arsinöe, who were holding wine-jugs and water-bottles and bread-platters behind the backs of these four persons, became as alert as if they expected this startling and oriental summons to result in the appearance of a troop of Harpies.

But, after a deep silence, the husky, hoarse voice of the old Nurse Eurycleia was heard from the end of the long dark passage leading to the kitchen. "What do you want?" were the direct and downright words that reached their ears.

"Send up Tis," was the king's imperative answer; and when Tis arrived, clearly somewhat disturbed and uncomfortable, Odysseus told him with a rough, humorous, blunt emphasis upon the word *maid*, to explain to the Lady Okyrhöe from Thebes how it was that he allowed a maid as young as Eione to go off on such an adventurous excursion alone with Arcadian Pan and two such formidable goddesses as Eurybia and Echidna.

Tis came forward to the left of the king's chair upon the arm of which he boldly rested his hand as he spoke. It was as clear to Okyrhöe and Pontopereia as it was to Zeuks that he was accustomed to doing this, and although feeling awkward and uncomfortable was so thoroughly used to speaking his mind before Odysseus that he was by no means tonguetied in the king's presence or in the presence of any guests.

"My little sister," he said, "like the rest of us, has been brought up to take care of herself. We have never been people to be afraid of the gods and where there are a lot of sheep-folds there have always been occasional visits from the great god Pan who likes the company of mortal girls as much as he likes the company of mortal or immortal Nymphs. My little sister Eione has always looked after her maidenhead shrewdly enough as well as briskly and boldly among the lads of the farms round us. So at our end of the island, if you understand, we would never be worried or scared if a sister of ours made friends with Arcadian Pan. Us all do know, ye must understand, that 'tis natural for Arcadian Pan to want a maid like she, and us all do know too that if Arcadian Pan did take she's maidenhead, and she did bear a child to he, that child would be, whether it were a he-child or a she-child, half a god and half of an ordinary person; and what we do feel at our end of this dumb little island is that when once a girl has got through her labour-pains and has laid her baby, whether that baby be a man-child or a god-child, a mortal child or an immortal child, safe on the steps of the altar, she's done pretty well for herself and has got a very nice start in life.

"Life's a hard game is what us do think at our end of this rocky isle, and if a girl like our Eione gets through the hard part of being had by a man and the still harder part of having a baby-man, what us do feel, at our end of this funny-shaped island, is that she hasn't done so badly for herself."

Having thus spoken Tis looked at his island's king, seated in the throne of Laertes, and wondered in his insular heart how it was that in so simple a matter as Arcadian Pan's attraction to Eione and her rural predisposition to his thin goatish shanks compared with the more human limbs of other possible lovers it should have been necessary to have called him from the scullery to set the mind of this strange Theban lady at rest. Did the woman think that compared with the great fashionable courts of the main-land the royal palace-cave of Ithaca was a poor thing, and its girls poor things and its herdsmen uneducated clowns? By Hades! I'd larn her to think poorly of Ithaca if I were Odysseus the son of——

His thoughts were interrupted by the sound of a crashing fall in the Corridor of the Pillars, the door leading into which had been left ajar.

"See what that was!" commanded the king; while Zeuks, who was beginning to grow sleepy after the well-cooked food and good wine, jerked himself up, and fumbling under his coat for his dagger sat sideways against the back of his chair, watching Tis descend the couple of steps, push open the door, and pass into the corridor. The door swung back and there was silence. Tis wore, for his indoor work in kitchen and scullery his softest sandals; so that the silence round that dining table at this moment was profound.

Then Telemachos deliberately got up. Having risen from his chair he crossed the room as noiselessly as he could. All the while he had been so intensely struggling to get his philosophical ideas into focus so that he might explain them to Pontopereia his eyes had been fixed on an ancient sword suspended from an iron nail in the wall. It was a sword of a completely different make from the sort used by Odysseus. It had been part of a collection of foreign weapons made long ago by the father of Penelope, who, like Zenios of Thebes, was a great picker-up of antiques.

Engraved upon the handle, as Telemachos remembered well from his childhood, was the word "Sidon"; but there had once been a travelling merchant at their table when Telemachos was a little boy who assured Penelope from certain metal-marks he knew that this unusual weapon must have been made in Ecbatana. Of this sword Telemachos now possessed himself; nor did he fail to note with a thrill of more natural and simple pride than he had allowed himself to feel for years—well! anyway since the death of his mother—how firmly and strongly and yet how lightly and easily, he found himself able to wield it.

Without looking at Zeuks, for he kept his eyes on his father with a quaint deprecatory half-smile, he managed somehow to convey to the humorous kidnapper of the divine horses that with two such broad-shouldered men as they were to guard that throne-room neither of the old king's lady-guests, however attractive, was in any danger of violence to her chastity.

Pontopereia, however, in place of catching such whimsical thoughts from her host's son, fixed her beautiful eyes upon Zeuks who, although he had screwed his head round against the back of his chair in the hope of being able to follow the movements of Tis in the Corridor, was quite capable of giving her a wink.

Nor was the daughter of Teiresias unaware of all it meant just at that moment to get a wink from "Zeuks of Cuckoo-Hill", as the king's mother would certainly have called him, although in reality Cuckoo-Hill never came down as near to the actual harbour as was the man's dwelling.

But Zeuks' wink said all that was necessary between them at that particular beat of the pulse of time. It said quite unmistakably: "O no! I know you've not forgotten about the pirates Strapping us to our chairs and chopping us to bits. And I know you've not forgotten the great word *prokleesis*."

But Zeuks and Pontopereia were not the only man and woman whose difference of sex was a cause of vivid feeling at that moment. Into the wine-fragrant air about her Okyrhöe was projecting all the seduction she could. In fact she was playing the unmitigated harlot at the expense of the old king. She had not missed his attraction to her specially rounded breasts; and thus, as she kept asking him certain simple and direct questions, questions which she selected for the absence from them of what couldn't be answered without an effort of thought—questions such as: "What was one of your earliest recollections, great King?"—she took care, in lifting her wine-glass to her lips, to reveal ever so little more of the rondure of one of these same breasts, whose perfect orb, culminating in a nipple as rosy as the wine at her lips, was never wholly revealed or wholly concealed, but was always, like the tip of a coral flagstaff in the heart of a milky isle, being partially glimpsed, to the most exquisite titillation of the old hero's amorous proclivities.

Telemachos meanwhile, with that remarkable sword in his hand from the collection of his maternal ancestor, continued to lean all his weight upon this rare weapon's gold-chased handle while he kept his attention absorbed in the effort to get its point firmly lodged in a convenient crack between two flag-stones. Pontopereia, having, so to say, settled her ethical account with Zeuks by a mental obeisance before the word *prokleesis* in exchange for a wink of recognition that if philosophy didn't bring the sexes together it wasn't of much use to mankind, had suddenly grown aware that by tilting herself a bit to one side and, though her chair was too heavy to be moved, by resting her weight on her left buttock, she could glimpse quite clearly at the end of the Corridor of Pillars the broad back of the spell-bound Tis.

"What on earth is the fellow staring at?" she asked herself. "Is someone lying dead at his feet? Has he killed some intruder —the first of Zeuks' pirates to enter the palace?"

Tis was undoubtedly—she could divine that much from the general pose of his figure—a trifle scared as well as intensely interested and arrested; and Pontopereia, herself stiff with nervous excitement, breathed quickly as she watched him. While all this was going on, little old Eurycleia, who, under all her weight of years, moved as lightly as Atropos, the oldest, smallest, but most to be feared and most to be relied upon of all the Fates, was now leaning against the door-post of the interior entrance to the dining-hall. Her expression as she leant there was one of concern but it was not an expression of alarm. Nor was it an expression of tremulous or jumpy nerves.

What her face showed was pure and simple annoyance. The old nurse felt indignant. Indeed you might say she felt extremely angry. For two, if not for three generations she had been compelled to behold her own peculiar and special world crumble down. She did not see it fall with a crash. She saw it disintegrate and crumble down. And she saw this happen without being able to lift a finger to stop it. What she was doing now was typical of the whole situation. She was simply standing with her back against the cold stones of the passage wall just as if they, these inanimate fragments of flint and quartz and these bits of chilly marble were arrogantly and in a new kind of contemptuous aristocratic haughtiness cold-shouldering her into an oblivious grave.

All this waiting lasted for a far less space of time than it takes to describe the emotions of the persons who were waiting; and when the waiting ended, the general relief that everybody felt, though great enough, was not as heavenly as it would have been had the thoughts and feelings involved gone on for as long as any chronicler, using those unwieldy hieroglyphs we call "words" to inscribe them, was bound to go on.

Whether it was a real son of Hephaistos who had carved the letters "U" for *uios*, and "H" for the aspirated vowel at the beginning of the name of the great god of fire, nobody could ever be absolutely sure, but that the Pillar on which those letters were engraved had had breathed into it some sort of sub-human or super-human consciousness was undeniable.

And at this particular veering between serious apprehension and immense relief it was given to the consciousness of the Pillar to note the difference between the attitudes to life and death of the three men in that dining-hall; how Odysseus never gave to either life or death a single thought, pondering only and solely on how best to carry out his immediate purpose, how Telemachos, although temperamentally longing to be quit of the whole business, kept forcing himself to retain, with regard to the meaning of life, and with regard to the question whether there was any life for the individual soul after its body was dead, a position of rigid agnosticism; and finally how Zeuks with his motto of *Prokleesis* or "defiance" and his practice of *Terpsis* or "enjoyment" held strongly to the annihilation of the soul with the death of the body.

Shamelessly chuckling, as he had seldom dared to do in the presence of Odysseus, and never before had done in the presence of lady-visitors to the palace, Tis came back into the dining-hall from the Corridor, and at the sight of him the whole company except Odysseus and Okyrhöe moved forward to learn what had caused that resounding crash. There was now no physical barrier between the king on his throne with his wine-cup in his hand and the low arch at the end of the Corridor of Pillars that led out into the olive-garden, out into the grave-yard of the slaves, and out into the darkness of night.

"It were thee wone club what fell, my King," explained Tis, as having mounted the two marble steps that led into the hall he advanced towards the foot of the throne; "and it did strike me silly old mind, as I did see the waves of darkness pouring in at far end, and these here lights of banquet pouring out at near end, that if us were all lying in the dirt, man-deep, under they olive-stumps outside thik arch,' stead of meat-dazed and urine-dizzened inside these here luscious walls, that what made the old club fall was fear of summat happening to all on us when this night's over and we get the people's word at the 'agora'!

"To say the truth I felt durned funny, my king, just now, when I seed thee's girt club lying face-down on they stones near olive-branch what have come up bold and straight, as you might say, out of floor!"

The first thought of Odysseus, when he heard all this, was the entirely practical and personal one of making sure that his most useful weapon was in its usual place and ready to his hand when needed.

"You propped it up again exactly where it always used to be, I hope—I mean between those bits of white stone in the wall?"

"Sure I did, my King, sure I did! Club do now bide exactly where club always did bide; I reckon about five feet away from that there up-growing olive-shoot."

And then, when Odysseus had nodded his obvious satisfaction at this statement, and when Telemachos had re-hung the antique sword picked up by his grand-dad upon its nail and resumed his seat, and when the combined voices of Tis and Eurycleia had died away in lively comment upon the club's fall as the speakers withdrew into the kitchen, it was left to Zeuks to swing the conversation back to the extraordinary expedition which the dead Dryad had originated.

"I've heard from some quarter," he told them all, "that the hundred-armed Monsters, Briareos, Kottos, and Gyes are now swimming about in the sunken cities of Atlantis, feeding upon the innumerable corpses of their drowned populations; and, do you know, the idea has crossed my mind that what the dead Dryad really hoped to bring about was that Typhon should join them down there. But how a fire-breathing creature like

Typhon could live under water like those Monsters is as much beyond my comprehension as——'"''

"As many other things, Master Zeuks!" murmured Okyrhöe with her silvery laugh. And it was during the general amusement that followed this sally that the Fly, having rejoined the Moth in their usual retreat, which was now safely propped up again, implored his lovely friend to listen intently. "For," said he, "the Pillar is now telling the club what is happening down there."

"You mean down in Atlantis?" enquired the Moth.

"Certainly I do," replied the Fly. "For you mustn't be so absurdly man-loving as to think that because the human population of a continent is drowned with that continent, nothing interesting can go on down there any more. There are the fish, my pretty one, there are the fish. Do try to realize that life doesn't end, Pyraust darling, when the human race ends. There *are* philosophers in the world—I won't at this moment emphasize their names or their species—who hold the view that it will only be when the tribes of mortal men are sunk into complete oblivion that the real drama of the Cosmos will properly begin."

"But," whispered the Moth anxiously, "and forgive my stupidity if this is a silly question, what I cannot see is how this drama of the future will be recorded if there's nobody to record it."

"Unrecorded things are as important as recorded things," said the Fly.

"But who hears of them?" commented the Moth sadly.

CHAPTER VIII

"How many are they?"

"How many of what, my beautiful one? Are you speaking of sea-gulls or crows?"

"People of course!" answered the Moth irritably. "Did you think I meant flies?"

"You'd have to count me out if you did," replied her friend grimly. "For I don't, and I believe it is a peculiarity shared by most of my species, at any rate those of the male sex, at all like being included in any plural category. Yes, indeed, my lovely one, I believe you'll find, as your experience thickens and your years increase, that you'll seldom meet a male who isn't at heart, though under various circumstances he may not appear so, an ingrained individualist. When I was younger I used to flirt with the wanton notion that to be really ourselves we had to move about in circles. I also played with the *spiritual* thought, as I understand they call it, that only when there are two or three of us the wind can be cozened and coaxed and cajoled to carry us to particular places, to certain river-banks, for instance, and to certain ponds full of special sorts of rushes, where we can find those extra delicate morsels of refreshment which our exacting senses crave.

"But after all the horrors I've seen, and after all the dangers from which I've been saved only by my constant and obsequious flattery of the goddess of Chance, I have learnt the supreme lesson of my life, that there is only one thing upon which a Fly can depend, namely himself."

"Do look what a lot of people there are! There must be more than a thousand! A thousand warriors who are skilled with the spear, not counting women and children!"

It was clear to the fly that his emotional friend was so hopelessly impressed by the number of the listeners that no appeal to reason was possible. So, giving it up, he confined himself to gazing out of the club's "life-crack" at that awe-inspired mass of islanders and to endeavouring to follow the words of the orator. This shepherd of the people was none other than Nisos' Father, Krateros Naubolides, who, mounted on an extremely old-fashioned and extremely shaky platform that had been erected by democratic settlers in Ithaca some sixty odd years ago, with the glittering marble Temple of Athene to its West and the deep blue water of the bay to its East, was explaining in a rough homely directness of speech, whose lack of intellectual subtlety and manifest honesty of feeling made his argument formidable, how bad for them it would be to use up all their precious sail-cloth, this divine "othonia" that took such expense to grow, such trouble to weave, and such art to prepare, for the ill-advised and indeed the absolutely crazy purpose of seeing off their aged and infirm king, in times when all experienced rulers were needed at home, on a wild fantastic voyage of his own eccentric fancy.

"It is our King's actual presence," Krateros bluntly and crudely shouted, "that we need at this juncture of our Island's life, not some fabulous glory from a mad adventure undertaken in a demented old warrior's last days!"

It was clear to the attentive fly that these rough and rude words uttered by a farmer, whose local breed was a good deal more purely local and insular than was that of Odysseus, was making a deep impression upon those among the islanders, both men and women, who were near enough to hear him; for they kept turning their heads to look at one another, and a considerable number of them actually clashed their brazen-pointed spears together in more than ordinary agreement.

Indeed the speaker himself, as the fly could catch in the tone of his voice, took it to be an indication that they were prepared, if this doting old hero went on insisting on his mad scheme, to rise in arms and dethrone both him and his philosophy-besotted son in favour of the more sensible if more insular stock of the House of Naubolides itself.

It was evident to Pontopereia that Odysseus was watching the assembly with inexhaustible attention, and was making, the girl decided, some special calculation with regard, not only to numbers and weapons, but to the quality and significance of the various farming families who were gathered here today, even if some were only represented by a male spearman whose relatives were all on the mainland. He had not dared to change the place of meeting and the girl could clearly see what were the chief impediments to this sort of democratic assembly in an "agora" that was at once old-fashioned in an unseemly, ramshackle, slovenly way, and modernistic in a cold, remote, indifferent way. For one thing, she noticed that however forcibly Odysseus had just now pressed his demand upon them for contributions of sail-cloth as if he were exacting the payment of tribute, it was only those quite near who could catch what he meant because of the purer language he used.

She noticed too that although Krateros Naubolides made himself heard, the agitation he created by the rough boldness of his rejection of the old king's claim was so great that little groups of men from nearby positions kept hurrying to further-off vantage-grounds where they would ardently enlarge on what had been said.

No sooner had the Father of our young friend Nisos Naubolides swung himself down from the platform of his Ithacan "agora", an erection that was really much too high to be a suitable speaking-place, than there ensued a rushing to and fro that made of the whole assembly a confusing if not a confounding hubbub of human bodies and human voices.

When "Government by Discussion", as you might call the flexible and casual manner in which the Ithacan natives had settled their affairs half a century ago, was working well, the population of the island was much smaller, and the half-circle of stone-seats for listeners had a much less extended circumference.

The result of this increase in numbers was that many of the most eloquent speakers took care to avoid the grotesquely elevated wooden erection on the speaking-rock and made their speeches from the ground, which meant that they often had to stand a good deal too near their antagonists, who frequently were a closely-packed crowd of angry and excited spearmen.

There had been no political meeting in this Ithacan "agora" for several years, nor had it been observed by any official person, or indeed by anybody, official or otherwise, before this meeting began that a couple of rungs in the wooden steps ascending the speaking-rock were missing. This gap in the ascent to the platform of oratory had been treated as negligible by Krateros. The old King too in his introductory talk, where he had briefly and succinctly suggested the possibility of every householder on the Island delivering a certain quantity of "othonia", had totally disregarded the shaky rostrum.

On this particular occasion it was before the handsome Father of our friend Nisos had reached the middle of his blunt and rude speech that the bulk of those who were listening to him became aware of the presence of the Priest of the Orphic Mysteries among the elders who stood at the foot of that dilapidated old-fashioned wooden erection on the summit of the speaking-rock.

The moment he was caught sight of, especially by the women, who were freely sprinkled among the men throughout the whole assembly, it was clear to the shrewd weather-eye of the watchful Odysseus that there was a palpable quickening of pulses. These manifestations of feeling in crowds are very queer phenomena. But of course this man possessed psychic powers of an unusually rare kind and he was insatiable in his quest for human converts of every age up and down the island; and, while a bogey-man to some, he was a redeeming angel to others.

Thus there now appeared over that whole assembly of men and women something resembling a many-coloured wind-blown ripple moving rapidly over a wide expanse of water, a ripple that was grey when it reached our horizon but had been a deep blue-green when it left the shore.

Had Nisos Naubolides arrived at the "agora" just then, he would have plunged at once into a veritable vortex of bewildering psychic problems, the chief of which would have been the extremely complicated question as to just what constituted an important enough crisis in the general stream of events, whether a waterfall, a cataract, a tributary, a marsh, a lake, or a "delta" of several river-estuaries, to justify an interference in the situation by the little old lady he had known as Atropos, and by what subtle understandings of the forces of earth and air and water and fire messages were duly despatched to the said little old lady, so that she could draw certain hints indicating in detail the issues involved and not failing to make clear at what exact point, if care was not taken, the wanton Goddess of pure Chance, whose name is Tyche, might snatch the occasion out of wiser hands.

But queerly enough it was neither blind Chance nor the oldest of the Fates who was now the disturber of the normal stream of natural events—this stream that flowed and eddied and circled and delayed and hastened across that old "agora". It was none other than the young girl, Pontopereia.

It was some while before Enorches fully realized that his most formidable opponent at this crucial pause in events was the awkward and ungainly damsel who was now shuffling so absent-mindedly up and down between Odysseus, who was leaning on his club, and Okyrhöe, who had accompanied them to this confused scene for some mysterious purpose of her own. As she shuffled back and forth in this odd manner Pontopereia couldn't help noticing a great many things that she had no wish to notice.

This business of "noticing" was the very last thing she wanted to be engaged in at that particular juncture. Her entire purpose as she shuffled to and fro was indeed the extreme opposite of noticing anything. What she desired just then was to make her mind as near a blank as she possibly could so as to offer it as a pure, clean, unfurnished sanctuary, of which, free from every distraction, encumbrance, or rival, her father's prophetic spirit might take complete possession.

But so astonishing were the forms and colours forced upon her senses by the spectacle before her that she struggled in vain to defend her attention from them. The sun just then was in mid-sky and was blazing down with such tremendous noon-day glare upon land and sea that it was difficult for her not to feel that she must yield up her whole being to the dazzling white opacity of Athene's Temple on the one hand, and to the dazzling blue opacity of the gleaming salt water on the other.

She had never seen bluer salt water in all her life. It seemed at one moment to lift her up to a yet bluer sky-zenith in the air above, and at another moment, just as if it were some vast, hard, smooth, magnetic precious stone, to draw her down to a petrifying abyss of demonic blueness in some enchanting but dangerous dimension of existence below Tartaros itself.

It was indeed, though nobody but herself knew it, a real crisis in the life of the daughter of Teiresias, this appearance of hers before the Ithacan assembly of which Odysseus made so much. Her real antagonist in the whole thing was not the father of her new friend Nisos but the Priest of the Mysteries who was even now preparing to take a terrific advantage of the old King's calm and unruffled assurance.

"How absolutely alone," she said to herself, "we all are! That old hero with his projecting chin and his sharp beard sticking out from it like the horn of a fabulous beast, what is he thinking and feeling now? I shall never know. Nobody will ever know. And that red and green gnat over there, sunning itself on that half-budded greenish-yellow willow-leaf, I would bet anything it is now, at this very moment of time, wondering whether its fate is destined to come by the violence of another insect not much bigger than itself, or by the sudden downfall of a rotten branch dislodged by a gust of wind, or by being snapped up between the upper half and the lower half of the beak of a bird.

"And has it perhaps just decided," the girl thought, "that it would be pleasanter to be trampled out of existence while it was asleep under a leaf than to perish in the disgustingly foul air of the crop of a feathery glutton? It's gone anyway; and wherever it's gone it's just as absolutely alone, in a multitudinous world without end in any direction, as I am, or as this old king is, or as Mummy Okyrhöe is, or any one of these men waving their spears and whispering to their wives and to the wives of their friends! Alone, alone, alone!

"And the same applies," thought Pontopereia, "to whatever grub that little hole contains!" And she struck with the side of her sandal a decaying fragment of tree-root that was half-covered by dark-green moss but had blotches of grey lichen on it here and there, and it was between two of these grey patches that the daughter of Teiresias detected a small orifice that was obviously the entrance to the dwelling of some grub-like creature.

"Are you at home, master?" she muttered; and then, digging her heel into the rubble beside that piece of decayed wood, she swung her whole body round, smiling to herself with a muttered exclamation. "Why," she told herself, "I am doing just what I said a minute ago I mustn't do! I'm noticing things! Only these things aren't exactly what I meant. I meant marble roofs and dazzling waves! But I must, I *must* get into the right mood for father's spirit!"

She straightened herself, clasped her hands behind her, stared at her sandals, and tried to imagine she was walking upon empty air. "If I can't make my mind a blank," she said to herself, "I must anyway get myself into the mood of being angry with this confounded Krateros who wants to make a fool of the old king by not letting him sail. I know exactly what the old man feels. He doesn't want to slide into an ordinary, conventional, tiresome, commonplace old age. I can follow *that* like a map!

"Heaven and earth! If *I* had a chance to sail in a ship over the drowned cities of Atlantis, wouldn't I snatch at it!"

She shuffled on, after that, with her head bent, repeating the word "Atlantis" over and over again. What she obscurely felt in her deepest consciousness was that, since this word contained the concentrated desire of the old hero who had appealed to her for aid at this crisis of his life, the best way of emptying her mind so as to make it a medium for the spirit of the dead prophet was to dissolve this actual word into a sacred mist, or even, and her eyes grew larger when she thought of this, into a sort of nectar such as would help to banish every emotion from her mind save the will to prophesy.

"Atlantis! Atlantis." Atlantis! And from the lovely head balanced on the ungainly little body, all the whole teeming mass of that portentous gathering, with its hosts of sullen-sultry spearmen and its agitated mothers and excited children in their blood-bright gaily-coloured clothes, and beneath them those blue waters that drew her down, and above them those white walls that lifted her up, were wholly and absolutely banished.

And it was at that very moment, for at such times strange

vibrations can pass between the oldest and the youngest among us, that Odysseus beckoned Pontopereia to his side.

Leaning with his right hand on his club, from the crack in whose breast both the moth and the fly were now gazing with absorbed interest at everything within the circuit of their vision, Odysseus told the daughter of Teiresias to use his left hand in place of the broken rung of that rotten ladder; "and make the devils, my brave girl," he muttered, "give me a good pile of sound 'othonia' instead of all this false flattery about 'wise old rulers'."

With this physical help and moral stimulus Pontopereia did manage in spite of her awkward legs and heavy thighs to get to her feet on that absurd wooden erection. But, once mounted there, a tragedy took place that was completely unknown to every consciousness in the whole world except the girl's own, a tragedy the mere existence of which justified up to the hilt what she had been feeling all that morning about the abysmal loneliness of every creature born into what we call "life".

For Pontopereia, as she gazed at those shining spears, and at that blue sea-pavement, that kept drawing her down, and at those white walls that kept lifting her up, was suddenly seized by a fit of appalling shyness. This convulsion of shyness paralysed her mouth as if with a ghost-fish's monstrous fins. It pressed against her throat as if with a bilge-smelling flattened-out whalebone snout.

And finally it brought the thousand-times despairing shipwrecked eye of a girl's frustrated life-hope to fix itself upon her! Yes, it brought it closer and closer and closer to the self within the self, to the Pontopereia within Pontopereia, to the living, shrinking soul inside the innermost sheath of her calyx-like identity, so that nothing less than what was all she was should be exposed to this searching, reducing, unsympathetic, sardonic eye, the eye of a shyness that at that moment had gone stark mad.

The poor girl was helpless. What had suddenly come over her could no more be struggled against than she could have regained her right arm if somebody had cut it off. And now quite independently of that fit of grotesque sub-human shyness, as if she had been a sparrow imagining itself a swan, she felt a natural, normal, overpowering human shame. She wanted nothing but to be allowed to hide her head and cry piteously. She could not even remember now, with the tears running down her cheeks and tasting salt on her lips and blotting out her sight, how she managed to slide down from that ridiculous wooden platform. But she did remember how the beard of Odysseus tickled her chin as the old king bent over her and tried to comfort her as she wept on the ground.

It was at that moment that the Priest of the Mysteries, who, like a holy and consecrated wolf, had been waiting for his chance to spring, snatched at his opportunity. And such was the power of this man's demonic personality that although the collapse of Teiresias' daughter had been followed by quite a lot of shouting and rushing hither and thither, accompanied by the angry brandishing of many spears in male hands and much high-pitched expostulation from female throats, the moment it was realized who it was who was now pulling himself up to the top of that shaky erection and using such obstinate determination in treading upon each broken rung and in clinging to each wretched bit of balustrade there was another of those queer gasps of mass-attention where the actual crowd itself seems to create for itself a unified Being with ears and eyes that can take things in, and get shocks of feeling from taking things in, just as ordinary personalities can.

Quite a considerable crowd of these islanders with spears, whose number had so impressed the moth that she had whispered the startling syllables "a thousand", were close enough to the speech-rock to see what a teasing thing it was to mount that platform. Pontopereia had only managed it by the help of the old king.

It was the complete absence of anything traditional or romantic about that wholly silly erection that took the heart out of its ascent and may even have been the cause of the girl's collapse when she had ascended it. One of the prices that had to be paid for the Trojan War by the Island of Ithaca was that there was neither time nor money to obliterate the finger-prints of the flagrant bad taste left by the rich citizens of that particular epoch.

It was lucky that most of the work of that bad time was not done in materials that by their own nature were especially lasting. It should also be noted that since then, the general taste of the islanders had improved so much that had any of the younger men, even the eldest son of Krateros Naubolides for instance, been called upon to speak they would have certainly spoken from among the old traditional stone-seats and not approached that fatal erection of ill-chosen wood. It was just because these preposterous platforms had already become laughing-stocks, that, when the Priest of the Mysteries in his struggle to ascend was observed to be hanging by one arm from the balustrade with his "chlaines", or professional philosophic cloak, flapping in the wind about his rump, till the wood-work broke and deposited him on his back on the ground, quite a number of the men in the crowd gave a vent to a rude burst of laughter.

The sound of this must have reached the priest's ears for he leapt to his feet in one of his fits of blind rage, fits that always endowed him with superhuman strength and were therefore an advantage to him rather than anything else. At this moment what he did was to seize the actual main floor of the platform with both his hands and to shake it for a while, as if he were a besotted giant capable of shaking a king's palace to dust and ashes.

Then with one grand shattering, heaving spasm what he did was to bring the whole erection crashing to the ground in pieces. This done the astonishing man completely regained his self-control, in fact more than his self-control, for he became a supernaturally competent commander with all the resources of an exceptionally brilliant orator at the absolute disposal of a perfect strategist.

He coolly kicked aside the relics of the dilapidated platform he had demolished, and advancing to the front of the marble eminence on which the thing had been erected, he made just the right gesture and uttered just the right appeal to the crowd to command total attention. Indeed he did much more: for he allowed no second to pass, no pulse-beat to intervene, between this beginning of things and the torrential flow of burning words that followed it.

"Let no wind," he cried, "O people of sacred Ithaca, fill any ship's sail that leaves your consecrated coasts! Keep this feeble, doting, maudlin, crazy, despotic, degenerate old man on his throne till old age makes him drop from it like a rotten apple and drop straight into his grave! Meanwhile let him stay where he is! Let him keep the throne warm for your brave Krateros who is a strong, sensible, natural man like any other man, and all the better for not being an herald-trumpeted, bard-celebrated, minstrel-sung, lick-spittle old legend-maker who doesn't think his cup of glory is full enough in just being accepted by you islanders as your king, doesn't in fact think that to be king at all over a crew of miserly farmers and poor fishermen, such as he considers you to be, is worthy of a deathless, immortal hero, like himself!

"What he wants to do by this mad voyage of his over the drowned cities of Atlantis is to win for himself a name beyond that of any of our famous men, a name beyond the name of Agamemnon, beyond the name of Achilles, beyond the name of Diomed, and of course far beyond the names of any of your most glorious Trojan enemies, such as Priam or Hector or Aeneas or Paris!

"O my friends, my friends, it is only yesterday we all heard, through the mediumship of earth and air and fire and water of the drowning of Atlantis. These murderous gods always like their news to reach us drop by drop, as it suits their god-almighty-nesses' cunning craftiness, and not for *our* interest really at all! But there's one little, obvious, simple, human interpretation of their trick of revealing their own murderous behaviour in connection with these hints from earth and air and water and fire that may not yet have occurred to you—I mean the double-dyed craftiness of suggesting that what they have done purely and solely to protect themselves was done in the interest of a faithful steering of human history, as it takes place on this old earth, and in the interest of progress on this old earth, or anywhere else in space.

"And now I would like to say something to you about this drowning of Atlantis of which we hear so much. I would like at this moment, my dear friends, humbly, patiently, submissively, and with all due respect where respect is due, to suggest to you that these curst Olympian rulers of ours recently made a great discovery. They discovered, never mind how, perhaps through earth or air or water or fire, or perhaps through some treacherous group of Atlanteans themselves, for there are traitors in every country, that some great Atlantean philosopher, who may now at this moment, for all we know, be wandering over the earth under a completely different name, anyway my suggestion is that somehow or other they found out that an Atlantic philosopher had got the secret of some new magnetic stone that can influence unborn embryos and that is probably called the 'Embryo Stone', and whose power—I am only humbly suggesting this to you, though, I confess, in my own philosophical researches I have discovered some very peculiar and very powerful magnetic stones that can change the sex of an embryo.

"The Atlantean philosopher's stone may have the power of making the embryo bi-sexual. In which case, as you can well imagine, you warriors of Ithaca, the influence, the renown, the glory and the power of this Sage of Atlantis, not to mention his wealth, would be very great indeed! And naturally enough the high Olympians would hate him. They have always been extremely touchy and sensitive on such points; as they may well be! For doesn't their authority with all of us ordinary mortals largely depend on their power over birth, and over the various issues of birth?—yes! extremely touchy they have always been about this whole problem of birth and sex; and if I may whisper this in your ears, you brave men and beautiful women of Ithaca, it is by the cunning trick of keeping sex, and birth, the issue of sex, completely under their control, that these Olympian gods retain their power over us.

"But they can be defied now and again for all that; and very successfully defied. You have only to visit the "Herm" of the great Goddess Themis, within a mile of where we are now, and as you can believe from my devotion to Eros and Dionysos I'm no fanatic champion of propriety and decency, to see the havoc done to her image by the hands of the chaotic Harpies; and yet upon the traditional order maintained by Themis the basic rule of these Olympians is declared by their champions to depend.

"Whereas I say it depends only on two things—on the Thunderbolts of Zeus and on the plagues sent by the Queen of Heaven. O my friends! if you would listen to me and boldly defy all these false gods; if you would turn to the only deities and divinities in the whole pantheon of godlike creatures who really have the power of giving us new life—not just murdering us with thunderbolts and with plagues and famines—but transporting us by mystic ecstasies and paradisic trances into Dimensions of Being, where what here we are deluded into calling reality is seen in its true light, and where nothing, I say again to you, my friends, where nothing is the secret of all the Mysteries beneath and above the Sun and the Moon, beneath and above the divine ether, except the mind that half-creates what it enjoys, except the mind that half-annihilates what it cannot enjoy!"

When Enorches had finished speaking he showed in the presence of that enormous crowd and in the presence, and before the steady eyes and pointed beard, of the unalterable old king, the same perfectly cool brain and perfectly poised intelligence that he had shown when he began speaking.

But neither the old king, who now held the awkward form of the daughter of Teiresias firmly by the waist while he slowly and indifferently swung the club of Herakles to and fro with his free hand, nor the agitated crowd of spear-waving men and excited women had time to note this serenity in their orator, for the attention of every person in that oldest portion of the "agora", including king and crowd and prophet's daughter, was suddenly and startlingly switched to a completely new occurrence.

ATLANTIS

This abrupt jerk to the particular set of nerves in them all that responded to dramatic events included in its field of operations, as may be easily supposed, both the moth and the fly who just then were peering out of the life-crack of the club of Herakles with concentrated interest. It also included the club itself who in following the rush of events at this particular crisis had the advantage of its vibratory contact with the Sixth Pillar in the Corridor of Pillars. This contact, based on a long series of experiences so homely and natural that they might almost be called domestic, was in its way as much of a philosophical discovery as any conceivable one made by the Atlantean sage, and neither the moth, whose silky wings quivered with the agitation of its emotion, nor the fly, whose great black head bulged with the intensity of its rumination, could do more than quietly accept such a verdict when they heard the club murmur aloud to itself what it had just caught from the massive Being that bore the signature of a son of Hephaistos, namely the words: "Hear therefore what the sage saith, "When the messenger flies or gallops, or drives, or runs, hope nothing, fear nothing, expect nothing, talk of nothing, till he's standing on the ground at your gate."

This messenger was indeed running at a speed that made some of the women who watched him fear he would fall dead the moment he delivered his message. And what was his message? This question, which was pulsing and heart-beating in that whole vast mass of people, did not disturb Odysseus in the slightest degree.

His plan of using the Prophet's daughter as a shaft of irresistible power resembling the shaft that originally separated the Heavens from the Earth had completely failed. Well! *That* had failed. *That* was over and done with. *That* was finished, closed, shut, settled, rounded off; but in its frustration, in its defeat, in its absolute *overness*, it left the great battlefield of creation and destruction open for something fresh from the root up!

Yes! the field was free for something that had not so far crossed the mind of any living creature, whether that creature were a god or a man or a beast or a bird or a fish or a reptile or a worm or an insect! Yes, the greatest gift the Earth had given to Odysseus at his birth was his power of accepting a crushing disaster and of starting freshly again, as the phrase runs, "from scratch".

Another great gift from the universal mother of men, who by many among us is called Nature rather than the Earth, of which this old hero was possessed, was the power of detaching himself from the agitations, confusions, emotions, desperations, terrors and exultations that might be absorbing and upsetting his immediate companions and not only of keeping his own spirit in the midst of the craziest hurly-burly and hullabaloo absolutely calm and unmoved, but of being capable under these conditions of so isolating his mind that he could go on coolly planning for the future, and calmly pondering on the future, and amusing himself by imagining what he would like best to happen in the future, with as much serenity as if he'd had nothing but lonely forests and untraversed seas around him for hundreds and hundreds of miles.

It had become clear to everybody now that behind the man who was running so fast, and who now was near enough to be recognizable as no other than our young friend Nisos, there was another man, quite different in appearance, attired in a manner wholly foreign to Ithaca and even to the main-land of Hellas, who clearly was finding it difficult to keep up with the younger man. Suddenly this first runner—"And it *is* Nisos!" thought Pontopereia, unable to stop herself from squeezing the king's arm in her excitement, "and he's coming straight to us!"—turned, saw how far off the other was, and stood still, so as to be overtaken.

It was indeed one of those curious occasions when the innate natures of the spectators at an important event reveal themselves to themselves, if not to anyone else, with what sometimes are quite surprising results.

"Can you see Enorches any longer?" enquired the moth of the fly. "I feel so dreadfully sure that the dear man may be wanting someone like me to make him happy about his beautiful speech and tell him how rich and clear his noble voice sounded."

"May the Great Hornet sting your confounded Enorches!" responded the fly crossly. "Why can't you, you little priest worshipper, look at the drama of life from a scientific distance?"

There was something so infinitely unpleasant to the moth, and so blighting and bleaching and blistering and blasting to her whole life-instinct, about this appalling "scientific distance" to which the fly was alluding, that she found it hard to be even polite to him.

"Well, my pretty?" he went on teasingly, for the difference of sex between them put *her* seriousness into one ballot-box and *his* into another, "why don't you answer my plain question about a rational view of life taken from an astronomical scientific distance?"

This was too much for the moth, and she lost every silken flake of her natural sweet and obedient temper. "Why," she screamed at him, "don't I look at life from the view-point of the furthest star in the firmament? I'll tell you why! I'll tell you why! I'll tell you why! Because I happen to be a Living Being on the Earth!"

The Fly sighed heavily. "How impossible it is," he thought, "to exchange rational ideas with a female! And yet they *are* clever. It would be absurd to deny it. They are extremely clever. They may even be called wise. But their wisdom follows a completely different track from our wisdom. It skips about from point to point, *matching things*. We look at life as a whole."

"You know exactly where the world comes to an end then?" shrieked the moth, making the fly feel as though she had read his thoughts. "What if it has trailing edges that lead to completely different ends? What if there's a jumping-off place, from which a person can leap into another world altogether?"

"Listen, pretty fool!" protested the Fly sternly: and once more there came to their ears the voice of the Sixth Pillar conversing gravely with the club of Herakles; on whose head Odysseus was leaning rather heavily at that moment as he watched Nisos approach with that fantastically attired foreigner.

"The Sage avers that if the difference between one man and another with regard to their bodies is so great that it passeth understanding, considering that all have a head and a neck and shoulders and trunk and arms and legs and hands and feet and eyes and ears, the difference between them in regard to their minds is so great that it bars any approach to an attempt to understand it."

"You heard *that*, sweetheart?" commented the Fly with satisfaction. "And if we can say as much as that about the difference in body and mind between creatures of the same species, what about the difference when you consider varieties of species? I tell you, little one, there's no more good in my hoping that out of the various tribes of Flies one will arise destined to conquer the world than in these people here thinking that some Hellenic or Achaian or Boeotian tribe will conquer the world. I tell you, darling little idiot, no species and no portion of a species will ever conquer the world. It's one of the tricks of Nature to put such ideas into people's heads so as to make great wars arise between race and race and between species and species. Such wars between one swarm and another swarm are deliberately worked up by Nature so as to thin out earth's population. Will you never learn, you lovely little goose-girl, that if a moth of your tribe wants her folks to rule the world there is only one thing for her to do?"

"And what may *that* be?" responded the moth in a voice so faint with sarcasm that it was hardly audible.

"Tell yourself a story about it happening," said the fly, "and die before you get to the last chapter."

"I sometimes think," whispered the moth, "that that's what I've done."

When Nisos and his oddly-attired companion reached Odysseus, Pontopereia took care to move aside and to be as inconspicuous a figure in that crowded landscape as was possible for a girl with her strikingly beautiful and intellectual face. Hardly conscious of what she was doing, however, when Nisos did begin to speak she kept on moving nearer and nearer to the old king; but since her reputed mother or at any rate her official guardian, Okyrhöe, also moved nearer, her interest must have seemed to Nisos entirely natural.

One thing about this new encounter of these two young people certainly showed the daughter of Teiresias in a dignified and admirable light, namely the fact that in her excited interest in what Nisos was telling the old King she forgot completely the shame and humiliation she had herself suffered so short a time before. In fact she forgot, as apparently Odysseus himself had forgotten, what a central dramatic part in turning the tide of popular feeling she had been brought there to play. And now it was all over and done with, as utterly as was the life of the old Dryad and her tree, both of them reduced to dust and ashes.

"It was when I had only just left the Cave of the Naiads that I first saw it." And here Nisos made a rather formal and yet quite a dramatic pause; and Pontopereia couldn't help noticing that the presence of the ornately-dressed, portentous-looking stranger who so punctiliously kept one of his brocaded knees on the ground while he watched the face of Odysseus with obsequious impassivity, did have the effect of stiffening just a little the unconventional naturalness of speech which the direct frankness of their master usually evoked in those who were closest to him.

And the girl also noticed that the spontaneous island-schoolboy attitude to all the fantastic ceremonials and the symbolic rituals of Persians, Libyans, Phoenicians, Babylonians and Assyrians, which she had marked in most Achaian and Hellenic lads, an attitude partly humorous, and partly fascinated and even a little awed, had resulted in this case in the way in which, though he did not kneel, Nisos stood respectfully before the king with his head bare and his hands clasped behind his back.

"I knew at once," the boy went on, "that it was a foreign boat. I knew *that* by its build and by its curious-looking sail. I knew also that it couldn't have come from very far away, for it was too small to have crossed such a formidable mass of water as that great Western Ocean in which we are told the gods have drowned the land of Atlantis. Well, O King, I climbed down to the sea's edge so as to direct them, by waving and shouting, to the estuary where they could lower their sail, fasten up their vessel, and land on our shore. It took a long time to do this for them. I had to scramble over a lot of steep rocks, didn't I, Euanthos?" And Pontopereia noticed that, instead of turning and giving a responsive smile to the speaker, this palatial individual, with one knee still on the gravelly ground and his submissively reverential gaze still fixed on the king, who by this time was crouching like a somnolent steersman on a rough lichen-covered ledge with the club between his knees, replied to the lad's appeal by making a solemn little bow, a bow which, in the relative position to which chance had brought them, might have been directed to the four staring eyes of the pair of fascinated insects.

"But when they were safely landed—when you were landed, Euanthos!" and Pontopereia, not to mention Okyrhöe, who kept edging nearer and nearer, noted a repetition of the same quaint performance—"I soon heard the great news. Thou, O King,"—and it was clear to both those observant ladies that this boy-messenger completely misread the relaxed attitude of the old hero he was addressing, taking his drowsy abstraction as a sign of nonchalant indifference, when all the while it was really an instinctive animal withdrawal into cover, under the mask of which the wily old warrior watched the course of events, noting with shrewd precision the particular direction in which, under the pressure of numberless conflicting entities, the tide of destiny was moving.

"Thou, O King, art about to be visited by a famous royal Princess from the land of the Phaiakians whose parents and brothers enabled you to sail for home in a ship full of rich gifts."

"And what, my young friend," enquired Odysseus, throwing into his tone, the two ladies decided, a deliberate weariness and tedium, "do those of her court who are with her say is the name by which she is known to her own people and by which she wishes to be known to those other lands whither her ship carries her; for among all men who live by bread there are none to whom their parents do not give names, whether they be rich or poor, slaves or free, tillers of the earth, or wielders of royal sceptres."

"The name," cried Nisos, in a high-pitched excited voice, "of this visitor to the shores of Ithaca is none other than Nausikaa, the daughter of Arete who was the daughter of Rhexenor, and of Alkinoos who was the son of Nausithoos."

Neither Okyrhöe nor Pontopereia missed the rather startling swallowing sound, as if he had been munching a too big mouthful of bread and having retained it till it was in an almost liquid form in his mouth had sucked it down in one terrific gulp, which the old man emitted as the word "Nausikaa" reached his ears.

But Nisos had a still greater shock in store for his king. "From a couch of purple at the bottom of their boat," he went on, "they helped to land the most noble figure of a man I have ever seen or could ever imagine. His hair was white with age and his shoulders were extremely bent, but the grandeur of his features and the beauty of his form, even in old age, were more like those of a god than of a human creature. I looked at him with awe and reverence, O king, and still more was I reduced to wordless amazement when the stately and distinguished Euanthos here"—and once again the two ladies were fascinated to watch this perfect courtier on his bended knee make that same masquerade-like inclination of his head without turning so much as the point of his beak-like nose in the direction of the person whose flattery he was acknowledging—"and I was impressed, O my King, to notice how superior to any of our modern Hellenic or Argive or Pelasgic or Danaan ways were the——"

"By Kronos, boy, you don't mean to say the man at the bottom of the boat was *Ajax*?"

At the utterance of this name both the ladies gasped audibly, and the elder one, with a shiver that ran clean through her, flung her arms protectively about the younger.

This time it was the turn of Nisos to nod assent while his gaze remained fixed on a different person from the one to whom he was responding. And at the receipt of this assent Odysseus rose from his seat abruptly.

"Ajax again!" he muttered. "It must have been a dream then that I saw him among the dead when the spirit of Achilles questioned me and went off with long strides among the rest in his joy that I could assure him his son had won glory! Ajax again! Well, well, well, well! He had Poseidon as his enemy among the Olympians, even as I have! And it may be that as I found help from Circe and Calypso and Leucothea, so he has found it from some great goddess at the bottom of the Sea! Poseidon must have overturned his ship in no ordinary way; not by just a wave out of the deep: very likely by flinging a mountain upon it, as the grandfather of Nausikaa prophesied the sea-god might do one day over their only good harbourage to stop their giving convoy and ships to the enemies of the Olympians.

"And very likely by doing that very thing Poseidon ruined his own abominable and murderous intention. The great *wave*, or the great *mountain*, whichever it was may have had the opposite effect to what was intended. It may have enshrouded Ajax in forests and ferns and mosses and vast leafy chasms and yawning flowery abysses and huge cracks and crevices in the green thick rondure of the earth.

"Well, well, well! So we've got Ajax on our hands again! What twists and turns of fate!—'Turns' do I say? What enormous, sweeping, astral curves this destiny of ours indulges in! *Ajax!* Well, well! We must all be as gentle and hospitable to him as we can—eh, ladies, my dears?—eh, Nisos, my lad? And to this purpose"—and at this point the old King swung directly round upon Euanthos, who had risen to his feet and with his hands clasped behind him and his shoulders squared was staring at some particular oblong of nothingness beyond which his preposterous politeness had erected its own private horizon—"to this purpose we are indeed—don't you think so, Ladies?— incredibly lucky to have a real live Herald from the land of the

Phaiakians actually here with us in our midst! He will explain to us, primitive islanders and settlers and farmers and fishermen as we are here in Ithaca, to what a stately tradition on the mainland of Hellas our ancestors look back.

"Yes, he will soon find, O my most gallant Hetairoi, that our old Achaian and Danaan ritual of life is as poetical as any he can discover in the most courtly cities of the orient. The first lesson he is destined to receive as to our power to show ourselves worthy of his respect will be the hospitality we shall now show to this noble princess, of whose coming he is the herald, and also the manner in which we shall entertain my ancient friend and once beloved rival, Ajax the son of Telamon!"

Odysseus leant forward as he spoke and as he did so he clasped with both hands the head of his club, pressing it against the pit of his stomach. It may be well believed how, as he did this, out of what the club itself always referred to as its "life-crack" and which was a slit in its gullet reaching as far down as its lungs and containing, as all its friends well knew, a sort of nomadic camp for two adventurous insect-friends of quite different species, there now issued a fine controversy.

Yes, out of the "life-crack" of the club there emerged and dissolved like recurrent waves of smoke into the hot afternoon air quite a bitter dialogue. It is curious how the voices of any living things as they strike air, or earth, or water, or fire, go through a change in their nature the perceiving of which, especially when such sounds happen to be solitary sounds, is a remarkable experience for the human person who perceives it.

Yes, it is when other sounds are absent and when the earth feels as if it were surrounded by an aura possessed of a singularly penetrating fragrance like nothing else in the world, that this change occurs. The sound may have been a cry of wild delight. It may have been a shriek of anger, it may have been a wail of sorrow, it may have been a whistle, a call, an appeal. It matters not what the sound was or what it conveyed. The sound has been changed.

And this change has come about by the thing having drawn

out of the element into which it rose or fell, and into which it dispersed itself, something akin to its own nature and yet something that no creature alive could apprehend through its sense of hearing. Into what has it been changed? Into a presence. Yes, there is no doubt or question about that. It has become a presence. What the listener is aware of now is the inexplicable and unaccountable effect upon him of a presence; not a human presence nor a godlike presence nor a titanic presence, and totally different from any conceivable animal presence.

But the point is that the effect of this presence is the etherealizing in some mysterious way of the material element, whatever it may have been, into which the sound has plunged. If into the flames of a bonfire, those flames become the purged and dancing spirits of all the leaves they are devouring! If into the air above the peaks of a mountain, that air becomes a particular region of pure space made of a more rarefied substance than the ordinary air which surrounds the earth.

If into water, that water becomes a pool of such perfect translucence that a consecration of all the places on earth where water springs up seems indicated by its mere existence on this planet.

And finally if into earth, every grain of sand, or atom of rock or speck of mud, or dab of clay, or chip of quartz, or crumb of dung, or grit of granite, or mite of mould, which that sound reaches becomes suddenly possessed by something akin to the mystery of consciousness, though it is not the consciousness of a man or a beast or even of a vegetable.

It was when the voice of Odysseus died away with the sound of the name of the father of Ajax that the moth enquired of the fly: "Why does the King go on so long about Ajax? Isn't the important person who has arrived not this half-drowned half-witted doting old hero from the Siege of Troy, but this great living Princess Nausikaa from the land of the Phaiakians?"

The philosophical contempt in the voice of the fly cannot be expressed in rational words. "Have you no idea, you funny little perfection of a darling, silly, little girl, as to the way we men take these things? Don't you see that he's making all this fuss about Ajax simply to cover up his feelings about Nausikaa? Have you forgotten, little stupid, all we were taught at school about men hiding up their strongest feelings, and about there having been a passionate romance between our King and some great Phaiakian princess? Why, you little ignorant silly, it's one of the great love-stories of the entire world! Of course he has to make a lot of fuss about this old crazy Ajax! Why, you lovely, delicious, heavenly, little idiot, what on earth are you thinking about? Ajax defying the lightning is a simple proposition.

"*There* is Ajax. *There* is the lightning! There is an Ajax in every single living creature on earth and when that creature is in the mood of defying the Great Gods, it may be on behalf of the Little Gods, or it may be in anger on its own account. I tell you, you little silky-soft priest-worshipper, there isn't a fisherman in all the coasts of Ithaca who hasn't heard about Ajax and the Lightning. The toughest, roughest, homeliest, rudest fisherman you could find in this whole island has heard of Ajax defying the Lightning.

"I tell you, child, I know what I'm talking about. Being as fond of rotten fish as anybody in the world, I used to go out with certain special boats, whose owners used to start earlier in the morning than the others and weren't as fussy as the others about cleaning out the bottom of their skiffs. Yes! I swear to you, you un-scientific, irrational, unphilosophical, little lovely, I heard the most savage and most primitive of these sailors, yes! the very rudest of them, cry out to some companion: 'Why, you're as upset by a storm as Ajax defying the Lightning!'

"But when it comes to our king's meetings with Princess Nausikaa of that land, it's a very different story! Of course he keeps the essence of it to himself. Look at him now! He's as ready to fall into a fit of reverie and fantasia as any youth in his beatified adolescence!"

The words of the wise fly had much truth in them just then; but the whole scene up there, from the place where Odysseus held his Heraklian weapon to the place where excitedly whispering groups were gathered on the furthest outskirts of that island-agora, was so confused and chaotic that it had become difficult to concentrate on any particular member of the heterogeneous crowd that was surging about in agitated waves of bewildered excitement.

As for the priest Enorches, he had become so invisible that he might have sunk into the earth after his tremendous oration.

"And now," cried Odysseus, raising his voice above its accustomed pitch, "the thing for us to do is to go and greet this heroic rival of mine out of my ancient past, thus risen like a ghost to keep my pride in its proper place but also to make it clear to my enemies that it is essential that the people of Ithaca should provide their king with sail-cloth!"

While his words died away in that incredible sunshine he instinctively began leading them down the slope at the foot of which lay his rock-hewn palace.

But Nisos had a further announcement to make. "It was while we were leading Ajax as carefully as we could towards the palace that we met Zeuks, O King, and it was to tell you how Zeuks had taken it on himself to be the guide and interpreter to my Lord Ajax that I ran to meet you. My friend Euanthos here objected very strongly to my leaving our Lord Ajax under the care of Zeuks. It seemed to him that Zeuks was not well-dressed enough, well-mannered enough, distinguished enough, or nearly aristocratic enough, to be able to explain our life in Ithaca to a hero of the ancient tradition and one who possesses the lofty habits of the past and those godlike ways of living and thinking that are now lost to the world."

Odysseus had inadvertently taken Pontopereia by the arm as he began to descend the hill, and this protective gesture of his had naturally brought Okyrhöe to his other side, that is to his right, where he prodded the ground with his club of Herakles. It was therefore, across the club's self-styled "life-crack" that the craftiest woman in Hellas murmured her seductive words to the craftiest man in Hellas, and what she said was as nectar to the moth and as gall to the fly.

ATLANTIS

"All the Achaian world will be waiting with eagerness, my Lord King," she murmured, "to hear the result of this encounter between you and the Lady Nausikaa. We forget sometimes how quickly news travels in these modern days. It's the quality of the sails the ships carry, I expect: O, and of course it's also because there are so many more merchant-sailors nowadays! Merchants are the great news-carriers and scandal-bearers. No doubt they always *have* been. But we mustn't forget all these modern improvements in the masts and sails and benches and keels of ships, and even in the sleeping-places below the benches.

"It is wonderful to think of all the improvements we have lived to see of which our fathers never dreamed! Yes, I have followed pretty closely the history of Phaiakia from merchant-sailors' narratives of what has been going on there, for in the history of any country what you pick up from travelling merchants is always nearer the truth than the speeches of official rulers and their ambassadors."

"It was at this point that the fly became convinced that if Okyrhöe went on for one single sentence more in this manner Odysseus would revolt against her influence. But the clever woman now made it manifest that she could practise a quite different strategy, and as soon as she began in this clear, definite, and concrete manner, to aim at convincing him, she had the king at her mercy.

"What I have been leading up to," she now remarked in a most emphatic manner, "is this. I have been, as I tell you, O King, following rather carefully the events in Phaiakia; and I have noticed that when Alkinoos died his throne was occupied first by one, and then by another, of the favourite sons of the widowed queen. But both these sons died before their mother —at least that is what my merchant-sailors have told me; though I fully admit they may have had, in each case, their own peculiar business-reasons for lying—and so when finally the mother herself died the only surviving child of Alkinoos was Nausikaa.

"She married twice and both her husbands died childless, a situation that set going various shameful rumours among the people, rumours that Nausikaa poisoned them both with the hope of sailing for Ithaca when they were dead and being wedded to thyself! Of course you will know, O great King, much better than a mere stranger and traveller like myself, how to treat such ignoble tales: but you must at least remember in excuse for such tales that you have, as few heroes ever have, become a legend during your life-time, and since many of us in our youth have read—and have written too, I'll be bound!—passionate love-lyrics about you and this daughter of Alkinoos, it is inevitable that when we hear of you two meeting again all manner of disturbingly romantic thoughts rush into our human-too-human heads!

"From a perfectly practical and sensible point of view the coming to Ithaca of this experienced and beautiful woman was indeed most cleverly planned. She too without any doubt has been collecting news from merchant-ships about Ithaca, just as I have about Phaiakia; and having found out that Penelope has been long dead and that you have never taken a second wife she naturally thinks of marrying you and of having those children by you which she clearly could not have by any other husband. It is a tragic and a touching hope; but I can imagine it proving a good deal of a nuisance and embarrassment to you."

Neither the fly nor the moth as they listened to these words could see the effect upon the king of this treacherous warning, though they couldn't help noticing how the beard of Odysseus kept giving curious little forward jerks. But then the king's beard had for some time clearly been trying to isolate itself from the rest of his appearance. Apparently its desire was to become a sort of advanced Body-guard, which, if it were not propitiated, or, as the school-boy mates of Nisos would say, "sucked up to", its owner would have to treat as an independent personality, or simply to cut it off.

As a matter of fact the old man's imperviousness at this moment had no connection with these ambitions of his beard. It was in accord with his whole character that, while he accepted every material detail of what Okyrhöe suggested, he disregarded, or postponed for later consideration, the lady's psychic interpretation of the same.

What did cross his mind at that moment was a definite regret that owing to his penuriousness, or to his poverty, or to a mixture of them both, he had for years contented himself with getting on without any more effective cook in his excavated cave of a kitchen than the family's ancient Nurse Eurycleia, who though she knew well enough what to prepare for his own meals, and even better how to restrict the appetites of Arsinoë and Leipephile, would lack both the physical strength and the culinary experience to cook for a visitor like the Princess Nausikaa.

"Nisos!"

"I am here, my lord the King!"

"Run *down* this hill as fast as you ran *up* just now. Make it as clear as you can to Eurycleia what kind of guests we shall have tonight. Explain to her that Ajax will be as old as I am and probably as fussy about his food. I take it, lad, that if you start now you'll get home before either of them have time to arrive, especially if our friend Zeuks, who's such a babbler, is the one you've left with Ajax. You *will* have time to get there first, sonny, won't you?"

Nisos didn't look at the sky above the slope on which they had paused nor at the tops of the trees at the foot of the hill. He looked at his own sandals and he looked at his own hands. And then he said: "Yes, I *think* I can, my King. I'll have a good try at it anyway." And with one quick glance at Pontopereia he set off at top speed.

But while Nisos was running at top speed down the wooded slope between the "agora" and the palace, dodging sharp-edged rocks and thick clumps of impenetrable island-bushes, and squeezing his way between close-growing fir-trees whose lower branches were spiky and dead from lack of sun, and as he ran was being sexually and emotionally almost pulled in half; for his feelings were tugged at in one direction by what might be called the golden cord of Eione's supple limbs and lovely gestures and in another direction by the silver cord of Pontopereia's expressive face, the middle-aged Zeuks was guiding the senile Ajax through the deserted but still haunted region that was called "Arima".

The heraldic master of ceremony from the land of Phaiakia would certainly have described our friend Zeuks as an egregious and unconscionable rogue; but it is certain that as this same Zeuks slowly and carefully—though chuckling very often as he did so over private quips of his own—escorted the old, bent, white-headed Ajax, by the nearest way he could think of, to the rock-hewn House of Odysseus, he had some startling shocks.

The nearest way that was familiar to Zeuks was the unfrequented path through that haunted region that from Time unknown had been, and to Time unknown would always be, called Arima, and which really seemed, now it was deserted by Eurybia and Echidna, almost more ghostly in its loneliness than when those two phantasmagoric Beings disputed in their dreadful dialogue who first, who last, had broken loose from Erebos.

"You are taking me a little, just a little, too fast!" murmured the aged Ajax as they passed the spot where Echidna used to be.

Zeuks stopped at once to give the old man a chance to get his breath and to look round. He himself also looked round; and in doing so he noticed a blaze of golden light not far in front of them. It was a peculiar blaze. It was like nothing that Zeuks had ever seen before. He stared at it in positive amazement. Then suddenly, though entirely without any rational cause, he associated this fiery marvel with the presence of the aged warrior at his side.

Nor was he mistaken. Ajax, though much taller and broader-shouldered than any of the other Greeks in the Trojan war, was now terribly bent. There was indeed something impressively pitiful, even you might say, grotesquely pitiful, about the way his white head—for his hair instead of having become grey like the hair of Odysseus, had become as white as hoar-frost—or rather about the way his bent spine, curved like a great bow, had come to bring down his white head towards his feet, which were now encased, as he stood looking up under his deeply wrinkled and majestically moulded forehead, in massive almost coal-black sandals.

Ajax took longer than his guide in discovering that mysterious blaze of golden flame isolated in this haunted place.

"What in the name of Hermes is that light over there?" gurgled the old man, in a voice the significance of which Zeuks had been trying for the last couple of hours, in fact ever since he had first helped him from the ship to the shore, to catch and understand. It wasn't that he couldn't understand the meaning of the old hero's words. The difficulty was not there. He couldn't understand the mental and psychological frame of mind, the temper of mood, the drift of feeling, that was giving the very simplest of the groans, cries, sighs, ejaculations, murmurs, whispers, repetitions, interruptions, protestations, that issued from that long, narrow, pointed, friable, brittle-looking jaw whose dominant peculiarity was its extreme sensitiveness to emotion, whether that emotion was one of attraction or repulsion, of satisfied complacency or furious irritation.

The longer Zeuks pondered upon the psychic implications of the old warrior's tone the more he became convinced that the picturesque apophthegm, purporting to give a characteristic idea of the man, that had already, long ere his death, spread throughout all Hellas, was substantially correct. You had only, Zeuks told himself, to observe for half an hour, as you followed the man, the twitchings, quiverings, tightenings, relaxings, compressions, releases, explosions, of his mouth, his lips, his jaws, to realize that the muscles which set these objects working were themselves set in motion by the drift of his whole spirit.

It became clear in fact that when Ajax in a fit of blind rage "defied the lightning" he was not in any mood of metaphysical rebellion, not, for instance, obeying Zeuks' own precept of philosophic *prokleesis*, but was quite simply giving way to a natural fit of violent human fury. But whether his mood at this moment was normal or abnormal the febrile nerves of his malleable mouth were now twitching like something subjected to an extreme emotional stress.

"It's an extraordinary light!" he cried. "I must go and see what it-is! It's like that dream I've always had since my childhood! And do you know what started that dream?"

At this Zeuks felt more interested than he had expected to feel in the outbursts of this white-haired hero.

"I would greatly like to know," he answered.

The tall, thin, bent figure swung round, using its left heel in its black sandal as a pivot.

"My father whose name was—"" The old warrior suffered from some impediment in his throat, an impediment which his attendants usually mistook for phlegm, but which was in reality the fragment of a golden arrow-head which the exceptional adaptability of the man's flesh and blood had appropriated to themselves and rendered innocuous, and it was now as he struggled with his father's name that a sound like a suppressed lion's roar burst from him.

"Telamon", interjected Zeuks patiently. "Telamon", the man repeated, —"who was king of Salamis, used to tell me of a rock on that Island near the village of Cychreus through which there was a bottomless hole.

"To this hole every infant born in Salamis was brought; and into this hole, whether it was a boy or girl, it looked, and sometimes saw nothing but impenetrable darkness, and sometimes saw a dazzling light; and its parents knew by its cries of joy when it saw the light and by its cries of sorrow when it saw the darkness. And once when I told my father—Telamon that is, and it's a good sign you've heard of him—when I told my father that I always dreamed of meeting a laughing man at the bottom of that hole he said it would be a son of the great god Pan I should meet and that when I met him I should die.

"He said—Telamon I mean, and it's a good sign you've heard of him—that the light in that hole came from a dancing-lawn of the Nymphs on the other side of the earth and that among the Nymphs the most beautiful of all was Maia who was the mother of Hermes, who himself was the father of the great god Pan. And now when it's such a good sign for me that you said

'Telamon', and when there is that light over there, I must go and see it."

Zeuks never forgot how Ajax looked, as once more, with that weird gurgling sound in his throat that resembled the suppressed roar of a half-dead lion, he cried that he must go to that light. What made the man look so specially grotesque—and yet he was the noblest-looking human being Zeuks had ever seen— was the manner in which, while his tall thin majestic figure was bent almost double, his snow-white hair and ivory-white forehead not so far away from his jet-black sandals, his head was twisted sideways in order that he might fix upon Zeuks the intense stare of his yellowish-green eyes, a stare that had about it just then a golden effect, as if that fragment of solid gold that had incorporated itself among the native elements of his throat had the power of emitting gold-dust rays, even as the terrible Typhon breathed forth fire and smoke!

Zeuks, who had no more idea than Ajax himself what it really was that burned so grandly in the sun's afternoon rays, moved with him now in the direction of the tree-carved Hector standing there in heroic isolation. But little did he guess for all his cleverness what was on the point of happening.

They had moved together about fifty paces from the point where they had, so to speak, stopped to get their breath, and had joined issue on the matter of the prophetic words of Telamon of Salamis.

Suddenly Ajax began swaying backwards and forwards as if he had been sprinkled with a handful of the holy dust from that Cychrean hole, and each time he swayed, first to the East and then to the West, just as if he were indulging in some ancestral and primordial ritual, he managed to accentuate into a grotesque distortion of his whole gaunt frame the way his white skull bent sideways to stare at Zeuks while it came bowing down from the mystery of the East to the mystery of the West.

And then with one single movement of his whole body the old warrior became as motionless as the Stone of Sisyphos, had Sisyphos been suddenly saved from the undying cruelty of Zeus.

And from that motionlessness, just as if some primordial vein of gold in that Cychrean hole had really uttered a cry, there rang out a challenge so startling, that any daring wanderer passing through that deserted Arima, where Eurybia and Echidna no longer kept up their reciprocal incantation, would have said to himself: "By the gods, I must get nearer to *this*! Something really exciting is happening in this queer place! *Hush!* I must creep nearer!"

And hearer such an one would have crept. And he would have been rewarded.

"A power tells me, you laughing one, that you are my dream come true! Yes, by the earth our mother, you are no servant of Odysseus! You are no farmer of Ithaca! I, Ajax, the son of Telamon, know you for what you are! You are a true son of the great god Pan! You are the son of Pan, who is the son of Hermes, who is the son of Zeus, who is the son of Kronos!"

Certainly if the person who called himself Zeuks had all along known his parentage he couldn't have acted differently. His fate it was just then to lead the desperately old Ajax to his fantastic end; and that is what he unhesitatingly did though without the faintest idea that death was hurrying there too. Straight up to that carved image of Hector of Troy he led the greatest Achaian. Full upon that figure shone the slanting afternoon sun in a blaze of burning light and all the artistry of Hector's own daughter flamed forth in her father's majestic person.

"Watch your sandals as you walk, my Lord Ajax. There are snakes in the grass."

It was because the Trojan hero heard this instruction and obeyed it to the letter that they reached the carved tree before he lifted up his eyes to see what it was that burned before him with such a flame.

"*Hector!*" he cried with a ringing battle-cry; and then almost querulously as he rolled over at the feet of the son of Priam, "so its you and neither the one nor the other of us who at the end has the arms of Achilles!"

CHAPTER IX

By the time the body of the white-haired son of Telamon lay still, and Zeuks, "the laughing man", had satisfied himself that this long, lean, fleshless form, whose mighty muscles had once hurled back from the hulls and bulwarks of the Achaian ships troop after troop of Trojans and Trojan allies, was really and truly dead, the sun had begun to fall horizontally upon the golden armour of Achilles, hanging now so easily and naturally on the ash-tree carved to resemble Hector. The Image of Hector, thus blazing in its blinding splendour, seemed to be exulting over the body of Ajax, as if it had stricken down that mighty son of Telamon not from the broken towers of a darkened Ilium but from the battlements of some new aerial Troy that were now emerging victorious.

And at this moment there came over Zeuks an unusual craving to get to the bottom of the old familiar mystery of his own birth. Those particular words which Ajax had evidently uttered under the direct impact and pressure of some sudden inspiration had sunk like a lump of adamant into the mind of Zeuks. He repeated them to himself—"The son of Pan, the son of Hermes, the son of Zeus, the son of Kronos"—and he even carried this liturgical genealogy a step further, and murmured the words: "the son of Gaia and Ouranos."

Murmuring these words like a ritualistic chant he knelt over the body before him and thrusting his arms beneath it lifted it sufficiently high as to be able to prop it up with its back against the shins and knees and thighs of the graven image of the greatest of the Trojans, still blazing like fire in the armour of Achilles.

In carving Hector's image out of that tree-trunk his unrecognized daughter had thought more of making the man's face resemble its original than of making his form as muscular as it actually was. So that now, when the real muscles of the tall emaciated son of Telamon were thus contrasted with the supple and pliant elegance of that sunlit golden "eidolon" of his famous enemy, there would have been plenty of excuse for Zeuks had he cried out: "Gods in Heaven! No wonder Troy was taken and destroyed if one leader was like *this* and the other like *that*!"

But the mind of Zeuks was at that moment far too full of its own private speculations to do more than place on the ground behind him his own personal weapon, which was a thick, short, double-edged dagger with a sharp point, and lifting both hands to the bowed sun-illumined white head above him that now hung down with a distinct droop towards the direction from which they had just come, that is to say towards the rocky coast where the Naiads had their cave, he began to tilt it up and thrust it back a little, so that it should be kept in an upright position by resting it against the heart of the inmost wood of the carved tree where it was supported on one side by Hector's left knee and on the other side by his right knee; and once having got it in that position Zeuks was as careful as a woman in the considerate manner in which he closed its eyes.

The afternoon sun was now projecting such a blaze of light that the armour of Achilles reflected it from every curve, whether convex or concave. In fact the incredible and miraculous gleaming of this armour which the cajoleries of the sea-goddess had extracted from the smithy of the fire-god, was so dazzling that whether it flamed back from the closed eyes of the son of Telamon or from the golden greaves of the son of Priam it compelled Zeuks to bend down till his own head was as deeply sunk forward between the knees of the dead Ajax as the head of Ajax was sunk backwards between the knees of the image of Hector.

Thus were the three figures united, one a corpse, one a work of art, and one a living creature; and this uniting of life with death, and of life and death with a graven image of human imagination had a curious and singular effect: for there came into the already confused and naturally chaotic mind of Zeuks one of the most powerful impressions of his whole life. In embracing those dead limbs and in drawing into the depths of his being the bitter smell of the old hero's scrotum, and the salt, sharp taste of the perspiration-soaked hairs of his motionless thighs, Zeuks completely forgot the dead man's announcement as to his own paternity. What filled his mind now was a sudden doubt about the wisdom of his proudly proclaimed "Prokleesis" as the best of all possible war-cries for the struggle of living creatures with the mystery of life.

But was it really the best? Was this challenging and this defying of life the wisest attitude for living creatures? Zeuks had long ago found out by bitter experience that *some* sort of habitual life-philosophy was absolutely essential for him. But was this mood of defiance and challenge the best he could find? He began to mutter all sorts of alternatives to himself as he buried his head between the thighs of Ajax.

By degrees he felt as if he were embracing both life and death, though like a bird swimming under water he had to rise to the surface every few minutes to get a breath of air. "By the waters of the Styx," he said, "whatever essence of living I make up my mind to embrace, it must be capable of being reduced to a simple surge of will-power and a simple clutch of enjoyment! And I must make it such a habit that I can summon it up at any moment and use it under any conditions!

"And since I've got to live out my destiny, whether I challenge it and defy it or simply submit to it, it seems silly to go on making this 'prokleesis' of mine the essence of the whole thing. No! I can now see well what the right word for my life-struggle is—not the word 'prokleesis', 'defiance', but the word *Lanthanomai*, or 'I forget', followed by the still simpler word, *Terpomai* or 'I enjoy'. For by the Styx, its a question if we can enjoy anything till we've forgotten almost everything!

"That's what's the matter with Odysseus"; and at the thought of the man who had won this golden armour from the sinews and bones that here lay dead, only to lose it all again to this graven tree-trunk that would never be able to know anything of these human rivalries, Zeuks lifted up his head from between those withered but still mighty thighs. "It is," he told himself, "as if I were embracing this corpse beneath that famous tree outside the great wall of Ilium; and as if I had been given by the gods the power to suck and draw and drain from the lapsing semen of this dead body such magnetic force into the peristaltic channel of my spirit that a fresh, and a new insight into the whole of life radiates through me."

Zeuks was not exaggerating what he felt; and indeed if the young daughter of Teiresias had been present at this moment she would have learnt as much, and perhaps more, from the motions of the man's arms and legs just then, as she had ever learnt from his discarded clue-word "prokleesis", or was ever likely to learn from his new clue-words, "lanthanomai" and "Terpomai". But then Pontopereia, being, for all her prophetic gift, a natural girl, she would instinctively put less confidence in the creative impulse of a clue-word than in the simplest bodily movement.

But it was with more than his out-flung arms that this queer son of Arcadian soil proceeded now to encircle in one and the same embrace both the dead man's neck and the base of that ash-tree out of which Hector's shin-bones had been so exquisitely carved. It was not indeed until the moment when he saw Ajax fall at the feet of that graven image wearing the armour of Achilles, that something in him such as had never before come to the surface of the "laughing man" rose up, and dominated his whole nature. And it was on the strength of this "something" that he now pressed against his ribs in the same desperate, embrace both the dead man and the carved tree.

"Why should I laugh at life rather than challenge it or defy it when all I've really got to do is just to enjoy it?" This was. what he was telling himself as he hugged the tree and the gold and the flesh and the bone together. And the very form of his. countenance became changed as he did so. The physiognomy of Zeuks has been, as we have seen, designed and dedicated, devoted and destined for the ribald reduction of everything in. existence to a monstrous jest.

But something had risen just then out of the depths of his being that was neither solemn nor comical; something that found its account in quite a different direction from that of either defiance or mockery. And the advantage of this direction was its freedom from the necessity of any effort except the effort of will. It needed absolutely no mental effort at all; not even the mental effort of realizing just exactly what it was he was defying, or towards what particular thing he was directing his mockery. "To will," Zeuks told himself, "is simply to do a little more vigorously what we are already doing spontaneously. These efforts naturally occur when we grow consciously aware of some exercise in ourselves of the life-energy which moves in every offspring of the ancient earth. All we have to do is to use our will to intensify this."

Nor was the expression upon the face of Zeuks that accompanied this revelation lost on the air. It was on the contrary inwardly digested. It was one of the luckiest moments in the philosophical life of the creature that always so proudly called itself "the Worm of Arima" that just when the adventurous consciousness of the son of Arcadian Pan had dived deep enough among the mysteries of the multiverse to discover a clue-word, or rather a clue-act, that was more intimate and more effective than "defy" or "mock", the protruding, perspiring, and palpitating proboscis of the Worm of Arima happened to be aboveboard rather than in any of its convoluted labyrinths below. For since the illumination upon the countenance of Zeuks at this second of time communicated itself by the usual aerial vibration to everything within reach, it was natural enough that the Worm of Arima, being so near to it, carried away into its underground world when it returned there, though the form of its own visage was so much simpler, a celestial exultation worthy of the noblest zodiacal sign.

"These motions of the will," said Zeuks to himself, "are motions of the life-energy within us, sometimes enduring and patient, sometimes violent and desperate. But, whatever these motions of the life-energy are, if they're to give us that thrill of enjoyment we need, we've got to acquire the trick of forcing ourselves to forget the particular afflictions that spoil such enjoyment."

And it was at this point in what might have been called his pearl-diving in the ensorcerized earth-mould of Arima that Zeuks felt himself to be, at one and the same time, a god, a man, a beast, a bird, a fish, a worm and an insect. And in his heart he cried out: "O gods, O men, O beasts, O birds, O fish, O frogs, O ferns and funguses, I, Zeuks, have you all in me, and I, Zeuks, am within you all! But, O Maia, mother of Hermes and grandmother of Pan, teach me to forget! Teach me, O youthful Maia, the heavenly tracks and heavenlier side-tracks of the sacred art of forgetting! Don't let me ever, O Maia most holy, O Maia most blessed, O Maia eternally youthful, don't let me forget how to forget!

"Yes, to forget the disgusts! Yes! to forget the horrors! yes! to forget the loathings! Mother of Hermes, hear the prayer of thy great-grand-son Zeuks, and grant unto him, and that not too late, the power of forgetting the madness, the loathsomeness, and the horror! I should require," thus did the thoughts of Zeuks run on, "I who am a god, a man, a beast; a bird, a fish, a frog, a worm, an insect, I who have suffered such horrors from the sky, my begetter, from the earth, my mother, from the elements, my aunts, from Space my grandmother, from Time my grandfather, I should require a draught of forgetfulness so obliterating that it could turn every hell that all my separate natures necessitate into every paradise that all my separate natures crave! Mother of Hermes"—thus did the heart of Zeuks still jerk forth its desperate prayer to the multiverse around it— "cannot you see that for a manifold creature such as I am, a creature who is a god, a man, an insect, a frog, a newt, an ass, a camel, a bear, a monkey, an elephant, if I am really to drink a draught of pure Lethe, if I am really to obtain the power of forcing myself to forget the horrors, it can only be done by my own *will to forget*!

"O thou 'still youthful Maia', cannot you see that what I need is to strengthen my will to forget till it is ten thousand times more powerful than any god as yet discovered by us whether in earth or in air or in fire or in water? If I had this power, O thou 'still youthful' great-grandmother of mine, I could enjoy sight, sound, touch, taste and smell, each one of them separately or all together, and in the pleasure of satisfying hunger and thirst, and in the pleasure of satisfying lust and desire, and in the pleasure of diving into earth and air and water and fire, and through them and out the other side, if there is another side, I beseech thee, O Maia, thou Nymph forever young, let me learn the greatest of all the arts, the art of forgetting!"

By one of those pure caprices and casual happenings that occur under the dispensation of Tyche the great goddess of chance such as we mortals call "a stroke of luck" when they suit us and "the cruel irony of things" when they don't, it happened that when Zeuks began heaving up the body of Ajax, with a view to carrying it to the Corridor of the Pillars, there occurred a faint but unmistakable flicker at the outer corner of the dead man's left eyelid.

This incident was solely and simply due to the sudden jerk to the corpse's head when Zeuks lifted up that long, lean, painfully muscular body preparatory to making the effort, which was not at all an easy one, of balancing it on his shoulder. But this negligible and unimportant accident made, for a special reason, a most agitating impression on the mind of Zeuks.

What it did for him was to set going a peculiarly morbid infirmity of his imagination; namely the fantastic illusion that his own automatic blinkings and pulse-beats and heart-throbs and blood-circulations, yes! and even the naturally drawn breathings from his lungs might suddenly be intensified to a degree beyond bearing and he might be driven so wild by all these reiterative pulsings, pumpings and poundings that he'd be sent raving through Arima like a naked madman!

His face was contracted into a desperately grim scowl as he staggered off from the Hector-Tree with the body of Ajax on his back. "And so," he told himself, "it has now come to the point;

and the question is, can the great-grand-son of immortal Maia keep his 'will to forget' intact when his whole taut skin drums from within to the tune of' remember!'

Staggering along for a dozen strides at a time, every few seconds Zeuks had to stop to take breath. His shoulders were broad enough; but his legs were short; and the corpse he carried was so tall that its toes, for he carried it face downwards, kept tapping against his own heels.

But it was the horrible feeling that at any moment this repetitive pounding and pulsing and blinking might split his skin that was spoiling that moment for him rather than any effort of carrying Ajax. And it was at his tenth stop that he made a really desperate attempt to deal with this insane attack. He planted his feet firmly in a patch of damp and mossy soil, not far from the spot where Eurybia used to exercise her curious sedentary witchcraft, and where she used to argue with Echidna from twilight to twilight as to whether this breaking loose out of Tartaros, about which all the Attic world was now talking, was due to feminine wiles or to titanic straining.

Having got the heel of one sandal hidden in that soft wet moss and the under-curve of the other sandal covering something brittle below that wet moss that might easily have turned out to be the ivory-white thigh-bone of a still-born child, Zeuks now took up his own consciousness, as if it were a massive plummet of lead sharpened at the end, and drove it down deep into the earth.

Had either of his youthful acquaintances, Nisos or Pontopereia, been at his side at that moment they would have had, in the case of the former a male inspiration, and in the case of the latter a female inspiration, simply from Zeuks' visage. It was literally distorted, contorted, convulsed with pure exultation when at last he hauled up into the light the mental self he had let down into the abyss. What pleased him so much was the supreme success of his supreme effort; for his horrid, loathsome, disgusting mental illness, revolting in itself and attended by the wildest and maddest terrors, had actually been left behind in the depths of the earth like an after-birth at the bottom of a weedy garden.

This was a relief so incredible that it confused him by its very beatitude. "Never again," he told himself, "never once again shall I have those horrors!"

And Zeuks remembered how when he was farming in the vicinity of Cuckoo-Hill he once heard Enorches, the Priest of the Mysteries, curse a rash young neighbour who had tried to seduce the neophyte-priestess Spartika, the daughter of Nosodea, and the sister of Leipephile; and how the pompously perverse and the necrophiliastically censorious tone of the man in his assumption of priestly authority had for long haunted him because it jumped with his own peculiar mental malady: "May your crime exude from every pore of your body like stinking pus! May it burst from every inch of your skin like gangrenous necrosis! May it reek from your body like putrid decomposition! May it cross every sight you see with a streak of fœtid blood! May it infect every sound you hear with an explosion of foul wind! May it taint everything you touch with vile and viscous glutinosity! May all you taste have the tang of brine and all you smell have a reek of the mortuary! May your consciousness of yourself become a consciousness of empty eye-sockets and rattling cross-bones! May the clock-strokes of annihilation record the hours of all your nights and the dust-motes of disillusion drift over the minutes of all your days!"

Zeuks could not only remember the shock he got from this curse, he remembered also the intensity of the particular prayer about his own fate which was his reaction to it. He had prayed to Arcadian Pan that he might become the supreme lord of the Island of Ithaca, dwelling, as Odysseus the son of Laertes did, and as Agelaos the son of Krateros Naubolides hoped one day to do, above the Corridor of the Pillars. "Why do I think of that prayer at this particular moment?" he asked himself as he staggered and shuffled under the weight of the tall corpse he was carrying, up the much-trodden path across the burying-ground of the slaves that led into the olive-garden.

ATLANTIS

But Zeuks the son of Arcadian Pan didn't hasten to leave the graves of the old slaves in order to reach the cradles of the young olives. On the contrary he moved more slowly than ever. He was clutching the dead man's wrists so tightly with both his hands that the warrior's toes still in heavy silver-clamped sandals tapped against his own bare heels causing him pain. In this slaves' cemetery Zeuks was on fairly familiar ground, for several of the farmers of Cuckoo Hill who were too poor to possess cemeteries of their own brought the bodies of their dead slaves to this spot.

Zeuks in his previous visits to the place however had never noticed that one of these graves and this a very deep one had not been filled up but was gaping wide-open. Now what, in the name of Persephoneia, the Queen of all the Dead, was the explanation of this? There were no inscriptions here at all and there had been none for centuries; so that the identity or identities of the occupant or occupants of this deep hole in the earth could only be revealed by such as had lowered him or her into this deep and narrow sepulchre or had recently robbed this nameless sanctuary of its inmate.

By this time the sun had already gone down below the horizon and night was rapidly approaching. "What in the name of Aidoneus and Persephoneia will our old man do with this other old man?" Zeuks now asked himself in perplexity. "He must be-entertaining the Princess by this time in the Dining-Hall and if that incredible old Eurycleia weren't the woman she is our old king would be in a fine fix! But that's just what this amazing old woman must have been doing again tonight, saving him from the shame of failing in any of his kingly duties! But what in the name of Aidoneus would the old man feel at this overpowering moment, when he's not only got the Phaiakians on his hands, along with that crazy Herald of theirs, but has had to confront this Princess of all Princesses, if I were to appear before him with the corpse of Ajax!"

Very carefully and very slowly Zeuks lifted the long lean body, all bone and muscle and sinew, from his shoulder and laid it on its back on the indescribable rubble and litter that surrounded that gaping hole. Then, with his eyes on a smashed pot that looked as if it might have been the first piece of pottery ever made by the hand of man, his thoughts turned to Okyrhöe, "I hate that woman. I *know* she's up to some game. Yes, I hate her! Oh, why is it that in this world there's always somebody we *have* to wish in Hades? It's not a matter of war or revenge or rivalry or just family against family, or tribe against tribe, or race against race. Those things are all part of the game, part of the way things are, part of the price we have to pay for being alive at all.

"Krateros Naubolides wants to keep the king here, so that without any trouble he can slip into his shoes when he dies. Odysseus on the contrary naturally wants *before he dies* to make such a thunderous commotion and such a roaring rumpus that his personality will go resounding on, like the beating of brazen swords upon brazen shields, till it's heard over both the horizons of the world; heard where the blameless Ethiopians at the Gates of the West cry their farewell to the burning sun on his nightly journey, and heard where the blameless Ethiopians at the Gates of the East cry their welcome to the burning sun as he rises for a new day!

"No, what's wrong isn't our having enemies, it's our having friends like this woman Okyrhöe! The old man will never be able to be happy again with Nausikaa while that cunning bitch is about. It's a wicked shame."

Staring with a frown at those smashed bits of discarded pottery Zeuks was now absolutely astonished to find himself sobbing. What in Hades' name did this mean? Was he not exultantly happy? Had he not shuffled off the coil of his worst horrors and left their scurf and their scum at the bottom of the abyss? "For what then—by all the Harpies"—he said to himself, "am I a grown man blubbing like a baby?"

He sucked in both his lips at this point which gave him an extremely odd expression, an expression which would certainly have interested his great-grandmother Maia if from some Valley

of Eternal Youth she could have seen it; and with this expression
—which was a mixture of fussy punctiliousness, touchy querulousness, and irritable contrariness, mingled together by a sort of
impish gravity—fixed upon his features like an actor's mask, he
placed his hands under the armpits of the dead man and lowered
him down feet foremost into the open grave till he was standing
erect in it.

Then Zeuks set himself to fill up the grave with the rubble that
lay several inches deep in every direction. This was an easy task
and Zeuks accomplished it in quick time, using both his extremities. What he didn't kick down into that hole from the litter
around it he threw down into it with his hands.

And when he had finished his job he stamped heavily and
obstinately on the rubble round the top of the corpse's head,
leaving, however, for the benefit of his own private and secret
knowledge and information, but only just recognizable even by
himself, the little bronze spike on the top of the small bull's-hide
head-piece that continued to surmount, even after all the knock-
ing about that that warrior-body had undergone, the snow-white
head of the dead chieftain.

With his lips still sucked into his mouth in that odd way
Zeuks spent several minutes covering and revealing, revealing
and once more covering, that little bronze spike, to conceal which
finally, and it was almost dark by now, he made use of a cracked
oyster-shell.

All this accomplished, he made the special ritual gesture practised for a thousand years at ceremonies where the dead had been
buried rather than burnt, and when this had been done he
moved cautiously through the olive-garden and bent his head in
the darkness lower than he need have done before passing beneath
the arch into the corridor of pillars. He felt in some odd way
humbled; and every sort of pride, whether human or godlike,
seemed to have been drained out of him simply by the fact of
having lived all these hours with Ajax, who, whether alive or
dead, was so natural and so true to his essential self, that he made
any other persons seem vacillating and wayward.

ATLANTIS

"Didn't somebody tell me," Zeuks said to himself, as he emerged from under the low-bowed arch into the corridor of pillars, "that there was an olive-stump inside here ready to discuss the newest and the most difficult problems in philosophy? But I smell meat! The old king must be already at dinner. Hades! But I mustn't make a sound or I'll have them all rushing out!" His sandals were of tougher leather than those worn by his neighbours on Cuckoo-Hill and he suddenly became fearful of their creaking. He felt better when he had slipped them off and was holding them in his left hand; but he felt better still when he had extricated with some difficulty from the lining of his outer vest or "chiton" his two-edged dagger, whose small bronze handle was covered with a particular kind of cloth specially adapted to soak up blood without letting it drip.

But the odd thing with Zeuks just then, as inhaling the rich waftures from Eurycleia's ancestral cooking he stared wildly at the Club of Herakles propped up between its two projecting quartz-stones, was the fact that his irresolution at that critical moment connected itself with a feeling that went beyond humility.

"What has happened," he cried out from the depths of his heart with a wordless, soundless cry, "what has happened to you, O Maia, the Nymph who gave birth to Hermes, the begetter of Pan? You were not one, O Maia my own, O Maia, my more than Mother! You were not one of those tragic mortal ones who die, as the old Dryad here must have died along with her aged oak! Of the fate of the Nymph of Master Dryops I know something; and of the fate of the Nymph who bore Pan to Hermes I have heard much: but whither, I implore you to answer me, whither, O whither, have *you* fled, immortal mother of my father's father, you for whose sake the lyre was first strung? Are you still being visited by the son of Kronos in some hidden cave in Arcady? Or perhaps at this very moment, beyond the reach of us all, caught by the rising flood in some royal chamber in Atlantis, your far-floating, filmy-textured, chestnut-coloured hair is washing backwards and forwards, while stiff-finned fish and scaly-tailed sea-snakes press their snouts against your cold breasts?

"Have I prayed in vain to you all my life as an immortal, and have you all *the time been* cold and dead as Atlantis itself? Surely you are immortal among the Nymphs, oh mother of my father's father? Don't they say that the great earth-mother bore you at the beginning of all things, before she was over-shadowed by Ouranos or knew what it was to have connexion with any elemental power beyond herself? Aren't you, along with all the Nymphs of the Mountains and the Springs and the Lakes and the Seas, different altogether in the hierarchies of the gods from a pathetic old creature like the family-Dryad of this place who has now perished with her oak?"

He must have been himself at that moment, poor Zeuks, a somewhat pathetic figure, with one hand clutching that double-edged weapon under his "chiton" and with the other pressing his sandals against his ribs. At any rate the easily moved moth murmured to her friend the fly: "I do so, *so* wish, my dear friend, that we knew whence this fellow Zeuks originally came. I don't mean *just now*, for, of course, we know *that* well enough! I mean at the beginning of his life. Do, for Heaven's sake, Myos, wake up, 'and see', as rude boys learn to say at school, 'what the cat has brought in'! I'm afraid you ate far too much of that beautifully-cooked bread-sauce! I warned you against it. Oh how I did warn you against it! For the same thing has happened to you before. It shows how we cannot be trusted not to fall into the sin of gluttony when we are safe at home and in no danger of being swallowed up alive by voracious insectivorous monsters. Listen to me, Myos, my only friend! Listen to me, most learned of revered teachers! I hate to speak of such tragic things: but don't you remember how often we've seen dead flies, lying mute and silent, never to hum, never to buzz, never to murmur again? And where, I ask you, have we seen them?

"On plates and under plates! On tables and under tables! On window sills and under window sills! You flies are far too sensitive and intellectual and highly-strung to take risks with your food. It's different altogether with us. We're made for risks like that! If *we* don't take risks every day of our lives we very quickly degenerate. I oughtn't to scold you, my precious wise one"—here the beautiful moth showed signs of emotion, for her right wing quivered and her left antenna groped freely in a whiff of steam-infected air from the hall within—"because I have myself been yielding so weakly to my admiration for your learning that I have not yet, though I heard his inspired speech, flown to enquire how the noble Priest of the Mysteries has borne up after his exhausting oration.

"But, O thou wisest of flies, I do feel such shame when I think"—It was then that there broke in upon their conversation the voice of their living and moving tent, namely the Club of Herakles, who when in the company of his special and most privileged associates always called himself "Dokeesis" a name which in that dark Nemean Forest, where he was brought up, has the meaning of "seeming", because there are so many shadows there that it is often hard to distinguish between appearance and reality.

"It is I who am speaking to you, again, Sixth Pillar, yes it is I, the Slayer of the Nemean Lion, and I want to know whether I heard you correctly, Sixth Pillar, when you spoke of receiving the news that the great Goddess Hera the Queen of Heaven, had suddenly left Olympos empty of her divine presence and had gone to Gargaros, the summit of Ida, with the intention of persuading the Son of Kronos, by the help of Desire, and by the help of Sleep after the satisfaction of Desire, to yield up his third portion of Power over the Kingdoms of this World to his two Brothers Aidoneus and Poseidon?

"And if I heard you correctly, O illustrious Sixth Pillar, who bear on your pedestal the signature of a son of Hephaistos, I would like to ask you if you could tell me what in your opinion was the secret purpose of the wife of Zeus in thus betraying her husband, the Ruler of the Upper Air, and through the air of the whole surface of the earth?"

There was no need for the little shame-faced silky-winged Pyraust to prod her friend the fly to listen to this dialogue whose reverberation shook the corridor. Indeed the fly's big eyes had begun to bulge to such an extent that the anxious moth-girl feared they might fall out of his head leaving two bloody apertures through which she would be staring into her friend's "frontal lobe", the last thing she wished to do.

"In my opinion," the two insects now heard the Sixth Pillar say, "the goddess Hera must have welcomed the return, completely unknown to her husband, of the Messenger she sent, namely the seven-coloured Iris, to find Pallas Athene among the blameless Ethiopians. In my opinion Pallas Athene must have assured her that if they worked together now and got the help, both of Persephone from Hades, and of Thetis from the Sea, they would be able to take the domination of the world out of the possession of men and hand it over into the possession of women where it ought to have been from the beginning."

After this there was dead silence in the corridor; until the shame-faced moth took upon herself to fling a question upon that wine-scented air towards the lusty olive-sprout that had dared to grow up between a couple of flagstones.

"Can you tell me, Olive-Branch, whether it will be the lady Okyrhöe or the lady Nausikaa who will win the love of Odysseus?" There was such a long silence after this dramatic question that the fly came near to spreading its gauzy wings and taking upon itself the role of Messenger from the Insects to the Olympians.

Well did the moth know what was in her friend's mind; and she couldn't help wondering what she herself would feel if she accompanied the fly through the flashes of light that wavered down from the hall above, and with rainbow colours flashing from point to point in *his* wings and mysterious gleams glorifying the lustrous brown of *her* wings, they were both to flicker up those stone steps and confront the revellers with the startling and momentous news that henceforth the world was to be ruled by women.

But the olive-shoot's wise answer brought back everybody's wits to the practical situation with which they were now faced. "The king will choose neither of those two women," announced the sagacious olive-shoot. "But you may be sure," he added with sturdy cynicism, "the King will use all the power he may have over both these ladies to be in a position to hoist sail without delay and explore the unknown West beyond Lost Atlantis."

Once more the boldness and rashness of the turn their talk so soon took brought down upon them all the same uneasy silence. But this time it was not from among any of them in the corridor that the interruption to their colloquy came; and it was Zeuks who was the first to be aware of it.

Zeuks was still standing against the wall clutching his formidable double-edged dagger in one hand and his sandals in the other; but he now imperceptibly moved his head so that his right ear might be directed towards the stairs that led down into the corridor from the dining-hall.

Zeuks heard steps descending those stairs, very, very slow and cautious steps, and very light steps, but with no vacillation or hesitation about their purpose. Somebody—a light-footed boy or girl—was coming as a spy or anyway as a scout. Zeuks listened intently to the faintest sound made by this explorer and he soon heard the hurried gasping breaths that the light-footed young person in his excitement was unable to suppress.

Listening with the divining rod, as you might call it, of his auditory intelligence Zeuks was soon rewarded for his concentrated attention by recognizing a particular click between two of these irrepressible gasps that identified the prowler without further question. He was Nisos Naubolides.

And then there occurred one of those curious moments, or rather seconds, in the experience of persons suddenly encountering each other in this particular dimension of our multiverse, persons familiar to each other and yet on the alert in regard to each other's immediate intentions. At such a second of time there is liable to happen an electric explosion between the life energy of the one and the life energy of the other, an explosion over which and upon which the consciousness of neither of the persons has the slightest influence or effect. What you might call the two kinds of life-levin or of life-lightning in these persons, thus confronting each other, must be far more different than the persons themselves are different and far more antagonistic.

Nisos, for instance, had always felt for Zeuks a friendly attraction and Zeuks had certainly felt for Nisos a protective affection. And yet no sooner did the lad descending those steps in the twilight catch sight of the familiar figure of Zeuks than he performed, or the life-lightning that was using him performed, some surprising acts. In the first place he put his fingers to his lips in the universal sign which means: "Hush! This little business is entirely between ourselves!" Then, though he was some seven or eight steps above the corridor, he made a wild leap like a young lion and landed on the corridor floor at least a yard beyond the Sixth Pillar; and then with a second and still more leonine leap he grasped Zeuks by the throat.

It was lucky for him that the impersonal life-lightning which seized upon Zeuks at that same instant confined itself, as if Zeuks had really been an animal, to physical contact. What Zeuks actually did was to thrust back, with a blind instinctive jerk, deep into the thick wool of the under-shirt out of which he'd drawn it, that dangerous two-edged dagger; and then with the whole strength of both his arms he tore one of Nisos' hands from his throat and treating this captured hand as a hawk might treat a butcher-bird he squeezed it into his capacious mouth and pressed his teeth against it, not really hard enough to draw blood, but hard enough to give Nisos the feeling that those doglike teeth *were* drawing blood.

Thus had the situation between these two resolved itself into one of those purely physical encounters which carry with them so large a current of earth-life that they seem to satisfy both the creatures involved with a sort of absolute satisfaction. And what happened then was so much what we can imagine any benevolent fate would have intended to happen that it is hard to believe that it was brought about by pure chance.

Feeling through every throb the one hand which was still on Zeuks' throat that he had only to press these fleshy sinews with a viciously increasing purpose to stop the man's breath for ever, Nisos suddenly thought: "But I am going to be a prophet; and all Prophets have the power of an absolute control over their rage. I shall therefore show this funny fellow Zeuks that I am letting him live when I could easily kill him and being a good friend to him when I could easily be the deadliest enemy."

And on his side Zeuks was now saying to himself, as he kept his dog-like teeth firmly pressed against his antagonist's hand: "What is the use of being the great-grandson of the ever-youthful Nymph Maia, even if in the end, for all the gods in my blood, I have to sleep the perpetual sleep of death, what, I ask you, is the use of it all if I can't detach my consciousness from my body far enough to be able to put up with a leaping, scrabbling, jumping, skipping, dancing kid like this without wanting to bite his head off?"

"Come up quietly with me, Zeuks, old friend," gasped Nisos. "The old man will be damned glad to see you. But, for the sake of all we both love best in the world, what has happened to Ajax?"

"Surely I'll come with you, my dear boy," replied Zeuks. "Ajax, did you say? Why, Ajax is wholly, entirely, absolutely, and altogether out of it. Ajax is in fact not only dead but buried. I found him dead and I buried him myself. But let us go now and let us go quietly as you and I know well how to go. But tell me this before we start and tell it me in your lowest and least heraldic voice. How are things with the old man over his wine? Have either of those ladies got him yet in her toils?"

Nisos gave him as well as he could a lively but rather a schoolboyish description of what he had seen; and as the older man listened he nodded many times and muttered varying rather cynical commentaries. Then did the two of them thread their way between the first, second, third and fourth Pillars, Zeuks leaning on the arm of Nisos as if he had been much older than he actually was.

"No, my dear friend," Zeuks said with a rapid downward glance towards the base of the Sixth Pillar as they passed that philosophic interpreter of elemental vibrations, "no! my impression from all you've told me about our old man's behaviour with those two women is that the Princess Nausikaa is shocked at the physical change in him. I don't want to mislead you, Sonny, for your impressions are vivid and you have described them mighty well; but my own feeling about it is that Nausikaa finds it hard to recognise in our old king the handsome hero with whom she fell in love when he suddenly appeared from out of the shadows of the rocks while she and her maidens were playing ball by the sea-shore. I don't think myself he is in the faintest danger of being seduced by the Okyrhöe woman. My idea is that the kind of flattery he uses in her case, you know the sort of thing I mean, that exaggerated praise of everything about her, is due to a mounting and intensifying irritation with the way she treats him."

"Yes! yes! yes!" murmured Nisos in a still lower voice as they drew near to the thick oaken brazen-barred door at the top of the steps, "yes! yes! I've noticed *that* about him too! He gets rid of his bottled-up rage just as some old people do of their bottled-up misery by the simple process of inventing exaggerated and fantastical fables. But I tell you, Zeuks, my friend, things are about as ticklish up there as they can possibly be. It's like balancing yourself on a tight-rope—no! not like balancing *yourself*, like watching them balance *themselves!* No! I haven't got it quite right even yet! It's like watching them dancing upon thin ice dangerously slippery and liable to break and let them into the water!"

"Well, Son, we'll soon be"—but Nisos couldn't catch the dying out of that sentence; for they were now standing before the massive brazen-fitted time-darkened door, the other side of which was that palace dining-hall which had already been for numberless generations, and would be for many more to come, a centre of intrigue and plotting, not only for Ithaca, but for the whole of Hellas.

This black-oak door with its four panels and bronze frame opened to them now at the first pressure of Zeuks' hand. It would have needed one of the minutest of all the dust-motes that danced so solemnly in that spear-shaft of a torch-ray across the head of the lady Okyrhöe, across the head of the lady Nausikaa, across the head of Odysseus himself, to thread that twisted path, beyond the cunning of the tiniest mite of sea-spray left by the sun in his descent, the twisted path to the heart of the old king.

It was clear at once to both Zeuks and Nisos that Odysseus was not so much drunk from the fumes of wine as drunk from the opposing sorceries of those two formidable women.

"You'd have thought," said Nisos to himself, "that Circe and Calypso between them would have made him harder to beguile; but of course—Nausikaa——""

He closed the brazen-framed door behind Zeuks and himself and made a hurried obeisance to the old bearded figure on the throne-seat at the table, but although the king looked searchingly into each of their faces as they came forward it struck them both that he understood nothing of what he saw save only that some terrible crisis of a fatal choice was upon him.

As to this choice it was abundantly clear to both Nisos and Zeuks that until some unexpected ray of light penetrated that bearded head the old king was simply incapable of choosing between his new temptress and his ancient flame. There was indeed to each of them something almost sickeningly painful in the sight of this tremendous hero of the greatest war ever experienced by the human race being lured to this unseemly turnstile of sexual cross-purpose.

Nisos and Zeuks were able to approach the table in whispered colloquy with each other, were able indeed to receive a wine-glass from Eurycleia and have it filled by Arsinoë, and finally were able to enter into an extremely punctilious argument with the Herald without attracting more notice from Odysseus than a vague, obscure, and taking-everything-for-granted nod.

"Yes, you will be interested to hear," said the Herald, "that your humble servant has been permitted to approach your King of Kings and Lord of Lords with a request for permission to visit in person the Royal Treasury and to see with my own eyes and touch with my own hands certain pieces of golden armour that actually belonged to Achilles the son of Peleus and which your King of Kings and Lord of Lords won from Ajax in a public competition presided over by the Olympians. This permission I hope presently to take advantage of, but this beautiful lady-in-waiting, who tells me she will escort me to the Treasury, begs me to await the moment when her lovely duty of dispensing wine to the King's visitors is over for tonight."

Zeuks looked at Nisos with a cold shiver of apprehension when Ajax was mentioned; and Arsinöe hastened to fill up the young man's glass the moment he had allowed himself in his embarrassment to empty it at one gulp.

"You haven't yet made it quite clear to me, sweet lady," they heard Okyrhöe say to Nausikaa, "what exactly is the change you are so struck by in my darling hero here, since you beheld him, after his escape from that accurst Bitch-Nymph, washed up naked on your shores. O what a shock to your chaste and virginal feelings that occasion must have been! A naked man coming forth out of the wild waves and advancing straight towards you! No wonder this romantic and bewitching story had already become a sailor's ditty in the docks of every port when I was a little girl!

"Little did I dream it would ever be my lot to be allowed by fate to succeed you in the affections of our little-girl-loving hero! O you must satisfy my childish curiosity, sweet Auntie Nausikaa; for my parents, you know, never allowed me to forget that I was descended from Nausithoos the father of Alkinoos who wedded your dear mother, Arete.

"O yes! it is indeed as if one of those impossible dreams in a young girl's life had come true that the very same hero of my childhood should actually have become now that I'm grown up and can realize all it means, yes, should actually have become, in spite of his old age, my lover and my beloved!

"O sweet Auntie Nausikaa, you *must* forgive my emotion in

meeting you; for you must realize how the sight of you calls up every glimpse and feature of my earliest visions of life, now so wonderfully satisfied, with him as my lover"—At this point Okyrhöe actually leant across the table and touched the stem of the wine-glass out of which Odysseus was drinking. "Yes," she told him, "your little girl is confessing all our happiness to her Auntie Nausikaa!"

It was at this point that Zeuks looked at Nisos, and Nisos looked at Zeuks; and never, in all the history of love has such savage derision been excited by such palpable humbug.

"We Phaiakians," began the Herald, his natural ritualistic assurance evidently emphasized by the long unnatural suppression which he had endured while his Phaiakian princess struggled to ward off without losing her temper the diabolical jibes of the weird woman from Thebes.

"We Phaiakians are more ready to enter into technical arguments on matters of science and on the navigation of ocean-going ships than any other race, and we find it very hard to argue on these important subjects with barbarians. That is one of the reasons why it is such a deep satisfaction to us to have the privilege of talking with real Hellenic gentlemen like yourselves."

"My own feeling is," said Nisos, trying to make himself a little more comfortable by leaning sideways against the table, "my own feeling is that it is better to work out our own personal system of philosophy as well as our system of navigation in private meditation than to offer them both for public discussion."

"Heaven and earth!" cried Zeuks. "What about impulsive fellows like me? I couldn't tell you by day or by night what I was going to do next!" Thus speaking, the great-grandson of the Nymph Maia hesitated not to take to himself a curious chair that stood empty, with its back to one of the richly carved alcoves of that stately hall, a chair that was actually formed out of the figure of a monstrously swollen dwarf from whose head a stag's antlers protruded and whose feet were elongated into tree-roots.

There was something about this chair so perfectly adapted to the personality of Zeuks that Odysseus seemed to accept him and the chair as if they had been one thing and not two things. In fact whenever Odysseus glanced in their direction he gave to this fantastical flesh-turned-into-wood man in a chair a half-humorous nod, a nod that seemed to say: "We are all in the same box; and if we don't grow horns and roots we grow fins and scales."

The easy way in which Zeuks was now enjoying life in that horned and rooted man-chair with which he had identified himself gave our friend Nisos an opportunity to take in more of the general situation than he had as yet had leisure to grasp. He noticed that more than half the seats round the table were empty but that the plates of their recent occupiers were still half full of untouched nuts and fruits and that their wine-glasses too were still only half empty.

It soon began to be clear to the young man that the cause of this desertion of the table was the simple fact that the three chief officers of Nausikaa's crew had been persuaded by Eurycleia, along with the half-a-dozen sailors who had navigated their ship, to join our old friend Tis and the Trojan captive Arsinoë in a wine-drinking revel parallel with the one that was now ebbing feebly to its close in this dilatory teasing of Nausikaa by the crafty Okyrhöe. Gay and lively were the cries and the laughter that kept reaching that quiet hall from the echoing passage leading down to the underground kitchen and wash-house.

As Nisos watched all that was going on he soon was made to feel decidedly uncomfortable by the absence of the familiar form of the beautiful Leipephile, who, quite naturally, was away somewhere with her betrothed, the elder son of Krateros Naubolides. Little physical things, too, as so often happens on such drastic occasions, were worrying Nisos now, and these were the more annoying and irritating because of Zeuks' excessive and exaggerated delight in identifying himself with that grotesque chair and its horns and roots.

Nisos himself, who had no chair and had begun to feel a fool as he stood alone by the side of the table like a child who has crept down from its nursery, had just got one of his bare knees into some sort of a kneeling position upon the edge of a high four-legged footstool, a position he endeavoured to render more secure by pressing his hand in the side of the table. He was unlucky in both these supports; for the footstool had once been covered by some sort of ancient rug, and an unpleasant knot left in its weaving chafed his knee to distraction, while at the precise spot where he pressed his hand on the table's edge there happened to be two or three brass nails that hadn't been properly hammered into the wood and one of these nails behaved as if it were trying to bite at the fleshy part at the base of his thumb.

Had Tis's little sister been present in this dining-hall just now instead of being carried on a crazy rampage on the back of Pegasos along with Arcadian Pan and that pair of appalling Phantoms, whose eternally-whispered wrangle seemed destined to be transferred from Arima to the drowned towers of Atlantis, she would no doubt have drifted to Nisos' aid.

Pontopereia, the daughter of Teiresias, who *was* present, was far too shy to speak to a soul except the punctilious Herald to whom she finally confessed her longing to climb up to one of the high windows under the roof of this great chamber and persuaded him to help her in this achievement.

While our friend Nisos was contending with knots in rugs and nails in boards there were other personalities in that hall, quite apart from the Herald and Pontopereia, who seemed to feel that the moment had come for the old little lady Atropos to draw near and give destiny a new turn. Among these other personalities were individual hairs in the beard of Odysseus: for though, like the branch of a tree, a beard, whether of a goat or a man, has its own general individual being, its separate hairs like the leaves on such a branch have identities of their own. Thus the king's beard in its general personality was not surprised to hear its separate hairs disputing.

"A spiritual impression has reached me," began one of its smallest hairs, addressing itself to one of the largest; "that before darkness covers the earth today you and I and every other hair in this beard may be homeless."

"May I be permitted to enquire," returned the big hair to the little hair, "upon what authority you base this somewhat startling prediction?"

"There's not the least reason why you should put on that patronizing tone just because you are a little older and a little thicker than I am," retorted the other. "The important question is whether we shall or shall not both be thrown into a bonfire of rubbish and there burnt up into invisible nothingness!" And as he spoke the smallest hair made a faintly fluttering motion, like a minute dandelion-seed, or some still more simply constructed airborne vehicle, towards the smouldering fire in the centre of the room that still contained a few red embers and a few wisps of grey smoke, and as he made this gesture he shuddered visibly through the whole length of his being; "burnt to nothingness," he concluded. "Go," said the biggest hair in the king's beard to an extremely active though almost invisible insect, "go and discover for the benefit of all of us whether there is still enough life in those smouldering embers to reduce even the scurf on the navel of a wood-louse to nothingness." The resonance of so commanding a word plunged all the hairs into silence.

"I would dearly like to see myself, Odysseus," began Nausikaa suddenly, "some of those golden pieces of armour, just a single shin-piece perhaps, or one of the lighter sort of thigh-pieces, if your treasury is handy, of the armour of Achilles, which by the adjudication of the Olympian gods was bestowed on you in preference to Ajax, the son of Telamon."

The bowsprit-shaped beard of the king was raised with a jerk at this demand. "Tell somebody, tell Arsinöe," the old man commanded, "to bring up here to show, to show to the Princess any of those pieces she finds herself strong enough to carry!"

"Yes, my lord the King, certainly, my lord the King," replied the stentorian Herald, scrambling back not only to the floor of the hall from the high window-ledge whither he had helped the daughter of Teiresias to find an uninterrupted refuge for her shy and unwordly mind, but to the reality of his own role in life from which he had been snatched by a sudden amorous illusion,

"I will certainly see that the lady Arsinöe brings up at once all that in her heart the Princess covets to behold."

It was then that young Nisos as he leant so uncomfortably against the table was led by the King's command and the Herald's reply to imagine that here indeed was the voice of Atropos herself. "It's I who will be the herald to Arsinöe!" he told himself as he hurried off. He found the Trojan captive helping Eurycleia in the task of washing the most precious of the vessels that had just been used; and taking her aside out of the riotous revelry of Nausikaa's officers and men he explained to her just what the Princess had said; nor did he hesitate to make his own comment upon Nausikaa's request.

"Don't you think, my friend, that what she really wants is to re-establish something of her old link with the old man? Don't you think that in this subtle battle between these two—and I confess, my dear, it's a surprise to me that this complete stranger from Thebes, of whom we know nothing except what she herself tells us, should presume to make such a bold move as to try at once to link her life with his in sexual love so as to forestall any natural return of the old romantic attraction between Odysseus and Nausikaa—don't you think that it's our business to help Nausikaa all we can and to put as many spikes as we possibly can in the wily path of this confounded sorceress?"

Was it Atropos again who now inspired the Trojan captive with a lie worthy of the old Odysseus himself?

"I have already, Nisos Naubolides, thought of this very thing. In fact I have been spending all the twilight hours of this long and heavy evening, while these sailors of the Princess have been making such a barbaric rumpus, in carrying out to a particular tree, yes, Nisos Naubolides, to a special ash-tree in our ghostly Arima here which for years I have been carving into a faint resemblance to Hector of Troy himself, one after another of these golden pieces of the armour that once belonged to Achilles."

Nisos stared at the woman for a second in absolute wonder, even with awe. How clever girls were! How they anticipated everything that could possibly happen, and long before it happened too! So *this* was the explanation of a premonition he had had for some while that something was going to happen here at home that would turn out to be more serious than any crazy excursions upon which Arcadian Pan might embark with poor little Eione, Tis's small sister!

"Listen, you wise one!" he cried, pulling her close to him by her shoulders and putting his eager lips to her right ear, "can't you think of some trick you and I might play upon this damned woman from Syracuse—no! from Thebes it was! And, by the gods I shall hate the very name of Thebes from now on! Yes, I shall always think of Thebes in future as a filthy city of rats, with walls of stinking rottenness, and towers and domes that are just heaps of dung!

"But tell me, Arsinoë, O please, please tell me, Arsinoë, how we can play some effective trick upon this scriggling and wriggling worm of a woman! You were so clever, Arsinoë, so divinely clever, in making an image of carved wood out of a living tree and hanging the armour of Achilles on it! Surely you can think of some device, some trick, some stab in the dark, by which you and I together could save the old man from this curst Theban Sorceress! Do, *do*, I beg and beseech you, Arsinoë, put your good Trojan wits alongside of my poor rocky-island ones and see what we can do! Never mind your coming from Troy. In a thing like this we are at one. Your grand old Priam would agree with me I know; and as for the noble Hector himself, why, he wouldn't hesitate for a second! I know it, I am sure of it, my sweet Arsinoë! Ithaca and Ilium can hold together as well as any civilized pair against this dock-yard Brothel Bitch from the slave-markets of the Orient! Think, think, think, all-wise one! I swear to you that you and I, if we can only put our heads properly together, can forget all that old Helen-of-Troy business and show this confounded Theban witch that she shan't meddle with us in our gratitude to these Phaiakian sea-farers and to their brave Princess Nausikaa.

"For the gods' sake think, my wise one, think out a cunning scheme that'll save our old man from this infernal witch!" Nisos then became silent for a while, holding Arsinoë by the shoulders and pressing her gently against one of the walls of that long narrow down-descending passage, illuminated here and there by richly-oiled and richly-ensconced torches, and echoing at intervals, as the door at the bottom of it opened to let someone in or out, to the excited voices of the Phaiakian sailors, who, in Eurycleia's subterranean kitchen, were enjoying her sagacious hospitality. Then, bending his head down gravely and seriously he touched Arsinoë's forehead with his lips. And it was at this moment that the thought first flashed through his mind that he was the kind of boy who could only be really happy if he had as his wife a woman a lot older than himself.

"For don't you see, Arsinoë, my darling friend," he went on, "don't you see, here there has suddenly come by the very will of Atropos herself, the grandest chance that the old man is ever likely to have to realize his desire to sail over the great Western ocean, under the waves of which Atlantis lies and to discover what unknown lands and continents and peoples and cities and fields of rich grain exist beyond those furthest horizons of water! For don't you see, Arsinoë darling, if this Princess Nausikaa can only be brought to see our old man as she saw him once when she loved him at first sight, why then, my lovely Trojan, let the armour of Achilles be left on your Image of Hector! Odysseus will be the Captain of Nausikaa's ship; and together they will sail into the fabulous memory of all the men who come after us—and, O my dear! may the old little goddess of Fate, Atropos herself, see to it that I am with him in this venture!"

Nisos was again silent, holding her by her shoulders against that wall. And then suddenly, freeing herself from him and throwing his hands back, she held herself erect and closed her eyes.

"I think," she said, speaking clearly and very rapidly, "that it's his beard that puts her off. What I would do if I were you is to make someone you happen to know, someone who wouldn't suffer the punishment *you* would have to suffer for such a thing in case it turned out badly, cut off with a sharp sword, or a polished knife, or a pair of shears, this teasing and intrusive and conceited and aggressive beard of the old man! Yes, Nisos Naubolides, *that* is what you must do! I see the doing of it clearly in the curious darkness into which at this moment the mental effort of trying to do exactly what is required has thrown around me. The thing to do is to cut off his beard!

"But one thing I know. The moment that beard of his has been cut off Nausikaa will see him as she saw him at the very first, when, while she was playing ball with her companions, he came straight to her out of the sea. Yes, Nisos Naubolides, that is the only way this witch-woman from Thebes who is already succeeding in enlarging the gulf between these former lovers, can be defeated. I swear to you I am right. I see it as if it were being done at this very moment. The love-light will come into Nausikaa's eyes the second that beard is gone. No, it is not your king's age that keeps them apart, now that they are together again. *It is the beard*. And Okyrhöe knows it very well and plays upon it. I have been watching her. She doesn't come between them herself if she can help it. She is too wise for that. She leaves it to the beard."

It was at this point—and, whether she was one of Hector's many illegitimate daughters or not, she certainly had a particular kind of intense and absorbed gravity, especially when there was a frown between her eyebrows, which anyone who had ever seen Hector would have recognized as his—that she opened her eyes and laid her fingers upon the young man's sleeve.

"Have you anyone in your mind, Nisos Naubolides," she asked him, "who would be the best person of all persons to do this bold and dangerous thing, whether a man or a woman, whether old or young? I mean," she went on earnestly, after a pause to let a couple of Nausikaa's ship's officers pass down the passage, and Nisos couldn't help admiring the way she instinctively let her fingers slip from his sleeve to his hand and let her head droop towards her shoulder—"I mean the actual cutting it off?" And when she saw he hadn't missed her gesture as the men passed, "Lovers, not conspirators, eh?" she added.

"Well, my beautiful one," he said, while his mind rushed off to the dining-hall and to the animal-shaped chair in which he had left Zeuks, "I think I *do* know the right one for the handling of this little job. But don't you think we ought to have two strings to our bow in so ticklish a thing? Why don't you go down to the kitchen and drop a few tentative hints in our old lady's ear? She's hand and glove with Odysseus, who treats her as if she were his Grandmother. She knows his mind, I should say, better than anyone else on this earth; and we may be sure she has as little love for Okyrhöe as we have: though I admit it's possible she's less friendly to Nausikaa than we are! However—the immediate business for us is to outwit this bitch from Thebes.

"Besides I think we're agreed, my sweet Trojan, that it would be sheer madness in the old king not to snatch at the heavenly chance of a perfect ship and perfect sailors?"

Arsinöe smiled; and having exchanged a kiss that was at once so friendly and so free from passion that they might have been brother and sister, she went down to the kitchen, while he went up to the dining-hall. He found Odysseus still sipping his wine and still keeping up a curious kind of cerebral dalliance with both the women; while from one end of the table to the other end of the table the two oldest of the Phaiakian ship's officers argued pedantically, technically and very loudly upon certain nice and difficult problems connected with the art of navigation.

Nisos slipped as noiselessly and as respectfully as he could to Zeuks' grotesque chair, and kneeling down before it muttered what was really a sort of extempore prayer, graver than casual listeners might have supposed, to Zeuks and Zeuks' chair, as if they were one creature or one sacred Image. To emphasize and enhance this anthropomorphic and fetish-worshipping gesture, which was one part humorous, two parts entirely serious, and only one part theatrical, he pressed his elbows against the arms of the chair and clasped his fingers in supplication; and then, afraid lest his queer friend should think he was making fun of him, he twisted his head round, as if to make sure that his performance was not missed by those at the table.

Meanwhile, having made sure that Zeuks was not in a trance of any sort, but sufficiently attentive, he whispered to him a realistic and rather grossly-worded summary of his talk with Arsinoë, feeling all the while that what he was kneeling before was neither a chair nor a man but a multiformed malleable monster ready to embrace whatever creature sank into its lap with such a transfiguring power of metamorphosis that it and the creature received into it were transformed into a new and monstrous identity.

Zeuks made no comment upon his friend's whispered monologue murmur save a constant murmur of the same words: "Go on. I understand. Go on. I follow you. Go on, Nisos Naubolides."

This completely passive acceptance of our young friend's startling revelation of what might have been described as "the Plot of the King's Beard" reduced a little the enormity of the sacrilege involved. It was only after they had gone on like this for some time, Nisos explaining, predicting, conjecturing, anticipating, enlarging, revising, and Zeuks listening and indicating that he missed nothing of what he heard, that there was a quite unlooked-for if not especially momentous interruption to the wine-sipping at the high table.

No less a person than the midwife came up the steps from the corridor, holding by the hand her now pregnant sister.

"I have brought to you, O king," she hurriedly announced, offering one of the empty table-chairs to her companion who sank into it with a groan of ineffable relief, "our well-known family prophetess, because they told me that there has come to you from Thebes the daughter of the great prophet Teiresias; and I wanted my sister, who is in the state you now witness, to exchange a few thoughts with her."

Round went the fine cranium and bowsprit beard of the old king as he looked for Pontopereia at the spot where she had recently been; but it was from quite a different quarter that her clear and unperturbed voice reached them. Tired of watching the deep and subtle struggle between the two ladies, the clumsy little wide-eyed creature, whose intellectual grasp of the whole state of the world at that juncture reduced—and how little either of those clever ones knew it!—both Okyrhöe and Nausikaa to a pathetically ordinary level of active, lively, beautiful, ambitious, practical women whose response to life completely shut out all the more cosmic reactions of the human mind, had boldly climbed into the high recess of one of the windows.

Having persuaded, and not without rousing some rather pathetic erotic illusions in that official breast, the pompous Herald to help her with his powerful arms and shoulders, the girl had succeeded in scrambling up into what was one of the most elevated of all that spacious hall's high window-ledges. From this vantage-ground she could not only amuse herself by watching the tricks of Okyrhöe and the shrewd hit-backs of Nausikaa, but she could see between the stalks of the creepers the blackened square of ground which was all that was left of the old Dryad and her oak-tree, after Zeus' angry thunderbolt.

"Something decisive for good and something heavy with the opposite of good are both on the verge of happening." Thus did Pontopereia murmur to herself the prophetic inspiration which came to her straight from that blackened spot in the forest where the old Dryad had perished.

"Something decisive for good, though it is also heavy with the opposite of good, is on the verge of happening," and as Pontopereia tried in these crude words, which she repeated twice over to herself in silence, to express what a breath of wind was now uttering in her ears and uttering a good deal more often than twice, she was suddenly arrested and fascinated by something else. It was a peculiarity of hers to make much of all the chance-shapes and accidental formations that presented themselves whether out-of-doors or in-doors; and what she saw now struck her as a real omen. The Dryad's blackened square of earth, which one general darkness of night had already made part of itself was scrawled over by a thin streak of light from the aperture at which she herself crouched, a streak of light with which chance or destiny was now inscribing, according to the lettering of a language not wholly different from hers, the fitful outlines of a disturbing "N"! Did this "N", the girl wondered, refer to Nisos or to Nausikaa, or possibly even to Nosodea the mother of Leipephile?

"It is in accordance with the ancient custom of our Grecian islands," the Midwife was now saying—indeed she had been uttering sentence after sentence ever since she first appeared but in such a loud, pontifical, assured, self-confident voice, that it was as if she were addressing a crowd of people outside who had no connection with Odysseus or with these two women or with Zeuks or with Nisos.

Odysseus, who had not taken the faintest notice of what the midwife was saying, now suddenly addressed the pregnant woman herself. "Your pains have not begun yet, have they, my dear?" The question was a foolish one and an extremely masculine one; for it was obvious that the pregnant woman's sister whose profession it was to deal with such cases would not have left her quite unassisted while she harangued the world; but there was clearly something about the exhausted creature that appealed to the old king.

Nausikaa rose from her seat. "Where's that old nurse of yours," she enquired; "the one you introduced me to a while ago? Hasn't she got a room in the palace where a poor woman like this can rest in peace and wait her hour?"

Odysseus put down his wine-glass and looked round the room. "Nisos!" he cried. "Please go down to the kitchen and bring Eurycleia up here. I want to talk to her."

Nisos leaned forward and whispered to the occupant of that grotesque chair, while the chair itself, as he did so, seemed to be perceptibly projecting its roots into the floor and its stag-like horns towards the roof.

"Shall I do what he says?" he whispered to Zeuks, "or shall I pretend not to hear him?"

It was Zeuks himself, however, who at that moment pretended not to hear Nisos; for in his own mind Zeuks was thinking, "Why is it that it gives me no great thrill to know I am the son of

Arcadian Pan? Is it because it doesn't make me immortal and independent of death? In such great matters we men are like animals and do not understand what is going on. If it did make me independent of death it would still be impossible for me to *feel* independent of it. And what benefit do I get from being the son of a god, I should like to know, when I *feel* exactly like everybody else?"

These thoughts so dominated Zeuks that they gave him the sensation that he was lost in them and that his personality had disappeared and that it was the chair he sat in that thought these thoughts and that he was merely the name for the language the chair used. The chair, in fact, thought in *Zeuks* instead of *in Greek*!

It was indeed the fact that Nisos had actually knelt down with both his elbows propped on the arms of this singular chair where tree-root-legs and hooded covering of stag-horn seemed so much more alive than the man who was sitting in it, that rendered both himself and Zeuks so lost to all that was going on that it wasn't until quite a crowd of Nisos' relations were standing round them, nor until the Midwife herself had commenced a formal supplication imploring the goddess Athene to return to them in Ithaca that the spell was broken.

Roused at length from his trance Nisos was amazed to see quite close to him not only Nosodea, the mother of Leipephile, but Leipephile's elder sister Spartika, the priestess of Athene, as well as the old man Damnos Geraios. His amazement indeed had hardly reached its peak when lo! standing alone behind the lot of them, but with the half-protective, half-mocking gaze he knew so fatally well fixed steadily upon himself he saw his own mother!

Pandea looked just as calm, just as confident and self contained and just as serenely poised, as if she had been in her own house. That she was in the presence of the king did not apparently disturb her; nor, though her shrewd gaze was fixed on her son, did she seem at all concerned when without taking the least notice of any of the new-comers Odysseus repeated his command that the young man should hasten to the kitchen and fetch Eurycleia.

When at length Nisos did remove his elbows and release his fingers from the clasp of entranced prayer, and stiffly and painfully lifted, as if his limbs had been in peril of growing as inanimate as the wood-work above them, first one knee and then the other from the floor, he found that the wave-length of excitement was still concentrated on the almost stellar arena where the old warrior's beard with Zodiacal precision was pointed first towards Okyrhöe and then towards Nausikaa.

It certainly was not pointing towards Zeuks or towards this enigmatic chair; though the words by which Nisos had been ordered to fetch Eurycleia were still echoing in the boy's head. No; that bowsprit beard had turned away from them all and was now quivering like a moonlit spear-head over broken water towards the towering figure of the white-robed Spartika.

"Has the old man forgotten," Nisos thought, "that he has told me to fetch Eurycleia; or is he getting blind and doesn't see me at all and fancies that I've already gone down there? Or do the wisest old men, even when they're as wily as he is, when between two ladies like those two and a jug of wine such as he's got there, grow queer in the head? O gods above and gods below!" the boy's thoughts ran on as he pretended to be too absorbed in the condition of his friend Zeuks to make any response either to his mother's questioning concern or to the echo in his ears of the king's unobeyed command, "What on earth", he wondered, turning his gaze with such a rapid jerk that he made it impossible to meet his mother's eye, "What on earth is Spartika up to?"

It was evident to everyone there, except perhaps to Zeuks, who had fallen into one of his deepest gulfs of egoistic self-questioning, that the king was amazed by this apparition of Spartika in her white robes, chanting rather than repeating her religious message to them all.

Nisos had acquired the habit, shared by most of his friends and relations, of thinking nothing of Spartika. To disparage her religion, to question her devotion, to minimize her gifts, to underrate her sincerity, to make sport of the grave intensity she always put into her worship of Athene had been the general custom ever since this girl grew up, among everybody who knew her.

It is indeed one of life's mysteries how this can happen with certain particular young people; and it happens to young men as often as it does to young women. The Goddess herself, however, had encouraged this young priestess of hers from the very start; and it had in recent years become a familiar joke in the Temple that if you wanted to catch a glimpse of the Goddess of Wisdom you would have to cast yourself down in front of the small side-chapel altar which it was Spartika's duty to decorate with fresh flowers.

If on the contrary you wanted to avoid any risk of encountering the formidable Goddess the thing to do was to say your prayers at her High Altar on the day when the Priest of the Mysteries of Eros and Dionysos was paying his perfunctory and conventional visit to the centre of the island's traditional worship.

As Nisos turned at this moment towards Spartika, praying that his mother wouldn't see through his pretence that he hadn't seen her, and that Odysseus wouldn't see through his pretence that he hadn't heard his command, he was relieved of one of his nervous fears by noticing that the pregnant fugitive from Italy had gone to sleep in the chair wherein her sister had ensconced her and that, though the poor lady's snores made old Damnos Geraios grin like a water-sprite, nobody else appeared to bother about her at all. Her midwife-sister was apparently absorbed in listening to Spartika's speech; but whenever the impassioned priestess paused to take breath the midwife would interpolate some high-pitched moralizing of her own. Nisos however found himself in a very short time heartily wishing that the midwife would hold her tongue; for it began to strike him more and more strongly that Spartika had been grossly underrated.

"O Great Goddess of Wisdom," prayed the white-robed figure, "send to thy faithful and devoted worshippers the power to hold fast amid all troubles and tribulations and against all enemies and traitors, and against all chances and accidents, and against all famines and pestilences and elemental disasters, that imperishable gift of pure reason which alone can assuage and mitigate and allay all the ills that our human mortality brings with it! Return, return, O greatest of all Goddesses, thou who wast born of the divine head of the son of Kronos, thou who hast merely to shake the tassels of thy glorious, equitable, thrice-holy Aegis, and all the howling, ravening, raving, blood-drinking, bone-cracking, flesh-devouring minions of mischief who serve the bigots, the dogmatists, the maniacs, the fanatics, the inquisitors who dominate this maddest of all possible worlds are scouted and routed into headlong flight!

"Here in this ancient hall while our world-famous king is entertaining two beautiful princesses and while Pontopereia the daughter of Teiresias—yes, my sweet child, I see that you're listening to me from your perch like a sea-swallow blown inland before its time in that high window seat!—here, I say, in this old hall, while our king is entertaining his beautiful visitors, have you, his faithful people, forgotten—hast thou our wily sovereign thyself forgotten—the noble, the heroic, the pure, the devoted, the religious-hearted Telemachos, son of Odysseus, son of Laertes.

"What, I ask you, is wrong with all you people, that you are dividing yourselves now into these accurst divisions, some of you wanting Odysseus to rot like a wounded stag till he lies dead in his bed and makes way for Krateros Naubolides, or for Agelaos, son of Krateros Naubolides, the betrothed of my own sister Leipephile, and some wanting him to catch the ears of the whole world with his voyage across the drowned Atlantis to unknown shores beyond the Ultimate Horizons, but none of you, no! not even thou thyself, O King! thou infinitely heroic and infinitely wise lord of adventure by land and sea!—have even so much as considered the claim of this noble, this calm, this beautiful, this dignified, this profoundly intellectual, this spiritual-soul'd, pure-minded only son of Odysseus and Penelope!

"Why, I ask you, my friends, why, I ask you, my sisters and

parents and neighbours, why, I ask you, my wily, secretive, many-natured, much-experienced, much-enduring, invincible Odysseus, have you narrowed down this ridiculous dispute to whether an old man is to risk mixing his bones with the bones of the lost populations of drowned Atlantis or is to be allowed to walk in the forests in sunshine and moonlight to listen to the winds and the waves, to survey the motions of the stars and risings and settings of the sun and the moon until he is buried by the side of his faithful wife, when all the while, only a few leagues away, there abides in the deep contemplation of the secret wisdom of the Great Goddess whose shining temple we have among us, the only son of this heroic king and his noble wife?

"I know well that Telemachos seeks no kingship and no kingdom. I know well that Telemachos has his courts and his palaces, his lands and his waters, his armies and his fleets in the high invisible world of the ancient philosophers and thinkers of the human race. I know very well that all you servants of our old heroic king, and thou O King thyself, I know would be with thy servants in this, would have difficulty in persuading Telemachos to add to the intellectual labours of his philosophical life by undertaking the more active and practical burdens of kingship.

"I know very well too that he has great respect for my sister's betrothed suitor, Agelaos Naubolides. But he is a much older man than my sister's Agelaos and if our old and much-enduring adventurer—I speak with all respect, most noble king!—were never to return from this incredible voyage upon which he has fixed his heart, his soul and his unusual brain—according to the natural ways of life it seems quite likely that my young friend Agelaos would not have to wait so very long for his turn at the game of Kingship. Therefore let us all, let every one of us, I say, be prepared for the future in the strength of our great Goddess Athene!"

Here the tall girl bent her head, smiled at her mother, Nosodea, who was taking the whole thing with the utmost matter-of-fact placidity and had just moved to the side of the pregnant woman who was now awake again, and quietly accepted the chair which the declamatory Midwife, talking quite hilariously now, dragged to her side.

And then, to Nisos' relief, Odysseus, who himself had risen from his seat and moved up close to the pregnant woman's side, once more requested him, but quite gently and apparently taking for granted that his earlier orders had been unheard, to hasten at once to the kitchen and fetch Eurycleia.

"And tell her, my boy," the old king added, "that I'd be glad if she could make up a bed for this woman so that her child can be born, even if the birth is delayed for a day or two, somewhere within these walls."

Lifting his head and straightening his shoulders while he whispered a hasty assurance to Zeuks that he'd be back in a pulse-beat, Nisos was just starting on this quest when Odysseus made a sign that he would like a private word with him before he left the hall. When he obeyed this sign and was standing so close to the old man that he could smell the wine he'd been drinking and even feel his own chin tickled by the foremost hairs of that still undaunted and still defiant beard, the old man took advantage of the Midwife's formidable back being momentarily bent over her sister to whisper to his young emissary that it was extremely likely that the father of this expected infant was none other than that king of the Latins whose defeat by Aeneas and his Trojan followers had, it seemed, led to the founding in Italy of a New Troy upon a group of Seven Hills, not without the aid of the most famous of all cave-nymphs and not without the help of human infants nourished by the dugs of wolves!

"So you can tell our nurse, my boy, if you find her in a difficult mood, that this baby, if a bed is made for its mother here, may turn out to be the heir to all the riches of the Italian Peninsula!" It was at that moment that Nisos became aware that his own mother, Pandea, was cautiously, slowly, obstinately, threading her way towards him, for, drawn as women always are, by the twin-shadows of birth and death, the wife of the rival claimant to their island-throne had naturally an extra magnet tugging at her bosom in addition to the loadstone weighted by both birth and death.

But so quickly had it got about among the neighbours that the most romantic as well as the most human of all the old king's adventurous lady-loves had suddenly arrived along with Ajax, son of Telamon, regarded by all the world as dead, that popular curiosity, most of all in the women, had already crowded the corridor and the steps with people and was now filling the dining-hall.

Pandea had always been one of the most neighbourly and gossip-loving of ladies and this made her present passage through the crowd to reach her son Nisos by no means rapid. She was in fact caught by the belt and by the folds of her gown at every step.

At any moment now Nisos could have hurried off, thus obeying the king, escaping from his mother, and precluding any untimely labour-pains for the woman here; but he suddenly felt himself powerfully seized by the left wrist. It was Odysseus. "Where," cried the old man in a husky, agitated voice, "where, in the name of all the gods, is Ajax?"

All Nisos could do in reply to this, for in his intense desire to outwit Okyrhöe, and in his new and sudden alliance with Arsinoë, he had forgotten Ajax altogether, was to blurt out all he knew.

"Zeuks told me just now," he cried, "that he had found him dead and had buried him with his own hands." The one word *"Where?"*, which the old king uttered on hearing this in a very curious tone, left a queer and complicated impression on the mind and nerves of Nisos. The boy could see that to the old man at this moment the idea of being confronted once again by his ancient comrade in arms of those long years of the Trojan War had touched something in his soul that was deeper and more essential and more important to him than all his romantic feeling for Nausikaa and all his libidinous feeling, or emotional feeling, or companionable intellectual feeling, for Okyrhöe.

The figure of Ajax, as the old man recalled it now, acted like a magic talisman upon him, restoring to him a whole existence of thoughts and sensations, of undertones and overtones of feeling, of desperations and ecstasies, so utterly remote from all he was experiencing at this moment that to plunge into them, and swim about in them, and inhale great draughts of their encircling atmosphere, was a startling shock.

Odysseus was indeed so affected by this sudden mental vision of Ajax that the one single view of himself and his whole life that he could endure, and that struck him as ground firm enough to fall back upon at a crisis, was the view of himself that accompanied his present resolution to sail across the ocean that had drowned Atlantis. This intention, this purpose did alone, the old man felt at that moment, justify his existence as nothing had done since in rivalry with the rest of the Greek leaders he entered Ilium in the Wooden Horse.

Escaping from his king therefore, with almost as much relief as he escaped from his mother, for he felt a sudden longing to be plotting and planning with Arsinoë again, Nisos pushed his way hurriedly through the crowd and was soon pleading passionately and eagerly the cause of the unborn babe, who might turn out to be the inheritor of the longest-descended racial tradition in Italy. "Well, if he's set his heart on it," the old lady finally conceded, "there's nothing to be gained by thwarting his wishes. O you men! you men! He has no notion, nor, I expect, have you, closer though you are than he is to the womb out of which you all come, how near to her pains this woman is, but if——"

Nisos interrupted her. "It was her sister, the midwife, Granny dear, who brought her to Odysseus, not I. I can't remember ever seeing her. But I daresay I may have seen her when I was little, and before she went to Italy. She lived with the Nymph in the Cave, Granny. You know about that Nymph in the Cave in Italy, don't you?"

But the old lady's contradictory mood wasn't soothed away by this. "I've known too many caves and too many Nymphs already!" she cried. "You and your Nymphs! What I would like to see, Nisos Naubolides, would be no more nymphs and no more caves but a well-built Palace in a well-built City with a well-trained army to protect it from pirates and murderers and thieves, and with well-trained servants to send on the King's business, without having to have recourse to—— But what am I doing, chattering here with a baby like you when an old woman's proper work's up yonder? Here! give me my cloak, girl; and you were best come with me too, foreigner though you be, for us can never tell with these cave-nymphs! This wench may be dropping a monster with horns and tail before we've got her to bed!"

As may be conjectured these words were addressed to the alert Arsinöe, who with a quick glance at Nisos helped the old woman into the garment she required and assisted her up the passage to the hall. Before he followed them thither, however, our young friend couldn't resist a word with his old comrade Tis whom he found naked to the waist working furiously between oven and wash-trough on his left and red ashes under a great cauldron on his right.

Dragging about with them across the floor their own foreign blankets, which they had brought up from the ship lest they should be stolen, were half-a-dozen sailors who had been so freely and hilariously partaking of the old nurse's hospitality that, now the feast was over, they found it hard to keep awake.

Nisos persuaded Tis to put on his tunic again and leave his wash-tub. Then in a voice too low for those of the foreigners who were not asleep to catch his words he tried to make clear to his friend the pressing necessity for cutting off the beard of Odysseus so that Nausikaa should see him as he was when she first set eyes on him. To his surprise he found that this daring stroke met with obstinate and determined resistance from Tis.

"I don't like it: I don't like it: I don't like it," he kept repeating. "It's an insult to the old man—an insult that I'd never consent to see practised on my old grand-dati Moros, an insult that you'll never persuade me to help you to carry through."

"But don't you see, old friend," pleaded Nisos, considerably disturbed by this unexpected opposition, "don't you see it's essential that Princess Nausikaa should recognize in our king the man she loved the moment she saw him coming out of the sea?"

But Tis shook his head. "You young folk always exaggerate and overrate the effect of any mortal thing that strikes you as romantic. How do you know that cutting off our king's beard will make him look young again? There are other signs of old age than the greyness or the whiteness of our hair. Odysseus had nothing like those deep lines at the side of his mouth, for instance, or those other lines, deeper still, in the centre of his forehead when he first met his princess. No, no! You know very well he hadn't! He couldn't have had.

"No, you're making a great mistake if you think our old hero's beard has anything to do with it! In fact, if anybody tried to meddle with our king's beard when his servant Tis was around that person had better take care! It wouldn't be that man's beard that would come off. It would be his head!"

"But don't you see, Tis, old friend, it will only be in the interest of our king, and for the sake of the happiness of our king, and in order that our king may have all the honour and glory he wants, that his beard will be cut off. Better lose a beard, than a kingdom! Better lose a beard than the enchanting Love of your proud youth! O Tis, Tis, don't be an obstinate Tis, a reactionary Tis, an antiquarian Tis! The world has to move on. Life has to move on. Customs have to change. Habits have to change. There was a time for beards. That time is past. Beards have to be—— "

But Nisos stopped suddenly. He was shocked at the expression he saw on Tis's face. He felt in the marrow of his bones a lively shudder of fear. "Then it is really and truly possible," he told himself, "for old Tis to give me such a clap across the ear-hole that my head will roll from my neck and go bouncing into—— "

But his thoughts were interrupted, and Tis's attention was turned by a sudden loud uproar which descended the passage from the hall above; and they both became aware of shrill cries and resounding tramplings and even of the sound of bronze striking against bronze and iron striking against iron.

The foreign sailors leapt to their feet and drew from their belts their double-edged knives; while Nisos couldn't help noticing, even in the distraction of that uproar, how carefully these men folded up the blankets on which they'd been lying and tucked them under their arms.

Both Tis and he were out of the kitchen and up the passage and forcing their way into the hall before either of them had time even to imagine what had happened. But it was soon plain enough to them both. There, confronting the king who was leaning forward across the back of the throne on which he had been seated, was Nisos' brother Agelaos, the eldest son of Krateros and Pandea, and close to him was none other than Leipephile the young man's betrothed, while, facing the pair of them, on one side of Odysseus was Nausikaa and on the other were Okyrhöe and Pontopereia.

The uproar that had reached the kitchen came from two opposing groups of angry armed men, one of whom was shouting abuse of the House of Odysseus and the other abuse of the House of Naubolides. Matters might have got worse at any minute and serious blood-shed might doubtless have ensued, if an event had not occurred so unexpected by both parties that they turned, as if by mutual consent, from their furious confrontation of each other; and both sides gazed with awe-struck amazement at what they saw.

And what they saw was indeed a sufficient wonder to quell the wildest altercation. Walking quite gently, slowly, carefully and quietly, his wounded wing evidently grown again, and its roots completely healed, while the long feathery tips of both wings were folded against the animal's sides like those of a colossal moth, there came up through the crowd, from the corridor of the pillars, the winged horse Pegasos. On his back, seated there with the utmost ease, and evidently in a mood of radiant high spirits, was the young girl Eione, Tis's little sister, who the moment she caught sight of her brother by the side of Nisos kissed one of her hands to them both while with the other she waved in the air an extraordinary-looking object which she was clasping in triumph.

Pegasos bore her straight up to the old king, the two contending groups of people automatically separating to let them pass. When they reached the throne, across the back of which Odysseus, with great practical shrewdness, was already leaning forward above its empty seat, his body wedged between the chair's back, across which he leaned, and the massive table which protected his rear, Pegasos stopped, and lowering his head, consented to enjoy the natural equine satisfaction of munching a couple of large lettuce-leaves which the old King lost no time in snatching from the table behind him and placing on the seat of the throne for the god-like creature's special delectation.

At that moment all the uproar ceased and so eager and anxious were both parties to catch every word of the dialogue between Eione and the king that in the silence which fell upon the whole company the sound of Pegasos munching the lettuce-leaves was audible from the door of the steps to the corridor to the door of the passage to the kitchen.

But everybody in the place was soon conscious of an absolutely different sound, a sound that closely accompanied the winged horse's munching of lettuce-leaves. This came from the mysterious object which Eione was now showing to Odysseus across the horse's bowed head. It was a sound like the sound of the wind. And the sound in this object was not limited to the sound of the North Wind or of the South Wind or of the East Wind or the West Wind. It was just the wind. It was all the winds together. And it was so powerful that it made many people at the back of the hall, who were unable to see that the sound was caused by what the girl was showing to the king, look up at the windows beneath the roof at one of which Pontopereia had been recently sitting and through which they supposed this wild rush of wind must be entering the hall.

The real power of it could only have been appreciated at that moment however by some observer who could read human thoughts; for this roaring, sighing, crying, wailing, laughing, lamenting, groaning, shrieking sound was so startlingly an embodiment of the real wind that it produced upon those who were nearest to the object out of which it came the identical effect that the hearing of such a wind, had it been real, would naturally have evoked. It made Odysseus feel more strongly than he had ever felt before his absolute determination to sail over the waters into which Atlantis had gone down. It carried Nausikaa back to her girlhood upon an irresistible rush of the wings of memory.

She had a hundred times recalled that day when she and her playmates were disporting themselves at their game of ball, in relaxation from washing their clothes, when the godlike stranger suddenly appeared among them and clasped her knees in a passionate appeal for help. O how well she remembered how he had followed up the impression he made upon her by uttering the hope that when she met her true mate, he and she together would soon find out how such a true union between lovers could be lucky to their friends and unlucky to their foes; and how they themselves would alone know what it really meant.

It brought to Pontopereia the feeling that she was gloriously giving herself up to a thrilling and convincing rush of prophetic inspiration. It raced through the mind of Nisos with the impossible romantic wish that somehow, somewhere, he would be triumphantly justified in possessing both Eione and Pontopereia as his Loves!

To Okyrhöe this sound of the wind, issuing forth from Eione's gift to Odysseus, brought a sense of deep, abysmal, desolate loneliness. She found herself identifying her own inmost being with this mysterious wind that had suddenly appeared, only the river Styx knew from whence, and which was associated with this ghostly "Arima" that sooner or later she would have to face if she remained with Odysseus.

While the wind of day and the wind of night were thus working upon various living creatures in various different ways, Eione was explaining in meticulous detail precisely how this extraordinary instrument worked; how it could be stopped, how intensified, how diminished, how directed, how reduced, and how expanded at the will of the wearer. Thus there was no special start or spasm of astonishment in that dining-hall when finally, just before Pegasos had lifted his head from the last lettuce-stalk left on the seat of the throne, Odysseus took the thing from the girl's hands and raising it carefully in both his own fixed it on his head.

Once on his head, though it had a certain vague resemblance to a brazen helmet from which hung long twisting snakes, it looked much more like a complicated, convoluted sea-shell, a sea-shell that might have been worn by the sea-god Triton, or even by some greater deity of the salt deep. After a few more less solemn directions from Eione as to its use, the old king removed it from his head and half-turning round placed it beside his wine-cup on the table. He then, in the face of the whole company, gratefully, respectfully, and devotedly kissed both Eione's hands, caressed the head of Pegasos, and instructed Tis, who was staring awestruck at his sister, to take the bridle of the winged horse and lead him, if his girl-rider saw fit, to a more restful feast in the royal stable adjoining the cow-stall of Babba.

When Tis had led away his sister and Pegasos the old king summoned Nisos, who had engaged Pontopereia in a whispered conversation behind the backs of Nausikaa and Okyrhöe, and told him to fetch Zeuks. This command he had no difficulty in obeying, for the son of Arcadian Pan had fallen into such a deep sleep in that queer-backed and queer-legged chair that it was easier to get him awake and to escort him, a bit dazed but no longer muttering in his sleep about "Ajax and the Lightning", to where the king and his two ladies were once more seated at the table with their heads close together, than it would have been to explain to him all that had happened since he had fallen asleep.

But if it had been difficult to arouse the great-grandson of "still youthful Maia" from his trance in a chair that had both roots and horns, Odysseus did not seem to have the least difficulty in seating him on the throne now calmly and resolutely vacated.

"Fetch me, child," he said to Nisos, laying a caressing hand on the boy's head and drawing up for himself, to the acute vexation of Okyrhöe, an empty chair to the side of Nausikaa, "my club of Herakles, the weapon called 'Dokeesis,' from the entrance porch."

There wasn't a person in that hall that night who didn't hear these momentous words; nor was there one who didn't catch their significance. This was in fact a declaration that, armed as he would be when Nisos brought "Dokeesis", and possessed as he now was of the Helmet of the Winds, the oldest and weakest and frailest, but far, O far the wisest, of the Fates, Atropos herself, the great-aunt of all the heavenly powers, had decided in an uncontroverted decree that, whatever the issue, Odysseus, King of Ithaca, was to sail over the towers of Lost Atlantis before he perished after the manner of men.

So intense had been the fascination and expectation throughout that great hall that when Nisos in a shorter time than seemed possible returned with the Club of Herakles and placed it in Odysseus' hands there occurred once more that curious kind of hush that is in truth when it falls upon any mixed crowd of men and women the most mysterious force for the working of miracles that exists in this solar dimension of the multiverse.

"Listen, wise Fly," murmured the Moth, as they peered together out of the life-crack of their wheel-less conveyance, "I think the Sixth Pillar is talking to our All-in-All."

The Fly did listen: and it heard the Pillar tell the club that Poseidon and Aidoneus had decided to break the covenant they once made with Zeus over Atlantis when they allowed him to drown it under the western ocean as a punishment for its refusal to believe he existed. They promised him they would let it stay drowned and that no man should ever cross the place of its drowning. This solemn covenant they have now decided to tear to shreds; and, if it comes to a fight, they say that Two are stronger than One.

"I am wondering," murmured the Moth, "whether it isn't my duty to leave you tonight and fly at my best speed to the

Priest of Eros, lest, my duty neglected, some world-disaster may overtake us."

"If you feel like that, you'd better go to him," hissed the Fly, in jealous rage. "And leave you alone in here?" "Where I am," replied the Fly in his metaphysical pride, "there is always Eternity."

The moth groaned. "I must, but O! it's so hard, learn to love Eternity;" and she stroked with her left antenna one of the fly's wings.

But the fly said to himself. "What shall I do if the King takes us down into Atlantis itself? There must be millions of dead flies down there."

Meanwhile Nisos was walking round and round the great table thinking out very carefully just what he would say to Eione to persuade her to go with them. In his heart he was so indescribably relieved at the disappearance not only of his own relations, such as his brother and his brother's betrothed, together with Pandea, his mother, and Nosodea, along with Spartika and the midwife, but of almost all the disputants and contenders of the general public of Ithaca, that he could only listen with amused and sympathetic satisfaction while the King explained to Zeuks that he had decided to put him into full, absolute, and complete charge of the Palace, the Temple, the chief Harbour, the lesser harbours, and all the caves, shrines, sanctuaries, and sacred places of the Island of Ithaca to guard, to hold and to sustain intact, until he, its only lawful sovereign and ruler, should return from his Voyage across the drowned Atlantis; "and take from you again the rights and privileges he now makes over to you and leaves unchallenged in your possession".

At this point Odysseus laid his hand upon the strange object brought to him by Eione. "The Princess Nausikaa, here present," he went on, "has consented to accept my company and that of my armour-bearer and Hetairos, Nisos Naubolides, together with my friend Okyrhöe the Theban and together with Pontopereia the daughter of Teiresias. At the moment I cannot tell you whether Eione, the sister of my Herdsman Tis, will also come with us; but I have the Princess's permission to invite her to do so, and my impression is she *will* do so. Just as I make thee, Zeuks, my vice-regent and sole representative among men, so, among women I leave my old Nurse Eurycleia in absolute and unchallenged control. I must add that there has just come into my possession the Helmet of Proteus, wearing which it will be possible for me to visit drowned Atlantis beneath the very waters that drowned her."

It was then that Nausikaa rose to her feet and said: "What my Lord Odysseus has told you is the truth."

CHAPTER X

"Well," said Nisos to Akron, the Master of the ship "Teras", "she's got through *that* anyway!"

"O she's a sly old bird, our good black ship, when matters get really serious," replied Akron, "and there's another thing about her which I wonder if you've noticed; I mean about her motion?"

"I *may* have noticed it and again I may not. Different eyes notice different things."

"They sure do; and they are also blind to different things. I was blind myself just now when the Pillars of Herakles vanished over the Eastern Horizon."

"Why, so they have! And I'd been watching so steadily to see them go! It's no use. You'll never make a sailor of me."

"I used to say that very thing once myself! But it passes, Nisos, it passes!"

Nisos looked at him gravely. "I take it you don't feel the slightest sensation of nervousness, or strangeness, not to speak of simple terror, when from this old black ship of yours you can see no sign or hint or trace of land? Don't you feel *any* fear, master, when with nothing between you and this black abyss but a few scrabbled bits of wood, if you don't mind my saying so, and a few shaky planks blown by the wind and tossed on the wave, you give yourself up to whatever fate awaits you?"

"Well, I wouldn't deny, my dear lad," replied Akron, the ship's master, "that sometimes, now and then, *I have that feeling*, just as we all have when a spear or an arrow comes too close to our head! I get it, for instance, when I see the spouting of a whale, or catch sight of one of those great sharks, or one of those terrifying Hekatoncheiroi, such as Briareos must have looked when he smuggled down in the throne of the heavenly father and spread out on all sides his appalling suckers, each one of which would be capable of squeezing to death a man like you or me.

"But I really think I've got over those first sensations of what you might call pure elemental panic. I think I've come to be more or less reconciled to there being, as you say, Nisos, so much water under us and so much air above us! But such a lot of water and such an immensity of empty air does make a person feel small."

"I don't think," Nisos went on in a meditative tone, "that its exactly the mass of water, or the infinity of air, that makes us feel small. I think it is the ceasing of accustomed labour and the idleness that leaves the mind free to follow its fancies."

The ship's master watched his young passenger with a shrewd eye as he talked in this way. He thought Nisos was trying to make him believe that he was analysing his feelings with the utmost calm, like an experienced traveller recording his reactions when the most dangerous and agitating moments of what he was going through had arrived and passed.

"The kid would like me to think," he told himself, "that he accepts these monstrous enormities of air and water without one single natural shiver."

Their ship was named the "Teras" or the "Prodigy" and its master with whom Nisos had already made friends was a man called Akron who came from Lilaia, a town in Phokis, and was of a reserved and reticent but of a decidedly philosophical turn of mind. Akron came, like Tis, of farm ing stock, and although his father had kept an Inn in the main street of Lilaia, he had a great-uncle, of about the same age as old Moros, who continued running the family farm.

The second officer, whose name was Thon, had quite a different temperament from Akron and a very different bringing-up. He came of an old military family in Phrygia with a long and turbulent history. The "Teras" had two decks below the top one on which Nisos was standing as he talked with Akron. It was from the upper one of these that the four long oars projected that kept the "Teras" moving when the wind failed.

The mast was fixed in the keel of the vessel and reached up through both the two lower decks to where, on the top-deck, quite close to the spot on which our friend was now talking with Akron, the huge sail, made of the same sort of cloth that Odysseus had tried so desperately to obtain in Ithaca, was now carrying the "Teras" over the waves in a style that must have delighted every true sailor's heart on board.

The way the vessel was behaving at this moment in a wind almost straight from the South-East, was certainly especially pleasing to the two men who just then were supervising the "protonoi" or "forestays", the "kaloi" or "halliards", and the "huperoi" or "braces". These men were a pair of brothers, whose names, Pontos and Proros, were enough in themselves to suggest seafaring ability, but whose home-harbour, Skandeia in Kythera, was known over all Hellas to breed the best deck-hands in the world.

As he listened attentively and politely, though it must be confessed just a little cynically, to our friend Nisos' rather prolonged but eloquent discourse on what particular feelings, whether enjoyable or the reverse, were aroused in him by air and water, Akron remained, according to the custom then prevalent in that best of all sea-going Hellenic circles, quietly, though not unsympathetically, detached from the chatter that was proceeding so happily between Pontos and Proros.

Both the brothers from Kythera were small in regard to their bodily form but they were smaller still in regard to the size of their skulls. Indeed so diminutive were these Kytharean craniums that the most studious and experienced of phrenologists would have been puzzled to say where there was room for any sort of bump of worship or for any sort of bump of mathematics or for any sort of bump of metaphysics in these quaint little rondures that resembled a couple of oak-apples as they kept bobbing up and down, rallying each other and making sport of the entire universe.

The oarsmen in the second deck, above sea-level, were not at that moment using their long, thick, heavy oars, which were the largest oars to be seen at that epoch in any harbour in the world, but had pulled them out of the water and were holding them across their knees while they themselves leant back in their seats, talking, or throwing "astragaloi", the special kind of dice that sailors preferred, or just settling themselves to sleep. There were four of these oarsmen, a couple for each side of the "Teras" as she breasted the waves, Klytos and Teknon on her starboard side, and Euros and Halios on her port side.

All these four men came from the immediate vicinity of the palace of Nausikaa's parents and their families were personally well-known to her. It was down on the third deck that the passengers' cabins were situated; and the present possessors of these cabins had to be selected without any exhausting consideration of personal feelings. One of them for instance was shared between Nausikaa and Okyrhöe; and another between Pontopereia and Eione; while a third was given up entirely to Odysseus.

The most striking thing about the "Teras" however was not the number of her decks nor the number of her cabins. It was her Figure-Head. If the beard of Odysseus, which already had played its part in one of the queerest palace-plots ever revealed by a chronicler, bore, as has already been noted, a strong resemblance to a ship's bowsprit, the real bowsprit of the "Teras" had no sooner entered the harbours of the world than it was recognized as the most striking of all figure-heads known to civilization. It represented a unique creature whose form and shape had been invented by the Ruler of Lost Atlantis who had concluded the work by placing on the creature's scaly neck his or her own head with all its striking features.

The name of this Ruler was unknown and the peculiarity of its unusual head was that it was hard to imagine it as the head of any mortal or immortal man, and still harder to accept it as the head of a god or head of the horribly scaly neck to which it was and is attached. This mysterious Being, whose extraordinary features were not those of a man or a god or a beast or a monster, was the author of a long poem about the beginning and the end of everything, a poem which still remains the greatest oracle of man's destiny existing upon the earth.

The unfortunate thing about this tremendous hieroglyph is that by reason of the drowning of the continent that produced it, and by reason of its being chained with golden chains to the altar of the Hundred and Twenty-Five Gods of that sunken continent, only those who were permitted to read it before the waves covered the altar to which it was bound know anything of its secret; and among these only the Seven Wise Men of Italy have so much as begun to penetrate its contents; and these have only revealed the fact that it is landscape superimposed upon landscape rather than rhythm upon rhythm that is the method of its message.

Since, however, when any of these Seven Wise Men perish the remaining ones appoint successors there is still a hope that in spite of the punishment inflicted by Zeus, the wisdom of Atlantis. will never be entirely lost.

While Nisos was struggling to be as prophetic as he could in his talk to the Master of the "Teras", Pontopereia, the daughter of a prophet, was doing the same sort of thing, only with more subtlety, in regard to Eione, as the two girls sipped the well-made red wine, mixed with plenty of pure spring-water, with which Nausikaa's stores provided them, not to mention nibbling a few particularly well-spiced biscuits from Arabia, a taste for which the princess inherited from her mother.

"Oh don't say *that*, darling Eione! I know so well the feeling you have that drives you to say it; but we women really must learn to slip under or slip over these crude urges of Nature that lift us off our feet and force us to utter things like that! The great thing is, I know I'm right in *that* anyway, the great thing is always to have *two* lives going; one of them the life we share with our friends, and the other the life we enjoy with our own mind and with our own senses.

"To keep this secret second life going, even while we are living the other to the full, is the supreme trick of existence for girls such as you and I."

Eione lifted up her shapely legs from the couch where hitherto the two girls had been lying face to face, each pair of bare feet resting motionless against the neck of the owner of the other pair. But the easy nonchalance of that chaste yet familiar position was completely broken up by this provocative movement on the part of Tis's sister. Their position blotted out from the daughter of Teiresias all view of her companion's face. All she could see of her now was a couple of white shins and the extremely intimate shadows and outlines between them.

"When you talk of the life we 'share with our friends'," enquired a girlish voice from behind these uplifted knees, "do you mean our lovers?"

"Certainly I do," replied Pontopereia almost sharply, "if we have such idiots; but what was in my mind was nothing as sexual as that."

"Would you advocate living this double life even after marriage?"

"Most certainly I would! Don't you see, my sweet, it is only after the actual moment of union has been consummated by the loss of our virginity that men, and women, can make love, as people call it, on equal terms. But does the ecstasy of such embraces so absorb us both as to completely blot out and obliterate our separate identities? Don't you suppose, my lovely one, that we still go on—I won't say thinking thoughts that have have no connection with the passionate pleasure we're enjoying, but thinking such a thought as—'oh how utterly and entirely this heavenly, this divine sensation beats all other sensations I've ever known!'"

"But," came the voice from behind the upraised legs, that is to say from behind the whole of Eione from the waist down, "but doesn't what you're now saying, my friend, reduce the passion of love to an extremity of purely selfish sensation?"

Pontopereia at this drew up her own legs with an abrupt jerk; but straightened her back as she did so, and leaned forward, sitting on her heels, and resting the palms of both her hands upon the uplifted knees of the girl before her.

"I confess, my dear," she said, "that I'm talking of something of which I've had no experience. But surely if this ecstasy of love's embrace, of which such a lot is made, is as transporting and enthralling as we're always being told it is, neither of the parties concerned can possibly have the detachment of consciousness left inside them to say anything to themselves around or about or above or beneath the absolutely absorbing sensation they are caught up in and which is blinding them to all else?"

A sudden outburst of silvery laughter came from the girlish face upon which, with her hands on the young creature's knees, Pontopereia now gazed with unpretended admiration.

"Aren't you confusing," were the words that issued from that radiant but extremely simple countenance, "what we feel when we're imagining a love-ecstasy in some hot exciting trance of deliciousness when alone by ourselves with what we feel in our first real love-night?"

"You mean, Eione darling, that when we're in the act of making love we think more of our lover and more of *his* feelings than of our own?"

"The gods forbid!" cried the excited girl. "Did I hear you utter the word 'more'? Of course we think 'more' of his feelings for us than of ours for him! Isn't it the delicious heat of his feelings for us that rouses ours and that alone has the power to arouse ours?" Pontopereia perceived that she had indeed entered a sphere of philosophic analysis where more intimate experience than had yet been hers was required if she were to see the thing in proper perspective.

ATLANTIS

So with a view to changing the subject she changed her physical position and sliding both her own feet to the floor she edged herself along the side of the bed, till bending down above her friend she was able to smooth the girl's fair hair from her forehead.

"You haven't half told me, you know, what happened after you rode off with Arcadian Pan and with Eurybia and Echidna. Where on earth did those two leave you? What happened to the horse with the flowing mane? Did Pan himself go down under the waves when you got to the place where the land of Atlantis had been drowned?"

Before beginning any answer to all this Eione thrust her friend's hand away. "Don't do that! It makes me nervous! It's what Thrasonika our school-teacher used to do."

Pontopereia hurriedly withdrew her hand. She had received such a shock that, hardly aware of what she was doing, she licked the longest finger of the hand that had not been to blame and with it gently stroked the erring hand as if to cure it of its impetuosity.

"I can tell *you* of course," went on Eione, seized by a sudden gust of confidential school-girlishness, "because you weren't at school in Ithaca. But it was because of Thrasonica going on stroking her hair that Amaryllis Leporides drowned herself."

Pontopereia's face expressed all the astonishment she felt, though by no means all the moral indignation she felt. Eione nodded vigorously. "Nobody but the three youngest of us know," she repeated; throwing into her tone the implication that in Ithaca a girl's sophistication decreased rather than increased as she grew up.

And indeed this was a view of insular as compared with continental education which struck Pontopereia as entirely correct.

"Nisos told me," announced Pontopereia, standing on her feet now, and sufficiently disturbed by the rebuff Eione had given her to hit back—woman *versus* woman—by dragging in Nisos, "that the great Epic Poem about the Beginning of All Things by the Ruler of Atlantis brings in the little island where Arcadian Pan must have given you the Helmet of Proteus and told Pegasos to carry you to Odysseus! But Nisos tells me this little island, which he says is called 'Wone' and must be pronounced so as to rhyme with 'tone' is really the top of the tallest of the mountains of drowned Atlantis, a mountain which used to be called Kunthorax and whose foot-hills rose from a vast fir-forest which was only a couple of days' ride from the great city of Gom which was—and I suppose still *is*, only it's under the water—the capital of Atlantis."

Eione had listened to all this with her eyes tightly shut and her whole face quiescent, as if, though perhaps not actually asleep, the treatment of this crucial subject by her philosophic friend had a somnolent effect upon her. But she was compelled to open her eyes, and open them pretty wide too, when Pontopereia seized the pole, with which they regulated the sky-light to the deck above, the sky-light from which came *most* of their air and, when they hadn't lit their oil-lamp, *all* their light, and opening it wider than they had ever done before, shouted in a shrill voice: "Is Nisos Naubolides up there? If he is, for the sake of all the gods tell him to come down here for a moment!"

So loudly did the youthful voice of the daughter of Teiresias ring through the whole interior of the "Teras" that it crossed the mind of Odysseus as he swung himself backwards and forwards in his cabin that it was possible that one of these two young creatures might have tried to put an end to the life of the other; and vaguely endeavouring to allow this imaginary supposition its full weight the old adventurer caused his hammock of small cords to swing rhythmically backwards and forwards to a sort of musical argument in favour of the advantage of being alive compared with the advantage of being dead.

The four oarsmen who while so fresh a wind filled the great sail were able to take their pleasure with their special dice or "astragaloi", and had just decided that until supper-time they would make the game more lively by making it less individualistic, turning it in fact into a battle between the starboard and larboard oarsmen of the "Teras", with Teknon and Klytos on the starboard side, and Euros and Halios on the larboard or port side; and it was this new and more communal game that was broken up by Pontopereia's cry.

Having put its violent lid upon the dicing of these astragoloi-players the girl's quivering cry rang from end to end of the topmost deck where Proros and Pontos, who were managing the ropes which held the great bulging sail upon whose one, taut, open curve their speed and safety of their speed entirely depended, repeated the cry at once, and not content with repeating it, they both imitated it, and did this so successfully that the first officer, Thon, who by general consent rather than by professional succession had become the outlookman of the "Teras", ransacked the sea's surface with his eyes in search of some broken-winged siren before he made it known to Akron the ship's master, that the young man to whom that same skipper was courteously listening was wanted below.

"Better go down at once, my boy! There's some serious trouble among your women-folk! I pray it's between those young ones, and *not* between those older ones! Down with you, my son! Down with you! No! no! Don't wait a second, *lad*! These troubles *inside* the ship are far more serious than anything that goes on in the City of Gom or at the top of Kunthorax; or on the Island of Wone. Oh, you'll settle this trouble, my lad, whatever it is! You've got the look of an ambassador. Down with you now; and quick about it!"

But it was several minutes before Nisos, buoyed up by feeling that it was especially exciting to be called upon to decide a quarrel between the daughter of Teiresias and the sister of Tis, managed to reach even the second deck of the "Teras"; and it was perhaps just because he kept telling himself that it was so quaint that a son of Krateros and Pandea should be the one destined by Atropos to hold these uncertain scales that he didn't clamber down the ship's first ladder with more headlong speed.

The ladder from the second deck to the third deck was at the stern of the vessel, whereas the one he had just descended was near the prow and the astonishing neck, scaled, feathered, wrinkled, infundibular, that belonged to the figure-head of the "Teras", the figure-head which so far he had only seen from the rear but which Akron assured him, when seen from the front, represented the most intellectual visage ever carved out of any substance upon earth by flint or stone or bronze or iron and was the face of "the unknown ruler" of Atlantis. Thus in order to reach the ladder to the lowest deck of the "Teras" where were the three cabins occupied at present by Nausikaa and Okyrböe, by Eione and Pontopereia, and by Odysseus himself, Nisos had to step over the big round oars, either of Teknon and Klytos on the starboard side, or of Euros and Halios on the port side; and he selected the latter.

He did this, as we so often say, "for a trivial reason" but as we all, especially those of us who are historians, know only too well, reasons like this always appear to everybody trivial before the result is revealed, and the event which is the result monumentalized, made clear to all. His "trivial reason" was that the oarsman Euros had that deep indentation behind his skull and above his neck, which certain experiences had taught our young prophet was an infallible sign of refinement and of quite special sensitivity.

Greeting Euros therefore with diffidence and respect and half-turning to address the man's up-tilted face as he paused, before stepping over the oar of Halios he continued to see, even while glancing into the man's eyes, that particular indentation at the back of his head which he held in such high regard, while behind it as if it were a symbol of all that was delicate and vulnerable in humanity, as opposed to all that was inhuman in Nature, rolled the enormous weight of waters. But it is dangerous, as his hero Odysseus could have told him, to philosophize too minutely when you are acting with a rush: and his pause at that second made him trip up so blindly over Halios' oar that down he came with a crash, sprawling absurdly on the carefully scrubbed deck, and uttering a blasphemous curse on the vindictive ways of Poseidon.

Halios lowered his great oar with rapid effectiveness as well as with exquisite nicety and helped Nisos to his feet while all their six eyes, joined now by the four eyes of Teknon and Klytos on the starboard side, turned simultaneously seaward, totally forgetting Pontopereia's wild cry.

And what they saw was indeed a sufficient marvel to justify any creature's obliviousness to all else. For on one side a flaming red sun sank behind the horizon; and on the other a pale full moon rose above the horizon.

What was indeed curious in this sudden possession by the sinking Sun and the rising Moon of the entire consciousness of four middle-aged men and one young man was the fact that each of the two celestial luminaries was only visible through one of the oar-holes on one of the two sides of the ship.

In each case the bulk of the hole was filled by its particular oar; and, since each of the heavenly bodies was of a circular shape, the golden segment of the moon, which encircled the oar of Euros on one side, and the blood-red segment of the sun which encircled the oar of Teknon on the other side, produced, when the eyes of all five men moved from one to the other, a visual effect so strange that it was doubtful if any of them would ever, though he lived as long as the Ithacan palace Dryad, see such a sight again. Each of the five men received the startlingness of this queer vision in a different way. Euros, for instance, felt pure annoyance over the advantage that the deck-hands who dealt with the ropes and the sail had over themselves in regard to what they could see, and this feeling was increased when first on one side and then on the other the oar-holes were not only lined and inlaid with bloody sickles and golden crescents but crossed and re-crossed by the obstinate and greedy flight of a small sea-bird, for whose feather-covered cranium these creaking orifices were associated neither with the sun nor with the moon, but purely and solely with the fragments of terrestial garbage which the oarsmen got rid of through them. As for Nisos, he played with the crazy and fantastic fancy that the whole universe was the body of the giant Atlas, that great Titan whom the Son of Saturn compelled to hold up the sky lest it fall upon the earth.

And Nisos imagined himself following his hero Odysseus in a

winged ship that had the power of forcing its way through the body of the earth, as well as through the body of the sun, as well as through the body of the moon; but in his present fancy these three bodies were one body, the body that is to say of the entire universe, which was simply the body of Titan Atlas. His pet hawk was with him; and in his fancy he and his hawk kept flying through the whole body of Atlas and out on the other side: that is to say—into the void and back again into Atlas.

It was not long, however, before this Atlas fancy of our youthful prophet developed into a much bolder imagination; the idea namely, that he himself was a universe-devouring dragon who lived on the elements and fed on earth and fire and water as he hurled himself through the air from one universe to another, devouring each one in turn, while, out of his excrement, vast-trailing protoplasmic embryos of new universes were eternally coagulated afresh.

The queer trance into which all five men on the rowing-deck of the "Teras" had fallen may have been caused by the fact that in their awareness that the ship was sailing mid-way between sinking sun and rising moon each man felt he was being pitilessly pulled in opposite directions by two sanguinary opponents and that the end of it could only be that he would be torn into two halves. He could already feel himself becoming both these two half-selves which were now feebly drifting in opposite directions, their ragged edges raw and bloody while the flesh nearest those edges grew more and more gangrened. Was it perhaps that the screams of this sea-hawk, a bird that might easily have seemed to a prophetess, like that Nymph in the Italian cave, to be the return of a creature that had for hundreds of thousands of years been visiting and re-visiting the earth, stirred up in Nisos a desire to plunge deeper and deeper into the mystery of matter?

At any rate one thing was certainly clear, namely that the wood-work of the "Teras" herself was slowly being aroused to a sort of semi-human consciousness. Whether this would have a good effect on those who were voyaging in her, who could say?

But Nisos now set himself to scramble down to that lowest deck of all, from whence Pontopereia's cry had ascended. It occurred to him, as he now rushed down, to wonder whether his delay in obeying her cry had hurt the feelings of the daughter of Teiresias, and as he climbed down the ladder, feeling slightly uncomfortable in his mind from remorse at not obeying her more quickly and slightly uncomfortable in his body from his crashing fall he cursed himself as a prize fool. "Where in the name of all the Harpies and Gorgons *is* the girl?" he muttered as he entered their cabin and found Tis's sister asleep on their couch and not a sign of the other one. "Has she," he thought, and as this fear shot through him he felt a queer sensation that he knew was different from any other feeling he had ever had before, "has she climbed up the ladder and thrown herself into the sea? And did she do this," and he addressed his remark not to himself but to the sleeping figure of Eione, "because of something *you* said to her?"

He stood staring at the sleeping girl in the bed with what he pretended to himself was a look of fierce dramatic reproach. The sleeping girl would have been gratified however to observe that this fierce look was directed solely at her face and that upon her incredibly well-moulded limbs, as fully exposed to his view as her extremely rustic and almost grotesquely simple features, the look that was drawn out of him was of quite a different kind.

Different or not, all that Pontopereia knew about Nisos' expression when she crept up silently behind him from her hiding-place among the hampers and nets and wicker cases and javelin-holders and quivers made of twisted root-fibres full of feathered arrows, which Odysseus had piled up outside his cabin and which —for the lowest deck of the "Teras" was anything but spacious— did more than just impinge upon the cabin of the two girls— all indeed that Pontopereia could possibly know of the feelings of Nisos as he stood staring at her enemy-friend and incorrigible rival was the simple fact that he *did* stand thus staring. And so when she spoke to him and he swung round to face her as if she had pricked him with one of Odysseus's darts, the look that was exchanged between them was one of those looks that young men and young maids exchange now and again and that are as the primeval Welsh Prose Epic expresses it, "like the colour of lightning upon a sword-blade".

But it was at this moment that Odysseus himself appeared on the scene, emerging from his solitary cabin with bare feet, and entirely naked save for the blanket he had wrapped round him and the extraordinary Helmet of Proteus which he had just clapped on his head.

"I want one of you," he whispered hoarsely, "to come here a second!"

"What in the name of Aidoneus," thought Nisos, "is in the king's mind?"

But Eione, who had already leapt from her couch so quickly that the imprint left by her head on the pillow contained a twisted couple of tiny fair hairs held together by an infinitesimal flake of cinder-dust that must have adhered to them when she was recently heating water for her bath, had not lived all her life with old Morus for nothing. She would naturally divine the sort of thing that the practical cunning of a wily old man would urge him to do at a crisis like this. She had therefore, in reading the mind of Odysseus, an advantage over both the daughter of a prophet and the young aspirant to be himself a prophet.

She therefore without a moment's hesitation, and as if it were a dedicated dagger for some pontifical killing, offered her slender wrist to the old king; who proceeded at once, and with no more hesitation than she had shown, to make use of this small wrist. He led her after an imperative gesture to Pontopereia and Nisos to remain quiescent, to the drawn curtain that covered the threshold of the cabin occupied by Nausikaa and Okyrhöe; and the moment he got her there he made a mute sign to her to remain absolutely still, and then, drawing the curtain aside with an imperceptibly gentle movement he set himself to listen to what was going on between the two women.

"O for heaven's sake don't make me have to go over it all again, Princess," Okyrhöe was saying. "I'm only telling you for the hundredth time that this whole mad voyage of this crazy old king is ridiculous; and that you who pretend to be his friend, instead of helping him, are driving him faster to his ruin and destruction! Why, my good, silly woman, before we started on this crazy voyage I talked to several of the sailors who are running this ship and I soon found out how hopeless the whole thing is. They told me that the very figure-head of this ship is enough to damn the whole business by showing the ship's destiny. They told me that the face of that Being at the prow is enough alone to prove to whom the vessel belongs! It belongs to the Ruler of Atlantis; for the face that looks out from that dreadful neck is the face of that Ruler himself!

"They *all* know that; yes! all the sailors on this ship know it. And they know too that it was because of the blasphemous inventions and impious intentions of this wicked magician that the divine Son of Kronos who wields the thunder plunged the whole continent of Atlantis into the depths of the ocean. You pretend that this ship is of your land and has inherited from the skill and the craft of your people its power of prevailing over disaster and of holding onto its strength. All this is false—in fact a lie! The 'Teras' with its officers and the best of its crew was a pirate-ship long before it fell into the skilled hands of your people and was converted into a vessel of the shape and style of your land.

"And now, my foolish woman, you must see how ridiculous it is to encourage Odysseus in this madness of his, when the truth is—"

At this point Nausikaa boldly interrupted her. "Come, come, my dear lady, why on earth should a couple of presentable females like you and me scold each other like a pair of fish-wives in the old 'Net-Alley' of the Piraeus?"

But once started in her torrent of vituperation it was impossible to silence Okyrhöe. "When I began", the woman went on, "talking to these people just now I soon realized into what a desperate and tragic business you had, with all your good intentions, betrayed this unfortunate old king. Don't you see how infinitely pathetic it is to watch this aged impulsive fool dressing himself up in this comical head-dress they call the Helmet of Proteus?

"What about all his fellow-countrymen who are now going to be led into such terrible peril by the pure chance that you came here with this ship? I'm not saying these things to you to torment you or to get any advantage over you. Do please, I beg you, lady, stop this vulgar abuse, and let us decide together how we can best help our mutual hero in this grand final adventure of his unequalled life!"

The two of them continued their word-battle for quite a number of minutes, though neither of them was unoccupied while their desperate dispute went on. They were both arranging their hair, their head-dresses, their robes, their jewels, and even smoothing out the creases in their soft leather sandals, to make which final adjustment they were forced to display to each other and of course, though unknown to themselves, to their three watchers, for, though the daughter of Teiresias still held herself proudly aloof, Nisos as it well may be believed, was unable to resist the temptation of joining in this espionage, the most intimate beauty of their figures.

Matters on board the "Teras" were further complicated at this critical point by the emergence from the ship's hold, which was reached by a short ladder of no more than three rungs from the cabin occupied by Odysseus, of the two black Lybian cooks staggering under their first instalment of food and drink for everyone on board; and as this plenteous repast was to be swallowed in what was now the cabin of Odysseus it can be imagined with what rapidity these two imperious ladies of fashion hastened to complete their toilet.

Along with the two black Libyans there came up also from the hold of the good ship "Teras", or "Prodigy", a couple of Assyrian boys of about thirteen whose business it was to act as general scavengers and excrement-disposers for both crew and passengers. On every deck of the ship there were containers for excremental liquids and containers for excremental solids which it was the duty of these Assyrian boys to empty into the sea; and for this purpose, each day of every voyage, they went the round of the ship at sunset.

Thus it was no haphazard or random coincidence but by one of those inevitable concentrations of the normal and natural forces of life that keep the world on the move that the whole crowd of human creatures, from the Old Odysseus to the young excrement disposers, who were divided from the waters of drowning by the planks of the "Teras" or "Prodigy", were gathered together when a clamorous shout went up, a shout that came from the throats of the general crowd and not from any professional group or any especially nervous group, a shout that was soon repeated still louder and by this time came from the deck upon which any boat-load of people coming from any direction at all would of necessity scramble on board.

Nisos was at Odysseus' side when the divine animal, Pegasos, flying with quite a company of people on his broad back, reached the "Teras" and therefore our young man had a unique opportunity of noting how the old king reacted to this impact. But he was so anxious to catch all the king's feelings that he couldn't help exaggerating much that he observed.

He exaggerated for instance many flickering changes of expression on the countenance of Odysseus. He exaggerated certain jerky and feverish gestures made by the King. The truth was that no one alive really understood the King except Eurycleia his old nurse. It was one of the results of Odysseus' abnormal self-control that he could feel deep down in his blood and bones reactions quite different from those which he felt in his more superficial nerves or along the surface of his skin, and more different still from those expressed in his face.

The scene on the "Teras"' top deck when Pegasos arrived was indeed something that might have reduced to a wild state of hysterical excitement any traveller less self-controlled and less artful than Odysseus. The human creatures whom Pegasos now shook from his broad back and from between his wide-stretched wings were obviously so confused by the whole experience that, as the saying goes, they hardly "knew their heads from their tails".

ATLANTIS

For the last couple of days a frantic longing to cling together like a frightened swarm of insects must have possessed them. But in spite of this they preserved their poise and endurance. Chief among these brave voyagers upon the winged horse was Zeuks the son of Arcadian Pan and along with him was none other than Spartika the Priestess of Athene's Temple, and in addition to these and holding herself with proud dignity a little apart from the rest was none other than Arsinöe the bastard daughter of Hector, who in her childhood had been befriended by Andromache, Hector's wife.

Nisos was astonished to see that it was not Zeuks but Spartika who held the proudest position on the back of the winged horse, nearest, that is to say, to his head, and he was still more surprised when instead of descending, as Zeuks and Arsinöe very speedily did, Spartika remained seated, and indeed began to caress the mane of Pegasos and to give that arching neck whose curves resembled a torrent of water released from rocks and roots and flowing at ease down a smooth declivity, a series of reassuring and yet authoritative pats.

Our friend Nisos, who still retained at the back of his consciousness an obstinate determination to be a real prophet before he died, and who was still alert to catch the most intimate ways of the mental rulers of our race, was deeply struck by the manner in which Spartika kept them all standing where they were, as if she had thrown a spell over each of them, while she delivered what evidently was a long-prepared and legally-involved discourse on the precise attitude she intended to take between the run-away goddess of that formidable "aegis", whose very "tassels" could bring new life to the half-dead, and that Priest of the Mysteries who had so successfully usurped the position of Telemachos.

And suddenly Nisos noticed, and he felt that he had really made a step forward in his private self-education in the art of prophesying by having resisted Spartika's priestess-spell sufficiently to be able to notice such a thing at all, that while with one hand she caressed Pegasos, preparatory to giving him the recognizable signal that would make him shake out his eagle wings and gather up his equine hooves beneath him, with the other hand she was active in helping some quite carefully shrouded human figure to edge itself off the horse's back on to the deck where the others were now standing.

Nisos alone among all the onlookers was therefore spared the shock of surprise when two startling events occurred simultaneously: Pegasos suddenly spread his wings and rose into the air with Spartika leaning forward, and clinging to his mane with both hands. And like a living bundle of villainously dirty rags the figure of Enorches rolled upon the deck, and after a minute or two of absolutely solitary twisting and turning, rose to its feet, took up its wrappings and conveyed them to the rail of the ship.

Here, with what struck Nisos as a deadly curse upon the whole gamut of existence, this destructive Priest of the Mysteries flung his bundle of filthy rags into the water; and then, leaning over the edge himself, just as if he were hugging the thought of following his garments—and how had he managed to make them heavy enough to sink?—he plunged his thought, if nothing else, after what he had thrown.

And while the Priest of Eros and Dionysos was staring blindly after his own imaginary corpse, that corpse of living thought which he evidently pretended to himself he could see sinking down and down and down, till it found the slit at the bottom of the ocean which led to the slit at the bottom of the world which led to the slit at the bottom of the universe, Odysseus, whose outward nerves, equally with the imperturbable recesses of his being, were totally unaffected by any of these mental horrors, addressed a quiet request to Zeuks that he relate to him what had actually happened in Ithaca since the "Teras" set sail.

Nisos never forgot the scene that followed this natural demand. All the living persons on board save Akron the Master of the ship were gathered round the mast from which that pair of perfect sailors, Pontos and Proros from Skandeia in Kythara, had wisely lowered all but a small fold of the great sail.

Thus the "Teras", or "Prodigy", was running lightly, easily, freely, but comparatively slowly before a gentle and cool easterly wind; while the full moon, which was now moving with that motionless movement which is unlike any other movement in the universe, over, under, and straight through cloud after cloud, after cloud, after cloud, flooded the whole of what was visible, as well as—at least that was what came suddenly into Nisos' head—the whole of what was invisible, with an enchantment that separated the real life of each separate living thing from the life imagined as its life by all other living things.

Nisos noted very definitely the extraordinary manner in which this flood of moonlight, which was as spiritual and mental as it was physical and emotional, held everybody at that crisis under such a spell that when the quiet voice of Odysseus called upon Zeuks to speak there came a strangely universal sigh from all present. The thoughts and feelings of Odysseus himself as he made this quiet request were more direct and simple, as they were more massively impenetrable and impervious to influence of any sort or kind, than his young follower Nisos could have believed possible.

Odysseus was prepared to humour and indulge to the limit all those who needed humouring and indulging if they were to be useful to him in the fulfilment of his purpose. He was also prepared to obliterate totally from his consideration, leaving them to go their way just as they liked, as he intended to go his way just as he liked, all those persons, creatures, tendencies, and forces, over whom or over which he had no control.

Unlike Zeuks as a man, and unlike Pegasos as an animal, there was, in spite of all the rumours to the contrary, no trustworthy evidence that any seed save that from the loins of Laertes was responsible for his begetting. What separated him from other mortal men was the adamantine weight and solid mass of what might be called Being, or Existence, or Entity, thickening out his Personality, which he put behind the purpose, whatever purpose it might be, upon which at the moment he was engaged.

The real essence of the man's shrewdness, for it was more like the measured sagacity of some huge sea-lion than it was like the wily cunning of a fox or the crafty vigilance of a hungry hyaena or the distracted desperation of a solitary wolf, had a super-animal obstinacy in it which had the power of keeping intact, like some monumental idol, the achievement towards which he kept advancing.

He had done precisely that with the taking and looting of Troy. The sack of this royal city must have occupied the attention of his whole essential Being and this perfectly calm yet terrific preoccupation, nourished on the very marrow of his bones, was the thing that made it possible for him to indulge in the most outrageous lies and monstrous deceptions, without, as the saying is, turning a hair.

And now it was the same with this voyage above the waters under which lay the lost Atlantis. Odysseus had the power of "jollying along" every mortal person and thing, whether divine, or human, whether animal, vegetable or mineral, that could possibly, by any imaginable twist or turn of coaxing, cajoling, cozening, condensing, dilating, liquifying, vaporizing, euhemer-izing, metamorphosing be made use of to help forward his individual purpose.

What would have needed the genius of Pontopereia's progenitor himself, yes! even of the great Teiresias, to unravel, was the convoluted connection between the definite, concrete, actual, realistic achievement at which Odysseus was aiming and the glory, honour and fame he would get by this achievement.

It seems to the present chronicler, though it is only too likely that both Homer and Hesiod would take a different view, that the grape-juice of the glory of achieving, and the fir-tree sap of having achieved, when the achievement has been accomplished, are so inextricably intermingled that not all the Sirens, Harpies, Gorgons and Erinyes in the whole cosmos could unravel them.

To capture Troy, to return to Ithaca while Penelope still lived, to plunge down among the sunken temples and altars and streets and markets of drowned Atlantis, each one of these triumphs of the individual will over all that opposes it, had become so completely all that was, all that is, all that shall be for evermore, to the man Odysseus, that to separate these events from this man would be like separating the moon from its light or the water from the waves.

Thus it was when Odysseus required of Zeuks that he should speak, Zeuks himself seemed conscious of some special quality in the moonlight as well as conscious of the abnormally dramatic weight of what he had to tell, for it struck Nisos who was watching Zeuks closely that this latter gave a sort of half-shrug of his broad shoulders and although he didn't remove his hands from his sides he opened them wide, with their palms exposed and their fingers widely extended, as if he were commencing to disclaim all possible responsibility for all conceivable events in this mad world.

And it was at that precise second that an infinitesimal and entirely haphazard thing occurred such as had happened to Nisos from his earliest childhood. The fact that he was watching Zeuks so closely sharpened his powers of observation to an abnormal extent. And the result of this was that his attention was caught and held by the fact that a small sea-swallow, swooping and swerving along this particular deck, had let fall upon the deck's well-scrubbed surface a little clot of bird's dung from which protruded not only the featherless stalk of a tiny feather but the clipt edge of a human toe-nail.

Nor did this extra discovery prevent Nisos in his moon-induced mania for minute observation, from noticing that Zeuks himself, as he straightened his shoulders to draw his breath before answering, laid bare upon his own chest a peculiar tuft of especially black hairs. "Is the sky going to fall when Zeuks answers?" thought Nisos: and certainly the general sigh that rose from the whole company just then struck him as curiously connected with all those aspects of human bodies of which human consciousness especially dislikes being reminded.

It was almost as if the unseemly parts of every corporeal frame in that whole company joined in that general sigh; joined in it indeed so pitifully that it seemed as if that sigh proceeded not so much from the lips of those gathered there as from those disparaged parts of their human bodies of which we only seem to grow fully aware when we are seized by an intense longing to escape from our bodies altogether!

It was a weird thought to come into a youthful head just then, but Nisos welcomed it, and indeed was proud of it, telling himself that his mother would have regarded it as an absolute proof that he was destined one day to be a prophet. Yes, he told himself, this great sigh from all these people came from every single one of the out-of-the-way hairs in their secret orifices of excretion and copulation, and from the ignoble hairs under their arms, whether male or female, and from every crushed, deformed, twisted, and squeezed-sideways toe-nail in that crowd, whether belonging to a male or a female.

Nor did the effect of the moon's motionless motion, through those indifferent clouds, affect only human beings. It was especially potent where small, disregarded, insignificant material objects were concerned, objects such as pieces of burnt wood, broken shells, wisps of wool, flakes of foam, strips of sea-weed, frayed bits of cordage, and even certain infinitesimal scoriae fragments risen to the surface of the water and carried in circles over leagues and leagues of salt waves from the burning craters of the great mountain Kunthorax which towered above the city of Gom, the capital of drowned Atlantis.

Yes, this curious universal sigh rose not only from the less honourable portions of the bodies of the people upon the deck of the "Teras", but from a host of derelict scraps and bits of scraps that winds and tides and sea-gull beaks had helped chance to collect at this particular moment and upon this particular deck. To the mind of our youthful prophet Nisos this heavy undulant sigh was drawn from every mortal thing there present that had, or could ever presume to claim that it had, suffered from the arrogance of immortal gods or the recklessness of mortal men.

A deep and spontaneous sigh like this was, he decided, clearly and unquestionably due to an obscure craving in existence itself to escape from every physical and every mental effort that was forever *"having to be made"* that it might remain what it was and not perish utterly in the abyss. All the animal, all the vegetable, all the mineral offscourings, castaways, shreds, patches, scrapings, splinters, parings, drift and flotsam, together with all the human abortions, misfits and degenerates and all the infected members of each particular corpus of corruption, seemed to Nisos just then as he tried desperately to unravel the psychic knot of that half-circle of suspended life and reluctant death under that intent moon as she passed those casual clouds, to be asking to be heard.

The universe seemed to be giving them some final pitiful chance that their breath should be audible and some broken syllable of their desire should be expressed, which, if Odysseus would only ask it or Zeuks would only answer it, might redeem all. But Odysseus was now repeating his question and Zeuks was now beginning to laugh.

Yes, it was with a laugh he commenced his answer, and with a laugh he finished his answer; and there were many there who must have thought that Odysseus would be overwhelmed by his answer. Zeuks told how it was soon after the "Teras" had sailed that the whole thing happened. Led by Krateros Naubolides, Nisos' father, and by Agelaos Naubolides, Nisos' brother, the enormous faction among the warriors of Ithaca who were opposed to the House of Odysseus swept down in a resolute mass upon the king's palace, ransacked it, scoured it out, gutted it, scraped it clean of every trace and vestige of the House of Odysseus, till from the Corridor of Pillars to the innermost caverns of its washing-chambers, sculleries, pantries, and kitchens, it became a primitive, antiquarian annex to the prosperous barns and picturesque enclosures and to all the long-reverberating rural and insular traditions of the autochthonous House of Naubolides.

"And Eurycleia?" enquired Odysseus, fixing upon the narrator a long, deep, quiet, steady look, not in the least degree an excited or emotional look, and not at all what could be called an inscrutable look. What it really was was a patient ritualistic look, like the look of a priest who has uttered the same words so many

times that his emotional reaction to them has the modified, qualified, calmly reverential feeling such as is really the reaction to their destiny of many generations of a closely knit nation, gravely, but not solemnly, honouring their past, guarding their present as something sacred, and facing their future with a massively unruffled assurance.

Zeuks clearly found it difficult to tell the truth as to just how Eurycleia perished; but after a good many noises in his throat that were too like the sounds in an ox-stall to be called laughing and too like the sounds in a cow-shed to be called crying, he explained that when the old nurse saw Leipephile by her betrothed's side among the foremost intruders she was unable to restrain her indignation and burst out in a rhapsody of vituperation. She abandoned herself indeed to such "shame-crying" and to flinging such "momon" or reproach upon Leipephile that Leipephile, who is, as we all know, a mightily big and powerful wench, lost her temper completely and struck her such a blow over the head with a large marble mixing-bowl or "depas" which she snatched from a side table that the old lady fell down and died instantaneously.

"In the confusion that followed, I fancy I began myself to behave in a wild and excited way and I think I must have drunk quite a lot too, for there was a great deal of wine floating round and I remember that the more adventurous of the intruders soon struck me as being a good deal more intoxicated than I was myself.

"Our Trojan Arsinoë here will bear witness to the truth of what I am narrating to you, O king; for in my tipsy folly I well remember thinking that it was my first duty to you to keep a tight hold on all your captives from the old Trojan War: and it was in the spirit of this sense of duty, O King, that I found myself clinging so closely to the maiden Arsinoë when we took our places on the back of the flying horse. It was your wise and cool-headed herdsman Tis, the brother of the maiden Eione who I understand is with you on board this ship, who insisted on our making use of Pegasos to follow you all this way across the sea.

"I tried to persuade him to accompany us rather than enter the service of the House of Naubolides but he maintained that his duty was first and foremost to the cow Babba, and that Babba's shed and hay-loft and her field of meadow-grass were, taken together, enough of a kingdom for any man to guard and fight for. He also said that if it was the will of Atropos that Krateros Naubolides should rule in Ithaca while its King was sailing where no mortal had ever sailed before, it might well be her will also that when you returned you would find your cow Babba as ready to give you as good milk and as perfect cream as she did before you sailed away.

"'The land,' said Master Tis, 'is my mother and my father and my grandmother and my grandfather. The grass growing on the land is my cow's salvation and the milk from the udders of my cow is my redemption. The bread, made of the wheat which grows on my land, is, as I munch it, the only heaven I need, and furthermore,' said Tis, the grandson of Moros, 'the sweetness of the bread I munch increases as it nears the crust. My bread needs neither honey nor sugar to make it sweet but it needs land as good as my land to make bread as good as my bread; and it needs a cow as good as my cow to keep me from following my King across drowned Atlantis.'"

It was at this point, just as if the mention of the name "Atlantis" had softened some tension in the minds of all, that as Enorches, the Priest of the Mysteries, left the side of the ship and began to pace up and down within the limited space left between the mast with its reduced sail and the half-circle of listeners to this weird scene while his chiton, or body-shirt, having become ruffled in his violent disposal of his rags, his nakedness, unknown to himself, was startlingly exposed in quite a flagrant fashion.

This shameless sight combined with its exhibitor's complete unconsciousness evoked a loud and profane chuckle from Euros which communicated itself to Pontos and from him extended to Klytos and Teknon. Whether Odysseus saw what they were laughing at or not this was one of those occasions when the root cause of all his triumphant endurances had a perfect chance to show itself. His senses might be stirred by the mischievous and provocative smile that Okyrhöe was now directing towards him: his anger might be roused by the thought of the murder of his old nurse Eurycleia, the one person in the world who had known him in the intimate sense in which our father or our mother knows us, or our mate knows us, and by the fact that the blow that killed her was struck by the woman who herself had been waiting at his table since she was a child: but as neither of these things seemed able to change by a jot or a tittle the obstinate bulk of his intention, so no burst of bawdy laughter, even though directed at the privy parts of his worst enemy, could distract him just then from the moon that covered the waters and from the waters that covered Atlantis.

"How did you come, my good friend," he now calmly enquired of Zeuks, indicating the grotesque figure of Enorches, "to bring this confounded fellow with you on the back of Pegasos?"

"I don't wonder, O great King," replied Zeuks, "at your asking how it was that *he* came with us! Well, I can soon tell you how *that* happened. Your herdsman Tis, the brother of Eione here—I'm right in *that*, aren't I, Eione?—was the sole cause of the whole business. None of us would be here now if it weren't for him; and you saw just now how submissively the horse obeyed the priestess Spartika—all owing to wise treatment he received in Tis's stable. Herdsman Tis must have learnt from that old cow Babba he so dotes on some secret language that all animals, whether mortal or immortal, make use of when alone with each other.

"It must have been painful to Tis to prepare Pegasos for leaving his stable so soon; but I can tell you, my King, you've got nobody in your palace-cave, nobody in your whole rock-bound island, more devoted to you and your best interests than this man Tis.

"Well! just as we were coming out of those stables and sheds of yours, that this Tis looks after so well—and only, as far as I can see, for the advantage of that one solitary old cow—lo! and behold! there came rushing up to us this egregious fellow who calls himself a priest of Orpheus and who sure is the most treacherous and teasing and tantalizing and tricky human being I have ever encountered in the whole of my life. Ye gods! and if he didn't go so far as to demand permission to sit alongside of us on Pegasos' back!

"For the moment, my lord, I can assure you I was flabbergasted by this request. I only knew the fellow as your enemy, and the enemy of my young friend Nisos here, and the enemy of your son Telemachos. Why then, you naturally ask, did I allow this arch-liar, this dangerous and tricky traitor, to have a seat with us on the back of Pegasos? I'll tell you exactly why, O my King, and you must decide for yourself whether I was right or wrong. This Priest-fellow, this Enorches-man, fell on his knees before me and tapped the earth with his forehead seven successive times! As he did so he swore an oath; and he even went so far as to presume to add to this oath certain terrible and dreadful words after the manner of the immortal gods: for the words he added had to do with the River Styx.

"It was this oath of his, this oath by the Styx that he was planning no harm to you, my King, that caused me to hesitate. And then I suddenly decided to put my dilemma—as to whether to refuse his request or to allow him to join us—before your herdsman Tis and allow him to decide. And, when I put the matter to him, shall I tell you how he answered me, O great King?

"He said quite quietly: 'Set him before me, my lord Zeuks, and let me ask him something.'

"So I did, and set the man before him. And your herdsman Tis said to Enorches: 'May I ask you one question, O great Master of the Mysteries?' And when Enorches nodded, for I could see he regarded Tis as not grand enough, nor famous enough, nor learned enough, nor royal enough, to have any part or lot in these high matters, this was the question Tis put to him:

"'If your will, Master, was done about Eros and Dionysos, it would mean, wouldn't it, that your will would also be done about the Mysteries?'

"You should have Seen the look the priest gave him. But he answered quick enough; and not sharply or angrily either: 'It *would* also be done about the Mysteries.' And it was then that the extraordinary thing happened that led to the Priest of the Mysteries to be marching up and down the deck of this ship as he is doing now in the eyes of all! Your herdsman Tis called upon the cow Babba.

"At the sound of his voice the cow Babba came straight from her stall and advanced among us, thrusting her cool wet nose into our bosoms, till we had, each one of us, pressed our lips against her upper lip with a noisy kiss.

"'Drop your token now, Babbawatty, my Holy of Holies,' said Tis in a low voice but a voice of the greatest authority I've ever heard since the day when I heard my grandfather addressing my father, and neither of *them* was an animal like Babba or a man like Tis; for indeed they both were and are immortal gods.

"At this command the cow turned towards us again as if she were going to repeat her recent nuzzling of us one by one. She did indeed move from one to another of us as before, but did no more nuzzling; and at that moment, O great King, there was one of those perceptible arrests, pauses, hushes, and sudden silences, as when the wing of a bird of omen touches the place where we are destined to rest in our final sleep. And it was after that weird pause that Babba stopped in front of Enorches, lifted her tail, straddled her legs and dropped on the ground the largest black-green cow-turd I've ever seen in my life.

"And, in the same pulse of time at which that huge dropping fell, Tis strode up to Enorches and said to him:

"'Master, you are holding something back from us. What is it?'

"And for answer the Priest of the Mysteries cried aloud in the hearing of them all:' What I am holding back can only be revealed when, once more, as formerly they confronted each other in Arima, Eurybia confronts Echidna above the sunken City of Gom!'

"Having uttered these words he begged to be helped up upon the back of Pegasos and there was none among us who found it in him to refuse."

Zeuks was silent: while Nisos, watching Odysseus with the closest interest felt as if the old warrior's attitude to all these upheavals was not so much abysmally super-human as it was fathomlessly sub-human. Odysseus by this time had seated himself on a coil of ropes at the foot of the mast where the brothers Pontos and Proros, as they turned from the "protonoi" or "forestays" to the "kaloi" or "halliards," were clearly obeying a sequence of silent signs from Akron, the Teras' master, who with one hand against the mast was staring at the moon-lit horizon in front of the ship.

From the expression upon his face Akron might have been saying to himself: "The chief thing when you are master of a ship is to keep your ship afloat and your eye on the water in front of her. And there is great danger you may forget both these objectives if you listen for a single second to the song of a siren outside the ship or to the voice of a Prophet inside the ship."

And it now suddenly struck Nisos, as he moved as near as he dared to the King's extemporized throne, that the way the old man was now watching the objects and persons round him was exactly the way the winged horse watched the objects and persons round him before he proceeded to obey Spartika and carry her back to Ithaca.

Yes, the old king had at this very moment the same expression as the winged horse before he rose into the air. And Nisos told himself that a sea-lion, setting off, or a whale setting off, or even a sea-serpent starting to cross the ocean would have a look not very different from this aged adventurer's as he contemplated the universe from that heap of ropes.

Nisos was too honest with himself not to admit to himself that along with this sub-human look in Odysseus' eyes there was a distinctly normal human look there also. It annoyed our young friend to have to admit this but he was simply forced to do so.

"It must be," he thought, "that in the look of a normal man there is something parallel to the expression in the face of a sea-lion or a sea-serpent." It annoyed him to have to confess this; but he held rigidly to the idea that a prophet had to be honest with himself and he was resolved that when he reached mature years he would be a prophet: yes! a prophet of something, though he could not yet say in any clear terms, or indeed in any terms at all, of exactly what. And it was obvious to him that whatever elements of heroic endurance Odysseus possessed, they were in a really absolute sense human ones and normal ones.

The time taken by our future prophet to reach the conclusion that Odysseus was absolutely human had been so lengthy that most of the crowd, including the deck-hands, had entirely scattered, and there was nobody left but a small group of ordinary human beings, who were anything but professional, and Nisos' friend Zeuks, whose personal obliquities were human enough in spite of his ancestry.

Nisos meanwhile moved nearer and nearer to Odysseus. What he felt at that moment he would have been extremely puzzled to put into words. There was in his feeling, mixed with many very different emotions, a definite protective instinct towards Odysseus. Watching him seated there with that absurd Helmet of Proteus on his head, and holding his Club of Herakles propped up between his knees, more like the staff of an aged beggar than the most formidable weapon in the whole Grecian hemisphere, that hemisphere out of which the ship Teras was now swiftly moving as she advanced into the unknown West, Nisos felt as if the old hero were some precious relic, being carried, for the purpose of using it as a charm, into some completely different universe.

Nisos himself was vividly conscious, as if it had been a magnetic hand laid upon his shoulder, of the intense pressure of the presence of Akron, the Sea-Captain, as the man with his hand on the mast stared with what might have been called a cool and competent stare, but with what at the same time was a desperate and frantic stare, at the moonlit water in front of them.

Pontopereia and Eione had evidently found some way of smoothing out their rather intricate knot of contrariety; for the two girls were now pacing arm-in-arm from one end of the deck to the other, talking eagerly and rapidly. Nausikaa and Okyrhöe also had discovered a way, perhaps the best of all possible ways, of bringing to an end, at least for a time, their convoluted rivalry: for Nausikaa had stretched herself out upon the arching back of the ship's tremendous figure-head, with her arms round the lower part of its scaly neck, and from this point of vantage she was watching with dreamy fascination the churned-up flakes of white and yellow-brown foam which followed one another to left and right as the proudly-cleaving neck, below the cosmogonic countenance of that sublime Being who had neither the face of a beast nor of a man nor of a god, cut its way through the water.

As for Okyrhöe, she had bent down gracefully in front of Odysseus and had snatched at a piece of sail-cloth that in some way had got itself entangled with the coil of ropes upon which the old man was seated. Spreading this piece of sail-cloth under the mast Okyrhöe plunged into the particular activity which had, since she was first grown up, been the ecstasy of her life, that is to say the arranging of her limbs in a manner to provoke intolerable desire.

Meanwhile the Club of Herakles, one of whose personal names was "Dokeesis", or *"That which Seems"*, and another was Prosdokia or "Expectation" and who had the power of thinking and feeling not only with what it called its "life-crack", within which the Moth and the Fly had taken sanctuary but with every portion of its polished surface, contemplated Okyrhöe who now lay at the feet of Akron, the Master of the ship, though he took no more notice of her than if she had been a captive from some island-citadel, a captive whom Odysseus, the Sacker of Cities, had carelessly carried off as they sailed West. But it was not Akron's attention Okyrhöe wished to catch, as, lightly and gracefully—but O so deliberately!—she threw back her head upon her soft white arm and drew up her limbs beneath her. And it was then, and not till then, that Odysseus heard, as long ago, in that dark Nemaean Forest, he had heard it, the voice of his Club of Herakles. The Club was in the midst of a hurried and agitated dialogue with the Sixth Pillar of that Corridor in Ithaca so well known to most of them there.

ATLANTIS

It was not Odysseus' nature, nor was it a habit of his in accordance with his nature, to enter lightly, casually, carelessly, easily, into a conversation with his most powerful weapon. Ever since he first heard that voice in the Nemaean Forest there had come moments when it was impossible not to hear the voice of the Club without a certain awe; and equally impossible not to reply to the voice without an inward submission to the burden of its utterance.

At this particular moment, seated on that coil of rope and turning his gaze first to the wide path of the moon on the water and then to a strange and shadowy Enormity that had suddenly appeared in front of them and that Nisos took to be a foreign ship with two colossal masts, but which might well have been a portion of the vast cranium of the Titan-Giant, Atlas, Odysseus was careful not to glance at Okyrhöe's seductive pose of slumber, nor at Nausikaa's slender limbs and passionate arms entwined about the scaly neck of the mysterious Ruler of Atlantis.

Okyrhöe's closed eyes above her rounded elbow might rest forever in sleepless provocation: Nausikaa's open eyes might be down-turned to the reflection of the moon and down-turned to depths below the reflection of the moon, and down-turned to depths below all reflection: it remained that Odysseus, the son of Laertes, calmly awaited what seemed like the imminent destruction of the ship "Teras" or "Prodigy" by her collison with an island, or with a monster of the deep, or with the head of the Giant Atlas, or with another and much larger vessel.

Odysseus and Nisos, as well as Akron, became aware at this crucial moment of agitated and extremely jerky words being exchanged between Pontos and Proros as they tugged at the outstretched sail of the "Teras". And, simultaneously with this dialogue between Pontos and Proros, Akron, the ship's master, gave expression to a long deep-drawn weirdly hopeless whistle and clapt his other hand upon the mast, to which he now seemed to be clinging, as if expectant of some terrific shock.

Meanwhile the Club of Herakles whose private and personal name was either "Dokeesis", "Seeming", or "Prosdokia",

"Expectation", translated the startling news he was getting from the Sixth Pillar for the benefit of the aged but absolutely normal human brain that now bent low above it. And the words from the Sixth Pillar that the Club of Herakles now repeated for the benefit of his King were terribly simple.

"The ship 'Teras' at this moment is running into extreme danger. The moon is full. And as she shines upon the water and as the water reflects her, the spirit of the Being at the ship's bow is stirred within that Being as it remembers all the long nights it watched from the summit of the mountain Kunthorax the moon as a crescent, sharpening her horns of inversion, and rounding her horns of reversion, in creating and uncreating herself as the orb she is; and this stirring of whatever it may be of the spirit of this Being that still clings to its image is full of peril for the ship 'Teras', and indeed in a moment or two she may be shattered to pieces upon the Island of Wone."

It was naturally only a weird murmuring that Nisos caught of all this; but there was something about the reverberation of the syllable "Wone" that struck his imagination as well as his ear; nor could he help being interested as well as faintly amused as he watched that familiar crack, in the very throat, as it were, of the great weapon the king was clutching, to see a beautiful moth flutter forth and fly straight to the troubled forehead of Enorches, who was now squatting on the deck, and, apparently absorbed in thought, was tearing into pieces a considerable handful of the particular kind of seaweed that has so many of those slippery little bladders growing out of it, which look as if they might explode at a touch.

Arrived at the forehead of Enorches which was such a prominent feature that it seemed to overhang the rest of the man's face like a menacing avalanche, the moth fluttered restlessly up and down as if asking for permission to enter this recondite citadel of metaphysical mystery. Getting no apparent response it flew straight back to the club of Herakles.

And now at last our young would-be prophet was rewarded for the trouble he had taken on first catching the finger-nails of the Harpies at work on the Image of the Goddess of Order, the trouble to memorize a few words of the language of Insects.

"Moan for the Island of Wone!" was what Nisos heard. But the Fly heard more. So much did it hear that it straightway flew to the ear of Nisos to inform him and to force him to understand. This took some time. But when he did understand Nisos felt it to be his duty as a loyal adherent of the House of Odysseus to let that hero, who was already on his feet with one hand upon the shoulder of Akron and the other on the broad head of "Dokeesis", know what he had learnt.

"When he sees," the Fly had buzzed: and Nisos knew that it was of Enorches he was speaking, "that terrible pair from Arima, facing each other and arguing about the drowned city of Gom, he will reveal his secret."

But it now came to pass that both Okyrhöe and Nausikaa sprang to their feet, while Akron, the master of the ship, uttering his commands to the brothers Pontos and Proros as if a great wave were at that moment hanging above their heads, joined with them to pull down the body of the sail, till it slapped the deck, as though it were slapping the back of some martial "hetairos", or comrade-in-arms, at the start of a dangerous crisis.

It can be imagined how the brown moth awaited in their moving citadel within the "life-crack" of the club of Herakles the return of her friend the Fly. She had slipped out of his clutches to flutter to the help of Enorches so swiftly and unexpectedly, that he hadn't been able to stop her. On *his* return therefore she greeted him with a protesting cry; pointing out how unfair it was that after scolding her for supporting the Priest of the Mysteries he yet should hasten to display just the same sort of partisan activity on behalf of those who were opposed to the Priest.

But the moth soon found that this particular moment was too tense with opposing currents of feeling to allow for their usual verbal dispute. "Hush, sweet fool!" cried the fly. And then, when she tried again: "Hold your tongue you flapperty twitter-thighs! Don't you see, little fool, that your friend the Priest is going to prick his own bubble?"

And indeed it was then that Nisos saw the Priest of the Mysteries leap up from the deck, throw away the seaweed with which he had been playing, and point with a pair of long bony arms at the flat, level, rocky Island that had suddenly risen out of the salt deep in front of them and now extended itself before the prow of the "Teras".

"There they are!" cried the Priest hoarsely. "But it's only another big ship with two tall masts!" screamed Okyrhöe. "It must be another ship! It *shall* be another ship! Those two things sticking up there, I say those two things there, *shan't* be anything else than two thick ugly Cretan masts!"

But Odysseus had suddenly swung round and was now addressing a quiet figure whose head, emerging from the ladder leading to the lower deck, had been followed by a pair of easily-shrugged shoulders and an active mobile body, clad, for this special occasion it would almost seem, in the most conventional attire.

"Zeuks! Zeuks! My good friend! Do you mind coming here for a second!" cried the old hero; and in all this whirligig of a phantasmagoric pandemonium Nisos was so hit by the old man's calm that while Zeuks hurried to their side he began scolding himself for the agitation he felt and for the fit of trembling that had seized him.

"Pray to Atropos, you immeasurable ass," he muttered to himself. "Pray that you may never forget what you now see, or, by the gods! that it may be the last thing you *do* see, before we're all drowned! . . . just a feeble old man with a pointed beard and this 'Jack-O-Lanthorn' on his head reducing the howling chaos of a wilderness of waters to something comparatively unimportant!"

"Can you catch," the king was now asking Zeuks, "what this priest of Orpheus is saying as he watches us strike this island?"

And Zeuks answered: "He is confessing to you and to Eros and to Diónysos and to all those he has drawn after him that he has only used his praise of Love and Drink and his Priesthood of Orpheus and of the Mysteries to conceal his advocacy of universal Death. Life ought never, he says, to have started; and the sooner it sinks back into Nothingness the better for us all!"

CHAPTER XI

For all his good seamanship the skipper of the "Teras" or "Prodigy" was at heart, much more than his second-in-command and much more than any of his crew, whether their business was with oar or with sail, a born carpenter.

Thus it was his, Akron's, crouching back that was the first object to arrest the attention of our friend Nisos when, not without having to overcome several physical and even a few mental impediments, he reached the bottom of the hold and was separated from the bottom of the sea by nothing but salt water and a double layer of inch-thick planks.

"More 'Kolla' I tell you! I must have a lot more 'Kolla!'" was the cry that issued from beneath that hunched-over spine. "Glue! More glue!" was in fact the word that in hoarsely groaned accents emerged from that massive head and hooked nose. These were bent so low between the pair of formidable hands now at work squeezing the stuff into place, that the image presented by the red flames beneath the cauldron of melting glue as they flickered over the kneeling man and over the group of dark-skinned boys who were helping him was really like that of a huge Raven, who, with its beak and claws working together, was engaged in the construction of the Gods alone knew what sort of impregnable nest.

"O it's you, is it?" Akron cried, straightening his back, though still remaining on his knees. "What I want now is one of those bronze hammers to smash this damned spike of rock! No! No!

Heavier, much heavier than that! Go in there, where they are, Nisos, will you, and bring me the heaviest you can find!"

Nisos looked round him in some bewilderment; for the intense blackness of the shadows, and the red flickerings from the fire under the cauldron that was keeping the glue fluid, made up between them such an Hephaistian Smithy, as might well have been started by an insane as well as a lame god of fire at the bottom of the ocean!

But one of the black Libyan boys was quick to see his confusion and led him at once to the recess referred to as "in there" out of which he was soon able to extract the sort of long-handled hammer that was the instrument needed. Armed with this he returned to the bent figure of Akron, handed him the huge hammer, and watched eagerly to see what he would do.

The effect of what he saw at that moment lodged itself in his brain so deeply that always, after that, when he found himself in a place where there was anything to remind him of black protruding shadows and cavities full of whirling tongues of scarlet fire, all the impressions of that moment rushed back upon him.

It was the presence of that burning fire under the cauldron of melted glue in connection with the bottom of the ocean that hit him so hard. The element of fire, though taking up only so small a space compared with the terrific mass of water that surrounded it, drew into itself and flung out of itself, as it whirled its bloody circles round and round, an essence of existence that was at once absolute and unique.

But the master of the "Teras" straightened his back, took the long-handed hammer in his hand, and struck that up-thrusting point of rock one—two—three—terrific blows. At the first blow that rough projection of time-crumpled, space-naked rock shivered and cracked. At the second blow a fragment was whirled away. At the third blow the whole piece of rock went crashing off and was sent hurtling through the air to one of the pitch-black corners of the hold. Then there came bursting out of the hole made by that pointed rock a violent spout of sea-water; and down above this jet of brine Akron crouched again, squeezing into that jagged rent handful after handful of "kolla", or semi-solid glue, snatched out of the cauldron. From a pile of carefully selected narrow slips of wood one of the black Libyan boys now handed Akron several freshly smoothed and rounded-off pieces of wood, by the aid of which, squeezed in with the malleable "kolla" or glue, this dangerous rent in the keel of the "Teras" was soon mended.

But they were now confronted by the yet more difficult business of getting the ship well away from the dangerous edges of the small island of Wone while they still kept within reach of it. Akron himself hurried to the oarsmen's deck; for he had already decided that for this particularly ticklish and hazardous undertaking of getting the "Teras" clear of Wone and yet circumnavigating the island till they were well to the west of it, they would be better and safer in the hands of their oarsmen than of the men who manipulated their great sail.

One special advantage which this choice of Akron's possessed Nisos realized to the full directly the two of them were on the oarsmen deck along with the four rowers. The crucial direction and management of the whole manoeuvre was now free from the presence of Nausikaa and Okyrhöe as well as of Eione and Pontopereia.

Zeuks however was still there, having deposited Arsinöe in the cabin of Odysseus, doubtless under the vague idea inherited from his immortal begetter, Arcadian Pan, that the only conceivable relation between a captive lady and a great sacker of cities was the sharing of a night's sleep. Fortunately for the "Teras" and for them all the sharply-pointed rock that had pierced the keel was at the extreme end of a little promontory; so that at the first strong pull of the four long oars the ship swung clear of the island and was in deep water.

Ordering the four men to go on with an evenly-timed spell of steady rowing, Akron now ran up the ladder to the top-deck followed hurriedly by Nisos; and, once on that deck, instead of approaching the group near the mast where Odysseus was watching events with the detachment of an alert sea-lion, he strode quickly to the ship's stern to join the helmsman. He didn't presume himself to touch the "Teras's" helm, as the business of steering a ship as big as she was was no light task, and required a man not only with a special training but with special endowments.

But it had been to Akron himself, who had spent a day and a night in his younger days voyaging to Kephallenia to find Eumolpos and persuade him to join them, that the "Teras" owed her incomparable steersman. It was fascinating to Nisos to see the reverential respect with which the Master of the "Teras" followed now every faintest movement of the rudder by an expert in that difficult art.

The rudder was made of a young fir-trunk, peeled smooth and white; and, by its exquisite pressure upon the carefully squared and polished piece of wood directing the ship's course beneath the water, it caused the "Teras" to obey the firm unswerving hands of Eumolpos of Kephallenia with a perfection that was indeed awe-inspiring.

Nisos edged himself as far back into the stern as he possibly could, so far indeed that the round pole of the rudder pressed against his left thigh. But from this position he was able to get an unforgettable view of the whole spectacle. The moon was obviously full that night and its lustre flooded everything with a liquid luminosity that had nothing ghostly or spectral about it and yet was decidedly unearthly.

The Island of Wone, when once they had got the "Teras" off that sharp-jutting rock, by no means towered above them. Its structure was indeed that of a flat table-land raised only three or four feet above the surface of the sea; and the single mast of the "Teras" rose so high into the air as to quite out-top the two weird Divinities from Arima, Eurybia and Echidna, who, as they had done from time immeasurable, were still arguing with each other in a tireless monotonous dialogue.

The object upon which Nisos finally fixed his attention was the neck of the terrific Figure-Head of the "Teras", which he had been assured he must regard as terminating in the actual head and features of its super-human designer.

These monumental features were at this very moment, so he had been solemnly told, no different from what they had been a hundred-thousand years ago and no different from what they would be a hundred-thousand years hence. "Had this supreme enemy of the everlasting gods," he asked himself, "been able to invent a way of surviving beneath a volume of water half-a-mile deep?"

And what had happened to that fire-breathing monster Typhon? Had *he* been, as it had been said, "intercepted", on his way to join the infernal foes of the gods who live forever? Nisos had been hearing, ever since he first came on board, extraordinary stories about this super-human Being whose features—and the legend ran that the Personage Itself had carved its own features—were neither divine nor human, neither of any conceivable Past or conceivable Future, but totally outside and beyond all we have heard, seen, remembered, imagined, dreamed, feared or hoped!

"It seems strange," he said to himself, "that I, Nisos, the son of Pandea the wife of Krateros Naubolides, should be squatting by this helmsman, staring at the curving neck of this creature beyond all creatures, created by this creator beyond all creators, whose dragon-swan neck ends in some ultimate vision, the vision of a Being that is both more Divine and more Titanic than anything we know, that is in fact outside all we know. And isn't it an unusually queer chance," Nisos now asked himself, "that I should know not one single person, except I suppose the men of the ship, who has ever seen the mysterious face with which the Figure-Head of the 'Teras' terminates?

"When this ship first entered the harbour of Ithaca was there not one single soul who saw her? When she was anchored in the harbour of Ithaca did no barge or boat or canoe or raft pass in front of her? Did no swimmer, swimming round her, look up at that face? Why haven't I asked this question of Odysseus, of

Zeuks, of Princess Nausikaa herself to whom the ship belongs? There is certainly something queer about all this."

Nisos shuffled his uncomfortable body a little further still to the rear, until his back was pressed against the actual jet-black cross-bar of the ship's stern, in which position every time Eumolpos of Kephallenia gave the rudder the particular push that swung the "Teras'" prow to the North our friend's thigh received something of a shock.

At one point indeed Eumolpos became aware of some sort of obstacle at the extreme reach of his helm's thrust, and turning his head for, as a man of good stock in Kephallenia, he was naturally courteous, he murmured an apology.

"O that's all right!" cried our friend. "It's only that I'm so unused to a ship. All I can do is to follow the master around."

But his word with the helmsman gave him the required incentive to put to Akron the question that was seething in his mind.

"By the way, Master, I suppose you've often examined the face of your ship's figure-head? Does it look like the face of a great philosopher, or like the face of a great poet, or like the face of a great scientist?"

Akron didn't even turn his head. "If I answered him properly you might never be able, aye, Eumolpos, to steer a ship again, all your days? But come along, Nisos! You said just now you were following me around! Well, I've got a bit of a job for you now."

Nisos disengaged himself from his cramped observation-post at the extreme stern of the "Teras" and followed Akron forward.

"No, seriously, my dear boy," the skipper said quietly, as they approached Odysseus, "it would never have done to start on all *that* business just then. The truth of it is that there's something funny about the whole thing." He grasped Nisos by the arm and they stood side by side for a minute, both of them watching, while he spoke, the wild half-naked figure of Enorches, the

Priest, who was clearly haranguing the old king about something; something that made it necessary for Odysseus to sit down again on his coiled ropes.

"He wants me," said Akron, "to put the Island of Wone well behind us before night. His hope is that a cloud may cover up this confounded Moon before dawn and leave us free to get a good vision of the special stars by which he wants us to sail or to row—whichever may be necessary—*due West*. No, my dear boy, we of the 'Teras' have a natural instinct against talking about that matter of which you enquired just now; I mean about the face of our Figure-Head. The truth of it is there has been 'borne in upon us', as one of us called it the other night, an absolute conviction that only someone who in everything else was so simple, so much of an innocent that people felt they must treat him as if he were a vegetable or an animal or a fish of some kind or an inanimate thing, would be able to face that face without 'getting', as we say, 'the horrors'.

"If you were such an animal-like innocent I'd let you, if we had our anchor out, swim backwards and forward in front of our bows till you could look face to face at this enemy of the Olympians; but you my dear boy are anything but an innocent! On the contrary in most things you're a damned lot cleverer than I am or any of the rest of us who run this old ship."

"What kind of horrors would come upon anyone who wasn't an innocent, and who dared to face the face?"

"Do you want a straight answer, lad?"

"Of course."

"Well, as it happens, I, who now am talking with you, can tell you of one case."

"O quick, quick, captain! Tell me, before that face, scaring the gulls, gets round the next rock!"

The master didn't turn his eyes away from their steadily advancing mast, with all its ropes in order, though without a sail, but as he spoke it was clear to Nisos that ninety per cent of his consciousness was at that moment in his words.

"It was the officer I had before we got Thuon. Poor old

Thuon can't bear even to look at the thing's neck from this side after what he's been told. The man's name was Teterix and he came from Zante and it was while I let them cast anchor for a while to catch some fish that this randy fool of a Zante-man began playing his games and swimming round the prow. I'd told him he weren't to do it, but he wanted to show off to the others; so as he swam he not only stared at the face but made faces at the face: and, in no time at all, there he was, climbing up on deck and dancing about in front of us with all his fingers pointing at his head. And such was the power of the horror on him *that he forced us to see him as he saw himself and as he felt himself*; that is to say with no human head at all, but with a raw bleeding neck out of which three bloated worms hung down who swayed to and fro and kept turning and twisting round.

"After this had gone on for several minutes the unfortunate Zante-man uttered one last piercing shriek, ran to the side of the ship and dived into the sea. So strong was the wretch's conviction that for a neck he had nothing but a gaping bloody hole with three bloated worms hanging out of it that it infected most of us who watched his dive; so that what we saw when he disappeared—and nothing of him ever reappeared—was a pool of blood on the water, with what looked like a blur of red worms squirming about within it."

"And you really and truly saw all that?"

"I really and truly saw all that," replied Akron.

Then it was that they both saw Odysseus beckoning to them and when they reached him they were, for the twentieth time that eventful evening, impressed to the depths of their souls by the old wanderer's self-control.

The excited priest of Orpheus, now entirely naked, was waving his long thin white arms, on which there was not a single black hair and which the moon seemed determined to turn to ivory. The madman was calling upon the whole universe to join him in his desperate incantation to Nothingness!

Not all the words of the priest's incantation reached Nisos; but those that did so sounded to him somewhat like this:

ATLANTIS

"Nothing! O Nothing! Thou god of all gods, thou creator of Silence!
God of all gods, and creator of Silence, thy daughter!
Nothing! O holy Nothing! O sacred Nothing, and Silence!
Swallow, great Nothing, all else but thyself and thy daughter!
Swallow air, swallow water, swallow fire, swallow earth and her children!
Swallow land, swallow sea, swallow all that in land and sea dwelleth!
Let the whole world be empty of all but thyself and thy daughter
Empty of all but thyself and thy daughter and darling!
Let nothing move in the height or the depth or the length or the breadth,
Save only thyself, great Nothing, thyself and thy daughter,
Only thyself and Silence, thy daughter and darling.
Let nothing sound in the earth or the air or the water or fire;
Let the whole world be empty of all but thyself and thy daughter,
All but thyself and Silence thy daughter and darling."

Nisos expected that Odysseus would react in some definite way to this nihilistic incantation; but he behaved as if he had not heard a word of what the Priest had been chanting, and as soon as Enorches realized that he was totally alone in his worship of Non-Existence he clung to the mast and became absolutely silent and still.

Meanwhile Odysseus had begun a long geological rigmarole on the chemical constituents of various kinds of scoriae substance; and he did this, Nisos decided, so as to reduce Enorches to the Nothingness he worshipped.

"It is an up-thrusting, up-pointing rock," Odysseus concluded, "a rock of black basalt, or of some blue-black adamantine stone, Master Akron. Have you heard what I've been saying in all this breaking of waves and splashing of water?"

Akron, followed closely by Nisos, who gave a grave little bow when he met the king's glance, declared that he'd heard perfectly every word.

"How well he lies!" thought Nisos. "I couldn't have done better myself. But no! He *must* have heard. What an ear he's got!"

"Yes, O great King," said Akron firmly. "You've said that we shall soon reach an up-pointing black rock, about a dozen feet inland from the island's edge, and that it is to this rock that you wish me to make fast the ship with our newest and strongest length of rope; for it is from there when this curst moonlight—have mercy on me, Selene!—is driven from the heaven by the sun, that you wish, my king, to make your first experimental dive with the Helmet of Proteus. Have I got your command clear, my lord Odysseus?" And the king murmured that he had. It struck Nisos however that the royal voice had grown perceptibly weaker since Pegasos had come and gone; but as the old man, after having risen to his feet for some minutes, had now re-seated himself on his pile of ropes, this change of tone may have been without any special significance.

"But how," thought Nisos, "how *can* the old man endure all this?" And then, as in obedience to a whisper from Akron he picked up the blanket that the Priest of Orpheus had dropped and wrapt it round the fellow's shoulders, he noticed that Enorches gave him a very queer look. All the same the priest wrapped the thing round himself with obvious relief and crouched down again, this time with his back to the mast.

"Stay and watch him for a while, will you, son?" whispered Akron. "I've got to go down now to the oarsmen to talk to them about this rock to which we have to tie up the ship for the night. And keep an eye, sonny, will you"—here Akron moved close enough to add this in an extremely low whisper—"on Zeuks, while I'm down below? He seems to think that as long as he's embracing that girl he's keeping her from some mischief she naturally will be up to the moment he lets her go! But it's much more about himself than about that poor worried-looking waif from Troy that I'm concerned.

"You know the man a lot better than I do; in fact, as far as I can see, you're the only one aboard our old 'Teras' who knows anything about him at all. He's a funny-looking fellow right enough; and he's got a look as if at any moment he might break out into a roar of laughter that would burst his skin! I don't like the look of him and I don't trust him. So keep an eye on him, son, will you? They'll be calling us down before very long to the old man's cabin for supper. I pray we'll be reaching this confounded rock he talks about before *that's* ready. But maybe not! Anyway I'm off now. I'll be seeing you later. At supper, if not before! I won't ask you now how *you* suppose the old man knew about this same 'pointed rock' to which we're to moor the 'Teras'? *He can't have been here before, can he*? Well! See you soon again, son! But keep your wits about you. I leave the old man, so to say, in your care. See you soon!"

Both pairs of ladies, Pontopereia and Eione in their cabin, and Nausikaa and Okyrhöe in theirs, were, in a leisurely, negligent, nonchalant way, preparing for the passengers' supper in the much larger cabin dedicated to the comfort of Odysseus.

"What do you really feel, Eione darling, when you see that queer-looking individual Zeuks, holding that grave, sweet Trojan woman on his knee?"

Pontopereia held her own not very shapely left leg balanced across the knee of her other while she carefully adjusted her left sandal so that a particular wrinkle in its leather shouldn't hurt a bunion from which she was suffering.

Eione screwed up her forehead, but gave her friend a very straight look.

"It wouldn't suit you, my beautiful one, to feel as I feel," Eione replied, "for you're a clever girl from a big city and are born with an intellect of your own; and if a man began fooling about with you you'd either want him to come to the point, take your maidenhead, as they call it, and have done with it, or to let you alone and come back to listening while you explained your philosophy to him.

"But country girls like me are quite different. We've lived so close to animals that we've sort of turned into animals. We're fond of our own human flesh just as animals are. And we're particularly fond of our own flesh when men are enjoying it, I mean feeling it with any part of *their* bodies. I know what I'm talking about, Ponty darling, for I've had an experience that doesn't happen to every girl in the world I can assure you! I mean I've been, as they call it, 'made love to'—not much 'making' and not much 'love' in it, but never mind that!—by no other than the most lecherous Being in the whole wide world, the great Arcadian god Pan, his own self!

"And do you know what happened? We just simply made friends. I begged him not to meddle with my virginity, for, as I told him frankly, I didn't want to be bothered with the consequence of that sort of thing yet! I wanted to enjoy my life before starting to be a mother and all that sort of business. Arcadian Pan fully understood what I said to him; and he fully agreed with my point of view. I told him it wasn't fair that our mother the Earth should just use us as procreating nest-eggs for her own purposes. And he agreed.

"He said that in the act of copulation a woman got more pleasure than a man the moment the pain was over and sometimes even while the pain was going on. But he said he'd make a bargain with me that he'd agree not to meddle with my virginity if in return I'd let him hold me on his knees and enjoy the feeling of my thighs pressed against his thighs and the pleasure of stroking my breasts. He said that the pleasure to male flesh of having female flesh pressed against it was greater than the most delicious taste to the tongue or the palate or the most exciting bathing in water, rushing through air, burrowing in earth-mould, or brandishing blazing fire.

"He said that to deny to masculine flesh its greatest possible thrill, namely the ecstasy of being pressed against feminine flesh, was the most cruel and wicked perversion in the whole universe, and that the whole idea of refusing our human flesh to each other, when the meeting of these two sorts of flesh, the male and the female, gave to each the greatest thrill of pleasure possible to all organic beings in the whole universe was a wicked and cruel denial to life of what life had come into existence to enjoy.

"'Life,' said Arcadian Pan to me, 'life is lured and attracted out of the inert and inanimate elements into its earliest existence by the promise of the indescribable ecstasy of sexual pleasure! And so, when we have lured life out of the inanimate, to go and deny to it,' thus spoke Arcadian Pan to me, 'its prerogative and privilege and proprietary right, is an abominable treachery to the mysterious pressure, whatever it may be, that brought life into existence!'

"And I must tell you this also, Ponty, my true and only friend. When Arcadian Pan had taught me the ineffable, the unfathomable, the infinite pleasure that comes from male flesh pressing female flesh against itself—and, mind you, this has nothing at all to do with' taking maidenheads', as they call it, or de-virginating virgins—he and I became excellent friends. I found his society extremely agreeable; and it seemed to me that he found mine the same! At any rate the result of our daily contact was that I got genuinely fond of him and sincerely attached to him as a friend; and I believe he felt exactly the same about me! That he was an immortal god and I a silly little mortal girl, doomed to perish in a few years, seemed to make no difference to him or to me! I can only tell you, Ponty dear, that if it weren't for meeting you, and your being so sweet to me, I should miss his company so much that there's no telling what silly things I might do. And what is more, I believe, though it seems conceited and vain to say so, that he misses me, though not of course as much as I miss him!"

At this point Pontopereia, as she lowered her not very shapely leg to the floor of that lowest deck of the "Teras" and endured with a little laugh the twitching pain she got from the contact of her sandal with her bunion, believed she beheld by the feeble flame of a flickering wick floating in oil, a real, actual, round pearl of a wet tear rolling down her friend's plain, simple, and the extreme opposite of what could be called a clever face and sliding from her retreating chin to the white hollow between her girlish breasts.

ATLANTIS

A very different dialogue was proceeding meanwhile in the cabin of the two older women. There was no inclination between those two to make the relation between male and female flesh the subject of discourse. *Their* talk was actuated by, and revolved round, and obstinately and viciously returned to, the intense heart-gnawing jealousy they felt with regard to each other and the old wanderer with whom they were sailing.

"You have no idea then, is that what you want me to believe, as to what you will do with me, when you and this ugly, badly built ship of yours have lured Odysseus to his death?"

"*Do* with you? I don't understand! I presume you'll stay here on board with us until you're tired of us? We shall, of course, when we've seen all we want to see of the ocean that swallowed up Atlantis, sail back to the land of my Fathers. If you think we're going to visit Ithaca just for the sake of ending where we began you're challenging the very mill-wheel of disappointment.

"And if you are playing with the crazy idea that you can persuade me to enter the harbour of the city of Thebes on your behalf you must be losing your head. What you ought to be asking yourself all this while is what you will do when we return to my country. I shall have no particular authority there; and if I *had* I doubt whether, from what I now am learning about you from personal contact, I should be particularly anxious to— *What was that?* The first call for dinner was it? Or was it a call for us to gather on the top deck again, before *something*—heaven knows what!—begins to happen?

"No, no! thanks all the same! You go on dressing; and be quick about it and stop talking! I can manage with this curst necklace if you leave me alone. Yes, you're welcome to all the hot water in that *pro-cho-os* over there. I've got all I want."

Meanwhile on the top deck the same sound of the same bell that had disturbed Nausikaa and Okyrhöe reached the ears of Odysseus. He had left his club propt against the bulwarks and had already begun to move, slowly and cautiously, as he always did when on board ship, from his seat of coiled ropes to the ladder leading to the oarsmen's deck.

Over the face of the priest Enorches as he lay naked in a couple of blankets, for some kindly sailor had brought him a second one, now that the only light in the sky and on the water was moonlight, there floated an unquestionable smile of pure comfort and relief. Most onlookers would have supposed this look to have been purely due to a draught of rich Cyprian wine which another kindly sailor had brought him; but our old acquaintance the Fly who was now in a position to observe these things at close quarters knew well enough that it was his friend the brown-winged Moth, who by deliberately fanning with her wings the wine-moistened lips of the Priest of the Mysteries, had drawn from him this genial token of well-being.

As to the Moth herself, she had no sooner returned to her friend in their familiar refuge than she was compelled to listen to one of those cosmic conversations between the Sixth Pillar and the Club of Herakles which the Fly's scientific mind always found so fascinating and illuminating.

"You must have noticed already, my dear old friend," the Sixth Pillar was saying, "how strongly and emphatically the four elements are joining in this multiversial revolt against the authority of the Olympians? Of course there are voices abroad and I can hear them in this corridor who declare that what is now going on is a world-wide revolt of women against men rather than of men against gods or of Titans against Olympians; but with my own personal nearness to the Four Supreme Elements I cannot share these eccentric opinions.

"To me it is clear that what is happening in the multiverse at the present moment is a revolt against Zeus the Son of Kronos by every other power in the wide world! The best proof of this is the definite news that Hera and Athene who have always worked hand in hand are now encouraging Poseidon and Aidoneus to join with Zeus in some final desperate act of authority and retribution.

"What I am most conscious of now," went on the Sixth Pillar, "is the mental awareness of what is going on by each of the Four Elements. Take the earth, to begin with, my good friend.

I assure you I cannot imagine anything clearer or more definite than the vibration of sympathy with the rebels in this cosmogonic revolt which I feel—yes! at this very second as I talk to you I feel it—emanating from the earth! The vibrations I feel, you must understand, my friend, are not spoken words. They are more like the deep, dim rumblings of an earthquake! They are thick and dense and dark, and convey to me something of what animals must feel when they fall and strike their foreheads upon the ground. On the contrary the vibrations I get out of the air are like a mighty rushing wind which seems in the fanning and flapping of its vast feathers to have completely surrounded me and to be carrying me into a boundless void.

"And then what I get out of the heart of the hot black fire of the darkened sun as he travels beneath the earth, and what I get out of the heart of the cold white fire of the ghostly moon as she rides through the clouds, are two infinite throbbings that are like thunder in my own heart!

"And strangest of all is the vibration that emanates from the massed volume of all the waters of the ocean, a vibration that is in many ways more important for us in this corridor of the rock-palace of the Island of Ithaca than all the other three; for it is a vibration from an element that resembles air made palpable, air thickened out into a tidal momentum encircling the earth, grey, fathomless, immeasurable, salt with all the tears ever shed, cold and ultimate as a universal grave."

The monotone of the Sixth Pillar's discourse as he thus informed his friend the Club of Herakles, to whom Atropos had given the name of "Expectation" and who had always had the name of "Dokeesis" or "Seeming", how the Four sublime elements of earth, air, fire and water responded to this world-wide revolt against the gods had scarcely died down, before there came, reverberating up from the depths of the "Teras", the second call for supper.

It was the custom on board this particular ship for the white crew and their black helpers to enjoy their evening meal in a haphazard manner, casually, and irregularly, and in no particular order, slipping down by twos and threes to the kitchen in the hold when opportunity offered, and lingering with a friend over a flask of wine down there when the wind was in their sail and the ship was moving quietly.

At the moment therefore when the second call for the supper went forth on this particular evening our young friend Nisos, who was to have a berth that night with the master of the ship so as to give the only remaining one-man cabin to Zeuks, was already wondering whether to obey the call alone or to beg Zeuks and Arsinoë, the latter looking half-asleep as she reposed partly on the knees of the son of Pan and partly against the base of the ship's figure-head, to accompany him.

If Arsinoë was half-asleep, Zeuks, as far as Nisos could tell, was entirely so, for his eyes were tightly closed and his face had the expression, already familiar to Nisos, that it always assumed when the man was asleep, an expression as if he were some whimsical creator of the world who had dozed off in the act of trying to suppress his amusement at his creation.

Pontos and Proros were playing some private game of their own at the foot of the mast, a game that was clearly one rather of skill than of chance; for they threw no dice, and seemed to be moving little bits of wood from one position to another across some geometrical figure scrawled on the deck.

Nisos had the boldness at this moment, so quietly and silently was the "Teras" being rowed along that rocky coast of the Island of Wone in that unearthly moonlight, to sink down himself upon the old king's seat of coiled ropes, as he watched in a sort of trance across the slowly changing rocky edges of Wone those two weird figures from Arima, whose unearthly and unending disputation with each other the wind must now be carrying back towards those old Eastern lands they were so steadily leaving as they sailed through the moonlight towards the unknown West.

It was a moment in his life, so our friend told himself, as he tried to arrange his limbs on his pile of ropes as comfortably as the king always did, that until his death he would remember.

"I don't believe I will go down to dinner at all tonight," he thought, answering, as he fancied, some call out of the moonlight that was more imperative for him than even the second call to the most important meal of the day, and in a flash of interior penetration he recognized that he still couldn't decide whether it was Pontopereia or Eione he would like best to have for his wife.

"I don't even know to which of them I am the more attracted! In fact, as I watch Arsinoë now, who is ever so much older than they are, I really think I would feel more at ease and more content if it were she rather than either of those young girls who was to be my mate. And she's not only older; she's a Trojan too! Of course I'd be thrilled to make love to either of those girls and overjoyed to sleep with either of them; but I'd be scared of being fixed up for good with that stupid little face of Eione's or with that heavy little body of Pontopereia's. I simply can't understand it! But there it is: it's the truth. What I feel now is that something—someone—a Presence of some kind—is calling to me out of this moonlight and out of this night-wind and out of these waves, though I'm damned if I know what kind of a Presence it is!

"Come! Tell me, you Unknown! Are you a living girl, you Mystery of the Night? Or are you a boy like me, alone and puzzled and not quite knowing what you want, but not wanting to go back to your mother, and hating your father and brother and your brother's girl? Are you a boy like me, you Mystery of the Night, serving one of the greatest heroes the world has ever seen and a hero who has seen more of the world than any other human being who has ever been born? Are you a lonely girl who want me for your mate? Or are you a lonely boy who want me for your 'Hetairos' or friend? Speak you Mystery of the Night! Speak and tell me which of the two you are!"

But there was no answer and the Moon grew steadily larger and larger and larger. And as Nisos settled himself deeper and deeper in the centre of that pile of ropes he began to feel as if it were the Moon herself, Selene the Moon-Goddess, who had selected him, as according to the rumours he was always hearing she had long ago selected Arcadian Pan and as she had lately selected, so the angelic scandal-mongers swore, the Carian shepherd Endymion of Mount Latmos.

He allowed himself to dally with this idea of having really attracted the attention of the Moon-Goddess on this night of all nights when her circle of white magic was full to the brim, until the inhuman murmur from Eurybia and Echidna, neither of whom seemed even remotely affected by their voyage through the air from Arima to Wone, reached such a point in their choreographic accompaniment to his fancy, as if—pair of ancestral Titanesses as they were!—they were about to vary the monotony of their immemorial argument by hopping up and down in the fury of their repartees!

It was at this point that Nisos fancying he saw Arsinöe, still in the arms of the now soundly sleeping Zeuks, throw him an understanding if not a companionable smile, replied to her by kissing his hand.

"I can't help liking this Trojan girl," he said to himself; and then, as his gaze returned to Eurybia and Echidna, and from them wandered back to the coast of Wone, and from thence to the moonlight on the ocean, there rushed through his mind like jaggedly forked lightning a startling philosophical speculation.

"Does everything come round in circles and repeat itself? Was there, when people first invented boats and ships, some boy like me ten thousand years ago who lay on a ship's deck, such as ships were in those days, with only one deck, and only a couple of oarsmen, and a sail made of the skins of seals and wild goats, and said to himself, just as I am saying now:' I don't want to go back to mother and father. I want to serve my King. I want to make love to that girl I saw on that wharf where we moored yesterday!'

"And will there be a boy like me ten thousand years hence who will lie on a much grander deck than this and say to himself: 'I don't want to go back to my mother and father! I want to sail round all the known West to the Isles of the Blest!' That boy who *was* like me; and this boy who *will be* like me, shall we three meet in the kingdom of Aidoneus?"

Nisos had only just begun to turn his mind away from thinking about boys like himself ten thousand years before and ten thousand years after, when he saw Arsinoë open her beautiful eyes very wide indeed and give a start that would have waked from sleep anyone in the world save the son of Arcadian Pan who was holding her on his knee.

At the same time Nisos felt himself touched on the shoulder. He twisted his head round, and there before him in the moonlight stood the figure of Odysseus!

"Hush!" whispered the old hero while his bowsprit beard tickled Nisos' chin: "get up as quietly as you can, my boy, and take a step with me!"

It was a comfort to Nisos to notice when he was on his feet that his friend Arsinoë had been shrewd enough to shut her eyes and pretend to surrender herself to what certainly looked like a sleep as deep as Zeuks' own.

"I won't take you with me just now further than the ladder, my boy," said Odysseus still speaking very quietly. "I came to fetch 'Expectation', my most valued weapon, with which, as you know, Herakles killed the Nemean lion. But I also came to tell you what my intention is. I have already told Akron, who is at this moment informing the oarsmen what I have in mind, and I have already told Eumolpos the helmsman. My intention is this. My son Telemachos received, when he visited the yellow-haired Menelaos, as a guest-gift from Helen herself, a little phial of Nepenthe which was given to her by the King of Egypt.

"When even a few drops of this divine Nepenthe, the enemy of all suffering, are dropped into wine, the wine into which the Nepenthe has been poured, takes away all thoughts that bring anxiety or pain or fear or doubt or suspicion or grief or envy or hatred or terror; and in place of these a beatific happiness fills our souls to the brim.

"A little of this precious Nepenthe goes a very long way; and I have brought some of it with me to this ship. Now what I propose to do is to put a few drops of this divine drug into the wine which our four Ladies, together with Nausikaa's official Herald, will presently be drinking in my cabin. You and I, however—and for heaven's sake, child, don't you go and get caught by the fragrance of the wine or lured into letting the least drop of it touch your tongue!—as soon as we see that the four ladies and Nausikaa's Herald have fallen asleep and are deep sunk in this blessed Elysium of happy visions, having taken good care—and don't you forget that part of it, my son!—to eat enough to last us, if need be, for a whole night and day, we, I say, will leave that lower deck and come up here, to be ready for, well, for whatever fate may bring!"

They had by this time reached the ladder which descended to the deck of the rowers, and it was not until Odysseus was half-way down that the necessity of asking him a most drastic and necessary question forced Nisos to make the old man turn round and lift up his head towards him. Never did the lad, through all the rest of his mortal days, forget the impression he received at that second as the unearthly luminosity of that night's omniscient moonlight poured down upon that old upturned face with that crazy "Helmet of Proteus" twisted about it, whereof the absurdly trailing "thusanoi", or "tassels" looked in that silvery gleaming as if they were the "tassels" of Athene's "aegis" transformed into long, slenderly-coiling, silvery worms.

"Do you wish me, my king," Nisos enquired, getting the words out with a gasping rush of breath, "to inform Zeuks of your intention? Is *he* to share your Nepenthe with the Herald and the four ladies? Or shall I tell him of your intention and recommend him to bring down the Trojan maid Arsinoë to wait on the four ladies and to share their supper and the sleep-giving wine?"

"You have done well in thinking as you have," answered the voice of the king from the white face above that moonlit beard. "Bring them both down to my cabin. We'll let them both sleep the sleep of Nepenthe. After all it was the gift of Helen."

A couple of minutes later, Nisos was standing close to what clearly had become an extremely agitating game of contending figurines above whose "Pessoi", or "inanimate men-at-arms", Pontos and Proros were now bending in intense concentration.

But Nisos was too occupied just then in obeying Odysseus to feel the faintest desire to "pessenize". "Arsinöe!" he called out in a clear though not a loud voice. The girl heard him at once. "What's the matter?" she asked, disengaging herself from the knees of the son of Pan and rising to her feet.

"You must wake him now," our friend answered, "for the king wants him at their supper."

And then he added hurriedly, catching a rather pathetic look, of bewilderment on her face, "And you too, Arsinöe my dear, I expect they'll all be glad to have you down there; for if I'm not mistaken there'll be more good wine than good manners at this precious supper of theirs!"

The girl bent down over Zeuks and shook him by the right shoulder. His body was squeezed between the metallic base of the famous figure-head which was at that point wrought into a number of shell-curved, beautifully carved dragon-scales, and the narrowing rondure of the rail of the ship's prow. Zeuks opened his left eye, gave both the girl and Nisos a glance that partook of the nature of a humorous wink and closed it again.

"Do wake him for heaven's sake, my dear!" repeated Nisos. "I'd do it myself," he went on, "only if I touched him he might fly into a passion and start hitting me; and that would probably set me off too and there'd be a fine row!"

Nisos felt deep in his soul that he wouldn't mind at all if there was a murderous row; but as he stared ahead he realized that the "Teras" had actually now reached the point at which not so far inland arose that nameless sharp-pointed rock to which their ship was to be roped. It certainly was a curiously shaped rock, like a tall lean man with a fantastically long neck and an unnaturally large head; and our friend began wondering just from where upon the "Teras" the rope would have to be conveyed to that figure and attached to it.

His speculations about the securing of their vessel were broken up by some change in the wind that brought to his ears—and apparently to Arsinoë's too, for she let Zeuks' head sink down again—what was unmistakably the culminating point of the unending dispute between Eurybia and Echidna.

Both Nisos and Arsinoë soon realized from the weird words they heard that Eurybia had finished her murmured contention that the reeling and rocking of the cosmos that was now the chief topic of what might be called the elemental gossip of the universe was due to a revolt of the whole Feminine Half of the world against the eternal Male; and that Echidna was now defending *her* notion of what was happening, which certainly was a startling and terrifying one, and entirely different from that of her sister phantom of this Arima in the midst of the ocean.

The gist of Echidna's view of what was occurring was that it was a grand revolt of the Titans, and, with the Titans of all those Giants and Dragons and Super-Animals and Super-Birds and Super-Fishes and Super-Reptiles and ancient long-forgotten insular divinities, such as Eurybia and herself, who, in comparison with the proud Olympians, must seem to some—"indeed" thought Nisos, "they seem to me"—hideous monsters and wicked antiquities—in universal conspiracy against the thunder-wielding All-Father, Zeus.

But what was probably to our friend Nisos' ears, and certainly to those of Arsinoë, who was doing her best to disturb the sleepy head of the unconscionable son of Pan, the most alarming part of this victory-chant of the Antediluvians was that it concluded with a phantasmagoric wail of prediction, prophesying—"falsely, O falsely! let us pray!" cried the look that was being at that second exchanged between our young armour-bearer of the King of Ithaca and the daughter of Hector—that the revolt of the Titans and the Monsters was destined to prevail!

And as the prophetic hiss of Echidna, the Snake-Goddess, floated away on the moonlight, it came with a considerable shock into Nisos' mind that it was no other than Arcadian Pan himself, the rustic god who had the horns and legs of a goat, who had carried off from Arima these two weird Beings who were like the ghosts of forgotten island Deities and had carried off Tis's little sister Eione as well, Eione, who was now safe in the king's cabin and would be shortly drinking the wine that contained Helen's Egyptian Nepenthe, carried them all off together on those two immortal horses.

"Whither now, then," the lad asked himself, "had Arcadian Pan gone? Had he dived down under the waters into the streets and temples and markets and shops and brothels of the metropolis of Atlantis? Impossible! Impossible! Who could imagine the goat-god of Arcadia playing on his flute in the fish-frequented streets of that drowned city? Impossible! Impossible! He must have made that other divine horse, the one whose mane was up-rooted by this naked wretch lying here now, dead-drunk in his blankets, under the ship's bulwark, carry him over sea and land home to his sheep-folds!"

As these thoughts crowded, like a swarm of small gnats, into our young friend's head he noticed that Akron, the ship's captain, was approaching them. This fact reached his intelligence indirectly but very quickly; for he saw all those little bits of wood that Pontos and Proros had been using as toy soldiers in their game of "Pesseia" disappear with a scraping and scuffling sound into the capacious folds of their tunics.

The unavoidable though quite faint sound made by these stalwart sailors as they disposed of so many handfuls of toy-soldiers made it clear to Nisos that the natural human passion for playing games was stronger than any intellectual interest in drowned cities or in the past or future of scientific civilizations. Pontos and Proros were ready for anything; but they did not want to see their precious "Pessoi" or draughtsmen cast into the sea.

"Well, my excellent land-lubbers!" exclaimed Akron in his most genial manner. "You'll soon have a chance to watch a little real seamanship, not un-combined, I hope, with a little unprofessional commonsense! You've already noticed, Nisos, my dear boy, that we've reached that rock——" Akron lifted his arm and pointed eagerly—"that the king calls the Atlas Rock because, so he informs us, only none of us on this old ship can corroborate his words, it resembles the giant Titan whose head, and shoulders too, you and I must have seen from this very deck beyond the Pillars of Herakles before the' Teras' made for the open sea; and the king swears it does actually resemble the Titan Atlas whom the All-Father punishes forever by making him hold up the sky.

"The king says that the Titan, though no weakling, lacks the broad shoulders and muscular neck that would render his task agreeable. The king says his shoulders slope like a woman's just as do those of this damned rock to which we've now got to tie up our grand old sea-eagle!"

It was clear to Nisos, if not to Zeuks, who had at last under the shock of the arrival of the skipper of the "Teras", shaken off his shameless tendency to respond to any increase in dramatic danger by an increase in undramatic drowsiness, that the four sailors on the deck below had stopped using their oars and that the "Teras" was now doing nothing but obeying the helmsmanship of Eumolpos as she followed the urge of those four men's final strokes.

"Odysseus told me"—and Nisos cried out his master's name with a voice to be heard in competition with the two sounds that just then were most dominant; in the first place with the whistling of the wind in the complicated rigging beneath the mast, rigging which, though doubtless less involved than Pontos' and Proros' recent "pessenizing" with soldiers made of splinters and slivers and shavings of wood, would have been enough to puzzle any landsman; and in the second place with the stentorian breathing of the poor blanketed Enorches.

Nisos must instinctively have said "Odysseus" instead of "the King" because, with this incredible moonlight flooding the rocks and beaches along whose edge they were moving and with that extraordinary rock wearing a human shape and those two phantom goddesses moaning forth into the moonlight their contrarious explanations of the present world-madness, it must have struck him that what was now happening was so dramatic that it lent itself better to the romantic name of the lover of Circe and Calypso than to the clanging monosyllable "King" whose only virtue was that it was the symbol of absolute law and order.

"Odysseus told me to say that both you yourself, friend Zeuks, and you also, Arsinöe my dear, will be welcome as soon as you can reach it, at the Passengers' Dining-Table in the King's cabin, and he told me to accompany you both as soon as——"

"What's the matter, baby-boy?" interrupted Zeuks, looking as if he were a human skin on the point of bursting and losing its human shape in one great bubble of laughter: "Have you got a flea in——"

"I pray it's not a poisonous fly!" cried Arsinöe, with unmistakable sympathy in her tone. "You may laugh my Lord Zeuks," the girl went on, coming hurriedly to Nisos' side and raising both hands to the spot just above his collar-bone where he was now scratching himself with positively vicious intensity, "yes, you may laugh, but there may easily have been a whole swarm of poisonous insects carried from our last 'port of call' which was of course your—or I suppose I must now say 'our'—island harbour."

But to the girl's astonishment, and indeed to the astonishment of both Zeuks and Akron, Nisos thrust away her sympathetic hand, though its delicate fingers were trembling with real concern. But Arsinöe was saved from feeling hurt at his rejection of her help by her amazement at what he proceeded to do when she withdrew her hand. Both Zeuks and Akron were as astonished as she was and all the three of them drew near to watch his antics.

Even Enorches, clutching his outer blanket with his left hand round his throat and his inner blanket with his right hand round his waist, woke up suddenly from his trance and stared with unglazed absorbed concentrated attention at what Nisos was doing. Nisos had clearly got possession now of whatever creature it was that had caused him to scratch himself to such a tune; and he now held it in his clenched fist close to one of his ears. The only sound that issued from his imprisoning fingers was an irregular buzzing; and Arsinoë smiled at both Zeuks and Akron, who were now openly smiling at each other, while the Priest of Orpheus began muttering the most formidable liturgical prayer he knew by heart that the most mystical swamp in the realm of Aidoneus should receive his purified ghost.

"You were indeed brave to come all this way from your club-tent, Master Myos," murmured our young friend; "though I hope your dear companion, the Brown Moth, won't be too miserable in your absence."

"Look at Enorches!" was the Fly's reply to this; and the moment our friend obeyed him he knew perfectly well that the Moth was anything but miserable; for it was indeed obvious from the beatific smile of paradisal bliss that now radiated from the Priest's curiously emphatic nose, mouth, eye-sockets, eye-brows, and ears, that the lovely little winged shadow that now kept hovering under and above and round and beneath the oddly-shaped chin of the oracle of Nothingness was nothing less than the Brown Moth herself playing at burning to death on the altar of truth.

That neither the worship of Eros nor of Dionysos nor even of Silence herself, oldest of all divinities in the world and the one most likely to outlive them all, could wholly satisfy the Priest's voracious mystery-maw, Nisos at that moment felt certain. The Orphic Priest could praise Nothingness; but the ecstasy he worshipped was a real, actual, concrete experience, which, if not given him by drink or by lechery, could be given him by the devotion of a disciple.

"She knows you are here, does she?"

"Of course. And when she's finished playing at 'wings in the candle' to pluck that poor devil out of his black blot of clotted ink, she'll come fluttering round us; and then together—'off we'll fly to drink with Helen before we die!'"

"With Helen?"

"I mean in a metaphysical sense, by sipping her Nepenthe."

"It's wonderful, Master Myos, isn't it, that I haven't forgotten your language?"

"Ah, my friend! Don't you know why that is?"

"I can't say I do."

"That's because"—and the Fly began to grow as academic as he always did with the Moth—"that's because it was Athene herself who taught you the syntax of it."

"You mean the peculiar way you always begin and always end with the adverb?"

"I mean the way we say: 'Beautifully fluttered round him the moth symbolically-speaking.'"

"But do go on, Master Fly, with what you were telling me you had just over-heard from the talk of the Sixth Pillar with the Club of Herakles."

"The Sixth Pillar told the Club that Princess Nausikaa had been chosen Queen of her Native Land and that those two Immortal Horses, that the Priest over there tried to maim, are even now on their way through the air to take her back to that country where her palace still possesses that famous garden which is the most beautiful garden that has ever been seen in the whole history of the world."

"Those two Horses *coming here*, do you say?"

At this startling piece of news Nisos jumped to his feet, removed his hand from his ear, opened his fingers, and let the Fly go free with a flourish of his wrist. The Fly was no sooner free than it was instantly joined by the Moth, and the speed with which the two of them flew off the top deck, down the ladder to the oarsmen's deck, down the next ladder to the cabin-deck, and thence straight into the interior of the great weapon that was their nomadic home, was incredible.

We human beings in our crowded life are more aware of the starting-points and arriving-points of insects than of the rapidity of their movements from point to point.

"Come along, Zeuks, for heaven's sake come along! And you too my lord Enorches! Fate will find a Community for you—don't you doubt it—where you can preach, if not practise, your nihilistic ideas, whether under the love-charms of Eros or under the Thyrsi of Dionysos!"

Our friend's voice was pitched so high, and he flung into it such a resounding intonation, that not only did Akron cast a sweeping glance from one end to the other of all the Horizon that was visible from their present position, but, to the evident surprise of Zeuks, Enorches actually did scramble clumsily to his feet, and even began automatically kicking at the skirt of his longest blanket as if to make sure that his sandals were firmly fastened.

Nisos then snatched instinctively at Arsinöe's arm; and followed closely by Zeuks, with Enorches lurching and shuffling after them, he turned his back upon the dragon-neck of the ship's figure-head and, avoiding the eyes of Pontos and Proros, for with a certain part of his mind he felt as if he were running away, he headed for that already familiar ladder leading down to the oarsmen's deck.

At the foot of this first ladder he paused for no more time than was just needed to get a glimpse of the face of Euros, a face that at that second looked vexed, irritated, touchy, anxious, full of the most sensitive perturbations, as he bent above his motionless oar, ready to give it the pull of a master oarsman at the faintest hint from the upper deck.

Arrived at that crowded, ticklish, furtively confused and terribly littered centre of all the gossip and eavesdropping that went on in the passenger's quarter, Nisos, who was followed closely by Zeuks and by Arsinöe, who once again had a tight hold of each other's hands, but who himself, since he had no hand to share with anyone, nor much thought for anything either, save to steer the wavering steps of the Priest of the Mysteries, had a moment's breathing-space. Now that this weird and disturbing individual was safely under at least temporary control Nisos couldn't help noticing the insatiable and unpleasantly greedy manner in which the man snuffed up and inhaled with, undisguised relish all the odours and all the smells and all the fragrances and all the airy essences and all the fetid stinks that challenged both the nostrils and the stomachs of any newcomers who dared to plunge from the upper deck into the stygian reek of these bowels of the "Teras".

And Nisos couldn't resist saying to himself: "Would this extraordinary creature advise us to lose ourselves in the madness of love or the madness of drink, and thus get to the Original nothingness, before the earth, before the sky, before the sea, before the sun, before the gods created man, before man created the Gods, if he hadn't forgotten the oracle that my mother used to tell me was what, by his obedience to it, made Odysseus the wisest of all men—*Meeden Agan*, 'nothing in excess'?"

"Why in the name of Aidoneus," the lad's thoughts ran on, as he watched his blanketed priest snuffing up with such a frenzy of maniacal sensuality the whirligig-reek of kitchen-fumes mixed with the contaminated sweat of the youthful disposers of excrement, "why in the name of Aidoneus was mother always quoting that *Meeden Agan*, 'Nothing in Excess', motto? It had nothing to do with the House of Naubolides, and was always on the lips of Odysseus. I can't understand it! Well, well! 'Nothing in Excess' will have now to be my motto, even when it comes to plunging into the revelry of this weird feast."

But it is easier to formulate a philosophy, even if we are destined to be a prophet in later life, than to apply it to a definite and particular occasion; and Nisos was puzzled by the sharpness of the pang of jealousy of which he became aware when Zeuks put his arm round the waist of Arsinöe.

The daughter of Hector and the son of Arcadian Pan, however, seemed wholly and entirely oblivious of the feelings they were exciting in their guide as they pushed on in front of him.

Nisos, indeed, had all he could do, apart entirely from his feelings, in steering the blanketed Priest of Orpheus through this packed and perspiring crowd. The most difficult place to pass, with Enorches as your self-absorbed ghost-walker, was the spot where a couple of elongated planks had been laid down to cover a slippery slope that led to the kitchens and pantries and sculleries as well as to the sleeping-quarters of the Lybian and Syrian ship-boys.

ATLANTIS

Nisos was struck at this particular point at once by the perfect opportunity which such a spot offered for the accumulation of filth, and by the noteworthy fact, which certainly spoke well for the crew, that those planks were so immaculately clean. As both white and black serving-boys, in spite of their trained politeness and of their evident terror of the blankets of Enorches, were pushed and jostled against him by their companions, Nisos decided that the sweat of the lads of the Greek islands and mainland had a completely different odour from the sweat of the lads from the more eastern Asiatic shores and harbours.

But he had no time to pause to philosophize now upon differences of human sweat for Zeuks had already got himself and Arsinöe into that unusual cabin crowded with people and it had fallen to the lot of Nisos to project the staring Enorches, blankets and all, into the presence of Odysseus and Nausikaa who were on their feet in that extempore dining-hall talking gravely together.

The old king and his ballad-princess of so long ago were, however, spared the discomfort of having to be polite to such a person as Enorches by the appearance on the scene, this time for just the sort of occasion Nisos had always prayed would never arise, of the super-official, super-courtly, super-distinguished, super-pontifical Herald; who at once, as a born authority in regard to all ceremonies that require magisterial handling, and as a practised expert in all those concatenations that need super-natural tact, greeted Zeuks and Arsinöe with a glance and a couple of words, and took the Priest of Orpheus under his impeccable wing.

As for Nisos, who was quite alone now, he found himself once more following Zeuks and Arsinöe with his eyes. Neither Odysseus nor Nausikaa seemed to notice him, although the king may have done so without revealing it. But the feeling that caused him to stand and gaze at the back of Zeuks' satyrish knuckles as they presented themselves to his view, with the implication that the palm of the man's hand was enjoying the curve of the girl's hip, was accentuated now by an uprush of self-revelation that nearly knocked him over.

The truth of the matter now must be, he now boldly dared to tell himself, that it was this Trojan woman Arsinöe, and not either his friend Tis's little sister, Eione, nor the prophet's prophetic daughter, Pontopereia, whom he desired for his wife.

"Yes," Nisos told himself, "though she must be years and years older than I am, she's the one I want! She understands me better than anybody in the world except Tis; and I like her better than anyone in the world. I like her better than father or mother or Agelaos."

Odysseus and Nausikaa, who now seemed completely absorbed in each other, kept moving a little nearer to him, though without taking any notice of him; and this went on till he was leaning with his back against several pieces of suspended armour and a couple of tunics woven in Ithaca but dyed in Tyre: it went on, in fact, till he began to feel, not so much hungry, as extremely sleepy.

What was indeed like a demonic teasing of him by fate than anything else was the fact that although he could just make out from where he leant, or rather crouched, behind the king and Nausikaa, the figure of Okyrhöe seated calmly, and with a face like a mask, at one of the long tables, with an empty place next to her, devouring with an absorbed and concentrated attention a somewhat over-ripe Sicilian melon, he could only just see, between the embroidered sleeve of the protective Herald and the bare neck of the protected Enorches the delicate waist and the left breast, the latter only half-covered with "linon" that specially lovely Achaian linen so dear to the ladies of all lands, of the girl with whom he now knew he was really in love as he had never been in love before.

This certainty reached his mind in close connection with those clutching knuckles of the lecherous son of Pan which he now could detect beneath that white linen and whiter breast; but it obtained its domination over him and over his destiny in connection with a secret resolve he now made that was totally different from any purpose or any vow or any dedication he had ever made before.

And with this new intention, with this new gathering together of the diverse forces of his soul into what he decided must be, from now on, one intense, strongly compressed *will*, a will most malleable, a will most adaptable, a will that lends itself, a will that adjusts itself, a will that conceals itself, a will that multiplies itself, a will that seeks its irrepressible level, a will like water, a will like air, our young friend made a convulsive clutch at the foot of the Heraklean club upon which Odysseus had begun to lean so heavily in his absorbed talk with Nausikaa that there was a real danger of its suddenly sliding along the floor and letting him down.

But no sooner had Nisos clutched it than the familiar tinkling voice of the scientific Fly was in his ears. "Oh how much easier it would be, this ancient language of yours," he thought, "if only there weren't all these accurst adverbs! It's the adverbs that spoil it. Why can't you sting without stinging violently or buzz without buzzing gently? Why can't you kiss without kissing tenderly? Why can't you even think without thinking stupidly or cleverly?"

Although he didn't relinquish his hold upon the club of Herakles, Nisos worked himself up into such irritation over the mania for adverbs in the language of insects, that in a whisper that contained something of sheer unkindness he called the attention of the Fly to the emergence from the club's "lifecrack", which was just above his fingers, of the priest-enamoured Moth.

But those adoring brown wings had barely fluttered twice up and down the sweltering space between the wet hairs of the man's blanket and the wet hairs of the man's chest, before, in her shrinking desire to comfort the Interpreter of the Mysteries without driving her companion to any regrettably rash act she had not only darted back to their lodging but had implored the Fly to translate for her what the news was that the club was hearing from the omniscient Sixth Pillar.

"Haven't you yet caught across that moon-lit ocean of yours, my adventurous friend," were the startling words that were now communicated to the moth by the fly and over-heard by Nisos, "the heavy breathing of Pegasos upon the wind and the quick gasps of his long-maned companion? And I presume Odysseus is already aware that his friend Nausikaa is now the Virgin Queen of her native-land, and that not only her parents' palace and garden await her return, but the whole country passionately wants her back?"

Nisos clutched the foot of the club of Herakles so fiercely that the force of his grip squeezed the club's attention out of his ears and reduced his Nemean senses to the same sort of deaf, dumb, and numb condition with which they had expected, washed up upon the shore of Ithaca, the reviving right hand of a new possessor.

And it was then that, more vividly than ever aware of those knuckles of Zeuks concealing from him so much of the bosom of Arsinoë, our young friend decided that he must learn from this queer rival of his, this fantastic child of Arcadian Pan, whose whole personality resembled an unburst bubble of purposeless laughter, the trick the fellow had of repeating some logos, some slogan of conduct, some motto of behaviour, by which a person's divided will-power could be unified and concentrated.

And Nisos then and there decided that the word he wanted was the word *spoudazo*. "Yes, yes," he muttered in his secret heart— "*that's* the word, *that's* the incantation I want! I want the feeling of being able to pull myself together till I'm like an arrow-head of intense will-power! Yes! yes! *Spoudazo* is my word, but I must add to it the word *terpsis, the sensation of enjoyment*, and I must throw into these words my whole self and with my whole self, I here and now must *will intensely* that Arsinoë the Trojan shall belong to me!"

Nisos had no sooner decided upon selecting *spoudazo*, "*I absolutely will*" as the logos that should henceforth represent the motive-power of his life, than Odysseus and Nausikaa having decided upon something that was clearly very important as the result of their prolonged and absorbed discussion, swung clear round and came out of the extempore dining-hall into that wretchedly littered ante-chamber where those carefully scrubbed planks led down to the ship's lowest hold.

Our friend followed the aged King of Ithaca and the middle-aged Queen of the Phaiakians till they paused at the threshold of the cabin that Nausikaa shared with Okyrhöe. The ever-watchful old warrior was aware in a flash that they were being followed, and turned indignantly upon Nisos. But Nisos, knowing the wanderer's almost supernatural self-control, flung himself on his mercy without a second's hesitation.

"You ought O my King," he cried, "to know at once what I've learnt by means of the weapon you now hold in your hand! For as you now are holding it, mighty one, this is news you will never share with the Sixth Pillar in the Corridor at Ithaca! If I don't repeat every word of it, O great Master, may I pass at once to the kingdom of Aidoneus!"

It was with an unclouded forehead and even with the beginning of a friendly smile that the Wanderer bade him speak; and hurriedly and breathlessly the lad told the two of them the whole story.

To the young man's astonishment it was Nausikaa who spoke first. "You had better tell him," she said, addressing Odysseus, "what you have told me."

"I have been telling the Queen," said Odysseus at once, "what no one in the world knows except your mother; namely, my dear child, that I, and not Krateros Naubolides, am your father."

Our friend stood for a moment just as if one of those golden antennae, for that is what those elongated tassels that hung from the Helmet of Proteus were really like, had got twisted round his neck. Then his whole face puckered up, in the manner of a small boy who has been slapped and told to go to bed and the biggest tears that Nausikaa had ever seen, though two even bigger ones formed, though they did not fall, in her own eyes, rolled down his cheeks.

Odysseus looked quietly from one to the other of them, while with the wrist of the hand that held the club, that club which sometimes was called *Dokeesis*, "Seeming", and sometimes "Expectation" he touched Nisos gently on the head. Then he said, while his bow-sprit beard turned with a queer jerk into the direction of the bed in Nausikaa's cabin: "Well, my son, what our new Queen and your old Dad have to do now is to plant between us the seed of a new brother for you since you've lost Agelaos! And he'll have to look sharp," Odysseus added, as he led the Queen towards her own bed, "if our friend Leipephile is to conceive a new King of Ithaca before you and I come home from Atlantis!"

The old man—and our young friend, for all his emotional agitation, had the wit to notice this, took good care to prop up "Expectation" against the edge of their bed, before returning to the threshold to draw the curtains of their chamber—said to Nisos with an extremely humorous expression on his face: "For the sake of Aphrodite's son, and by him I do *not* mean the good Aeneas—stay on guard here, my boy, and make sure that that terrible woman from Thebes doesn't break in upon us! O yes! and don't fail to remind me, before those Immortal Horses do carry them off, to see to it that that poor devil of an Enorches has a couple more blankets to keep him warm! He hurt both those creatures, you must remember, and flying horses, like ordinary horses, have long memories."

CHAPTER XII

It was at the upper portion of Pegasos's wounded shoulder that the hypnotized stare of Nisos was fixed. With his own back to the mast Nisos had accepted for a moment the serious responsibility of two important ropes while Proros as the natural result of the unusual amount of wine he had drunk went to the side of the vessel to relieve himself.

But after handing back the ropes Nisos still stared at the shoulder of the flying horse; for not only was he amazed to see that the outraged wing had grown fresh and strong but there was something else going on that astonished him even more. For while Nausikaa took her place in the centre of that god-like back, and while, behind her, the meticulous Herald discoursed earnestly and authoritatively to Okyrhöe, evidently explaining to her many matters of which she was completely ignorant with regard to the political situation among the Phaiakians to whose land she was now to be transported, to his bewilderment Nisos actually beheld, stretching out of the blankets with which the priest's nakedness was covered, a bare arm with extended fingers clutching a piece of solidified ointment wherewith he was furtively rubbing and moistening the roots of the newly-grown feathers of that resuscitated wing.

"Is this insane fellow," Nisos thought, "actually trying to wither up this new growth of feathers as he destroyed the original ones?"

But when, turning his gaze upon the Flying Horse's god-like head, he caught the creature's calm, alert, self-composed and liquid eye, he recognized the true state of the case; namely that the crazy priest was desperately trying to redeem the harm he had done by doctoring these miraculous feathers so as to make them resemble those of a supernatural albatross.

When once he was satisfied that the Priest was not playing any wicked game with Pegasos, Nisos gave himself up to the pure fascination of just watching the winged horse, as the creature patiently stood on that top deck of the "Teras". His length was such that four of him would have reached from figure-head to stern and his width was such that four of him would have reached from the starboard rail to the larboard rail. The rippling flow of the muscles under his skin was apparent with every breath he drew; and as Nisos watched him with increasing wonder and told himself that there weren't many boys in the world or men either who would ever live to see such a sight, the divine creature's grace became yet more astounding as the animal twisted his neck round to see Zeuks lift, first Eione, whose thighs he clearly enjoyed caressing as he assisted her, and then Pontopereia whom he hoisted up bodily by her waist, and who, taking no more notice of him than if he'd been a Mill-wheel or a Wind-mill, fixed her beautiful and intellectual dark eyes upon Nisos and breathed the words, unmistakably audible, though wafted to him on the prematurely engendered twin-sigh of a final farewell: "You are my boy and I love you!"

Nisos was standing now so close to Odysseus that he could feel the quivering outer edge of the great wave of intense erotic vibration that was passing between the old king of Ithaca and the new Queen of Phaiakia.

That Odysseus' emotion was unusually strong could be seen by the manner in which he squeezed the head of "Expectation" alias "Dokeesis". Herakles himself could have hardly clasped his fingers round that wooden skull with a fiercer clutch. The consequence of this natural action while the lithe and limber, the glossy and sinewy, the delicate and perfectly equipped body of the most athletic creature in the Cosmos rested on the deck of the "Teras", was to produce such a vertiginous shock in the interior of the Heraklean Club that the Fly was forced like so many other great scientists to forget himself in his profession, and at once began interpreting, to the Moth and to all the world, in his high-pitched adverbial tongue, the information which the familiar voice of the Sixth Pillar in the old Corridor was conveying to the club.

"The son of the Midwife's sister here, she who formerly served the famous' Nymph in Antro' until she was made big with child by that King of the Latins who is building in Italy a New Troy upon Seven Hills, has been weaned from his mother's breasts and can now be fed by hand. There have been rumours in the Palace that the marriage of the Maiden Leipephile to Agelaos the son of Krateros Naubolides will shortly take place. It is also reported that the other divine horse, the beautifully-maned one who has so often accompanied Pegasos when not using his wings or crossing the sea, has on several occasions been heard exchanging human speech with the Herdsman Tis. This strange event which seems to be unquestionably true has had the effect of greatly increasing the already high esteem with which Herdsman Tis is regarded, not only by Krateros Naubolides and his son Agelaos, but also by Nosodea the mother of both Leipephile and Spartika the Priestess of Athene's Temple."

Here the Fly's lively rendering of the conversation between the Sixth Pillar and the Club of Herakles was broken up by the Fly himself. As a scientific translator of the measured monotone in which the Sixth Pillar reported to the Heraklean Club the elemental gossip that reached it through earth and air and fire and water the Fly, for all his extravagant "adverbialism", was intelligible and sensible.

It was, in the manner of most great scientists, only when he enlarged on his purely personal grievances that his emotions tended to erupt in spasms of disconcerting spleen. "The bitch! The bitch! the bitch! the bitch!" he now buzzed in our friend's ears.

"Excuse me, O thou newly-proclaimed son of abysmally-enduring Odysseus, but I must incontinently go to emphatically warn that adulterously-and-slavishly-behaving whore that I've got my eye on her!"

It was indeed clear to Nisos that what the Fly feared was that Pegasos might suddenly spread his tremendous wings and create such a rush of wind that the Moth would be perforce carried off through the air to the land of Phaiakia and that he would never see her again. And as the pair of them, for like other fluttering priest-worshippers the Moth was susceptible to firm handling, returned to the weapon in the old hero's grasp, it struck the boy's mind as a topic upon which it was really incumbent upon him to ponder carefully in view of his future as prophet, namely as to what part the material size of a living Being ought to play in diminishing or increasing that Being's moral responsibility. To put it plainly, should the conscience of an insect be as tender and as quickly touched by remorse as the conscience of a whale?

A rasping stab in the vitals not so much of his conscience as of his intelligence hit him at that moment; and to the end of his days he always associated it with two things whose logical connection was merely that they belonged to the same animal. Something in the mast or the rigging interfered with the fall of the moonlight upon that glossy-dark supernatural form, whose fibres and muscles and tendons and curving sinews seemed to ripple in their relaxed quiescence not unlike the way the surface of the ocean itself was at that moment faintly stirring, but whatever it was that caused it, some kind of phantom-foam-drop appeared on the left front hoof of Pegasos gleaming with a light which seemed, in spite of it having descended from the full moon, to be an inner light, the light of a mind rather than of any external luminary.

And what became for Nisos a life-long memory, what became for him yet another symbol of that *spoudazo-terpsis*, "my whole will to enjoy what happens", which was now his war-cry, was the strange fact that this inward gleam in the left front hoof of the flying horse corresponded with, and answered to, an inner light in the fathomless depth of the liquid eye which Pegasos turned upon his passengers as he twisted his flexible neck round to see whether everyone was comfortably and securely mounted.

But no metaphysical war-cries and no mystical symbols can keep certain painful and jarring jolts and jerks from destroying our peace; and the splinter that now pierced our young friend's ideal chain of reasoning was a teasing and academic kind of question following closely on the childish one he had just asked himself about the conscience of a fly compared with that of a whale.

And the point was this. How far were the gods, by nature, by tradition, by custom, by international law, and finally by the necessity of the case, exempt from the moral law that all human beings of every tribe in the world feel an instinctive imperative, wherever it comes from, to obey?

ATLANTIS

When for instance Zeus swallowed the great prophetess Metis for fear of a fatal rival, was he breaking the moral law? The result, our teachers say, was the birth of Athene from his head. But does that redeem his murder of Metis? Athene was not Metis. To be the daughter of a mother born out of the head of the person who swallowed her does not make you your mother. It makes you a woman with every reason to avenge your mother on the person who swallowed her.

Themis the Goddess of Order may have been forced to yield to the embraces of Zeus, but it was she who named her daughter *Dike*, "Just Retribution" and all his thunderings and lightnings cannot save the All-Father from the penalty of his crimes.

"By Aidoneus, no! When the time comes for me to be a Prophet the great test of my truth and the truth of what I prophesy can be only one thing, whether I do or do not make it clear that not one of the gods—no! not even the Son of Kronos himself—can escape from the Law of Retribution. Shall I really be what I so long to be when I return from this voyage? O Atropos, thou great little goddess of Fate, give me——" His thoughts, and, we are compelled to add, his prayer to Destiny too, were broken off short by seeing Zeuks rush to the stern of the ship and disappear down the ladder. "He is after Arsinöe! He is after my girl!"

Every muscle in Nisos' tall slender frame grew stiff and tense. "I forgot her! I forgot her! I forgot her!" And he *had* forgotten her. Hypnotized by the fathomless moon-stone of that unnatural eye in the hoof of the Flying Horse, and quivering with excitement, as indeed was Pegasos himself, in anticipation of the spreading of those tremendous wings and of the immortal creature's leap upwards into the air, Nisos had not only forgotten his deliberate association of his newly formulated life-logos, *spoudazo-terpsis*, with Arsinöe rather than with Eione or Pontopereia; but he had completely lost the image—though it now came back with a rush and filled his whole consciousness—of the Trojan maid herself.

"God! What a 'kakos', what a cad I am!" But it was no use

dancing a remorse dance, or calling upon Dionysos or Eros. What he had to do, if he had anything left in him but downcast *aidos* or pure "shame", was to go after this incorrigible Zeuks and snatch Arsinoë away from him. But how could he, though he *was* the son of Odysseus and not of Krateros Naubolides, contend with the son of an immortal god, and that god none other than Arcadian Pan, whose passion for girls and obsession by girls amounted to an absolute mania?

"But you never know," he told himself.

"For not only is 'all fair in love and war', but in all earthly struggles, whether between races, or persons, or things, it is Chance, sometimes at the beginning, sometimes in the middle, sometimes at the end, who changes the wind, and gathers the rain, and loses or saves the day.

"What a curious nature mine is!" Nisos said to himself, instinctively making use of all the analytical intelligence he had, and he had a good deal more than most young men, to put an end to the smarting sting of self-reproach. "Here I am shivering with intense interest to see Pegasos mount up from the deck of the 'Teras' and yet I feel if I am to keep any self-respect at all I ought to invent some excuse, any confounded excuse, such as a desire to use a bucket down below, or to get a weapon from the pile of them in the big cabin, or to ask one of those Libyans to lend me his pocket-knife, and, muttering this same invented excuse, I ought to throw an easy self-contained glance at Odysseus, and slip off past Akron.

"By the Gods, this is what I will do!" For some reason he thought at this moment of his dead pet sea-hawk whom he would never behold again; and he also thought—it must have been the idea of his own death that brought such things into his mind—of the old dead Dryad about whom nobody any more seemed to give the least thought. Then he moved towards Akron. But what in heaven's name was the man doing?

The captain of the "Teras" was indeed acting in a drastic manner. He was slowly and deliberately divesting himself of his clothes, and with the help of Proros and Pontos he was tying round his waist a long rope. Nisos paused for a moment as the East Wind and the Moonlight isolated their intrepid skipper and held him in their crystal embrace, and then to the young man's spell-bound gaze seemed to plunge with him into the water from a bow-sprit now as bare of ornament as the beard of Odysseus.

On their naked captain now boldly swimming, with the rope behind him passing, as he swam, through the hands of both Proros and Pontos, Nisos saw Odysseus fix a well-pleased and proudly satisfied look, a look that said: "Well done, faithful one!" But the old man was evidently so certain now of the result that he soon turned his gaze back to Pegasos, and to his silent dialogue with Nausikaa, who was now resting as securely on the divine horse's back as she would soon be doing on her expectant throne in the land of her fathers. Nisos however kept his eyes steadily on that moon-lit swimmer, kept them there indeed till the "Teras", quickly enough when the man had once climbed out of the water, was strongly and firmly moored to that human-shaped rock on the island of Wone, about fifteen yards inland, and about the same distance from those primeval Beings, who in their "Arima" of a forgotten Past could remember the days before Zeus and his thunderbolts, or the Titans and their mountains piled on mountains, had begun to disturb the world.

"I think, my Lord the King," Nisos now began, edging himself forward between Pontos and Proros, "that I'll just run down, if I may, and tell Zeuks that our ship is now safely moored."

Odysseus however was too absorbed in his final farewell to Nausikaa to hear his youthful adherent's courteous mutterings; and indeed it was not till Akron was back on the ship and had begun to dress and even to swallow a glass of wine that the casual words: "Just as you like, my son," came from the old man's lips.

As he went off Nisos told himself rather crossly and maliciously that at that moment the man's beard looked as if it were the horn of a sea-unicorn, an appendage which, in the case of this singular marine beast, protrudes not from the creature's forehead but from beneath its jaws. The absent-minded permission to be, as children say, "excused", was however, as can be surmised, enough to send our friend hurrying down two ladders and past four oarsmen. "Suppose," he said to himself, "Zeuks has taken her into Nausikaa's cabin and is even now enjoying her in that sumptuous bed."

Nisos knew so little about the actual details of sex-adjustment between boys and girls that he was apt to wander off into completely fanciful paths when he thought of such a thing as the ravishing of Arsinöe by Zeuks. "I shall simply," he told himself, "hit him with all the strength I have, and if I can't crack his skull I ought to be able to stun him. But perhaps that might excite Arsinöe's sympathy. God! I don't know!"

It happened however, that at the moment when Arsinöe came flying towards him with anything but a desperate cry, with, in fact, a welcoming and laughing salute, he had just bent down to lift up the corner of one of those well-scrubbed planks leading down to the hold; for he had seen a wounded rat with the lower part of its body a mass of crushed flesh and blood feebly moving its front legs down there and making a faint and piteous appeal to an indifferent universe.

"Nisos! My dear, my dear! What is it? O the poor little thing!" And once having embraced the situation she not only allowed Zeuks to overtake her and with some trepidation to salute his rival but she gripped that rival's arm, and, stooping down beside him, snatched up a piece of broken pottery that some sailor had dropped a minute ago, and in a few well-directed strokes sent the soul of the rat to the kingdom of Aidoneus.

Was it the royal blood of the House of Priam in her veins, pulsing through the cells of her brain, that gave Arsinöe on this occasion so much more spontaneous grace of gesture and so much more swiftness of mental apprehension than was possessed by either the Son of Arcadian Pan or the son of Odysseus, or was it a new feeling in her own heart? Anyway, the rat having been disposed of, there passed between Arsinöe and Nisos, almost as if the dead creature's blood had brought it about, a strangely swift understanding. This understanding was so deep and complete that our friend Zeuks, while he grew aware of it, found himself, in a manner which if it had been less complete he could never have attained, able to disregard it.

"Excuse me, you two," he ejaculated casually and carelessly, "if you don't mind, I'll rush up now and see what's been happening. You can follow as leisurely as you like."

The daughter of Hector smiled at the son of Odysseus; for since a couple of Libyan lads had just scrambled hurriedly past them on the way up, and three elderly sailors had shuffled uneasily past them on the way down, it was clear that however strong their instinct might be to snatch a moment of quiescence at this crisis in their lives, this particular cross-road corner, dominated by the mutilated rat and the piece of broken pottery that had ended its misery, was not a good place to stand aside in out of the mid-current of events.

Arsinoë felt a sensitive woman's natural reluctance to confuse the background of one man's love-making with the background of another man's love-making, so she hesitated about letting Nisos lead her back into the cabin of Eione and Pontopereia, while the one where Nausikaa had recently given herself to the old king struck the Trojan imagination of Hector's daughter as already dedicated to the heir of the Latin ruler whose New Troy was even then rising upon its Seven Hills.

Thus it was that driven by her own sensitivity to the particular background of any sexual emotion she automatically steered the ardent Nisos towards the ladder leading up to the seats of the oarsmen; and it was upon the oarsmen's deck, as far as they could withdraw themselves from the great motionless oars of the four rowers, that they threw their arms round each other.

Never in his life had Nisos felt as he did now after they had unclasped their arms and had sunk back against the side of the vessel. He held her by her two hands and with their knees touching he stared at her with vibrant intensity but as if from a tremendous distance. What he was really beginning to approach at that moment was simply and solely the everlasting mystery of the feminine.

And what struck him above everything else in this connection was the fact of the unfathomable and impassable gulf between the whole being of a man and the whole being of a woman. Her bodily life and its particular quality, the physical, chemical, elemental nature of her flesh and blood, was as different from his as was the substance of a fallen star or a meteorite from the stalk of a burdock. "The extraordinary thing about it," he told himself, "is that this femininity exists in exactly the same things, like hair, and finger-knuckles, and veins, where veins are apparent, and the bones of wrists, and the rounded bones of knee-caps and the curving bones of chin and of jaw, and the more remarkable curves of shoulders, yes! in exactly the same things that in a corresponding manner exist in our male bodies as when I look at Zeuks or Akron or at my own reflection! And yet there is this startling, upsetting, disturbing difference between us!

"And all this is quite apart from the fatal, everlasting, tragic difference in bodily shape, which has to do with a girl's breasts and hips and all her softer and more undulating curves." So Nisos thought; and the more he gazed at her in this curious, special way the more did this mystery of her femininity grow upon him and envelope him. "What is it? What is it? What is it?C The spirit within him called aloud. But as he gave himself up to her he ceased to look at her. What he was now looking at were not the round knee-caps against which his own hard bare knees were pressed, but what seemed in that dim light to be a small ivory box or bottle—he couldn't be quite sure which it was, but he leaned to the view that it was an ivory box—out of which Euros kept shaking certain small, pearly shells upon a square wooden tray and examining them with extreme care as they lay side by side, before he gathered them up and shovelled them back into their glittering container.

Arsinoë herself was in the vague, dreamy, passive, resigned mood which had been her only happy mood for many a long year. She hadn't made friends with Zeuks in the way Eione had done with Arcadian Pan. But to be the son of a god is a very different thing from being a god. Besides, the great love-affair of Arsinoë's life had been her devotion to her father Hector, a devotion that couldn't have been tenderer or more ardent if Hector had responded to it but all he did was to take her away from her nameless mother and place her under the care of his wife Andromache.

On this deck of the oarsmen they could only embrace with their eyes a very narrow space of sky; so that neither of them had the least idea whether Pegasos had or had not spread his wings. The Trojan girl had really come to like Nisos quite a good deal and to feel a solid trust in him; but if some woman-friend had asked her point-blank: "What *do* you feel for this kid?" she would have probably revealed the truth that she felt a strong protective instinct for him and a desire to look after him. She would in all probability have made her woman-friend laugh, if she had not started a regular giggling-fit between them, by confessing that there had been moments of late, since she had known him better, when she had got the same sort of pleasure from his company as she used to get when she played with a special boy-doll of hers she was accustomed to call Ottatos.

Whether characteristic or not of the difference between the sexes in every human tribe beneath the sun, this interlude, or siesta, or metaphysical sticking-place in the dramatic story of the "Teras" or "Ship of Marvels", was a noteworthy experience for Nisos whatever it may have been for Arsinoë.

It struck him very forcibly that the extraordinary good luck — and he prayed it really was, from whatever far distance flung, the impact of the wisdom of that wisest of all old little maids his ancient patroness "Atropos" that had brought it about — of his having been thrown into contact with this Trojan captive was the greatest event in his whole life.

And it was so because, since his own entire intention was to be a prophet when he became a mature man, the last thing he wanted for his companion through life was an energetic,

ATLANTIS

assiduous, industrious, conscientious, formidable, inexhaustibly active and indefatigably competent. What Nisos wanted or some would prefer to say needed, was someone whose whole nature had the unusual power of being able to devote itself to the one perfectly simple and mysteriously wise act of drifting. Such an one, whether a man or woman, is able to act in a heart-whole and independent way only once in their life; but this act is the infinitely complicated one of stripping themselves stark naked, diving into the deep salt sea and there drifting wherever the tide carries them.

Compared with the people who put purpose after purpose before them and continue struggling energetically until they attain each of these purposes, these once-acting, once-stripping themselves, once-diving into the deep-sea Drifters seem allowed by Atropos the privilege of being porous to more than one universe and being aware of more than one Space and of more than one Time.

Yes! The winds of a million systems of things blow across them and one infinity calls to another infinity through them. And the singular thing is that among male children only those who are lucky enough to be born under the special inspiration of that funny little goddess, the old maid Atropos, whose abysmal intelligence has not been killed either by child-bearing or by playing the bitch, know that for life to *be* life and for the universe to *be* the universe it is essential that there shall be two embodiments of womankind. Each of these embodiments must have that everlasting mystery in her skin, in her flesh, in her hair, in her bones, in her milk, in her milt, in her mensuration as well as in her mind. But the one must be actively competent and divinely creative, the other incompetent and divinely passive. Nisos felt no longing for a mate who was protective of offspring and eternally producing offspring and keeping the human race alive upon this earth. It was the second type of female, the type protective of dreams and fancies and wishes and longings and illusions and imaginations, and ideals, and rebellions, and destructions, and insurrections, and redemptions, and recoveries, and re-births, and by means of all these things eternally changing the movements and explorations of the energy of life from one generation to another, towards which he felt drawn.

"What is it," he asked himself, at that crucial moment, "that this Trojan girl has got in her that neither Tis's little sister nor the daughter of Teiresias possess, but which I *must* have if I'm to be happy in my choice?"

It was at that very pulse-beat of Time that the young man became suddenly aware that Arsinöe was watching him with concentrated attention. Previous to this moment she had preserved the same friendly passivity that had always been her mood with Zeuks and had lasted throughout his recent amorous handling of her. But something, whether a flicker of romantic seriousness passing across the face of Nisos, or some thought or feeling of her own that may very well have reached her from the psychic work-shop of Atropos had suddenly drawn, the girl nearer to the young man.

Nor was he oblivious of this change in her. But the curious thing was that while each of her successive moods, favourable to him or unfavourable to him, were of startling and piercing importance to herself while they lasted, to him, as he watched them come and go, they seemed, each of them in its entirety and intensity, so much a part of her that they endeared her to him in absolute remoteness from their tone, whether for him or against him, in relation to himself.

What particularly struck him at that moment was an odd relief that she was neither as pretty as his friend Tis's little sister, Eione, nor as beautiful as Teiresias' daughter, Pontopereia. "Your preciousness to me, my dear," he told her in his heart, "is that you are *not* particularly graceful like Eione or particularly intellectual like Pontopereia, but just simply a sweet-natured extremely feminine woman whom fate has handed over to me for my very own and who has come to entirely belong to me and to no other man in the whole world. It's because you're completely and entirely mine," so his improper, indecent, and outrageous thoughts ran on, "that you're so entrancingly lovely.

What I worship, what I have always worshipped, ever since as a little boy I had a laurel stick called 'Sacred', which, though it hadn't any vital crack dividing its breast and supplying moths and flies and gnats and midges with a refuge from wind and rain, had one end resembling an idol's head and another end resembling a dragon's tail, is some object, possessed of an individuality that separates it from everything else in the world, and yet which is absolutely and entirely my very own, not to be shared in any way at all with anyone else. You *are* mine, aren't you, you tender, soft, mysterious subtle, enduring, unique creature? Gods in Heaven! if you weren't, I'd be so alone in this mad, aching, bruising, biting, scratching, stinging cosmos that I wouldn't care what happened to me! It's having found you, and having got you as both my idol and as my secret private personal toy that makes you what from now on you'll always—"

"Come on, you two! Come on, for the sake of your poor old Zeuks, if not at the command of cloud-compelling Zeus! Come on, or Odysseus will be jumping into the sea with nothing but that ridiculous 'prumneesia' on his silly old pate!"

They both leapt to their feet, followed him at a run to the ladder, scrambled up helter-skelter, Arsinoë clinging to Nisos, while Zeuks, his left hand on the small of the man's back and his right on the woman's waist, pushed them violently from the rear.

Yes! Odysseus was standing alone at the base of the figurehead gripping "Expectation", otherwise "Dokeesis", firmly by the middle, and disentangling from the extraordinary object on his head what looked like a couple of dangling, elongated, devilfish tentacles. Of these tentacles he was earnestly and gravely testing the strength, giving them a series of sharp tugs and using for this purpose both the hand that held the club and the one which was free and unencumbered.

Close to the mast stood Akron, watching over the curved spines and quiveringly extended arms of Pontos and Proros who were holding the swaying and dripping rope by which the "Teras" was moored to the rock that in shape resembled the Titan Atlas, and, as he watched those quivering arms and that massive rope, repeatedly turning his head away from the rock and towards Eumolpos at the helm.

Zeuks led the agitated and excited lovers straight up to Odysseus who swung round at once and regarded them from above his beard with a quiet and approving look, a look that said: "You're doing very well, my children. Go on as you've begun and all will be well."

It was only when Nisos realised the direction in which both the eyes and the pointed beard of the old man were now turned that a cold shudder of terror ran through him amounting to something like sheer panic though it didn't quite reach that point.

Odysseus was calmly regarding the water, his body stone-still, while both from the hand that held the club and from the other hand trailed those two weird streamers. What these streamers really resembled were the long-drawn-out single hairs of a certain prehistoric creature that swam the salt seas aeons of centuries ago and lived by devouring monstrous cuttle-fish which floated in chasms of water that descended to the centre of the earth.

Contemplating the greenish-black depths, into which Odysseus kept dangling these streamers from his fantastic helmet and testing their strength, Nisos began to feel more real nervous dismay than he had ever felt in his life before.

"By Aidoneus if this isn't worse," he said to himself, "than when I was in that prison of Enorches!" And then as he stared at that black-green swirling water, into which some deadly intimation told him Odysseus would soon force him to plunge, it suddenly came to him how the image of that mark on the base of the Sixth Pillar—"the Son of Hephaistos"—had acted like an incantation or a magic spell to free him from that cruel Priest's prison. And wasn't Hephaistos the god of Fire?

Well then, wasn't this mysterious Son of Hephaistos, or rather the Pillar raised up by him, the very saviour dedicated to come to the aid of a person in peril from Water? Thus, just as he had suddenly seen those two Letters on the wall of his prison, so he now saw them in the midst of that swirling green-black water.

And it was at that second that Odysseus swung round and shouted to Akron: "Keep her off the rocks till we come back!" and then in the same tone addressing Zeuks, just as if the daughter of Hector had been, like the "Teras", another "Prodigy" of a Ship, "Guard my son's Trojan as carefully as if she were Helen herself till we return!" Then turning his back upon everything but the miles of water that covered Atlantis: "Now you, my son, watch me carefully and do exactly what you see me do."

Thus speaking the old king disentangled the long single hair, that was his Ariadne's clue, from his Helmet of Proteus and placed the end of it between his teeth. Nisos, after one last hurried glance round, in which he saw the moonlit tips of Zeuks' knuckles at Arsinoë's waist but also noted that the knuckles of both *her* hands were pressed violently against her closed eyes, thrust the end of his "clue" into his mouth and shut his teeth upon it.

It was at that indrawn beat of the tense heart of their ship "Teras" that Arsinoë snatched her hands from her eyes, fumbled with the clothes of her companion, drew forth Zeuks' habitual defence, his short double-edged sword-dagger, and thrust it into Nisos' hand, thus it was not weaponless that our young friend, imitating to a nicety every movement of the old man, followed him over the ship's side, and plunging feet-first into the water, disappeared from view.

What did not disappear, however, and it can be imagined the queer feeling the sight of these things gave to Arsinoë, were the two elongated single hairs, so vividly suggestive, whether or not such was their real origin, of some aboriginal prehistoric feminine monster, of that grotesque Helmet of Proteus. These objects remained on the surface of the water; and it was the weirdest thing Arsinoë had ever seen in her life to observe these thin streaks of moon-lit silveriness, bobbing up and down and round and round each other, and every now and then shooting off a certain distance from each other, where, although separated, they would recommence their sport of bobbing up and down and round and round, as if the other one were there, when in reality it was completely outside that particular radius of the game.

Zeuks was also watching this ocean dance of a couple of moonlit filaments constituting themselves a curious sort of comic-cosmic choroio; but his attention was so taken up with the delight he got from pressing Arsinöe's body against his own that this dithyrambic crescendo-diminuendo upon the water became merely an outward projection of the deliciousness of the dalliance in which he was indulging.

To Arsinöe on the other hand, though she could no more help staring at it than she could prevent her senses responding to her Companion's caresses, it was as if the everlasting elements themselves were mocking her and making sport of her; but when Zeuks' ecstatic embrace subsided and she had once more to deal with the less wrought-up occurrences of the more normal succession of things she forced herself to recall what she had felt when in that "Arima" of Ithaca day after day, with the carving-tool tight between her fingers, she had carved the indomitable features of the defender of Troy out of the heart of an island ash-tree.

While the son of Arcadian Pan and the daughter of Hector of Troy watched the dance of those nameless things that were like the antennae of some primordial insect-monster of the ocean, our friend Nisos found he needed every gasp of breath, every drop of semen, every throb of blood, every microcosm of will, every spurt of energy, every burst of blind desperation he could call up if he were to remain "cheerful", as his island school-teachers had always taught him must be at the root of the philosophy of life of every pious son of an Achaian father, while side by side with Odysseus he sank through the water to the roofs and streets and temples of the capital-city of Atlantis.

They landed on a vast expanse of grey pavement and what was really an enormous space of perfectly smooth and carefully fitted flagstones; and while Odysseus was slowly turning round on his heels and with very little shuffling or stretching or stumbling was making a hurried but obviously a pretty careful survey of the panorama around them, the first thing that came into the head of Nisos to do was to snatch at his own silvery and swaying life-line. When once he had clutched this gleaming object at about five yards distance from the Helmet of Proteus, he glanced quickly at Odysseus for permission, and proceeded to give the glittering thin thing a bold twist round the cavity in the bosom of the Club of Herakles as the weapon reposed horizontally in the hand of Odysseus.

Noting his son's action and divining that it had something to do with the curious "life-crack" or naturally-engendered slit in the bosom of "Dokeesis" *alias* "Expectation", the old hero raised the weapon into a more perpendicular position and gave it the sort of brandishing shake that Herakles himself must have given it before between them they killed the Nemean lion.

Held quietly and firmly now at a slanting angle to the bottom of the ocean, and tangled in a twist of one of the two parallel life-lines that reached from the Helmet of Proteus to the surface of the sea, it was possible for our two world-voyaging insects to appear at the mouth of their unusually-shaped caravan and even plunge into verbal relations with their almost equally bewildered fellow-travellers.

"My friend the Moth keeps imploring me to tell her," murmured the Fly, "just where in the circumambient trail of our cosmogonic excursion she may know she has arrived. I tell her that this is the only ship upon the sea that fulfils the longing of real adventures all over the world who long to exchange earth for air, air for fire, fire for water, in their natural, heaven-blest longing for new life.

"My friend the moth suffers unfortunately from one of those troublesome manias that so often afflict lovely and sensitive females. She maintains that the Orphic Priest, who confessed just now, when he saw Eurybia and Echidna on the island of Wone, that the gods he really worshipped were not Eros and Dionysos but Death and Nothingness, had been driven mad by the way we all treated him and by the hatred we all felt for him.

"She actually went so far as to say that if she could have spent a whole night when he was asleep caressing with her silky wings the frontal bone of his skull she could have restored him to sanity! I think myself that it is the pressure of all this dreadful volume of water upon a creature as delicate as she is that has disturbed her own brain."

At this point Odysseus intervened, but quite carelessly and lightly. "If you don't mind," he said, "for this confounded weight of waters, in spite of our Helmet, makes me feel a trifle dizzy, I'll rest here for a moment." Saying this he seated himself upon a stone bench on a long, low wall; but he continued to keep the club in the same position and took care to hold it so that its "life-crack", out of which the two insects were peering, might point towards Nisos.

"Please, O please, thou son of Odysseus," cried the agitated moth, quickly recovering, under the powerful protection of the Helmet of Proteus, the spontaneous passion of her feelings, "don't let him traduce by his terrible cleverness a person as holy, a person as chaste, a person as devoted, a person as spiritual as this great Priest of Orpheus! Where is he now, I ask you? Carried away by brute force on the back of a titanic animal who hates him even more than any of you do! Is that the way to treat the greatest Priest of the Highest Mysteries that the history of our world has known?

"If *he* were here now, instead of having to crouch as we are doing on the lowest bench in the lowest bottom of the world, we would be marching proudly across these bridges and in and out of these vast temples and forth and back down these sumptuous terraces and across these colossal squares and up and down these palatial flights of gently curving and softly undulating stairways, or we might even have found a chariot to ride in, for that would be the proper fashion for a man as old and famous as our sovereign the King of Ithaca!

"Please, O please, thou Son of Odysseus, call on your father to use his power to lift us out of this humiliation!"

"Is it not clear," protested the fly, while the moth at his

side quickly recovered her equanimity, "that the poor darling has suffered a serious shock? Think of her assuming that an aged hero who has lived, loved, and fought with the gods and whose capture of Troy, as the Pillar in the Corridor has been telling me, is included in the poetical recitations of all the master-reciters in Hellas, is less poetical when resting by the wayside as an ordinary tired old man, than if under a gorgeous canopy he were riding on the back of an elephant followed by a procession of camels as the emperor of a host of jewelled Barbarians!

"It can only be, as you can see at once, my noble Lord Nisos, that our beautiful friend is suffering from a shock caused by the pressure of this appalling mass of water; and it would be very kind, as well as most appropriate, if, in order to turn her attention to other things, you would tell your King that the Sixth Pillar has just informed me that the fire-breathing Monster, Typhon, half-Dragon and half-Giant, and the arch-enemy of the Olympians, whom Zeus buried under a mountain in Italy, but who had been loose for several months, has now been decoyed by the Being who lives down here, and whose image is the Teras' figure-head, into serving Him or Her or It, after the manner in which an obedient Beast serves its master. In fact, O most noble, O most loyal, O most sagacious grandson of Laertes, if you will forgive my turning for a moment from the philosophical aspects of life to those of more immediate concern"—and Nisos noticed that the head of the fly grew suddenly larger and blacker than usual and that both its orbicular eyes were gazing into the distance—"I believe the Monster I have just referred to, not the figure-head Being, if you understand, but the half-ophidian and half-human fire-breather, has smelt human blood down here and is hastening in our direction."

The hand with which Nisos had hurriedly touched his master's elbow, pointed now at a convulsive cloud of smoke and fire that he could see bending its course towards them over a sort of under-water aqueduct, and then, drawing from a slit in his own shirt, in a manner worthy of Zeuks himself, that dagger-sword with two edges that had been pressed into his hand as he went over the side, he gave a little straightening jerk to the club in the old man's hand as if indicating to it that battling with a Monster rather than philosophizing with a Fly must now be the order of the day.

It now became obvious once more to our friend what a perfect fellow-voyager and fellow-adventurer his new father was. Apparently Odysseus had so shrewdly and so quickly taken in the immediate topography of their position and the general nature of this astonishing metropolis of a drowned continent that he had no sooner caught sight of the Fire-breathing Typhon advancing towards them, swaying and heaving and writhing like a serpent with the lower half of its body, but steering itself with human arms and keeping a straight course along a sort of aqueduct, which perhaps still, though it only had the thirst of titans and monsters to quench, carried fresh streams in spite of all this intolerable weight of salt water: then with "Dokeesis" otherwise "Expectation" or the Nemean club in his right hand, and his son's arm gripped tight above the elbow in his left, he hurried off in a straight line towards the advancing monster but upon such a different level of ground that to reach them Typhon would have had to risk a plunge of about a thousand feet, a leap which for all his dragon scales and serpent tail and the fearful strength of his gigantic arms was evidently beyond his power.

What struck Nisos most about Odysseus as they advanced side by side towards this writhing and twisting cloud of fire and smoke, till it was almost exactly above their heads, was the man's absolutely amazing gift for adapting himself to a staggering and overwhelming situation with complete calm and balance of mind.

"As for myself," Nisos thought, "I believe I might just manage to carry things off with a rush and be brave enough to scare my enemy with brandishings of my dagger as I flew at his throat; but what I couldn't do would be to get rid of my secret dread, my stalking and skulking terror, the horror I'd feel in my jumpy nerves and the heart-beating throbs of my jittering pulses.

"Why, the old man behaves as if this terrifying dead city at the bottom of the sea were the friendly haunts of his family dryad. He seems able to note things and examine things and analyse things with as much calm and as much lively interest as if he were observing the beasts and birds and shrubs and trees and plants and rocks and stones of a new tract of totally unknown country that we had invaded and occupied."

"I don't like the idea," said Odysseus at last, lowering his head after having kept it thrown back and tilted upwards with his bowsprit beard pointing to the world they had left, "of that creature up there dropping his *kopros* on our heads."

Nisos in his turn lifted his head; and there did indeed seem to him a very potent probability that from the under-belly of Typhon or, worse still, from beneath his serpentine tail, extremely unpleasant excrement might descend upon them! From that unwieldy body gusts of the foulest-smelling wind, collected for long in those over-replenished bowels, were already beginning to explode in startling and menacing bursts of spluttering thunder; and it certainly wasn't a pleasant prospect to imagine themselves being chased from one end of the ocean to the other by the droppings of this fire-breathing fugitive from the wrath of Zeus.

"I don't know, my son," the old man continued, "whether you can make out the width of that fresh-water aqueduct under his coils as he comes on; but from what I can see of the situation it strikes me that this final rebellious child of our old Earth has got himself on a road that's too narrow for him to turn till he arrives at the end of it. It's too high a jump even for him, and I really believe, now he's once on that aqueduct, that there's nothing he can do but go on to the end of the thing! We shall, no doubt, my dear boy, have many other vexations before we've got to the end of *our* aqueduct; but I think we're in no immediate danger from that outrageous Man-Dragon up there."

Forward therefore with free steps the father and son moved. They had to walk independently of each other because each held his weapon in his right hand, and when by any chance they moved too close, the hilt of the son's sword-dagger kept grazing the knuckles of the father's left hand.

What Odysseus was thinking as they went forward in this way Nisos would have given a lot to know; but he had by this time discovered that one of the fundamental characteristics of this greatest of all leaders was his power of keeping his wandering and philosophical thoughts wholly and completely distinct from his practical thoughts, that is to say from his tactics, stratagems, decisions, and plannings for future action.

For himself, as father and son advanced in this manner, both cautiously and impulsively, along the bottom of the deepest of earth's seas, Nisos was too absorbed and spell-bound by the external overpoweringness of what he saw to have any spirit left for mental reaction to it save awe and wonder. He decided that it must have been on the ground-floor so to say of the ocean-bed that they had found themselves after their dive.

But what a place it was, far more impressive than any city he had ever seen before, or ever was likely to see! The stones it was built of were all the same colour; but whether this was due to the action of the water or to the particular kind of rock or of marble that the builders had used he wasn't enough of a traveller to know. But all the visible masonry, including the roads and the pavements, was certainly of one and the same tint, and this tint was of a grey shade, but quite unlike any other grey shade he could ever remember having seen.

What struck him most about this whole drowned city as it rose up before him now was, strangely enough, its suitability, its fittingness, its adaptability for being a drowned city. It lent itself to its doom. It was in fact the most perfect realization of a drowned city that could have entered, or the idea of which could have entered, any great poet's imagination.

What especially struck Nisos about it was its unity with itself, the fact, namely, that it rose in so many levels, with its stair-ways and bridges and squares and platforms and tiers and terraces, as if conceived and created to support the pedestals and pillars of the metropolis of the universe with temples and theatres and dance-halls and council-chambers and academies and ecclesias and arenas and hippodromes and senate-halls, towering up, one above another, towards the surface of the water that covered them, making in their colossal entirety one single isolated palace-house, where reigned and ruled in undisturbed supremacy the mysterious Being who had revolted against Heaven, defied the Human Race, and adapted its own unfathomable consciousness to a secret submarine life, with no companion but the Man-Dragon, Typhon.

It was the extraordinary way in which this city beneath the waters satisfied the whole deep-breathing desire in the ultimate chemical elements of existence that they should have nothing within them to the end of their days save what in silence uttereth speech and whose speech is the speech of air, water, fire, and earth, an elemental language which in its essence is the music of enjoyment, that gave the thing its real secret.

It was queer and quaint to notice, as the two of them progressed onwards in what they both divined would probably turn out to be intricate curves returning by degrees to the region of the city from which they had set forth, how the various fish and sea-creatures they were constantly encountering showed not the faintest alarm at their appearance and even came so close that they sometimes brushed against their necks and arms and faces with their fins and tails. One star-fish for instance struck Nisos so violently in the mouth that it made his lip bleed, and it gave him a very queer shock when this sudden taste of blood mixed with salt-water brought back to his memory an occasion when as a child he had picked up a jelly-fish on the sea-coast, and then, falling on his face as he tried to bite it, had bloodied his mouth.

A much more obscure memory may have been released when he saw the extremely elastic and singularly delicate skin of one queer-looking sea-creature, skin that resembled the caul with which new-born babes are sometimes covered, rent and torn by the stab of a small sword-fish. But it was when he noticed one luckless fish whose eye was gone that he suddenly remembered how when he was questioning Eione as to the way the Helmet of Proteus, the thing that at this moment he and his father were using to such good effect, had come into her hands, she told him that Arcadian Pan had stolen it from the great Hunter Orion, whose consequent lack of it had resulted in his being blinded.

"The blinding of Orion! How very odd that I should never have given that piece of news a second thought!"

By one of those queer coincidences that it is always almost impossible to regard as *just* coincidences he had no sooner thought of the injury that Tis's little sister had unwittingly done to the great Hunter Orion than his father suddenly turned to him and said with a smile: "I was just wondering why it is, my son, that only once in my life I've composed a line of poetry, while from my memory I can repeat so many lines."

"What was the line you once composed?" enquired Nisos. "It would interest me so much if you'd repeat it to me now! Do, please, please, my father, let me hear that line of poetry you composed. Had it to do with what at that moment came into my head? I mean the blinding of Orion?"

Odysseus swung slowly round. "It's curious," he said, "that you should have spoken of Orion; for the line I composed, and I really do consider it a proper, authentic, natural line, though the only poetic part of it is the fact that it is rhythmical and runs smoothly, *is* about Orion. Well, I can't really say it's *about* him. But at any rate it refers to him, and the syllables of the line run musically together! In fact it's because they run so musically that I can repeat the line now. It's the simple sound of it that works the trick. In fact it's the sort of thing a child could invent without having to give it any particular significance.

"Yes, a child, if it tried to make up a story in poetry would be delighted if a line like this suddenly came into its head. It would probably even try to compose a second line, such as in its rhythm and smooth flow could follow the first.

"It was when I was in the Garden of Alkinöos to which Nausikaa guided me and when I was telling her father and mother, indeed when I was telling them all, about the ghosts of the Heroes I saw in Erebos, that this line suddenly came into my head.

"I had been explaining to them how I beheld the holy and upright Minos, that great son of Zeus, acting as Judge among the Ghosts in Hades when suddenly I thought: 'I must tell them how I saw the great Orion'; and it was only then, when, without premeditation, I uttered the words 'Ton de met Orionay pelorion eisenoeesa', that I realised I had uttered a line of real poetry. And yet all I'd said was just quite simply that 'after him'—by which I meant of course after Minos—'I beheld the gigantic Orion'. But I must have instinctively realized that the words I was using had suddenly, like a boat from a muddy ditch into a flowing stream, emerged out of prose and into poetry; for I knew the poetic rhythm in what I added to this, namely:
> 'Chersin echone ropalon panchalkion aien aages.'
> 'In his hands holding his club, all-bronzed and
> ever unbroken.'"

Nisos spontaneously brandished his double-edged dagger as Odysseus, moving on with a firmer stride, mounted a short flight of broad stone steps and began to cross a marble square of immense size in the middle of which must have been a grove of enormous trees. It was painful to observe the lost and condemned trunks of this grove, not merely blackened by the salt water but curst with a peculiar shade of blackness to which an exquisitely faint blue tinge had been in some way added.

As they followed the marble roadway between these weird tree-trunks that were like ghosts gathered in a desolate flock by some invisible enchanter, Odysseus turned to his son. "I can't tell how it is, my boy, but I have an instinct that it's not for nothing that you and I were brought at the same moment into contact with the name 'Orion'."

Nisos stood so still that he might himself have been one of those ghastly tree-trunks with their weird metallic glitter in that pale light.

"Do you mean, my father——" began the young man. But his words, whatever they were going to be, dissolved in that circumambient greyness; for as he met his father's glance he knew without any exchange of words what the older man was thinking. In fact their separate thought-streams at that critical moment in their lives whirled together in a silent circular eddy. "You think, my Lord," the younger man whispered, "that we're in the line of the great Hunter's arrows where we now stand; and that we might be hit and turned into ghosts ourselves at any second?"

Odysseus lowered his club till it rested on the pavement of the road they were following and they both gazed with instinctive apprehension at a group of colossal Sea-Weeds that rose, tough, wiry, weltering, succulent and elastic into the water, and seemed to be treating the water itself as if it were a thick undulating mass of weirdly smelling rubber that bent into curves and grooves and hollows as they pressed against it, and *into* it too, as you might say, without causing it to split or crack or bleed or sweat or melt; causing it to yield where it was pressed against, but always finding it impossible to prevent it returning, like a squeezed bubble, or like a vast impressionable bladder, the moment the pressure was relaxed.

"Have you realized, my Lord," whispered Nisos; and it showed the nature of the intimate crisis that was intensifying itself about them, like an elemental process, parallel to, but not the same as, the process of freezing, that the young man without consciousness of what he did reverted to his mood of utterance before he knew his parentage, "have you realized that we're on the edge of—"

His voice died away as he looked down; and there came no responding reply from the old man, as he too looked down. And well might the two of them—mere mental human animals of fibres and nerves as they were!—look down and look long, at what lay before them. They were indeed confronted by what might have struck them as a vast reserve of creation-material out of which all the multitudinous formations of earth-life could be replenished, reproduced, refilled with pith and sap and blood-juice.

ATLANTIS

They were indeed standing on the brink of a vast precipitous chasm that apparently descended to the centre of the earth but which the water of the ocean had now wholly filled. Huge rubber-like sea-growths protruded so thickly out of this indescribable gulf that it was clearly a horrible possibility that impulsive wayfarers might mistake the tops of these elastic weeds of the great salt deep for just a rougher portion of the paving-ground of the road they were following; but the idea that at any moment they might catch, carried to them by this weird element that could scarcely be called water, the twang of an arrow's flight from the bow of the great Hunter Orion, subdued to a minor degree of tension their reaction to this precipice beneath their feet.

Once more Nisos was, as they used to say in his island-school, bowled over by his new parent's calm. For the old man turned his back upon this cosmic chasm in the floor of the world just as he might have done if it had only been a muddy ditch near their old Dryad's decayed oak-tree.

"Well, sonny," he said, "we must go back a little way, but it won't have to be far. We'll find a way of getting our direction again if I'm not mistaken when we're at that arch." He was not mistaken. They soon found, exactly at the point he'd mentioned, sweeping upwards from that same arch, a tremendous flight of steps, a staircase, in fact, that soared up and up and up with such a stupendous urge that, in the process of their mounting it and ascending its grandly sweeping curves, neither of them, neither father nor son, could help feeling a curious exultant pride in belonging to the same type, if not to the same race, of human animals, who were responsible—quite apart from the Being who had tyrannized over them—for the building of this amazing city.

They had only to pause for a moment with their elbows on an ebony balustrade to realize what a sublime achievement this Metropolis of Atlantis was. The wonder was not only in the fact that its stairways and bridges and great squares and vast market-places were supported by the same colossal pillars, as the towering

ATLANTIS

temples, which themselves, in their turn, were over-topped by yet more bridges, bridges above which still mightier and higher platforms had been erected, platforms which had been made the floors for still loftier towers. It was also in the fact that the whole mass of them, yes! the whole volume and weight of all these amazing constructions, were connected with one another, forming, so to speak, one vast musical composition in marble and stone. And if this drowned super-city was indeed by far the most remarkable creation that the world contained, how was it that the human race could calmly look on while some Titan built and some Olympian drowned its sublime structure? How was it that no desperate prayers to Atropos, who was the oldest and wisest even if she was the smallest and the most easily exhausted of the three Fates who govern the affairs of men and of nations, were not uplifted by the prophets of the people? But it now seemed to both the father and the son as they contemplated this spectacle, leaning upon that ebony balustrade with its summit disappearing in the salt water above them and the foundation disappearing in the salt water beneath them, that they really could hear the terrifying twang of the bow-string of Orion.

But Odysseus wasn't one to remain paralysed and confounded even though in the presence of a menace from Orion on one side and from Typhon on the other. "If *that's* the Hunter," he remarked quietly, "*that* is, without question," and he jerked his beard in the opposite direction, "the breathing of the Monster. So I suppose we'd better leave this point of vantage and swing round again, whether eastward or westward, or northward or southward; for I have now absolutely lost all sense of direction, and I expect you have too, my son! But I know we were just now following that damned Dragon, so, if I'm right to assume from the noise I can hear that the brute's coming back this way we've got to return to our first direction, sonny, which was certainly directly opposite our present one."

They turned their backs therefore to the still faint but extremely unpleasant sounds of which they both were now fully aware, and made their way, the father with Herakles' club and the son with

Zeuks' double-edged dagger, back once more in the direction from which they had just been hastening.

"Was it an omen, my father, both of us thinking of Orion at the same time?" enquired Nisos rather timidly, for he was not sure, as nobody who knew Odysseus ever *could* be really sure, what his precise reaction would be to any question that had a mystical or religious over-tone.

In one sense this famous hero's character was abnormally simple, as simple, you might almost say, as that of an animal, in another sense it was unpredictable, yes! not so much complicated, or subtle, as wholly unpredictable. Even here it might have been argued that there was something animal-like, although to anyone who has a long experience of any particular species of animal the absolutely incalculable never occurs.

But it was precisely this, the absolute incalculable, that did occur with Odysseus; and it was upon this peculiarity that the popular idea of his wiliness and cunning rested. Human cunning, like human honesty, is one of the hardest of all qualities to catch, isolate, hold, and clearly define, especially so when we agitate our measuring scales by the introduction of our moral emotions. Odysseus' unpredictableness resembled in fact both the unpredictableness of the sort of super-animal we call "good", like Pegasos, and the unpredictableness of the sort of super-animal we call "bad", like Typhon.

But now to his son's question about Orion the old man's reply was both very gentle and very definite. "I have noticed," he said, "that the intimation of a great friend's approach or of a great enemy's approach reaches us through the intervening space much more quickly and much more unmistakably when the personage arriving finds us entirely alone and with nothing around us and about us except the elemental, the mineral, the vegetable forms of existence. Get away, you little idiots!" and he brushed aside with his left hand a shoal of tiny fish who had evidently mistaken his projecting beard for a growth of the sort of seaweed that might be expected to harbour the particular kind of small creatures that were to these scaly little mouths and distended gills a veritable heaven of feasting. "Of course in this case, my dear child," Odysseus went on, "you and I, since we have the same friends and enemies, can well, for the argument's sake, count as one person. To both of us, therefore, the presence of Orion down here at the bottom of the sea, exploring the metropolis of Atlantis, just as we are doing ourselves, is without question a menace to you and me. That he is, no doubt, much more of a menace to our enemy Typhon makes no difference to us. It is known that Orion was blinded for ravishing his mother and only restored to sight by the power of the Dawn. It is known that he has an insane passion for killing anything and everything with bow and arrow and that on one occasion he set out to destroy in this manner the whole human race. Whether he is here as a friend or as an enemy of the Being who rules this place and whose mysterious countenance our ship carries as her figure-head is completely unknown to us.

"Whether this mysterious Being to whose machinations, directed against the Son of Kronos, Atlantis owes her drowning, has the power to dominate Orion I have not the remotest idea. I can only assure you that when I saw Orion in Hades after my vision of Minos judging the Dead I felt very hostile to him. Ghost himself, he was killing for the second time, and for an everlasting Second Death, every creature he could discover, in a blind ecstasy of universal murder.

"Thus, my dear boy, when I hear you ask me whether the fact that the image or the eidolon or the actual living form of Orion coming into our two minds at the same moment when he is stalking through these deserted buildings in one of his insane murdering fits, is an omen, I can only answer, emphatically and definitely, *no*!

"*No!* It is no more an omen than when Polyphemos killed my companions and tried to kill me. It is a struggle, a battle, a contest, my little son. It is a fight! And everything in Life is a fight, Nisos my friend, *everything*! That the idea of this savage Hunter, this madman, who some say raped his own mother, and whose very name means 'to pour out semen', and who others say had neither father nor mother, but was born of the semen of Zeus and Poseidon deliberately thrust into the hide of some slaughtered beast, and left to ferment there for the necessary nine or ten months, came into our minds at the same moment only shows how the eidola of dangerous men, who are threatening us, can pass through air and water and earth and fire till they fling themselves upon us like horrible projected shadows, warning us that very shortly the men themselves in their own flesh and blood will be upon us!

"Omens? It is the fight for life, the fight in life, the fight of life, and, by all the gods! the fight *with* life! But what we must set ourselves to do now is to discover the palace, the dwelling, the temple, the throne, the hiding-place of the Being who rules this place."

He gathered up his own trailing cord of the Helmet of Proteus more effectively round his head and watched his son do the same for himself and also for the club of Herakles; and once more they went on with their exploratory journey. But their quest was soon at its end. Without warning, without the faintest hint of premonition, they were suddenly standing on a platform of green marble, marble that through all this water had itself the look of water and of water in motion too; while in front of them, but to their surprise not on the tremendous and awe-inspiring throne they were expecting and looking for, but on a heap of long-dead, long-decayed, long-rotted, long-dissolved, long-degenerated, filthily-stinking, foully-crumbling, horribly-putrifying mass of sea-weeds in accumulated decomposition, reclined, or rather sprawled, the god-titan, or goddess-titan, for this horrific and terrifying rebel against all Deities was completely bi-sexual and androgynous, who was by reason of his, or of her, or of its defiance of Zeus and of Poseidon and of Aidoneus, those three Olympian Rulers of Sky and Sea and Hades, responsible for the drowning of Atlantis.

This mysterious Being, whose physical appearance struck Nisos as more shocking and also more feminine than human words could convey, fixed her eyes upon the young man as he stared in stupefied horror and made with outstretched and inwardly curved fingers a series of gestures, of a dangerously magnetic nature, compelling him to approach her. This summoning gesture he felt unable to resist, and first with one of his feet and then with the other—and as each foot advanced he felt himself forced to move his arms, in a fumbling and groping manner, mechanically forward—he slowly and steadily, while he trembled from head to foot at what he was doing, advanced towards this indescribable creature's embrace.

And then, evidently as much to the surprise of this terrifying Being as to that of its intended victim, Odysseus calmly stepped forward and stood between them with his broad back towards his son and his face towards the Being crouching on that pile of rotting seaweed.

Nisos experienced an extremely odd sensation as he allowed his right hand grasping his two-edged weapon to sink down by his side and contemplated the broad back in front of him. It was to him a completely new sensation and one which made him feel a little foolish. He liked to be the active one, the most active one, in any group or in any company. He had been brought up to feel it his duty to serve, guard, protect, and defend his parents; and also to serve, guard, protect, and defend his King; and furthermore to help, aid, sustain and champion the very old.

And here he was standing weakly, feebly, passively, stupidly, behind the back of a person who was both his Father and his King and at the same was a very old man. Used to analysing his feelings he found it more than a little difficult to decide whether it was better to submit and obey on this occasion, when so old a man who was both his father and his king placed himself between him and the present danger and did so too without uttering a single word, did so in fact purely by the silent and practical and significant action of facing this appalling Being himself and turning his back upon the child of his loins, or whether he ought, with one desperate leap and a wild rush, to fling the old man aside, raise high his own arm, and plunge Zeuks' deadly double-edged dagger again and again into what he could only pray would prove to be the heart of this living Mystery of Horror.

Why he thought of her, what put her into his head, what power concealed in the depths of his own nature called upon her for help, Nisos could no more tell than he could tell whether she would have been, in any case and entirely independent of both Odysseus and himself, exploring, as many another powerful Deity might well want to do, the deserted Metropolis of a drowned world, but she who now came suddenly into our friend's head was none other than Atropos herself, the oldest and the smallest, but far the most powerful, of the three Goddesses of Fate.

"O Atropos, O Atropos!" Nisos prayed in his heart. "Great Goddess of Fate! Thou who once didst let me struggle with Gorgons and Furies on thy behalf, help Odysseus and help me against this Horror!"

He had no sooner uttered this prayer than he was aware of a curious hush in the humming and murmuring waters around them. He shuffled sideways just a little; in fact just enough to be able to choose to see or to choose not to see, according to his wish, the magnetic eyes of the Being reclining on that foul heap of stinking seaweed. From this position he could see that the Being in front of him had got its eyes fixed steadily upon the face of Odysseus and was still making with its semi-human, semi-vulture-like finger-claws a monotonous, repetitive, ritualistic pantomime of silent motions, which clearly gesticulated what in words would have been: "Come to me! Come to me! Come to me! You and I, when once we are one, will conquer the universe!"

The Creature's "Come to me!" was repeated over and over and while this appalling sorcery of repetition went on Nisos' glance wandered to a half-revealed object that lay amid that rotting dark-brown seaweed. What it was, when once he caught sight of it, was evident enough, though the seaweed in which it was entangled covered many portions of it. It was the skeleton of a man or woman. Nisos didn't know enough about anatomy to know to which of the sexes it had belonged, and the light that shone from the couple of swaying cords that emanated from the Helmet of Proteus was not strong enough to reveal with certainty whether the owner of the flesh that had once covered that skeleton was a tall or a short person; but those white bones entwined with dusky seaweed made him, as the Helmet's flickering light fell upon them, wonder why he had never asked the all-knowing old hero how it was that considering the thousands of people who must have been drowned in that sunken city he hadn't seen until this moment a single dead man or woman. Anyone would certainly have supposed that if the thunder-loving Son of Kronos had caused the sinking of a crowded city like this as a punishment for impiety the whole place would be full of dead people caught and drowned without warning in the midst of their daily business and profane pleasures.

If only he had the power of reading the thoughts that were passing to and fro within the living skull of Odysseus under that fantastic Helmet! What *could* the old hero be doing with his mind and his will to counter this gesticulated spell by which the Ruler of Atlantis was seeking to enthral him?

It was hard enough for Nisos to take his eyes away from those twining and twisting fingers, but he was too scared as well as too prudent to risk more than a series of snatching, switching, twitching glances at the appalling beauty and over-mastering power of the face above those flickering hands and that androgynous breast.

What on earth would the old hero decide to do? It was certainly a weird state of things for a person as inexperienced as he himself was to have to face. But here was his father facing it in deadly silence; and he told himself that if he intended to be a prophet when he grew older he must force himself to face what was happening now. He must in fact force himself to see himself cowering behind his father who held the Heraklean Club but who could do nothing in the presence of this Being but simply stand his ground, while round about them both, wandering up and down these towering bridges and triumphant bastions and tessellated battlements roamed the titanic Dragon-Monster Typhon who had shaken a whole Sicilian mountain from off his shoulders and who breathed such fire from his belly that no mortal man could face him, and yet, huger than he, and armed with a club not of wood, but of bronze, here also was the greatest of all the Hunters of the world, enormous Orion, threatening not only Typhon but all that lived and moved upon the earth and all that lived and moved beneath the waters! And here was he, Nisos, cowering behind the back of his father. But he must, he must without shirking his own shame, force himself to visualize this living group of heterogeneous Beings, human and divine and demonic and bestial, isolated there in drowned Atlantis, but as compared with the infinite extension of the sky, and the infinite extension of time, of no more importance or significance than if it had been a group of toads and tadpoles and newts and stickle-backs and dragonfly-grubs in the minute estuary of a small pond.

His half-conscious pride in being clever enough to think thus of himself and of the rest of them lifted his spirits considerably and once again, and this time with more faith and hope than before, he prayed to Atropos, the oldest and smallest, but by far the most powerful, of the Three Fates.

And lo! such was the regard which this aged directress of mortal lives had for our young friend, and whether he knew it or not this personal link with the old lady was the best omen and the deepest intimation that could possibly have reached him that one day he really might prove to be a prophet to the people of Hellas, —lo! there suddenly swam past them, following a straight line between Odysseus and the god-demon of the drowned City, a large and peculiarly handsome Dolphin, upon whose back, and clinging to him with a certain nervous intensity, was Atropos herself!

She gave our friend as she passed, and she looked at nobody else and took no notice of anybody else, a look he would live to remember all his days, and probably would recall on the day of his death. It was then that Odysseus swung round at last, turning his back upon the god-demon, as if the ripples made by the passing of that Dolphin had broken, independently of any effort he had to make for himself, the whole of the spell which was now in the process of being thrown over him by the twining and twisting of those appalling fingers.

But when, in the radiation of each of the Helmet's hollow cords that gave to the calm old hero and his agitated son all their light and all their air, Nisos looked at his father's face he was surprised to see upon it an expression quite different from the expression he expected; for what he saw was not satisfaction over something that had just happened but expectation of something that was just going to happen.

And this became yet more evident when the old man held up before his son, in the full light and air of both those hollow cords that sprang from the crazy-looking object upon his head and went wavering upwards till they reached ocean's surface, his wooden Heraklean club.

"Expectation's acting true to his name, eh, sonny?" murmured the old man, speaking as quietly as if in place of a glowering horror there was nobody present but Tis and his faithful cow.

Nisos looked at the life-crack in the great weapon's bosom. Yes! There, as of old, was the big head and staring black eyes of the scientific fly; and there were the wavering antennae of the mystical moth!

To the son's astonishment the old hero begged him to enquire from the fly if the Sixth Pillar at home could still hold converse with "Expectation", and, in case it could, had it any news for them at the bottom of the deep sea? Nisos, though in his nervousness he felt as if the weaving fingers and the appallingly dominant eyes of the Being behind his father were keeping up a threat that nothing could dispel, gathered about him, as if it were the aegis of Athene herself, that look of Atropos and implored the fly to tell him the news.

Drawn back in a second were the quivering antennae of the moth, evidently under her friend's pressure, while with all his usual adverbial emphasis, the fly announced that the essential drift of the Sixth Pillar's news was that all the dimensions and all the elements of nature were at that moment waiting in an hushed and awestruck suspense the result of an ocean-deep contest between the immortal hunter Orion and the creator and survivor of Atlantis.

"The fly," Nisos continued, translating the insect language as carefully as he could, for like all very ancient classic tongues this insect one, which was far older than any of those used either among the defenders or the destroyers of Ilium, was full of subtle shades of meaning, "the fly tells me that the Pillar is at this moment warning its friend the wooden club that the club carried by Orion is made of something heavier than wood. It is in fact made of bronze. And the fly is now telling me all that the Pillar says about it to the club. I beg you, my father, to listen for a second to the voice of the fly, so that you can see, but if anybody in the world knows that already, it's you, what a grand teacher our goddess was when she put into my head, on the day the the Harpies attacked that stone with their nails, the trick of understanding this insect-tongue.

"Anyway, from what the fly says I gather that the Pillar has been assuring the Club that in the hands of wisdom wood can beat bronze, and that——"

But Odysseus interrupted him at this point with a violent movement, a movement that flung them both down upon the ground. Then in a hoarse whisper the old hero bade Nisos help him, covering both of them with as much seaweed as they could gather up and strew over themselves, as they lay where they were with the club between them.

"Is it Typhon or Orion?" whispered the son. "Both of them!" groaned the father. And then with a sound that was half a curse and half a chuckle: "But its worse for this Atlantis-Bitch than for us!"

Vain and useless as he well knew such trifling things as double-edged daggers were in the presence of such Beings as he now peered at from under his heap of seaweed and across the heap that hid his begetter, Nisos couldn't help clutching his only weapon, such as it was, and he couldn't help feeling relieved when he saw by the light from the two Protean cords that swayed above their heaps of seaweed that his father had a tight grip upon their only real weapon, the club that in its day had drunk of the blood of the Nemean Lion, the club that sometimes bore the name of "Dokeesis", "Seeming", and sometimes the still simpler name of "Expectation".

"*Both of them!*" Odysseus had gasped, with that queer sound that might have been a groan and might have been a chuckle; and as Nisos, feeling a human superiority to the fly, as the fly in his turn had felt a metaphysical superiority to the moth, peered out from under one heap of seaweed and across another, he did indeed behold "both of them". And they were a really overwhelming sight. Typhon, the largest living creature ever born on land or in sea or air or fire, Typhon of whom even his mother the Earth was afraid, Typhon who had come so near to defeating Zeus that Zeus was only saved by a trick that was not a trick of his own, now approached from the South, breathing fire upon the spot where the Creator of Atlantis sprawled on her seaweed throne and where the son as well as the grandson of Laertes crouched at her feet as if within two seaweed graves.

The fortunate thing for our seaweed-hidden humanity just then was the fact that this colossal Monster with the arms, head, breast, hips and belly of a man, had, in place of the legs of man or beast, the terrific, curving, twisting, writhing, scale-covered tail of a dragon. Typhon's hands were garnished with the most vulpine and vulturine claws that were ever seen before, or during, or after the Great Flood that drowned Atlantis; while the gleam of the flame and the reek of the smoke that poured at all times from his throat in place of air kept making this ocean-deep water, through which he was now moving, steam and bubble round his too-human mouth, in a fashion that was as fascinatingly weird as it was, in some other queer way, disturbingly shocking.

But if the physical appearance of Typhon not only terrified but attracted Nisos after some mad and inexplicable fashion, the appearance of Orion, the greatest Hunter there has ever been, or ever will be, caused him to shiver under his rank-stinking shroud of slippery-slimy sea-refuse with a much more definite tug-of-war sensation between two conflicting emotions than he felt about the fugitive from beneath Etna.

It was indeed a certain concentrated, absolutely absorbed, gravely exultant enjoyment, held back as if by a leash just this side of ecstasy, which he read in the almost touchingly boyish features of the great Hunter that tore his sympathy into two halves of almost equally intense repercussion. O how he wanted to see that vast bow the Giant carried in his left hand bent for a shot and strung with one of those deadly arrows he wore in his belt! O how he longed to see that huge bronze club he swung in his right hand brought crashing down on the fire-breathing, water-bubbling visage of this Monster, who awaited his approach without a trace of perturbation!

So completely capable did Typhon evidently feel himself to be of clawing to death, or crushing to death, or squeezing to death, or burning to death with his fiery breath, or biting the head off any pursuer who dared approach him that Nisos was scarcely surprised to see him presently curl his gigantic tail in a vast circle round his ophidian loins and, deliberately clutching with outstretched human fingers handfuls of shells and pebbles and seaweed and sand, squat down in relaxed ease with his back against one of the colossal ammonites of which there are many in that deep bosom of the ocean.

What struck our young watcher, in spite of his boyish sympathy with every variety of hunter, as a really sublime spectacle of indifference in the hunted as to the final issue of the hunt, was the placid position in which the fire-breathing refugee from his living grave beneath Etna awaited the terrific Orion.

And like a mountain of submarine marble that has been washed smooth by the waves till it resembles a block of rainbow-gleaming ice, the great Hunter was now exposed to the petrified stare of our young friend under his counterpane of striking seaweed. The tremendous figure in the foreground was engaged, it was plain to see, in adjusting an arrow to the string.

ATLANTIS

Through the wavering atmospheric lustre that emanated From the fantastic object on his father's head the whole spectacle struck the prostrate lad with a strange sense of some vast world-history reaching some long-prognosticated moment, where life in its mysterious essence, human, sub-human, super-human, cosmic, and astronomic, had arrived at some pivotal point where the whole business, inscrutable, unspeakable, absolutely real, but beyond both mind and matter, gathers itself together to become something for which naturally enough there is as yet no name.

Then he saw Orion draw the arrow back on its quivering bow-string against his naked breast and let it fly. It flew with a reverberating directness straight towards the reclining Typhon and past the very feet of the recumbent Creator of Atlantis. It passed clean through one of the outstretched hands of the Man-Dragon, nailing it to the ground; and Orion perceiving this and glorying in it had the same look upon his face as when with his arrows he drove the Pleiades into the sky, and again when he came at last upon the sun-god Helios newly-risen over the edge of the world and was cured of his blindness.

But the latest and greatest of the primeval children of our Mother the Earth was not overcome by this shock. He didn't roar, nor did he howl; he didn't shriek, nor did he bellow: he didn't curse nor wail, nor yell, nor rumble, nor weep, nor moan. He only lifted as high as he could his right shoulder, for it was his left hand that had been hit, swung his right arm downward across his bent torso, seized the arrow and struggled to pull it out. The arrow, however, after piercing his hand, had gone deep into a very obstinate piece of rock, and pull as he might with that powerful arm and that powerful shoulder he couldn't pull it out.

While he struggled with it Nisos could see the vast figure of Orion approaching with long strides and brandishing his bronze club. At that particular sight the young man's mind moved very fast. He recalled what his father, lying now by his side, had told him, and how the words he used had of their own accord, so he declared, taken upon them the rhythm of poetry. In fact simultaneously with the approach of that tall terrifying figure, Nisos seemed to catch again the very syllables of what the old warrior had muttered at that moment.

"Tonde met' Orionay pelorion eisenoeesa."

"Chersin echone rapalon panchalkeon aien aages."

What astonished the young man most in himself at that crucial second was that in spite of all tradition, convention, propriety, decency, law, order, education, custom, and harmonious necessity, he found that his sympathy was with the hunted and not the hunter, with the ugly and not the beautiful, with the Monster, and not the destroyer of Monsters, and he suddenly felt in himself a mad, wicked, rebellious, reckless impulse to jump up from the side of Odysseus, clutch the double-edged dagger that had belonged to the son of Arcadian Pan, leap on the shoulder of this god-defying Man-Dragon, and spur him on with a mocking and resounding challenge to withstand Orion to the death!

Odysseus must have become aware, by some psychic vibration passing from one light-giving Proteus-cord to the other, of this rebellious impulse in the life-blood of the child of his loins, for he suddenly handed to him his club, leapt to his feet with astonishing agility, crossed the few yards between them and Typhon in a couple of strides, and kneeling on one knee, and using both hands, pulled out the arrow! Nisos who was instantly at his side gave him back the club and helped him to his feet. But they now found themselves, while they watched Orion's steady approach, standing so close to the Creator of Atlantis that this incalculable Entity was able to try its dangerous magic upon them both just as it pleased; one deadly-white phosphorescent tentacle of a finger being laid on the shoulder of Odysseus and the other on the shoulder of Nisos.

All three of them for a brief space, while every pulse-beat of time brought Orion nearer, were in any case reduced to helpless inactivity by the choking cloud of fire and smoke with which Typhon covered his retreat. But a retreat, and a very shrewd and very rapid retreat this enemy of Zeus was able to make under cover of his own fiery breath, so that when Orion, brandishing his club of bronze, arrived on the scene he had not the remotest idea whether his fugitive had fled east or west or north or south.

Nor did it appear to him that either of the two men he found awaiting him were in a condition capable of replying intelligently to any question he might ask as to the direction of the flight of the Enemy of Heaven. They were both, at least so it seemed to the simple mind of the great Hunter, so confused, so dazed, so numbed, so completely metagrabolized by the leprous white, death-worm-white, sarcophagus-toad-white dead-sea-eel-white fingers that rested upon them that he might equally well make enquiries of a heap of ordure dropped by the fugitive.

So he addressed himself to the Being who had reduced them to this condition.

"Tell me, you creator of drowned cities, you hypnotizer of men, whither has that monster whose belly-flame no water can quench and whose bladder-smoke no ocean can quell, shogged off on his wriggling tail?"

Neither the father with his unbelievable past nor the son with his doubtful future appeared able to utter a word. But the mental vibration between them was so aided by the cords of the Protean Helmet that Odysseus indicated to Nisos in a whisper below a whisper that the club of Herakles had begun to make curious little jerks, abrupt stirrings, and quiverings quite independent of the hand that held it. "Feel him, will you, son?" whispered the old hero, "and tell me what you think!"

Nisos laid his left hand on the club's head, just above its life-crack where the hollow cord, clinging closely to it, still protected the sheltering insects from the pressure of the water. "If it wants to act on its own, my king and my father," the young man whispered, "I would risk it and let it do so!"

And the club, whom some called "Expectation", and others called "Dokeesis", said to itself: "That bronze affair which Orion is whirling about over our heads may be all right for breaking stones. It is far too unwieldy, mechanical, automatic, and impervious to all suggestion, to crack the skull of a dangerous magician. If I can only make Odysseus give me my complete freedom I'll show him and this lad too how to deal with wicked and horrible Beings! I came near it at the cave of the Naiads; but this Living Horror lying on that dead seaweed is worse than the oldest natural-born monster. But I, Dokeesis, can deal with it! Only let me go, and you shall see!"

And then, as his own hand on the club's head and his father's hand round the club's waist relaxed a little, Nisos heard the fly say to the moth: "It's hard for a thinking person like myself to go on studying life while these gods and men and monsters make such a stir; but I'm at least lucky to have someone like you, not quite indifferent to philosophic conclusions. Before the Pillar stopped talking to the club just now, it revealed the real cause of all this hullabaloo. It said it had learnt from earth and water and air and fire that the death of every deity in the world was at hand. It said that the world, what it always calls 'the Pillared Firmament', would outlast every creator that was supposed to have made it. This boy Nisos thinks that our ancient classical language is too *adverbial*. Adverbial! How else, I should like to know, could any language express how perfectly, beautifully, intelligently, clearly, and completely the club, in whose bosom you and I are at peace, understands our old and subtle tongue? Anyway the Pillar has now revealed that as a result of a spontaneous and natural revolt all over the world against god-worship, all the gods that exist, from Zeus downwards, and all the goddesses that exist from Hera downwards, including Athene herself and Eros and Dionysos and of course including Aidoneus the god of the dead, and Poseidon the god of the sea, are fated to perish. They are not fated to perish rapidly. Some indeed, Athene and Hermes for example, will perish slowly.

"But perish they all will. And the fatal sickness that must ere long bring them to their end is caused by this growing refusal to worship them. If mortal beings depend on the sun and the rain, immortal beings depend on our worship of them. If we stop worshipping them, the juice, the sap, the pith, the oil, the ichor, the very blood of their life vanishes; and like plants without sun and air, and plants without earth and water, they simply wither away."

The fly now became silent; but Nisos heard the moth answering him in her most vehement manner. "I don't see the use of dead things like sand and rocks and air and water and fire going on when living things like gods and men and insects have vanished away. That would mean that nothing would be left; for if no one knew they were there, there'd be nobody there and everything would be nothing."

"Your voice, beautiful one," said the fly, "sounds as if you'd rather like everything to be nothing."

"I would! I would! I would!" cried the moth; "for then the greatest Priest who has ever lived would be right, and the Pillar and the Club and all the rest of you would be wrong!"

Nisos decided in his own mind that it must have been the abnormal excitement of the club itself that had communicated this tension to its inmates. "Shall I," he said to himself, "take my hand off its head, and see what happens? My Father's hardly holding it at all! Suppose I *did* take my hand off its head would it move of itself? Would it go for this horror?"

Nisos had never in his life been aware of so many cross-currents of thoughts and intentions, of revelations and counter-revelations, of insurrections and counter-insurrections. He was conscious of feelings that whirled one way and of feelings that whirled exactly the opposite way, through his consciousness. It was like being torn in half. With one part of his soul he longed to lift his hand from the club and see the club plunge itself with all the power that killed Nemean Lion into the face of this Mystery enthroned on this dead seaweed!

With the other part of his soul he felt that to see the terrible beauty of this majestic face mauled, crushed, churned up, smashed up, beaten up, pounded up, hammered up, reduced to an indistinguishable paste of pestilential mud and blood would be to assist at the most savage crime that his wickedest imagination had ever pictured. But there was an "I am I" within him that was deeper than his divided soul; and with this he felt that the only conceivable alternative to letting the club obliterate this Ruler of Atlantis was to let the Horror have its way, to give up himself to it with absolute submission, to give up his father Odysseus to it, to give up his friend Zeuks, the son of Arcadian Pan, to it, and, worst of all, to give up to it his girl Arsinoë, the daughter of Hector of Troy. No, no, no, no! He couldn't let this Being, whatever the mystery of its creative power, whatever the ineffable beauty of its face, whatever its justification as the arch-enemy of Olympos, triumph over all he loved, unresisted!

He felt too agitated, as the quivering of "Expectation" *alias* "Dokeesis" under the pressure of his hand indicated that at the withdrawal of his hand the club would act on its own and leap at that unspeakably lovely face bending towards them, to have the calm of mind to do what Odysseus was doing at this moment, namely keeping his eye fixed, not on the Creator-Survivor of Atlantis, but on the great Hunter Orion, who, towering above them, was now examining with the utmost nicety each arrow in his quiver, and as he did so kept turning north, south, east, west, and snuffing at the air for the direction of Typhon's flight.

But he was absolutely amazed when he heard his father, who like himself was now on his feet, addressing Orion in a calm, quiet, but extremely authoritative voice.

"We have met without meeting, O mighty Orion, and I must request you to kneel down here for a moment at my side. I must ask you to do so in the name of your island of Chios. I must ask you to do so in the name of Merope. I must ask you to do so for the sake of the hide of that sacrificed bull, filled with the mingled semen of Zeus, Poseidon, and Hermes, and buried in the earth for ten months, out of which you were born."

If the tone of Odysseus and the substance of his words were an astonishment to Nisos it was a still greater wonder to the boy when the towering giant submissively obeyed and knelt down by their side apparently quite indifferent to the fact that while he, a demi-god, was on his knees, they, a pair of mortal men, were on their feet.

ATLANTIS

Nisos now became painfully conscious of what might have been called the psychic helplessness of the four of them, Odysseus, Orion, the Nemean Club, and himself, arranged in a convenient row, as if they were Hesperidean Apples, to be devoured, one after another, by that Being reclining on the dead seaweed. Nor, it appeared, were any of the four of them very surprised by what they heard, though the tone of the Being's voice when it first came forth might well have pulverized, or, at any rate, petrified, any one of them, caught by it alone.

It was not only the most scraping and jarring voice that Nisos had ever heard. It was the most mechanical, automatic, and metallic voice. It was a voice like the triumphant screaming of steel when in contact with tin. It was a voice like the voice of every instrument in the Smithy of Hephaistos if they had revolted and taken over for themselves the whole resounding and echoing place. It was not the voice of a god, or a man, or a beast, or a bird, or a reptile, or an insect. It was the voice of a vast reverberating arsenal full of every kind of instrument for every kind of creation and every kind of destruction.

"From now on, to the end of your lives," the voice from the Entity reclining on the dead seaweed grimly grated like a wheel, or grievously groaned like a plough-share, "you three migrants to my kingdom, of which, as you know, having once come you are forever the loyal subjects, will go about the world proclaiming my kingdom's laws. These laws will, in their own time and in due course, become the law of the whole earth, the law of every country and race and tribe and nation and people. This law will be absolutely and entirely scientific. As it is born of science, so it will grow, century by century and aeon by aeon, more purely scientific. Its one and sole purpose will be science for the sake of science. It will care nothing about such trifling, frivolous, unimportant matters as faith, hope and charity. It will care nothing about the happiness of people, or the comfort of people, or the education of people, still less, if that be possible, about the virtue or the righteousness or the compassion or the pity or the sympathy of people.

"It will use people—that is to say men, women, and children as it uses animals. It will practise upon them and experiment with them, not for their sake, but always purely and solely, as it ought to be, for the only Purpose, the only Religion, the only Object, the only Ideal, the only Patriotism, the only Cause, Reason or Consideration worth anything in the world—*to understand everything that exists in every aspect of its existence.*

"For the sake of Science we must create. For the sake of Science we must destroy. For the sake of Science we must go so deeply into the secret of the power of one human mind over another, and of all human minds over the substance of earth, the substance of air, the substance of water, and, above all, the substance of fire, so that in the final event the whole earth will be as completely under control as my ship of state the 'Teras'. As completely, do I say? O much, much more! For though it will be worked and handled by human beings, just as the 'Teras' is worked by Akron and Teknon, and Pontos and Proros, and Klyton and Halios and Euros, they will be scientific human beings, that is to say every man, woman, and child, in the whole world will be dominated absolutely and entirely by me, or by someone appointed by me; and, in this new 'Teras' of mine, I shall sail to the furthest limit of the Cosmos carrying my war-cry of 'Science or Death!' to the end of Space and Time."

"Shut your eyes, darling!" murmured the fly to the moth, "for *our* 'cosmos', or whatever you call our old club, is going to hit this Science-Horror pretty heavily, furiously, bloodily, murderously on the head!"

Nisos was so close to the "life-crack" within the club's bosom that in the dead silence following the voice from that terribly beautiful countenance he couldn't help catching, as the adverb-loaded buzz of the fly ceased, the moth's contribution to the crisis, which, as can be imagined, was contained in two monosyllabic sighs—"priest"—"death". But such was his sympathy with the club's emotion that the boy now deliberately removed his hand. "Like son, like father," might have been a proverb among flies, for Odysseus also completely relaxed his hold upon the club. Whether the savour of "poisonous brass and metal sick" from the brazen club held by the kneeling Orion, who with his height thus reduced by half was still taller by a head than the father and son who were on their feet, had anything to do with the violence of its wooden rival neither Odysseus or Nisos ever knew; and the bronze and the wooden weapon never met again. But, after a desperate, whirling circle, the self-brandished pine-tree-stump from that Nemean wood crashed down head-foremost full into the forehead of the mysterious Being on that seaweed heap, breaking its skull to bits.

And, not content with this, the self-moved slayer of the Nemean Lion, just as if a ghost or "eidolon" of Herakles himself, wrenched forth from the dead past of that hero's madness, had been wielding him, continued to strike at that indescribably beautiful and majestic face, till there was nothing left but a revolting mixture of blood, flesh, bones, seaweed and sand, streaked with filthily bedaubed tufts of hair.

The whole business was over and the gigantic Orion with his club of bronze was already striding off, without a word to Odysseus, in a south-westerly direction whence he must have caught, on some far-carried stir of the waters, a trailing cloud-wisp of Typhon's breath, when a couple of Dolphins, a great deal larger than the one that had carried Atropos, but evidently, Nisos quickly told himself, sent to their aid by that timely-interfering Mistress of Particular Destinies, stopped with a slant-sliding pause of their triumphant witchery of movement close by their very side.

On the backs of these elegant sea-horses it was not long before it was possible for them to see, on rising to the ocean's surface pretty well in the identical place where they dived down, the familiar single mast and complicated rigging of the "Teras", not to speak of those tall, weird, eternally arguing goddesses "of an infant world", Eurybia and Echidna, who still stood, disputing with each other as to what was happening on earth at this crucial time, disputing with each other in their new "Arima", near to the Atlas-shaped rock to which the "Teras" was moored.

"Look! O my father! Look, for the sake of Aidoneus and Persephoneia, look! *It is gone!*" Gasping and spitting out the water from his throat and stomach, Nisos, keeping himself afloat with both legs and one arm, for their Dolphin-steeds were soon a mile away, shouted this news to Odysseus, to whom the watchful Akron had already thrown a rope.

Turning his steady gaze as well as his bowsprit-beard towards his son, the old adventurer, who with Akron's help was only using his left hand to climb on deck while under his left arm the club of Herakles was squeezed against his ribs, signed to Nisos, who was treading water in an unruffled sunlit sea, to detach from his shoulder, as he himself with his right hand was now detaching from his head the Helmet of Proteus.

The sight that had made the youth utter that cry was nothing less than the complete disappearance of the figure-head of the "Teras" so long renowned in all the harbours of all the Islands. "There's something here," the boy told himself, as he watched the Helmet of Proteus with its elaborate apparatus of hollow cords, sink out of sight, "that deserves more thought than I can give it till I'm warm and dry."

But as in his turn he was helped by Akron to reach the "Teras'" top deck he couldn't help wondering why it had been necessary to sacrifice this elaborately worked-out method of remaining for an indefinite time beneath the ocean.

"That awful Being," he said to himself, "had certainly no sympathy with anybody or anything. We were all the same to it! It would cut to bits, it would burn to cinders, a hero, a lion, a dolphin, a bird, a frog, a worm, a maggot, a flea. And all this to understand life!

"It didn't enjoy anything, or like anything, or admire anything, or pity anything. And yet it wanted to explore everything and understand everything. What a perfectly appalling way of understanding things! All it could understand of anything was how that 'anything' reacted to torture and compulsion. Well, well: I have learnt from the bottom of the ocean even more than from the ancient and adverbial language of flies. I now know what I shall be a prophet of when I am a man. I'll be a prophet for the putting of Science in its place! And what is its place? Its place is the servant, not the master, of life, the friendly 'doulos', or obedient slave of living things, not their pitiless 'basileus', or 'royal despot'."

That day, with all the following days for several months, turned out to be one of the happiest epochs in the whole life of Nisos, the son of Odysseus. He grew more devoted to Arsinoë, the daughter of Hector, than he had ever imagined that it was possible for him to be to any girl. In a physical sense, in a romantic sense, in a psychic sense she appealed to him; and on her side all she had endured in her captivity had left her with so much subtle knowledge of the pathetic simplicity of masculine self-esteem that not the most teasing obstacles, the most stupid jealousies, the most ridiculous suspicions, the most childish egotisms, could spoil for her what she saw of honesty, loyalty, and simplicity in her boy-lover's nature.

He also came to understand Odysseus as he had never dared to hope was possible; but it was not so much the mental enlightenment he got of the great Adventurer's character as the simply boyish delight in the endless stories the old man would tell out of his inexhaustible memory, as they sat together under that single mast and outstretched sail in the most fortunate wind that ever wafted a vessel towards an unknown, but O! so passionately imagined, shore!

What was most fascinating of all perhaps to the boy was the way the old man would correct and qualify, and sometimes even indignantly contradict, the ballad ditties that had already been scattered abroad throughout Hellas about so many of his exploits. Of these ballad-tales Odysseus hesitated not to explain to his son that the ones about the Trojan War itself were far grander as poetry than the more modern and more domestic ones, full, though these latter were, of the realism of daily life, and more concerned with his own private and particular experiences.

Certainly if their luck-blest sailing from East to West was a specially dedicated time for Nisos, it was an even rarer period of exquisite human happiness for Arsinoë. She had by this time come to profoundly understand, not in a scientific manner, but in a much subtler, wiser, and entirely feminine manner, all four of the chieftains on board, for no sea-faring chronicler ought to omit Akron; while our friend Zeuks, like his father, Arcadian Pan, had the power of enjoying a young woman without spoiling her chances with other men: and finally, since she was the only girl on the "Teras", the ship itself, devoid of a figure-head, was her only rival.

As for Zeuks, he had for the whole of this happy voyage from East to West exactly what his peculiar turn of mind liked best in the world, that is to say, for Arsinoë would never express herself with him, an old man, a middle-aged man, and a very young man, all well-educated, with whom he could discuss his favourite problems forever, problems that were at once erotic and metaphysical and that lent themselves to a humorous elaboration which any woman's mind spoilt. For the feminine intelligence, brought on the scene, swept in its direct realism so fast over both his logical hieroglyphs on the sands of time and the pantomime-stage overlooking them, that it spoilt the whole humour of his game.

And so when Arsinoë was helping Odysseus take his bath, or was learning something about navigation from Akron, Zeuks would argue with Nisos about that life-logos idea which was summed up in those two significant words "spoudazo terpsis", which Nisos loved to translate, in the adverbial language of the fly, "I powerfully throw my whole will into enjoying myself under all conditions," while in his own secret mind Zeuks would struggle to find, though he never could find it, some pregnant aphorism that would say to the whole regiment of all the thinkers and all the prophets that have ever been: "to laugh at everything is the prerogative of man, and we must acquire the art of doing it quickly before everything laughs at us."

By good luck, or rather by the profoundly wise premonition of Nausikaa, the "Teras" had sailed with provisions enough to last the whole crew for half a year, so that even Akron, cautious as he was, felt no fear that they would reach the end of their resources before they reached the coast of some island or country or continent. And even supposing the ocean stretched on and on as far as the Isles of the Blest where those favoured by the gods lived forever in perpetual happiness, what could happen to the "Teras" before she reached those isles need not trouble them now. Akron indeed went so far as to confess to Eumolpos the helmsman that when he experienced a certain shudder of apprehension at the idea of having to encounter such world-famous favourites of the immortals, he overcame the uneasiness of his respectful awe by the idea that these Blessed Ones might get some kind of a human thrill at being greeted with news from home.

But months passed by and the "Teras" reached no Isles of the Blest or any other Isles. Days followed days, weeks followed weeks, and they met nothing but the same monotony of unending waters. At last there came a day when there arose such an angry controversy among the crew, who had never bargained for a voyage as long as this, that Odysseus himself had to help Akron in restoring order. It was a quite natural nautical dispute about this everlasting fair wind. There certainly was something queer in a wind that never stopped filling their one great sail. Too well they all got to know that old familiar expanse of sail-cloth as it bulged out, so full of that never ceasing wind! There was even a dark stain upon it, in the shape of a man's hand, made by the blood of a seagull.

But it really was wonderful how quickly the aged adventurer restored order. And he didn't do it just by his bawdy jests; though there were plenty of those. He did it by holding their fascinated attention while he regaled them with one enthralling episode after another drawn from the actual stream of memorable things. It had been about this wind that their dispute had arisen; and, as so often happens in these contests, in each of the opposing arsenals of argumentative weapons, more were drawn from temperament than from experience.

In the matter of his own adventures Odysseus had come to realize as he grew older, and in doing so he had been greatly assisted by his old Dryad's intimacy with the Naiads of the Cave, that there were already a number of tavern-and-harbour ditties, school-boy catches, ballad-minstrel songs, and even longer and more scrupulously measured verses, that made very free use of him and of his adventures, just as they did of those of Agamemnon and Achilles and Hector and Ajax; and he now quickly understood, as he caught the drift of this present dispute, that it had to do with an entirely false and rather ridiculous tale that had been rumoured abroad about an ox-hide bag, in which Aiolos, the King of the floating island of Aeolia, bound up the four winds of heaven; and about this bag being given to Odysseus to carry with him on his ship, and about Odysseus's ship-mates, imagining it contained gold and silver, untying the knot and letting the winds go free, and finally about the frantic fury into which the foolish Aiolos flew when their ship was blown back to his fantastic brass-bound floating island!

Odysseus explained to both sides in this airy dispute that the winds had nothing to do with any such preposterous potentate as King Aiolos of Aeolia, this portly despot with his over-fed six sons married to his pampered six daughters, none of whom did anything but eat and drink all day long.

He explained to them that the mother of the winds was Eos the Goddess of the Dawn, who had married Astraios the son of that very Eurybia they had left on the island of Wone disputing with Echidna; and he warned them that unless they wanted the Hunter Orion on their track they had better cut out this silliness about ox-hide bags.

"I can't interfere," he told them, "with what the minstrels and tavern-singers make up about me. But inspired poetry is one thing and a versified fairy-tale, however entertainingly told, is another thing."

"Land! Land! Land! Land!"

By divine good luck—though Nisos had his own secret thought that his old helper Atropos had something to do with it—it happened to be at the exact hour of Noon with the Sun high above them and the water calm when the whole lot of them crowded on deck to welcome this most heavenly of all sights to those in the air or on the water, the simple sight of the solid earth. It was not a mountainous coast they beheld nor a particularly rocky one. It was just a coast, just a shore, just land at last.

Akron wisely decided not to let his helmsman steer them straight in at the first approach. "I prefer to wait," he told them—and Odysseus bowed to his opinion—"till we find a really good landing."

It is a curious thing but "what happens" as we say, often takes the course of events out of the hands of any particular power, even out of the hands of Tyche the Goddess of Chance herself, and yet doesn't yield it up to Fate or Destiny or the Will of Heaven. The event is not so much stranger than fiction as more appallingly natural than the natural, and to our amazement redeems all sorrows in the sweetness of its silent finality.

Probably no one will ever be really able to explain what there was in common between three extremely vital Entities on board the "Teras" that caused them all three to die of pure delight at their approach to land.

None of the three was entirely human, and it is possible that this was the reason; for it often happens that when plants and insects and half-gods die, ordinary human beings go on living. Ordinary human beings must have a certain mixture of fat and gristle in them that has the power, just because it is—well! *what it is,* of completely absorbing certain deadly vibrations.

"It's the end of me!" Zeuks murmured, as Nisos, fancying that the son of the great god Pan was merely drunk, bent rather irritably over him. He wanted to go to Arsinöe who was standing where the Figure-Head had once been, and was talking to Akron and Odysseus; but his conscience had compelled him not to desert his friend the Fly, who was stretched out on its back upon one of the wings of the Moth, who had beaten herself to death in an ecstasy of happiness against the wooden edge of the "life-crack" in the bosom of the club of Hcrakles.

"And of me also!" faintly whispered the Fly feebly moving

one long thin leg backwards and forwards along the surface of both his translucent wings.

Nisos was tempted to cry out for Arsinoë. "It's funny," he thought, "that all death calls for women; and yet all life depends on women!"

"Is the Pillar saying anything to the Club about our landing?" he asked the dying Fly, feeling instinctively that it would like to die talking.

But the Moth being dead and its own end near the Fly was disinclined to report on the world-events. "I have been thinking," he whispered, "about our burial; and it is of this I wish to speak."

"I take it," said Nisos, "you mean yours and the Moth's?"

"I do," whispered the Fly.

"Have you decided upon the exact spot?"

"I have."

"Do I know it?"

"You do."

"You don't mean the Sea?"

"No! No! No! No!"

"Where do you mean?"

"Put your ear close."

Nisos obeyed, though it meant his pressing rather awkwardly against the motionless Zeuks. "You don't mean you want me to finish you off first?"

"Of course," groaned the Fly. "Don't you understand that I'm done for and want to—to—be in one blob *with her*?"

"Blot did you say?"

"Call it what you like. I *said* blob."

"Where is it you want me to bury you both?"

"I want to be swallowed. I want to go into a god's stomach."

At this point Zeuks lifted his head with a chuckle. "I am no god of flies," he said, "but I can follow this little beggar's buzzing. Squeeze the two of them into a pellet and I'll swallow it right now!"

Nisos gravely and reverently obeyed. With his finger and

460

thumb he killed the Fly; and then of its body and of the body and the surviving wing of the Moth he made one blot or blob and held it towards Zeuks.

"Kiss it!" murmured the great-grandson of ever-youthful Maia.

Nisos kissed it and placed it between the lips of Zeuks who swallowed it with a pleased smile.

"Kiss *me*!"

Nisos again obeyed and kissed the grandson of Hermes with so much feeling that a tear fell on a cheek that looked as if it might at any moment be split from one side to the other by a burst of profane amusement. When this world-deep bubble of irrepressible jocularity had subsided, Zeuks, who was far too weak to do anything but just murmur the words, told Nisos that it was curious to think that at this moment all over the world there were entities dying in their loneliness, who were without a friend to help them and who had moreover an awareness of their loneliness that was so definite and clear that it was painful to think about it. "When you consider," Zeuks murmured, but Nisos could see, below the tragic pity of his words, a bubble of such defiant, mischievous merriment bursting through the whole body of the man that it seemed to arise out of the heart of life itself, "when you consider all the men and women and all the beasts, fishes, birds, reptiles and insects, isn't it awful to think of creatures dying in the panic terror of loneliness? Did you know, my friend"—Zeuks' speech by this time was so low that Nisos had to bend down to catch it—"that there are vibrations from one organism to another throughout the entire universe? Well! There are! And do you know what I'm going to do now? And please don't disturb me in it! I give you my word I'll die the moment I've done it. I'm going to tell every dying one in this whole crazy and confounded world that they've got me, Zeuks, the son of *Pan*, that is to say of the rebel who is everywhere, *on their side against Zeus*, and that the best way of fooling him and the whole lot of them is to die laughing, yes! laughing at this big, bloody, beggarly joke of a world! Stand back now, my dear!"

Nisos simply and silently obeyed the fellow; but the burst of stored-up ribaldry with which Zeuks died was so explosive that there was no corpse left to bury or burn. Out of world-dust he'd come, and into world-dust he dissolved, and the tiny blob of insect lovers he'd swallowed, melted with him into thin air.

Long afterwards Nisos and Arsinoë would spend hours asking each other about their memory of that landing. "What exactly did you feel," that luckiest of middle-aged Prophets would cry, "when Odysseus stopped us from lifting a finger against the Red-Skins crowding round us? Do you remember how he looked when he came back to us, after talking with them in some words they understood that he'd picked up, Heaven knows where, to tell us that we'd landed on a place called Manhattan, whose Ruler was a very very old Queen called Nokomis, whose only child had already sailed away to a Kingdom they called Ponemah, which was the land of the Wind they called Keewaydin? And, O my Love, my Life, *you* know as *I* know what we both felt when he cried aloud to us all, he, Odysseus, the son of Laertes, among all those Red-Skins: 'Now that our wind from the East has dropped at last, and the only wind that we feel is the North West wind Keewaydin, shall we hoist our sail again? Never, never, never, never! Come my friends, all of you, white, black, yellow, and red, let us pour out all our wine upon her and then burn her! Yes, let us burn our ship!'"